St. Martin's Paperbacks Titles
By Leslie LaFoy

The Perfect Seduction

The Perfect Temptation

The Perfect Desire

Her
Scandalous
Marriage

Leslie LaFoy

St. Martin's Paperbacks

HER SCANDALOUS MARRIAGE

Copyright © 2006 by Leslie LaFoy.

Cover photo © Shirley Green

ISBN: 0-312-34770-7
EAN: 9780312-34770-3

Printed in the United States of America

St. Martin's Paperbacks edition / May 2006

St. Martin's Paperbacks are published by St. Martin's Press, 175 Fifth Avenue, New York, NY 10010.

10 9 8 7 6 5 4 3 2 1

For Joan Hohl and Marcia Evanick

Wonderful writers

Extraordinary friends

❧ *One* ❧

CAROLINE STOPPED FIDDLING WITH THE DRAPING OF A gown and watched as the black vehicle rolled to a stop in front of her shop. A town coach that fancy didn't belong in this part of London. God only knew why the man climbing out of it was studying her sign, but his pinched nose and curled upper lip clearly indicated his disdain. Proving, Caroline decided, that some days were doomed from the moment you opened your eyes in the morning.

Mrs. Hobson had been waiting for her to open so she could change her mind about the fabric for her walking outfit—for the third time that week. Mrs. Ferrell had come in on her heels to complain about a side seam that hadn't withstood, much less contained, what had to have been, at the very least, a thirty-pound weight gain. She'd no more than stomped out when Mrs. Smythe had sashayed in with all four of her daughters for the final fittings on the dresses they were to wear to a cousin's wedding next week. Caroline had seen poodles less pampered than the Smythe girls. And less inclined to bite.

Now . . . Well, if the stranger ever stopped scowling, he'd be an incredibly handsome man. Tall, dark haired, pleasingly chiseled jaw and well defined, rather high cheek-bones. Not young, but not middle-aged yet, either. He had long, straight legs, a narrow waist, and a well-proportioned chest and broad shoulders. In short, he was a tailor's dream walking about in custom leather boots. And obviously there was a grateful tailor somewhere because the suit the man was wearing was well made out of a very fine—very expensive—wool cloth. Given the quality of the suit, the hat he wore was most likely made of the finest beaver.

Yes, all in all, the man coming through her shop door was a man of means and good taste, a man who moved with a natural grace and power.

"Good afternoon, sir," she said a bit breathlessly as he cleared the threshold and removed his hat. "How may I be of assistance?"

"You might summon the owner of this establishment."

His voice would be very rich and deep and pleasant if the haughty edge to it could be chipped away. "I'm the owner," she supplied, thinking that he had the most kiss-able mouth she'd ever seen. What would he taste like? She wondered? What flavor was carnal delight?

"You are Miss Caroline Dutton?"

He knew her name? Good Lord, had Wilamina Ferrell been serious when she'd threatened to contact her solici-tor? "Yes," Caroline admitted, her heart thumping. "How may I be of assistance to you, sir?"

"I am Drayton Mackenzie, Duke of Ryland."

Ryland? Well, that said volumes. Her heart settled back to a normal beat. "And you are here because . . . ?" she asked coolly.

"Because I am cursed."

"I'm afraid that I can't help you," she countered as she went back to adjusting the pins on the dress of the eldest

Smythe poodle. "But I have heard of a woman in White-hall who will cast and remove spells for a bottle of gin."

"I've been cursed by your father."

"Haven't we all," she quipped, tweaking the fabric and then leaning back to study the effects of the change.

"From the grave."

Why didn't she find that surprising? Why did she care enough to even wonder? "I must admit that I'm impressed."

"I am not here to impress you, madam."

That I'm-better-than-you manner of his was really insufferable. She glanced over at him. No, no one appeared to have broken his nose for it. Unfortunately. "Good, because you haven't impressed me at all." *At least not favorably in any sense other than the purely physical,* she silently added. Carrying the dress through the curtain that separated workroom from showroom, she clarified, "I was referring to the awe inspired by my late father's ability to make people dance to his tune despite his passage to the Great Beyond."

Drayton clenched his teeth and watched the curtain settle into place behind her. Yes, dear old Cousin Geoffrey had been one of the best at pulling strings. Damn him. As though it weren't bad enough that Geoffrey had played people as puppets while he lived, he'd transferred the paddles to a barrister at his death so the manipulation could continue for the next decade.

Maybe even longer, God forbid. Not that it was going to be hellishly difficult to meet the requirements where Caroline Dutton was concerned. She was pretty. She was tall and she was breathtakingly shapely. Add in flawless, fair skin, honey blond hair, strikingly blue eyes, and a deliciously saucy defiance . . .

He didn't have the slightest doubt of her ability to turn male heads wherever she went. And the hopes and fantasies she stirred when she did . . . He reminded himself that his task was not to make a mistress of her. No, he was mandated to make a regal, untouchable lady out of her and then hand her off to the highest, most deluded bidder. What a waste of a naturally seductive female. But since Geoffrey had decreed and the law was prepared to enforce it . . . When she came back into the showroom, he said, "Let me begin again." At her glance, he charged forward into the matter from the top. "I am here to discharge the duties attached to the inheritance of your late father's estate."

"Ah, I see," she said, as she went about straightening the chairs and footstools.

"You see what?"

"Why you've come to a place so obviously beneath a person of your importance," she answered. "You were compelled to do so by the lure of a fortune."

His importance? Ha! "I am not unfamiliar with environs such as this."

"Your upper lip apparently hasn't become accustomed to them."

He blinked and barely resisted the urge to lift his hand to his mouth. "Pardon?" he asked, more irritated by her dismissive manner than he was interested or mystified.

"Your upper lip," she repeated, picking up a basket and checking the contents. "When you climbed from your carriage, it tried to crawl up your nose."

Drayton tried to suppress the shudder and largely failed. If Geoffrey hadn't been dead, he'd have killed him. "If," he said crisply, determined to take the situation firmly in hand, "I might have your complete attention."

She sighed heavily, closed the lid of the damn basket, and looked at him. "Do go on," she instructed tightly. "And then do go on your way."

Her eyes darkened considerably when she was angry. At the moment, they were terribly close to the color of a well-blued gun barrel. And they were fixed on him with about the same sort of deadly intensity. He took a slow breath and met her challenge full on, saying, "As your father saw death approaching, he resolved to rectify what he considered the wrongs he'd done to others over the course of his long life. In addition to making several generous bequests to charities, he set aside funds for the proper maintenance and support of his children."

Her smile was barely civil. "I'm sure they're appropriately grateful. What does all this have to do with me?"

"You are his daughter."

"His illegitimate daughter," she countered icily.

"His direct legitimate descendants did not survive to assume the title."

"Or, as they say, they failed to survive *him*."

Well, yes, that was probably a fair statement. From all that he'd ever heard, Geoffrey's expectations of others had been considerably higher than any of those he had ever imposed on himself. "We were distantly related," Drayton offered, choosing his words carefully, "and I met him personally only once in my life. I can't say that I came away with the impression of his being a particularly ogreish or deliberately hard-hearted man."

"You're one meeting ahead of me in the tally," she said, her voice sounding oddly strained. "What impressions I've formed of him over the years are from my mother's life in his wake. Forgive me if I'm not giddy with the thought of dancing off to the south of France to live a life of carefree abandon with the buckets of money he left behind for me. I know enough of my sire and his tendencies to keep a very firm grasp on reality. And that reality is that, like my mother, I must make my own way."

"I believe I mentioned that he had something of a change of heart at the end of his life."

"Yes, you did," she allowed, heading for the curtain again, this time with the basket in hand. "You may leave the bag of coins on the counter and consider your task fulfilled."

The woman was maddening beyond belief! This shouldn't have been anywhere near as difficult as she was making it. He followed her through the curtain saying, "Madam, I would appreciate it if you would stop walking away from me while I am talking to you."

Standing at a worktable littered with scraps of fabric and tubes of vellum, she looked over her shoulder at him and arched a brow.

"If tossing a bag of coins at you were sufficient," he declared, "I would have handed the matter off to a solicitor and not made the effort to appear here personally. As a condition of inheritance, your father has charged me with the personal responsibility of seeing you formally recognized as his offspring and situated in an advantageous marriage."

She tilted her head and blinked at him in a manner that was unexpectedly, stunningly coquettish. "What?"

"If tossing a bag—"

"I heard what you said," she interrupted, straightening her head and obliterating the brief moment of femininity. "Quite clearly. My amazement is over the part relating to recognition and the arrangement of a marriage. Why would he suddenly care about such things?"

"I can only deduce that he was motivated by a keen sense of regret."

She arched her brow again and there was a decidedly sarcastic edge to her voice when she said, "Having to give an accounting to Saint Peter undoubtedly figured into it as well."

"Perhaps," he agreed with a slight shrug. "I can't speak to the spiritual beliefs he might have held. Whatever his deeper motives were, the fact is that he intended for you to use his name to secure an elevated station in life and the financial certainty which attends it."

She rolled her eyes. "And how many men of substance are there who would be interested in marrying the twenty-three-year-old bastard daughter of a dead-as-a-doornail peer?"

"You will be amazed."

"The bastard daughter who has spent the last five years of her life in . . ." She tilted her head slightly back and pressed the back of her wrist to her brow. "Oh, gasp," she whimpered in patently feigned distress. "Trade."

"You would be amazed by what men are willing to overlook in the light of a substantial dowry." *And be willing to give for a taste of you.*

"I would rather be left alone, thank you."

"Unfortunately, neither of us has a choice in the matter."

She considered him, an odd, almost taunting smile playing at the corners of her mouth. "Do you intend to take me from my shop by force, hold me in chains, and auction me to the highest bidder?"

Well, no, but he couldn't afford to admit it. "If need be."

She laughed—the sound feathering over his senses—and walked past him saying, "And to think that you appear to be such a civilized man. You must be in desperate need of money."

And once again he found himself standing on the wrong side of the curtain, watching it fall back into place and facing a choice between trotting after her like some damn cocker spaniel or standing his ground with no one to witness or appreciate the show. He scrubbed his hand over his chin, pivoted on his heel, and stepped to the other side of the curtain.

"My circumstances are not relevant," he lied as he crossed the showroom. With the counter between them, he met her gaze squarely and said, "I am required to see you properly wed and settled and I will employ whatever means are necessary to achieve that end."

"Really?"

That one single word, the disdainful, mocking tone of it . . . He reached into his coat pocket, took out his ace, and laid it on the counter in front of her.

"And this is?" she asked even as she picked it up.

"Notice from your landlord concerning the sale of this building," he explained.

"Do let me guess," she countered, putting it down without having looked at it. The color of her eyes was like that of a pure blue flame. "He's sold it to you. And you are fully prepared to increase my rent to an utterly astronomical level if I refuse to play my part in assuaging my dead father's conscience and securing your claim to his estate."

"That would be it in the proverbial nutshell," he admitted, nodding. "The rent is now two hundred pounds a month. Payable semi-annually, in advance. Which means the sum of twelve hundred pounds is due at the present moment." He put out his hand, palm up, and added, "In the absence of my business manager, I will, just this once, set aside convention and accept your payment."

Caroline drew a slow, deep breath and considered her possible courses. None of them were pleasant. If she had a bit of chain and a padlock, she could fasten herself to the coal stove in the workroom to keep him from hauling her out. But she didn't and now that he'd made it a contest of money . . . It wasn't a fair fight at all and she knew good and well that she was going to lose in the end. But surrendering without so much as a whimper . . . She lifted her chin. "Please consider this notification of my intent to immediately relocate my business."

"There is the matter of the unpaid balance on this month's rent," he countered instantly, apparently having anticipated her plan. "I'm afraid that I will have to seize your inventory in lieu of that payment."

Of course. A man every bit as ruthless as he was handsome. "Are you a bastard by birth as well as by temperament?"

Anger flashed in the depth of his dark eyes. It didn't, however, show in his voice when he said coolly, smoothly, "Casting aspersions will not alter my course. Or yours. You are the daughter of a duke."

"I have always been the daughter of a duke. Not that it's mattered one whit until today."

"Ah," he drawled, as the tiniest of smiles lifted one corner of his mouth. "But today has arrived and your destiny has been forever altered. Please get your wrap and whatever personal items of sentimental value you might wish to bring into your new life."

I have snapped my fingers. Obey. Caroline counted to ten and brought her anger under control. "I can't walk out the door right this instant, lock it behind me, and hand you the key."

"Why ever not?"

"This is a business," she explained tightly. "I have clients to whom I owe goods. They have made deposits and I have made promises. Aside from their disappointment, my professional reputation will be ruined if I simply up and leave."

"Your reputation as a modiste is now . . . pardon the pun . . . immaterial."

"And my assistant?" she posed. "What of her? She's to return from her shopping within the next hour or so. What's she to do when she finds the shop closed and locked?"

"Leave her a note telling her that she's free to find herself another situation."

"And my personal reputation?" she demanded, her voice higher pitched than she liked. She paused to swallow and drag in a settling breath. "What of it? Is there a proper chaperone waiting in your carriage?"

He shrugged. Barely. "Appearances do not matter overly much until such time as society becomes aware of you. Now please gather your belongings. We have much to do yet today and this has already taken far more time than I intended."

Far be it from her to inconvenience him. She folded her arms across her midriff. "And what will you do if I refuse?"

"Your trinkets will be left behind when I sling you over my shoulder and haul you out."

Trinkets. The pompous ass. "I'd kick and scream," she threatened, not caring that she sounded like a peevish child. "The public spectacle would be horribly embarrassing for you."

"Probably so," he admitted with a full-fledged, heart-tripping smile. "Which would mean, of course, that I could never appear in this part of town again. A tragedy I will simply have to bear as best I can."

Oh, to win against him . . . There had to be a way. Simply had to be. Perhaps she could make a pretense of gathering up her things and—

"Yes, you could easily slip out the rear door while you are collecting your belongings. But please be aware that my footman is waiting there for you."

How he'd known what she was thinking was a mystery she'd ponder later. At the moment, she was too frustrated and resentful to see anything except the trap in which she'd been caught. "You appear to have considered all of my likely reactions."

"I believe in being thorough," he admitted with a nod. "But I must admit to being surprised by your resistance. Why do you feel the need to be such an obstinate creature? I'm offering all the stuff of grand, girlish dreams. Wealth, privilege, marriage. What could this . . ." He glanced around her shop and made a weak gesture to encompass it. "What could this *place* offer you that would be of equal worth?"

Place? *Place?* She gripped the edge of the counter in front of her in a desperate effort to contain her anger. No, her shop wasn't a high-priced, self-important salon that decided who they'd deign to serve and who wasn't good enough to darken their door. But neither was it a dark and dingy and sweaty back room where clothes were assembled by women who were slaves in all but legal status. How dare he dismiss her shop as though the efforts to build it hadn't amounted to anything. How dare he walk into her life and expect her to happily—no gleefully, instantly!—abandon everything she and her mother had worked so hard to achieve.

"I'm not a girl," she replied tautly, inwardly seething. "I'm a woman, full-grown. I don't pine to be a wife, to either a rich man or a poor one. As for dreams of castles and houses with names and attending fancy balls in elegant, obscenely expensive gowns . . . My father couldn't be bothered with my dreams while he lived, couldn't be bothered with *me*. My dreams died long before he did. As for what this *place* offers me . . . Independence and protection from the whims of selfish men like my father. Of men like you."

He cocked a brow and tilted his head, studying her for a second as though she were some exotic Egyptian bug in a display case at the museum. "Have you ever heard the expression, cutting off one's nose to spite one's face?" He didn't give her a chance to reply. "Your father is dead. Refusing to accept his largesse accomplishes nothing that will make the least bit of difference to him or to anyone else. It will simply ensure that you spend the rest of your life as you have spent the first part of it, existing on the margins of respectability and clinging by your fingertips to economic survival."

He was right, of course. Damn him. But there was something so terribly humiliating, so patently desperate about throwing away all the efforts as if they'd been mere diversions while she waited to become a fairy-tale princess.

"Perhaps," he went on, "it might help to think of acceding as the fulfillment of your late mother's greatest hopes."

She sucked in a deep breath, furious that he'd stoop so low, weakened by the realization that her mother would have had her out the door and into his carriage before he'd even gotten out of it. "And how is it that you know anything of her aspirations?" she asked, stalling as she tried to weigh her pride against her mother's dreams.

"As I said, I am thorough. I came here to take you away by any means necessary. I prefer, of course, to accomplish the task through reason and an appeal to your intelligence and sensibilities. To that end, I made a point of learning all that I could about you and the history of your parents' relationship."

"Such as it was," she felt compelled to add testily.

"True." He dredged up a smile that actually seemed slightly apologetic. "Unfortunately, 'brief' and 'irresponsible' seem to be the words to characterize all of your late father's more . . . intimate relations outside his marriage."

"He had others?" she asked, stunned less by the fact that her mother hadn't been the man's only victim than the fact that she'd never considered the possibility.

He nodded. "Three that produced offspring. There may well have been more, but the other ladies involved did not make claims of paternity and ask for maintenance."

"Three," she said softly as Lord Thorough continued his monologue. "I have two siblings."

"Two sisters," he clarified, looking at her as though she'd suddenly become another kind of bug entirely. "Collecting them is next on my rather pressing list of tasks to be completed today. So if you could be so reasonable as to abandon your pride and understandable resentment of the past so that we may get on with it all, I would be most appreciative."

Part of her brain recognized that his request was a slightly milder, quieter version of a finger snap. Another part of her brain was whirling with childhood memories.

Yet another was cringing at unacceptable possibilities. "Are my sisters older or younger?"

"Younger," he supplied crisply. "Miss Simone is reportedly fourteen and Miss Fiona only eleven."

Oh, dear God. Babies. They were nothing more than babies. "And do you intend to see them established and married off as well?"

"When the time is appropriate."

Perhaps she was being needlessly concerned for their welfare. It could well be that their families wouldn't relinquish them. Or at the very least have the resources necessary to check the new duke's influence and control. "What are their present circumstances?" she asked.

"Let it suffice to say that I do not anticipate any difficulties in acquiring them."

Acquire. As he undoubtedly acquired a new suit. Or a title. Or a mistress. God, fourteen. She remembered being that age. It had been horrible. Part woman, part child. Not sure which would surface in any given situation. Hideously, acutely aware of how her body was changing. Minute by minute, it seemed. And how her new body had changed the way men looked at her and how that had changed, overnight, all the rules for dealing with people.

And eleven . . . She remembered that time, too. It had been awful in a different sort of way. Life had stopped being simple then. She'd realized there were ugly things in the world at eleven. Not that she'd understood exactly what they were then, but she'd sensed the shadows keenly enough that the distraction of old childhood games had started to feel like a dangerous thing. It was when you weren't paying attention that the monsters under the bed would grab your ankles and drag you off to hell.

She wouldn't go back and relive those years for all the money in Christendom, all the tea in China. She'd gotten through them and past them, but only because her mother had been such a strong and steady presence at her back. If she hadn't been there . . . If she'd been handed into the care of a stranger who issued decrees and saw to her care only because he *had* to . . . Caroline swallowed away the tickle of tears in her throat and surrendered to the whisper of her conscience.

"And where," she asked, "is it that the three of us will be . . ." She faltered, overwhelmed by a sense of hopelessness and the weight of unexpected responsibility.

"Ensconced? Housed?" he suggested.

"I was thinking more along the lines of imprisoned," she admitted.

He ignored her lack of enthusiasm. "The current Season is over and everyone has retired to their country estates. Your father had one, of course, and it was among several properties that passed into my possession at his death. It is my plan that we all take up residence there and spend the coming fall doing whatever is required for young women to be considered socially acceptable."

It didn't bode well that he didn't appear to have any better idea of the specific tasks that lay ahead than she did. But the die had been cast and there was nothing to do but make the best of things. "I'll accompany you, willingly, on three conditions."

His brow shot up. Warily, he asked, "And they would be?"

Believing that the strength of conviction accomplished far more than mealy pleading and hopeful suggestions, she said firmly, "The first is that you will place my account ledgers into the hands of an able manager to be settled fairly. I won't have those who have supported my mother and myself over the years treated shabbily."

"Consider it done. The second condition?"

"My assistant will see that the orders due in the next week are completed and delivered as promised. After that, she'll join us in the country."

"Why?"

"Don't ladies have personal maids?"

"Yes. Does she have experience at that sort of thing?"

"No, but then, I have no experience at being a lady, so it's not as though I'd notice any shortcomings on her part. Either you agree to bring Jane to the country, or I won't go."

"What is one more female in a house full of them? Your third condition?"

"If it becomes apparent that I don't have the temperament or the ability to become a socially acceptable woman, you won't persist in humiliating me. You'll allow me access to the money my father set aside for bribing a would-be husband so that I can reestablish an independent life for myself."

He narrowed his eyes. "Doing what?"

"The difference between being a modiste and a couturier is the price of the creation," she explained. "It takes money to make money. With adequate funds, I'm quite capable of designing and creating with the best in London. In Paris, too, for that matter."

He laughed. The sound was soft, but it was full and deep. More importantly, it brimmed with obviously sincere amusement and eased the knot around her heart. "You certainly don't lack for confidence," he observed.

"I'm the daughter of a duke," Caroline replied. "Nobility is often just as much an attitude as it is the good fortune of being born on the right side of the sheets. Do we have an agreement?"

"We do," he said, nodding slowly, almost . . . well, appreciatively.

"I want it put into writing."

His brow shot up again. "You don't trust my word?"

Oh, she liked taking him by surprise. There was something decidedly satisfying in knowing that he didn't have complete control of all the world and everyone and everything in it. "It's nothing personal, Your Grace," she assured him, coming around the end of the counter. "It's simply that the last duke who promised a woman in my family something proved himself a liar. I learned from my mother's mistake not to trust them any further than I can toss them."

Drayton watched her head toward the curtain, certain that she was walking away just because she knew it irritated him. But since he'd won the larger battle of wills, he could afford to be magnanimous and let her have her little demonstration of defiance. "I will have my solicitor draw up the papers when I give him your ledger to settle. Fair enough?"

"Fair," she said, disappearing without so much as a glance over her shoulder at him. "I won't be but a few moments."

He tilted his head and considered the curtain. If it was all a ruse and she bolted . . . He really should have thought of bringing his footman along to guard the rear door. It wasn't as though he hadn't inherited one. He had a slew of servants. Enough that he was constantly either tripping over them or bumping into them. At some point he was going to have to learn to think like a nobleman and actually use them.

And given the apparent intelligence, willfulness, and self-confidence of Caroline Dutton—no, it was Lady Caroline—he needed to get his feet under himself as quickly as possible. If he didn't, the charade was going to be blown to tiny, embarrassingly public bits.

❧ *Two* ❧

HIS GAZE VERY STUDIOUSLY FASTENED ON THE WORLD outside the carriage—on anything other than the woman sitting in the opposite seat—Drayton mulled his predicament. Caroline was what? His cousin three times removed? Which surely qualified them as hardly related at all. It certainly wasn't as though she were a sister or a first cousin. So given all that, there really wasn't anything unholy or grossly unnatural about noticing her physical attributes and imagining what might come of their forced companionship.

Brown wasn't the color he would have chosen for her if he'd been asked for his opinion. And there was something rather off-putting about wool; silks and satins and fine, thin lawns were ever so much more inviting to the touch. But the fact that her traveling costume was made of brown wool and covered her from neck to wrist to ankle didn't do a damned thing to detract from the wonderful curves it encased.

Neither did the little grosgrain-trimmed cape, the ruched overskirt, the fashionably sized bustle, or the straight skirt with the narrow knife pleats in brown satin around the hem. Combined with the perfectly proper and matching brown kid gloves and the feather-adorned hat that hid most of her hair and made her eyes impossibly huge and her skin look like alabaster . . .

God, he was doing it again, he silently groaned. She was legally under his protection until a suitable husband could be found for her. Ogling your ward and wondering just how much of her incredibly tempting shape was due to corset boning and lacings and how much was the woman herself . . . It was not only socially unacceptable, it was a sign of complete mental depravity.

He had to get control of himself, firmly and quickly. And the surest way to do that, he knew from experience, was to become immersed in a battle. He slid a glance in her direction and squelched the idea of commenting on the drab color of her clothes. With his kind of luck, she'd retaliate by stripping naked and throwing them out the window. How a woman who'd been suddenly handed far more than she could have ever dreamed possible could sit on a plush seat in a private carriage and look so beautiful and so put out by it all . . .

He cocked a brow and seized the opportunity. "Are you planning to sulk for the rest of today?"

"Yes," she answered crisply and without bothering to look at him. "And, quite likely, tomorrow and the next day, too."

"Just as a point of information, gentlemen prefer their companions to be cheerfully distracting."

She slowly turned her head to meet his gaze. "I see a series of great disappointments in your future."

Yes, well, so did he and he preferred not to think about them. "You said that your Jane has a key to the shop," he countered, pressing on with his plan for distraction. "You wrote her an excruciatingly long and detailed explanation.

You have more than adequately fulfilled all of your obligations as a proprietress and as an employer, and are being whisked off to a life of considerable luxury and great privilege. Forgive me, but I fail to see what it is that you have to sulk about."

"Forgive me," she said dryly, "if I'm less than delighted to be on a course I wasn't allowed to choose for myself."

"And do women in your world commonly get to chart their own ways?"

"Yes, until a man enters their lives and ties a millstone about their necks."

Ah, yes, money and privilege were such burdens for women to bear. "I don't think that you can honestly characterize your situation as being a hideous trial of feminine independence and prerogative. I have acceded to your every condition and allowed you far more time to accommodate your thinking to the changed circumstances than I had originally intended."

Acceded? Allowed? How very much like a man. "The fact that—" Caroline bit the rest of the words off and looked away. "Never mind," she finished tartly. "I'd have a better chance of reasoning with a post than I do with you."

"I think that I've given a highly credible performance of a reasonable man."

" 'Performance' being the key word," she countered, remembering how he'd looked her up and down when she'd come back into the showroom, ready to go. How he'd cocked that damn brow of his and then not only pointedly looked away, but made patently obvious efforts to avoid looking at her again. "But credible? Reasonable? I'm afraid not. Imperious I would be willing to concede, though. Pompous and disdainful, too. And thoroughly underhanded."

"Underhanded?"

Out of all the less than sterling qualities, *that* was the one that concerned him? "There was no footman guarding my back door," she reminded him.

"Oh, yes, that."

He'd all but waved his hand in dismissal! Marriage to a stranger wasn't looking quite as awful as it had earlier in the day. "And the purchasing of the building so that you could seize my business and force me to bend to your will."

His brow went up again. "Do you always keep such detailed score?"

"Yes," she supplied as the coach angled out of traffic and slowed.

"It's going to be a very long autumn."

"It is, indeed. Unless there's a God and you spend much of your time traveling about to inspect all the various and wondrous estates you've inherited."

"No weather will be too foul," he muttered, leaning forward to turn the door handle. He was already out on the walk when he said, "I shouldn't be overly long. Stay there."

Sit. Heel. Roll over. Be a good dog. Her teeth clenched and her blood pounding, Caroline grabbed a handful of her skirts and vaulted out of the carriage door before he could get it closed behind him.

He blinked. His gaze dropped to the vicinity of her waist and then snapped back up to her eyes. Closing the space between them so that she had to tilt her head and arch her back to see his face, he glowered down at her and said, "I must insist that you get back into the carriage."

"You may insist all you like."

He bent his head to snarl into the side of her bonnet, "No lady should be seen entering a house of ill repute."

Caroline glanced past him to the sagging façade of the

building—the building with the red curtains and the half-dressed woman standing in the open doorway. Her stomach went queasy in realization. She'd blundered. Hugely. How many times had her mother warned her of the consequences of not controlling her temper? Enough that she'd become very good at hasty but strategic retreats. She took a step backward and lifted her chin. "But sitting in a carriage parked in front of one *is* acceptable?"

"If you hadn't gotten out, no one would have known you were here," he said tightly, taking her firmly by the elbow and turning her toward the still open carriage door.

She climbed back inside because it was the only dignified thing to do at that point. "Is one of my sisters in there?" she asked to cover what was, in the final analysis, a retreat.

"Lady Simone," he answered, releasing her elbow. "Now, kindly let me be about getting her out of there with the least amount of embarrassment possible to any of us."

He didn't wait for her to offer approval or a pithy comment before he closed the door. Through the open window, she watched as he resumed his earlier course. He didn't get much farther than he had the first time.

The wooden steps squeaked as a large woman in a shockingly red, horribly crushed velvet dress descended with deliberate speed and altogether remarkable agility. "You be Lord Ryland?" she asked, coming to a winded stop right in front of him.

"I am."

Shoving the loose knot of gray hair back onto the top of her head, she said, "I'm Essie."

"A pleasure to put a face with the name, madam," he replied with a slight ever-so-genteel bow. "Would you care to step—"

"Twenty pounds is what we agreed to," she interrupted, sticking out her hand. "The money first and then you can have the chit."

Caroline watched him reach into the pocket of his coat and hand over a small leather bag. "Please feel free to count it if you would like."

Essie did, yanking open the drawstring and pouring the coins into her hand. She plucked one up and bit it before looking over her shoulder and nodding. Two burly men in billed caps instantly filled the doorway. Between them, held firmly by the arms, was a glaring bundle of squirming rags. Simone, no doubt.

Caroline considered her sister. She was small and rail thin and filthy from head to toe. What she lacked in size, though, she made up for in spirit. Somewhere there was a fishmonger in awe of the depth and breadth of Simone's vulgar vocabulary. The men marched her down the steps, ignoring her efforts to twist out of their grasp, and planted her between Essie and Lord Ryland.

Caroline leaned forward, trying—unsuccessfully—to see Simone in the knot of much larger bodies.

"This is the man that bought you," she heard Essie say harshly. "Don't make no problems for him, or you'll be coming right back here and I ain't gonna be happy to see you. Understand what I'm telling you?"

She couldn't see or hear Simone's response, but Lord Ryland's was immediate and swift. He turned with Simone's upper arm firmly in one hand as he reached out and wrenched open the carriage door with the other. In the next second, Simone's trouser-clad bottom was on Caroline's seat and sliding toward her.

The smell was beyond horrible—a combination of sewage and rotting garbage and heavy smoke. Gasping was the instinctive reaction, but most definitely the wrong one. Her stomach heaving, Caroline quickly and quietly expelled the breath and tried not to sag in relief as Simone recovered her balance, scrambled to the far end of the seat, and packed herself into the corner of the carriage.

Lord Ryland pulled the door closed and barked a command to his driver in the same second. In the next, the carriage shot forward, its sudden momentum making his effort to get onto his own seat a bit less than graceful.

Simone's chuckle drew Caroline's attention back to her. The stench was still strong, but the desperate bravado in the dark eyes peering out through an unruly, greasy mop of black curls was heart-wrenching. As Simone's gaze darted warily between her and Lord Ryland, Caroline summoned a smile and resolved to do what she could to put the child at ease.

"Hello," she said gently. "My name is Caroline. I'm your half-sister."

Simone raked the back of her right hand under her nose, sniffed, and announced, "I don't got no sisters."

"I believed the same thing until an hour or so ago," Caroline offered. "Until Lord Ryland informed me otherwise."

Her gaze snapped to the man in the opposite seat and her eyes narrowed. "I ain't no whore."

"You cannot know," he said dryly, "how very relieved I am to hear that bit of information."

"You even look like you wanna touch me, I'll rip your balls off."

He blinked. "Good God."

Well, if nothing else, Caroline decided, hiding a wide smile behind her hand, *she* had to look like a highly cultured princess compared to Simone. At his glare, she managed to sober enough to ask, "You didn't explain the true circumstances to dear Essie, did you?"

His brow inched upward. "Would you have opened that Pandora's box?"

Since they both knew the answer, she didn't bother with admitting it aloud. Instead, she turned to her sister. "Simone," she began soothingly, "no one is going to touch you inappropriately. Or even look at you in a manner they shouldn't. You are perfectly safe with us."

"Then what did you two buy me for?"

"*I* secured your freedom," he answered, his tone hard-edged, "because there are conditions on the inheritance of the personal fortune of my late cousin, twice removed—may his soul burn in the deepest, hottest fires of hell for all eternity. One of those conditions is you."

Simone studied him for a second or two, her face scrunched. Finally, she looked over at Caroline and asked, "Huh?"

"What Lord Ryland could no doubt say better if he would control his anger and frustration, is that the late Lord Ryland, his cousin—"

"Twice removed," he inserted, staring out the window, his jaw pulsing. "Don't tie me to the scoundrel any closer than I have to be."

"Yes, of course," Caroline said to placate him, and then turned back to Simone. "Anyway, as I was about to explain when I was so rudely interrupted . . . The Lord Ryland before this one had three daughters out of wedlock."

"You mean bastards."

"Yes. I am one. You are another. We have another sister whose name is Fiona."

It took less than a heartbeat for her to digest the information, shrug, and say defiantly, "So what?"

Well, in the child's favor, she was quick-witted enough to know that they hadn't reached the crux of the matter yet. "The old Lord Ryland felt bad about ignoring us—but not before he was dying, of course—and said the new Lord Ryland . . ."—she gestured in the general direction of the opposite seat—"had to take us under his wing and make ladies out of us. If he doesn't do that, he can't have all the money that goes with being a duke."

Simone looked Lord Ryland up and down. "Why'd he hate you so much?"

"Damned if I know," he replied without looking at his young ward. "If you ever discover the answer, I do hope you will share it with me."

She snorted and scrubbed the back of her hand under her nose again. "I ain't no royal, you know."

He closed his eyes and—with what Caroline considered far more gloom and doom than necessary—said, "Our blood line does not descend from the House of Hanover. A fact for which I am sure the queen has always been grateful and will soon be even more so."

"Huh?"

"He means that we aren't related to Her Majesty," Caroline clarified, growing more annoyed with his airs by the second. "Our ancestors apparently did something that a past king or queen really appreciated and were given a title as a reward."

"So this Ryland that cocked up his toes was our da?"

"That's what he claimed."

"And you believe it?"

"Well . . ." Caroline allowed.

"Pointin' to just one man as my da would be one helluva trick. How'd my ma manage that one and make him believe it?"

"I have no idea," Lord Ryland said. "It's not my place to make judgments concerning the accuracy of the claims. Geoffrey believed that you are his daughter and that's sufficient. I'm to make a lady of you and see that you marry well."

"Marry! I ain't about to spread—"

"Not for a long, long time!" Caroline hurried to assure her. "And never if you really don't want to. No one's going to force you into a relationship that you don't want."

"I don't want to. Not ever." She leaned forward to glare at the man on the other seat. "You try to make me and I'll—"

"Yes, I know," he said with a sigh of greatly strained patience. "You will unman me. It is not necessary to repeat the threat at every opportunity."

Simone slowly eased back into the corner and shifted her consideration to Caroline. "You gonna let him marry you off?"

"I have very serious doubts as to his ability to find anyone who would want to marry me. He says that he can, but . . ." She shrugged. "We'll see how desperate I am to escape come spring."

The look he slid her across the carriage was somehow both wounded and challenging. Even as she puzzled it and how to best respond, Simone asked, "How long before he cuts me loose?"

Yes, of course Simone would think that the arrangement was only temporary. The odds were good that nothing in her life to this day had been anything but moment to moment. "If you prefer not to marry," Caroline assured her, "you'll be provided for for the rest of your life."

"Huh?"

Caroline was trying to decide whether Simone didn't

understand the wording of the explanation or if it was simply a matter of the child not being able to grasp the concept of being cared for on a reliable basis, when Lord Ryland cleared his throat and said, "When one doesn't understand something or wishes for it to be repeated, the proper response is to say, 'I beg your pardon?' "

"I don't beg," Simone retorted, her voice granite hard. "Not for nuthin'. *Ever.*"

Caroline looked between the two of them, noting their steely glares and thinking that they might go to physical blows at any second. "Ah," she said, chuckling softly, hoping to break the tension. "Spoken like the true daughter of a duke."

Still holding Simone's gaze, the supposed adult said, "Do not encourage her."

"In answer to your request for clarification, Simone," she went on, refusing to be cowed, "Lord Ryland will see that you never want for anything for as long as you live."

"I want a lot."

"For instance?" he asked icily.

"Shoes with no holes in the bottom."

"That can be arranged."

"And supper every single night."

"There shouldn't be a problem with that, either."

"A *hot* supper," she countered. "Fixed *that* day."

"I will make sure the staff is aware of the expectation."

She hesitated, as if, Caroline thought, she'd exhausted the full range of her dreams and was having to dredge the realm of utter impossibilities. "And a *real* bed," Simone added, sounding a bit triumphant. "That I don't have to share with anyone."

"You will have a choice of a private chamber and the bed in it."

The girl's eyes narrowed. "Nobody gives away shoes and food and beds for nuthin'. What do you want from me for it?"

"You will be expected to undertake your lessons diligently and cheerfully."

"What kind of lessons?"

"Reading and writing, basic arith—"

"What do I need to know how to do that for?"

As he drew a breath to retort, Caroline made another attempt to diffuse the conflict. "Oh, Simone," she said breezily, "all ladies need to know how to read and write and how to do basic arithmetic. It's necessary for managing the household accounts and absolutely essential if they ever own a business."

"Not to mention vital," Lord Ryland contributed dryly, "to having the ability to carry on a conversation that someone might actually find interesting."

Caroline clenched her teeth and was promising herself that she wouldn't lift a finger to help him if Simone went for his throat, when her sister asked, "What if I'm no good at it?"

"Then you won't eat," he quickly supplied. "And I'll take away your shoes."

Simone sucked a breath through her teeth as she lowered her chin.

Caroline reached out and laid her hand on the girl's knee. "He's joking. Badly," she assured her. "You'll do fine with the schoolroom lessons. I can tell that you're a very bright young woman. And we'll both suffer through the social lessons together."

Simone gave her nemesis an especially hard look before very deliberately turning her attention to Caroline and saying, "Social?"

"How to walk like a lady, sit like a lady, talk like a lady."

"How to part the Red Sea," Lord Ryland muttered.

They both ignored him and Caroline added, "How to dance without stomping a man's toes to jelly and how to flutter and use a fan without accidentally slitting someone's throat with it. That sort of thing. Do you know how to embroider or needlepoint?"

"I ain't got no patience for that lah-dee-dah stuff."

Oh, dear. But surely she had domestic skills of some sort. She was, after all, fourteen and female. "What do you do with your days and evenings?"

"Mostly larkin' in the Thames durin' the late part of the day if the tide's right."

"You don't," Lord Ryland drawled, even as Caroline easily pictured the girl wading in the river mud, searching for bits of salvage.

"Do, too. Mornin's I have to spend moppin' up after Essie and her girls and their customers to pay off what my ma owed Essie. Evenin's . . . I make myself scarce so no one gets any ideas 'bout stuffin' me in a dress and hangin' a sign 'round my neck. I can shoot dice with the best of them and Jock's been learnin' me how to use a knife proper like."

"I suppose," he offered, looking away with another of his insufferable sighs, "there's little hope that Jock is a master chef."

"He's a cutpurse. A damn good one, too."

"Of course. Why am I not surprised?"

"The better question," Caroline snapped, her patience with him gone, "would be why you're being such an openly caustic snob, your grace? It isn't our fault that we weren't brought up to be ladies of the court. We've done the best that we could given the circumstances of our births.

It isn't our fault that our father found his conscience late in life and only to foist us off on you."

Simone opened her mouth to say something, but Caroline wasn't in the mood to let him off the hook by distraction. Her gaze pinned on him, she held up her hand to stay the girl. Simone went silent.

It took a long minute, but eventually he lifted his chin, took a slow deep breath, and turned to face her squarely. "Very true," he offered tightly. "My sincerest apologies. I will try to be more accepting."

"Thank you." She turned to face the girl in the seat beside her. "And my apologies for having to cut you off, Simone. What was it that you were going to say?"

Her head tilted to the side and what might have been the shadow of a smile lifting one corner of her mouth, Simone watched Lord Ryland as she asked, "What does 'foist' mean?"

"To force something off onto someone. Usually against their will."

Nodding, she said, "Carrie's right. It ain't our fault. None of it."

He swallowed and offered them both an obviously forced smile. "As I have agreed."

"Where're we goin'?"

"To the country house," he supplied, looking back out the window. "We will be stopping for the night at an inn along the way. Fiona's family has agreed to meet us there."

"You buyin' her, too?"

"They did not ask for money."

Caroline blinked, stunned by the reality. "They're simply giving their child away to a stranger?"

He sighed, gave up looking out the window, and stared at the floor between Caroline's feet as he explained,

"Apparently Fiona's mother handed her into the care of her sister when the child was quite young. The mother then disappeared and has not been heard from, or of, since. She's presumed dead. The aunt and uncle do not want to care for the child any longer. Why, I don't know."

"Maybe she eats too much," Simone guessed.

He looked up to meet his young ward's gaze. "I suspect that it may be a case of their not being able to feed her at all. My agent reported that they are extremely poor. And yes," he added, shifting his gaze to Caroline's, "before you can plant your dainty foot in the backside of my conscience, I intend to offer them a sizable sum for her anyway."

"Maybe there's something wrong with her," Simone theorized. "You know, maybe she got kicked in the head by a horse."

They both looked at her, but it was Lord Ryland who managed to ask first, "Do you know very many people who have been kicked in the head by a horse?"

"Two. Ada and Sally. Their das sold them to Essie 'cause they couldn't do nuthin' else. Ada came from a farm and Sally's da's a tinker."

To be sold into prostitution by your parents. It happened all the time, Caroline knew, but still . . . "How very sad."

"It's the way life goes sometimes," Simone offered with a shrug. "Nuthin' you can do to change it. Some's lucky and some's not." She paused, shrugged again, and added, " 'Course what's luck and what's ain't depends on how you look at it. Ada never had shoes till she came to Essie's place. For her it was good to be sold off like she was. Sally . . . I don't know nuthin' 'bout Sally. She don't talk."

"How long have you been there? At Essie's?" Lord Ryland asked quietly.

"This would be the third winter a-comin'. Ma rented a room from her for a little while. She died a few months after she moved us in there. Essie takes a cut out of those what comes through the door and picks from the parlor, so lots of the girls go out to make extra that Essie don't know about. Essie said my ma didn't have no sense about how to choose her customers. One afternoon she went into an alley with the wrong one and . . ." She lifted her chin and drew a dirt-encrusted finger across her throat. "That was that."

And that was that. Caroline couldn't think of anything to say. The child's mother had been found dead in an alley, her throat cut, and that was that. How long had it been before Simone had noticed that her mother was missing? Had she been distraught? How long had she had to search until the grim truth had been found? God, what sort of life had she lived that the gruesome murder of her mother was a simple fact of life?

"I'm very sorry," she heard Lord Ryland say gently. "No one's end should be so brutal and so unexpected."

"Not unexpected," Simone countered. She shrugged again. "Like I said, some's lucky and some's not. Some's smart 'bout people and some just ain't. Sad to say, but Essie was right 'bout my ma. Wasn't anythin' I didn't know already."

"Still," Caroline offered, thinking of her own mother's passing, "you must miss her terribly."

"Can't say that I do." She sighed, smiled thinly, and turned to look out the window. "How long till we get to the inn?"

"Fairly soon," Lord Ryland said.

"That's good. I'm tired a talkin'. It's makin' my head hurt."

No, Caroline thought, it wasn't her sister's head that hurt; it was her heart. But in the world in which Simone had grown up, being vulnerable was dangerous. Pretending that you were carved of stone wasn't an easy way to live, but openly caring and hurting made you easy prey. Better to be stone cold and alive than stone-cold dead.

But, as Simone had said, some were lucky and some weren't. And to Caroline's thinking, Simone had to be the most fortunate young woman in all of England. She'd survived long enough to be plucked from the edge of hell. From here on out . . .

Caroline stole a glance at their benefactor, their guardian. He sat looking out the other window of the carriage, his expression pensive, almost sad. Yes, he was pompous and far too arrogant to be tolerable. He could raise her temper faster and more effectively than any man ever had. He decreed, he pronounced, he instructed, he expected everything to go his way, on his schedule.

On the face of all that, he wasn't the least bit likable. Devilishly handsome, roguishly tempting, yes. But not likeable at first blush. There was more to him than the Great Commander, though. He'd seemed genuinely distressed by the tale of Simone's mother's death. The condolences he'd offered her had sounded utterly sincere. And now as they rolled on toward the inn and the collection of Fiona, he seemed preoccupied with worry. She could make several guesses as to what concerned him, but she preferred not to. No, it was much more comforting to wrap herself in the illusion that, down deep, he had a heart.

❧ *Three* ❧

CAROLINE CONSIDERED THE STRUCTURE LOOMING AT THE end of the gravel drive; to call it an inn did it a great injustice. Built of white stone, two stories tall, and as long as a London block, it was, to her mind, closer to a castle. The sun was setting, bathing the front wall in the softest, peach-tinted light. And the flowers . . . Never in her life had she seen anything as beautiful as the gardens that lined the drive, as the riot of color that spilled out of the carved stone planters that marched up both sides of the wide steps to the massive wooden doors. If Ryland Castle was just half as beautiful, putting up with its master might be worth the effort.

"And what don't belong here?" Simone asked from the other end of the seat.

Caroline leaned forward so she could see out the other window. A battered, weather-beaten wooden cart had been drawn up to the far side of the inn and parked in the shade of an ancient tree. A gray horse, who looked not one year younger than the tree, stood in the traces, his head hanging. Beside the cart . . . Had they been dressed better, they might have passed for a circus. A man, a woman, three dashing, yipping dogs, and a bounding horde of dark-haired children raising every bit as much noise as the dogs. Except for one child. A little towheaded thing dressed in what looked like a flour sack and standing as silent and still as a post between the man and the woman. "Oh, dear," Caroline whispered, knowing in her heart that the little girl was the one they'd come to collect.

"S'pose that's Fiona they got on that lead rope?"

Rope? Caroline looked closer as the carriage came a halt. Yes, there was indeed a rope tied around the child's waist. The other end of it was in the man's hand. "The poor baby."

"You will both remain here," Lord Ryland instructed as he let himself out of their vehicle. "And allow me to deal with these people without interference."

The instant he closed the door and walked away, Caroline slipped to the other seat and closer to the window.

"He always declarin' like that?" Simone asked as Caroline saw the little girl look at the stranger advancing toward them and then try to take a step back. The man shortened the rope and held her in place.

"It does seem to be his initial, preferred approach to matters."

"I don't like bein' barked at."

"No one does," she replied absently, watching the child hang her head and roll her shoulders forward so that the curtain of stringy, dirty blond hair fell over her face. "He's going to have to make some adjustments in his manner in the coming days."

"Well, it oughta be interestin' watchin' you two butt heads over it."

"I don't know that 'interesting' is the word I would choose to describe the contest," Caroline admitted as Lord Ryland removed his hat and bowed slightly to the

woman and then shook hands with the man. "I'm afraid
that it could become a bit explosive. He's already
proven that he can be quite devious in the pursuit of his
objectives."

"Your mouth ever get tired of puttin' all those words
together so fancy like?"

"No." How very odd. Fiona was clearly made uncomfortable by all the attention focused on her and yet she
didn't reach out to either her aunt or her uncle for reas-
surance. It was almost as if she were trying to become in-
visible instead.

"He's a looker, ain't he?"

Caroline blinked and brought her gaze back inside the
carriage. Simone was grinning from ear to ear. "He's pass-
ably handsome," Caroline allowed. "His snobbery and
high-handedness rather offset it, though."

"He married?"

"I have absolutely no idea. He hasn't mentioned a wife
and I haven't thought to ask."

"Maybe he's thinkin' of marryin' you."

Caroline rolled her eyes and then turned back to the
scene in the side yard, saying, "I very seriously doubt
that."

"He likes lookin' at you. Or ain't you caught him doin'
it?"

He liked looking at her? Ha! He made a point of not
doing so. And if Simone thought otherwise, the child
needed eyeglasses. "He's a duke, Simone," she pointed
out, addressing the larger issue. "If he isn't married already, then he can have his pick of all the ladies in the
land. There is no reason whatsoever for him to choose a
bastard modiste over a proper lady with a substantial
dowry and titles of her own."

Simone laughed—a deep, throaty, completely unaffected sound that really should have come out of someone considerably older than she was. It suggested a wisdom about men and relationships that Caroline knew she didn't possess herself. Not in sufficient depth to be of real value, anyway. That Simone seemed to be so sure of what she saw, what she knew . . . It was, to say the least, disconcerting.

Yes, Drayton Mackenzie, Duke of Ryland, was a handsome man. Terribly handsome, actually. And yes, he could be very irritating when he put his mind to it. But when he didn't—like now, as he squatted to speak to Fiona on her level . . . Sliding into his bed wouldn't be the most horrible thing that could ever happen to a woman.

Caroline closed her eyes and took a slow, deep breath. No, Simone came from a world in which relationships between men and women were nothing more than fleeting physical transactions, where they weren't complicated by titles and dowries and a thousand years of social rules and expectations. That simple world wasn't the one she and her sister found themselves in now. Not the public one, anyway; the one that mattered as far as they were concerned.

Simone had so very much to learn. They both did. Keeping her head squarely on her shoulders and the realities firmly in sight would make that task ever so much easier to do. And the most fundamental reality of all was that Drayton Mackenzie was her guardian and that was all he was ever going to be.

"HELLO, FIONA," HE SAID SOFTLY, ACUTELY AWARE OF how quickly the child's chest was rising and falling. "I'm

Drayton. Your father sent me to find you, to bring you to my house to live."

She didn't move, didn't make a sound.

"Your sisters are in that carriage over there. They'll be coming to my house with you."

"Like we said before, you might as well be talking to a rock, your lordship," Fiona's uncle said. "You can save the breath."

Drayton slowly rose to his full height and reached into his coat pocket. "I appreciate that you were willing to bring her to me here," he said, removing the leather bag of coins and adding, "Please allow me to pay you something not only for your time and trouble today, but for the child's keep over the years."

"That's real nice of you, but we can't accept—"

His wife countered the assertion by snatching the bag from Drayton's hand and saying, "Money makes it legal, Henry. She's his now, proper and forever. Give him the lead and let's be on our way while we still have some light." She turned away and barked at the boys, "Get in the cart! Now!"

With a shrug, Henry held out the end of the frayed rope. Drayton considered the little girl on the other end of it and all that her aunt and uncle had told him about her. He couldn't be sure how much was truth and how much was the product of their obvious resentment and frustration, but he was absolutely certain that he didn't want to take that rope and continue her humiliation.

"I'm sure you have other uses for the tether," he said. He held out his hand to Fiona, saying, "Shall we go meet your sisters? And then get something to eat?"

Her head slowly came up and from between the strands

of greasy blond hair, a pair of breathtaking green eyes warily considered him.

"You may have whatever you want to eat," he cajoled, his hand still out for her to take. "Whenever you want."

"We'll go with you, mister."

Fiona's gaze snapped to the ground at the sound of the young male voice. Drayton kept his hand out and his gaze fixed on her while silently cursing Geoffrey Turnbridge for all the hells he'd created. "Please, Fiona," he whispered. "Come with me and get something to eat."

"Take us, mister," said another of the boys, this one practically bellowing in his ear. "We'd be glad to eat."

All right, enough; if the parents had been willing to control their children this might have gone more to his liking, but since they weren't inclined to discipline and the unruly mob was pressing closer, the time had come to just be done with it. He'd win over Fiona when there was the peace and quiet the task required. Drayton let his hand fall back to his side with a resigned sigh. With the other hand, he reached out to accept the end of the rope. His fingers had barely touched it when one of the boys, the biggest of the bunch, stepped between him and Fiona, planted his hands on her shoulders and pushed, saying, "Talk, stupid!"

Fiona stumbled back from the assault, pulling the rope out of Drayton's loose control. In the fraction of time it took for her bottom to land in the yard, total chaos erupted.

"Hey, stop that!"

Simone? Drayton didn't spare a backward glance to be sure. Fiona was scrambling to her feet, her head whipping from side to side in an obvious frantic effort to decide where she was going to run. He darted forward, desperate to catch her—just as one of the other boys went to kick her, missed, and planted his foot in his mother's shin. The woman howled, the boy howled, and they both stumbled into Drayton's path. The bullying boy wasn't impeded, though, and he managed to snatch a handful of grimy dress and blond hair. Fiona gasped and froze.

"You little son of a bitch!"

Yes, Simone. And damn if she wasn't impressive. She took Bully Boy from his blind spot, flying through the air to plant her shoulder hard into his ribs and take him cleanly off his feet. Fiona was gone before they hit the ground—a flash of gray and dirty yellow and blackened soles headed toward the rear of the inn.

He'd barely had time to blink in realization when a brown blur passed him, headed after her. Caroline, he realized in a strangely calm sort of way. Well, that answered the corset question. No tightly laced woman could run like that. Nice ankles. And calves, too.

A painful yelp brought his attention back to the moment. And at that moment, Simone was giving the boy the pasting of his life. A beautiful right jab to the midsection. Followed immediately by a solid left uppercut to the jaw. The boy went off his feet again and Simone went down after him, doing a wonderful job of pummeling his head and shoulders as he tried—futilely—to shield himself from her vengeance. Since his parents were too busy getting the dogs and other boys into the cart to save him, Drayton felt compelled to intervene.

"Enough," he said as he slipped his arm around Simone's waist and hauled her off the hapless lad. She kicked and struggled to get out of the hold, but the boy was quick to seize the reprieve. He scrambled for the rear of the departing cart, launching himself into the grasping hands of his brothers and mother.

Simone yelled after him, threatening his anatomy and promising to wreak havoc on the entire family if they ever came within her reach again. Drayton didn't want to grin, he really didn't. It was a horrible situation. The daughter of a duke being involved in fisticuffs in full view of any one of the inn's guests or staff who happened to have been looking out a window . . .

But, God, what a show they'd have seen if they had. Simone had a sense of righteousness every father would be proud to see in a son. And incredible fighting skills to back it up. Chuckling quietly, he set her on her feet. It took supreme effort to keep himself from saying, "Well done," but he managed.

"Son of a bitch. Pickin' on her like that."

He nodded, pleased all over again. "Speaking of Fiona," he said, straightening his jacket. "We should be seeing where she went."

Simone turned without a word and strode off toward the rear of the inn. Drayton followed, feeling an odd mixture of resentment and pity for a nameless, faceless man standing at an altar in the distant, blessedly fuzzy future. He sighed and shook his head, amazed and a bit disgusted with himself. He wasn't the domestic type, had never once in his life had so much as a fleeting thought about the virtues of settling down to a hearth and home of his own. And here he was feeling positively paternal about a fourteen-year-old girl who'd come into his keeping less than three hours ago.

But better paternal, he decided, as he rounded the corner of the inn, than the feelings the sight of Caroline's backside ignited in him. Christ on a crutch. Did she have any idea of what went through mens' minds when they saw a woman on her knees and elbows, her derriere angled up in . . . Well, it wasn't an invitation. Not a conscious one, anyway. He needed to pretend he didn't see it. He needed to erase the searing fantasy from his mind. Which would be a hell of a lot easier if it weren't such a good one and if she'd get up from there and stop fueling it.

"It's all right, sweetheart," she was saying as she peered under the smokehouse. "Please come out."

Simone dropped down on the wooden steps, looked back at him and then down at her sister kneeling in the dirt. "Lord have mercy," she muttered, planting her elbow on her knee and her chin in the palm of her hand. "Ain't this gonna be fun."

"Caroline," he said, pausing to clear his throat. "If I might have a word with you, please."

She didn't get up; that would have been kind. Instead, she turned her head to look up at him. Her prim little bonnet was gone; to where he had no idea and didn't care. The tumble of her golden hair around her face and shoulders was beyond perfection. Her face, flushed rosy pink from running . . . The fantasy was so provocative that he had to strangle back a groan of appreciation. There was nothing he could do about the intense heat and instant flow of his blood, though. He carefully shifted his stance in accommodation. In desperation, he extended his hand, saying tightly, "Allow me to assist you up."

She put her gloved hand in his and the current surged from his fingertips to his toes. Swallowing, he put on a smile and balanced her as she gathered up her skirts and got to her feet. Once she was upright, matters improved considerably. At least his brain could think of something other than proving that he was a complete cad.

"According to her aunt," he began, keeping his voice low so that the hiding child couldn't hear herself being discussed, "Fiona is . . ." He touched his fingertip to the side of his head.

"Crazy," Simone translated. "Bet it was a horse. Got her foot, too. Did ya see how she limps?"

No, he hadn't, actually. Caroline nodded. "They said she was born crippled," he explained, thinking that it couldn't be all that bad if the girl could run. "But they didn't elaborate on the nature of the deformity. She can hear and speak, but rarely chooses to do the latter. She has always preferred the companionship of animals to that of people. They said that if she's not tied up, she'll wander off into the woods and not return."

"A faerie," Simone declared.

Her sister sighed and looked down at her. "Surely you don't believe such nonsense."

"Not until I seen her."

"Stop it, Simone," she said. "You're an intelligent young woman and know better. The poor child needs all the acceptance we can give her. Lord knows that she's probably never had so much as a dram of it in her life."

"Undoubtedly true," Drayton agreed. "However, I don't think standing here, cooing and smiling in acceptance, is going to lure her out from under the building."

Simone brightened and lifted her chin from her hand. "Want me to go in after her?"

"No," he said, unbuttoning his coat. "I will go after her."

The touch was light, but just as jolting as the last one had been. He went still as he looked down at the hand on his forearm, then up and into the pair of softly earnest blue eyes.

"She cowered the instant she saw you get out of the carriage," she said, drawing her hand back now that she had his attention. "And she withered into herself as you spoke with her aunt and uncle. To me, the reactions suggest that she hasn't been treated all that kindly by men in the past. Why don't the two of you go inside, see to our rooms and the ordering of baths and a meal for all of us, while I try to coax out our frightened little hedgehog? If I'm unsuccessful, then you can scramble in and drag her out."

It made sense. He'd noted the reactions, too. "Fifteen minutes," he offered. "No more than that."

She nodded and turned to the sister perched on the steps. "Simone, please be a dear and get me a lap robe from the carriage."

Simone stood, asking, "You gonna throw it over her head and grab her?"

"No. I'm going to offer her warmth and gentle compassion."

With a roll of her eyes, Simone dutifully trotted off toward the carriage. As she went, Caroline dropped gracefully to her knees in front of him. Drayton turned away as nonchalantly as he could, pretending that he was far more interested in watching Simone run her errand than he was in the new fantasy searing his imagination. To further distract himself, he cleared his throat and spat out the first coherent words that drifted through his awareness. "You're going to ruin your gown if you go under there."

"It can be laundered," she assured him. "And mended, if need be. I refuse to put concern for clothing ahead of a child's welfare."

Of course. It had been an incredibly stupid thing for him to mention. She had to think that he had all the depth of a rain puddle and all the compassion of a rock. Simone's return saved him from having to think of something redemptive to say. She zipped right past him with the lap robe, and without thinking, he turned. And promptly lost all awareness of Simone. Of breathing, too. He was, however, acutely aware of his tightening groin.

"Thank you," she said, gathering the blanket close to her chest as she leaned down—on one elbow this time—and peered under the smokehouse again. "Now the two of you wander off so I can speak with Fiona without the distraction."

As if she had any idea of what a real distraction was, he silently grumbled as he stuffed his hands into his trouser pockets and headed toward the corner of the inn.

"Fiona ain't the only one who's crazy," Simone offered from beside him. "Carrie's oars ain't exactly in the locks, either. Could be we ain't gonna see either of them ever again."

"Lady Caroline has full possession of her faculties."

"Her what?"

"Her faculties," he repeated. "Her mind. She also possesses a rather indomitable will."

"Huh?"

"I believe that I have already instructed you on the proper manner in which to request clarification."

"And I told you that I don't beg for nuthin'," she countered jauntily. "What does 'indomitable' mean?"

"That she is not easily dominated, controlled."

"I figured you was one of the ones smart 'bout people. It's in the eyes, you know. You don't miss much."

"No, I do not."

"I don't, either."

"A fact I concluded not two seconds after you planted yourself in my carriage."

"What do I call you? Da? Uncle?"

"My name is Drayton. It will suffice."

"So, Drayton, how come you're workin' so hard at being such a prig?"

He stopped dead in his tracks, his stomach chilling. It took Simone a second longer to come to a halt and he waited until she turned to face him before he asked coolly, "Pardon?"

A grin slowly spread across her dirt-smudged face. "Yeah, I figured you ain't the sort to beg any more than I am. So how come you're workin' so hard at being somethin' you ain't?"

It occurred to him that he could claim not to know what she was talking about. It also occurred to him that it would be a completely wasted effort and that there was an advantage in having her talk to him rather than to her older sister. "There are expectations and I must meet them."

"Why?"

"Money. I need it."

She nodded knowingly. "World us'ly boils down to pretty much that, don't it? You really a duke?"

"Yes. To my great surprise," he admitted. He drew a deep breath and looked back at the smokehouse. Thankfully, Caroline had disappeared into the shadows under the floorboards. "You and your sisters are not the only ones who will be taking lessons."

"I figured as much."

It was that obvious? He silently groaned. Just what was Caroline going to think when she discovered the truth? Was it even remotely possible for Simone to keep a secret? Or was it too late and Caroline had already recognized him as the fraud he was?

"Naw, I ain't said anythin' to her," Simone said softly, apparently able to read his mind. "She'll figure it out on her own, though. Once she takes a good look past them big shoulders and long legs of yours. 'Course, she could see that fire you got goin' for her and bolt for the hills without holdin' up to figure out what's botherin' her 'bout you besides what's makin' her all warm and gooey."

Sweet Jesus. He'd only thought he'd had problems before. He hadn't counted on Simone. "How old are you?" he asked, resuming their course.

"Fourteen. Or thereabouts," she said with a shrug. "Don't know that anyone's ever really cared all that much 'bout keepin' track."

"You have a wisdom uncommon in those with so few years."

"That's 'cause I seen a lot in my so few years. You know how to sword-fight?"

Sword-fight? Uh-oh. "Pardon?"

"I'm thinkin'," she drawled, "that I might be willin' to keep my uncommon wisdom to myself if you'd be willin' to teach me how to sword-fight."

God had taken pity on him. "That's blackmail," he observed, thinking that appearing too eager to accept the terms wasn't a particularly good idea.

"More like askin' for a bribe to my way of thinkin', but then, I don't much care what we call it as long as I get what I want."

"You are a ruthless child."

She grinned up at him. "Means I should be pretty good with a sword, huh?"

"Yes, it should," he admitted, suddenly wishing his father were still alive. The man had loved the old weapons, the old ways of warfare. How many times had he claimed that the young men of today had no appreciation for the *art* of killing and maiming their fellow men? Robert Mackenzie would have been delighted to meet Simone.

"And I like winnin', too," she said. "So does Carrie, in case you're interested in knowin' that. But she fights like a girl."

"She fights like a woman," he corrected, remembering. "There's a considerable difference."

She laughed softly. "You married, Drayton?" she asked as they came around the front corner of the building and started toward the main stairs.

"No," he declared crisply, wondering what the hell she was getting ready to ask for now.

"Why not?"

It was complicated and not a subject he was willing to discuss with his ward. Not today, not ever. "That's none of your business," he announced.

They were at the base of the stairs when she finally said, "I'm thinkin' you probably figured out a long time ago that there ain't no reason to buy the cow when you can get the milk for free."

Damn if she hadn't nailed a good portion of it square on. Admitting it wasn't the thing to do, though. This was most definitely not the kind of conversation one had with a lady. Of any age. He slid a warning look in her direction, saying, "You think quite a bit, don't you?" as they went up the steps.

"Yep." She grinned from ear to ear. "And right now I'm thinkin' that I've done 'bout all the talkin' that's safe for today."

"You have a most remarkable sense of self-preservation," he observed as the door was opened for them.

"Yes, I do."

"In," he commanded, gesturing for her to precede him and wondering how long he had before she decided to do some thinking around Caroline. Probably not long, he realized as the butler stepped forward to greet them. Which meant he had to do some thinking and deciding of his own and quickly.

⋙ *Four* ⋘

IT HAD TAKEN SURPRISINGLY LITTLE EFFORT TO GET Fiona to creep into the blanket. And when that sliver of comfort had proved non-lethal after just a few minutes, the little girl had been willing to crawl out from under the smokehouse. What she hadn't been willing to do was to ease her death grip on Caroline's hand for so much as a heartbeat. For a slight wisp of a thing, she was amazingly strong.

She was also exceptionally dirty. But unlike Simone, it wasn't the unpleasant odors of the city. Fiona smelled like dirt. And smoke. Both of them did now, actually. Caroline glanced down at her skirt as they made their way toward the front of the inn, and half smiled at the ground-in ash, thinking that it was a very small price to pay for having earned Fiona's trust.

She was a beautiful child. Or would be once she was scrubbed clean and the mats had been cut out of her hair. Those eyes of hers . . . It wasn't so much the striking green color of them that took the breath away, it was the look of sadness in their depths when she dared to meet a gaze. A single second had been all it had taken to twist Caroline's heart around her youngest sister's tiny little finger.

Whatever Fiona needed, she would get and heaven help Lord Ryland if he had any miserly inclinations. The child did limp. Rather more noticeably when she walked than when she ran. It was the right side that seemed to be the problem. A stolen glance at the little bare feet told Caroline that they were both finely boned and perfectly normal in appearance. Which left the possibility of the leg being shorter as the most likely cause of her rolling gait.

Perhaps a physician could fix the problem so her sister could walk normally. She'd insist that Lord Ryland find the best to treat the girl. And if all the medicine that money could buy couldn't help, then they'd simply see that Fiona had carefully crafted shoes that compensated for the difference so that she never once felt as though she were less than absolutely perfect. If anyone ever made fun of her . . .

Caroline smiled, remembering the hell that had broken loose when the boy had knocked Fiona down in the yard. All of London would someday fear the Wrath of Simone and anyone who was foolish enough to make Fiona the brunt of a joke or the object of a cruel remark would be missing crucial body parts.

What a strange lot of offspring they were, she realized as they rounded the front corner of the building. Her with her dark blond hair and rather grayish eyes. Simone with her fair skin and dark eyes and raven curls. Fiona the embodiment of a woodland sprite. And their temperaments! Were there ever three sisters so different?

Having never seen their father, she had no idea if either Simone or Fiona favored him. She had been the image of her mother—both in appearance and, for the most part, demeanor. If Simone and Fiona also favored theirs . . .

Well, it certainly suggested that their father's taste in women had been eclectic.

That the three of them came from such strikingly different worlds said that he had been a man who hadn't hesitated to cross all class barriers when urges came upon him. And the fact that his daughters had been unacknowledged until now said—very plainly—that he'd deliberately used those class differences to insulate himself from financial, moral, and ethical accountability.

Yes, altogether, they were bastards by birth, but their father had been one by privilege and choice. It was his loss, though, she reminded herself, gently squeezing the little hand in hers.

Fiona stopped and then took a full step back, jerking Caroline to an awkward, unexpected halt. She looked at her sister and then followed the alarmed gaze to the front steps of the inn. Or more accurately, to the base of them where Lord Ryland stood every bit as still as Fiona.

His gaze met Caroline's and he arched a brow. Not in sarcasm or disdain, she happily realized, but in silent question, in a tacit surrender to her judgment on how best to deal with Fiona. There was hope for him after all.

"He won't hurt you," Caroline promised quietly, smiling down at her sister. "He's a good man."

She nodded in a very tentative way, but she did step back to Caroline's side and let herself be drawn forward. As they approached, Lord Ryland eased toward the flower pots so that they passed with Caroline between him and Fiona. She wouldn't have guessed that he'd be so considerate of the child's fears.

"Which room is ours?" she asked softly as they passed him and started up the steps.

"Upstairs. The girls are in number five. You are in six."

She nodded in acknowledgment and kept going. The door opened at their approach and she managed to get Fiona across the threshold before the child's wonder overcame her ability to keep her feet moving. As she stared around the grand and gilded foyer, her mouth hanging open and her green eyes as big as saucers, Lord Ryland slipped in behind them.

He paused at Caroline's left side and whispered, "I will have some bread and cheeses sent up to tide you over. Our meal will be served in the private dining room whenever you and your sisters are ready to dine. I will await you there."

"Thank you, your grace," she whispered back.

He leaned closer, his jacket lapels brushing her sleeve, his breath warmly caressing her ear as he said, "Drayton."

It wasn't an unpleasant shudder. Not even remotely. She closed her eyes, savoring it, knowing as she did that she shouldn't. He was her legal guardian, she his ward. They were distant cousins. The thorns of reality didn't make the sensation any less pleasurable, though. Just more unseemly.

She forced herself to open her eyes, breathe, and focus on what was going on around her. He was talking to the man at the door, the low rumble of his voice sending another warm shudder through her body. Caroline swallowed and lifted her chin, determined to control herself. Lord knew she'd make enough missteps in the days and weeks ahead that she didn't need to compound the embarrassment by doing something so utterly unladylike as go weak kneed and pliant at the merest touch of a man.

Her resolve firmly in place, she smiled down at Fiona and winked. "Let's go see our rooms, shall we?"

Fiona nodded in her tentative way and allowed herself to be led across the black-and-white marble floor and up the carpeted stairs to the second floor. A long hallway stretched out on either side of the landing, doors opening onto them from both right and left. Caroline paused to find the numbers and determine that they should go to their right. As they turned, a movement from the foyer below caught her eye. She looked back to see Lord Ryland standing there alone, his hands stuffed into his trouser pockets, his gaze following them.

She offered him a smile and mouthed "thank you" in appreciation for all the consideration he'd shown her and Fiona in the past few moments. He rocked slightly back on his heels before he managed to summon a smile in return—a smile that looked more strained than anything else—and then promptly turned and walked out the front door.

She had no idea what she'd done that so obviously bothered him, but since there wasn't anything she could do about fixing it or apologizing for it at the moment, she set the issue aside and focused on finding room number 5. It was midway down the hall and on her left. And its door was standing wide open.

There were two big beds in it, a large draperied window and a table between them. Simone was standing on one of the beds, in the center of a down coverlet on what was apparently a down mattress. The whole thing had puffed up and around to hide the lower half of her legs and make her look decidedly sawed off. Fiona wasn't the only one the sight brought up short.

"Hello," Simone said, jumping off the bed to land neatly in front of them.

Caroline gently squeezed Fiona's hand in assurance, saying, "This is your other sister. Her name is Simone and she's not as wild as she looks."

Simone laughed and bounded off toward an open door

on the far side of the room, saying, "You have to see this, Carrie. C'mon in here." And then disappeared from sight.

She glanced down at Fiona and was relieved to see that the child didn't seem to be at all distressed by Simone's exuberance. In fact, if she had to guess what the tilted angle of the little blond head meant, it would be that she was intrigued and wanted to see what wonders Simone had discovered. Not that she was going to let go of Caroline's hand and scamper off on her own to do it.

Still, Caroline considered her open interest a sign of remarkable progress and gladly took Fiona across the room and through the tall doorway. Again they both stopped short. "What in the world?" Caroline muttered, staring in awe at the giant copper tub sitting lengthwise in the room. A lacy curtained window flanked it on either side, and on the wall in between them, two smallish, banded wooden pipes ran down, each with a shorter pipe sticking out at a right angle over the tub and with what looked like a copper doorknob sitting atop each one.

"Watch," Simone instructed, turning one of the knobs. Water instantly gushed from the end of the pipe and splashed into the tub. Fiona gasped and bounced on her toes in excitement as the steam rose and Simone exclaimed, "It's hot! And if it's too hot, you turn this handle, too," she added, cranking the other knob and sending water gushing out of the second pipe. "And it cools right down. Come feel!"

And Fiona did, releasing Caroline's hand and darting forward.

"Not in the stream," Simone said, catching her younger sister's hands. "The hot'll burn you. Down inside is perfect," she added, turning Fiona to face the tub.

Both of them leaned over the edge to place their hands in the rapidly deepening water and flat against the copper bottom. Fiona's feet came up off the floor and she giggled in delight. "Ain't it just magic?" Simone said over her shoulder, grinning from ear to ear.

Yes, it was. In so many ways. "I've heard of such things, but I've certainly never seen . . ." Words failed her and all she could do was smile at the contraption and shake her head in awed appreciation of the genius who'd created it.

Simone pushed herself upright and then, chuckling, reached over to pull a struggling Fiona back onto her feet. "See that plug there?" Simone said to them both, pointing to somewhere under the frothing water beneath the pipe ends. "You pull it and all the water drains right out the bottom. I know 'cause I've already done it. Twice."

She'd take her word that it was there and how it worked. "Oh, how absolutely wonderful. No hauling tubs and buckets. No having to heat water on a stove. No having to bathe in a teacup. I could kiss someone."

"How 'bout these, too?" Simone offered, snatching up a white sheet from a pile of them on a table beside the tub. "Ever seen anythin' so white in your life?"

No, she hadn't. London soot turned the best efforts of the strongest lye to a dull gray within moments. A hot bath, a white bath sheet . . . Oh, dear God, clean water for her after the girls had had their baths! At the turn of a knob! "Have my bags been brought up from the carriage yet?" she asked, her heart racing in giddy anticipation.

Simone shrugged and then pointed to a closed door opposite the open one that led into their room. "Heard some bumping and dumping a minute ago over on that side of the door."

"I want to get some things from my bags so we can have proper baths," Caroline announced, turning. Fiona's panicked little cry stopped her. "I'll leave the door open so you can see me the whole time I'm gone," she promised. "And I won't be gone long at all."

"We can play in the water while she's gone," Simone cajoled, leaning back over the edge of the tub. "Look how you can see your hand through it, Fiona. Have you ever seen anythin' that clear before?"

Fiona looked over at Simone, down into the tub, and then back at Caroline. With a tiny, tremulous smile, she turned and leaned back over the edge.

"OH," CAROLINE BREATHED ON A SIGH OF DELIGHT AS SHE eased down into the water. "Pure decadence." Life simply could not get any better than this. Simone was right; it was magic. Leaning her head against the back of the tub, Caroline closed her eyes and slid down until the water came to her chin. If this was typical of the lives of the wealthy, she'd fought way too hard to keep her independence.

Not that she would ever admit that to Lord Ryland, of course. Well, maybe she would if he threatened to deprive her of baths like this one. She'd be willing to swallow a bit of pride to have such a divinely sinful pleasure anytime she wanted it. What else she might be willing to give up if he demanded it, though . . .

He didn't strike her as the vindictive sort—despite the business of buying the building her shop was in and saying he'd posted a guard at her door when he hadn't. They'd been strangers then and he'd been coming into the negotiations without knowing how she'd react and needing to have some leverage just in case she proved obstinate. Which she had. In looking back at the day, she had to allow that if she'd been in his position, she'd probably have done the same thing.

It was amazing how a deliciously warm bath in a huge tub could change how the world looked—especially the men in it. Well, it wasn't just the bath, she amended. She'd begun to see him in a completely different light when he'd squatted down in front of Fiona and so patiently offered her his hand. It had been such a compassionate, understanding gesture. And he'd made it with what had looked like—admittedly from a distance—a natural kind of ease.

Simone insisted that Drayton wasn't what he appeared to be on the surface, that underneath all the "prigginess"—as Simone put it—he really was a regular man. Caroline grinned. She'd been in the process of trying to get Simone to describe just what being "regular" entailed when the tray of food had arrived and Simone had elevated him straight to sainthood.

It was only logical to assume that the youngest two of his wards would be starving, but that he'd actually thought to do something about it spoke volumes about his basic decency and sense of kindness. All in all, he certainly was shaping up to be a bit more human than she'd first thought possible.

Whether that was a good thing or not . . . Monsters breathing against your ear didn't turn your insides to delightfully warm jelly. And you most certainly didn't remember the moment with any sort of wistful sigh and then wonder what the chances were of it happening again. On purpose the next time. And perhaps with an actual slow, deliberate brush of the lips. It would feel so very good. It would be absolutely divine.

And absolutely, unforgivably scandalous.

Caroline fanned her cheeks with her hands, sat up and reached for her bar of sandalwood soap. French milled and exotically scented, it had cost a small fortune. It had been a luxury she'd regretted not ten feet from the merchant's shop, but she hadn't been willing to take it back to plead the belated common sense of poverty. Instead, she'd tucked it away for a special occasion. In the two years since, nothing had met her criteria of "special" until tonight.

If Drayton Mackenzie, the Duke of Ryland, was willing, she'd meet him halfway and declare a truce. She'd agree to do whatever it took to be considered the proper daughter of a peer. She'd do whatever was necessary to see that Simone and Fiona were brought up respectably and had everything that they would ever need or could possibly want. She would swallow her pride and put fulfilling her mother's plans for her future on the shelf. She would, if required to do so, even agree to sincerely consider any offers of marriage that might come her way.

If that didn't make the evening a special occasion, there was no such thing. Hopefully, Lord Ryland would appreciate just how much she was offering him and accept it all with some grace.

She rinsed and rose from the tub, wrapped herself in a bath sheet that smelled of sunshine and lavender, then laughingly called to Fiona, reminding her that it was her turn to have the honor of pulling the plug.

There was silence in response. Caroline's heart went to her throat. She'd given them each a worn but clean chemise to wear after their baths, with the promise of fashioning something makeshift from her wardrobe for them to wear down to dinner once she'd had her bath. If they'd taken off on their own dressed as she'd left them . . .

Clutching the wet sheet around herself, she stepped to the door of their room. They were both still there. Thank God. Both on the same bed with the cheese and bread plate between them, just as she'd left them not fifteen minutes ago . . . But now the plate was empty and they were sprawled out, not just sound asleep, but snoring like little puppies.

They were both such beautiful girls, Caroline thought, her heart going from pounding to swollen with appreciation. So different from each other and yet so much alike in their ability to seize the wonder of their suddenly changed circumstances. Fiona still hadn't uttered a single word, but she'd smiled as her hair had been washed, only winced once as it was combed out for the first time in heaven only knew how long, and then skipped around the room in the chemise as though she'd been dropped into a diamond- and pearl-studded evening gown.

And Simone . . . The girl who could swing a fist with bloody accuracy and make sailors blush with her frankness had taken up the game with her little sister, holding out the thin lawn of her borrowed chemise at the sides and dropping into exaggerated curtsies.

And there the two of them were now, fast asleep. Full and warm and clean. Bless Lord Ryland for having plucked them from the hells their lives had been. She'd make sure that he never once regretted it.

DRAYTON CHECKED HIS WATCH AND THEN RETURNED IT to its pocket with a sigh.

"More wine, your grace?"

"Is the bottle empty?" he asked, picking up his glass and looking at the firelight through the ruby red liquid.

"Yes, your grace."

Well, either it had evaporated or he'd been waiting even longer than he thought. Odd that he didn't feel the effects of a full bottle of wine, but then, the day had been one of the oddest of his life so it wasn't all that surprising. "Another one, then," he said. "In the event that my eldest ward might want a glass with her meal."

The sommelier uncorked the bottle in his hand, replaced the empty bottle with it and then departed the room, leaving Drayton alone with his thoughts. Or, more accurately, with his battle to control them. Which hadn't been going all that well for the better part of the day, but had gotten infinitely more difficult as he waited for Caroline and her sisters to join him.

Hopefully the woman didn't own a proper evening gown. It would be absolutely impossible to sit here and carry on something approximating a civil and circumspect dinner conversation if she arrived in a low-cut, sleeveless, waist- and hip-hugging dress. And God help him if she actually wore a necklace with a drop that fell into her cleavage.

Cursed. That's what he was, cursed. He'd been living the perfect life—no commitments or obligations to fulfill except those he made himself. No grand expectations to meet except those he set for himself. And then, through no fault of his own, the bloody world had been upended.

But he'd been a true Englishman and shouldered his duty and trudged on, making the best of the disaster and doing a fairly competent job of it all. Until Caroline.

His sense of mastery—marginal though it was—had begun to unravel the second he'd walked into her shop. Ever since then, good judgment and healthy male desire had been bludgeoning each other senseless. Because it was a rather evenly matched battle, it hadn't overly preoccupied him until his damn imagination had joined the fray and taken the bit firmly between its teeth by the smokehouse steps.

God, it had been only hours and already he was tired of trying to keep it reined in. And more than a little put out by the necessity of having to do so. Failing at the effort—even just a little and for a fraction of a moment—provided rewards that were infinitely more enjoyable than any self-control had ever given him.

The whisper in her ear in the foyer, for instance. He'd acted on the impulse before reason could intervene. And good God Almighty, the woman had practically purred and fallen into his arms. And what had he done with that sweet opportunity? He'd backed away from the luscious temptation and turned to speak with the footman at the door. He'd exercised self-discipline and decency. He'd been a goddamn gentleman and chosen being honorable over satisfying his instincts.

It wasn't as though she were the first woman who'd ever set his senses on fire. And she wasn't the only woman he'd ever met who could make even the softest smile look positively carnal. But she was the first woman he couldn't allow himself to seduce.

The only reasonable, workable solution to the dilemma, he decided, emptying the contents of his wine glass, was to keep as much distance as possible between them. And to find someone within the next month or so who wanted to marry her.

As he reached for the bottle to refill his glass, she stepped into the doorway. Distance wasn't going to be possible, he realized as he took in the bare shoulders and arms, the royal blue satin barely covering her breasts. No, there were only two ways he was going to be able to keep his hands off her. One was to see her married and on her way to the farthest corner of the empire before the week was out. The other option was to put a bullet in his brain.

∾ *Five* ∾

HE LOOKED AS IF SOMEONE—OR SOMETHING—HAD JUST kicked him in the stomach. Caroline was about to ask him if he needed assistance of some sort or another when he took a deep breath and asked, "Where are the Spawn of Satan and the Faerie Child?"

Well, "You look ravishing" had been a rather high expectation. She laughed and advanced into the private room, saying, "They attacked the food like little wolves and with their stomachs full and their bodies clean and warmed from their baths . . . They both fell sound asleep while I was taking mine and I'm afraid that I lacked the mental fortitude to wake them."

He swallowed down another just-kicked look to say tautly, "It has been a rather long and eventful day."

"It's been grueling," she allowed, wondering what on earth was wrong with him.

Picking up a glass and the wine bottle, he poured, his attention keenly focused on the task as he said, "A good glass of spirits might help smooth the rougher edges from it."

"Thank you," she replied softly, taking it from him and growing even more puzzled when he refused to meet her gaze.

"I've been quite impressed with your maternal instincts," he told the far wall as the gloved and liveried
wait staff entered the room carrying silver-domed plates.
He cleared his throat, instructed that two of the meals be
returned to the kitchen, and announced that they wouldn't
need attending during the meal.

As the staff cleared away the extra place settings and
removed the domes over the two remaining plates, Caroline sipped her wine and studied her dinner companion—
the dinner companion who seemed determined to look at
everything in the room except her.

"Thank you, again," she said, resuming their conversation as the staff left them. She lifted her glass to him.
"May I say that you've acquitted yourself admirably as a
responsible, respectable male."

He offered her a smile so tight that she wondered if
he'd been sucking lemons before she got there. "And now
that we've each expressed the appropriate compliments,"
he said, gesturing to the table and their cooling meal,
"would you care to be seated?"

"Yes, please." She put her wine glass on the linen-
covered table as she admitted, "I'm well beyond famished."

"The wolves didn't share?"

"I was afraid that if I reached between them for a
scrap," she confessed, smiling and smoothing her skirts
to settle onto the chair he held for her, "they'd take off my
hand. Not intentionally, of course." He moved her and the
chair closer to table with admirable skill and she looked
up over her shoulder at him. "Thank you, your grace."

His hands on the back of the chair, he finally met her
gaze. The tension didn't seem to so much ebb as it . . .
well, settled. He slowly cocked a brow. "Drayton," he said

softly. "I thought we'd covered this point in the foyer ear-lier this evening."

Heat flooded across her cheeks at the memory. Is that what they'd been doing? She watched him move around the table and take his own seat. They'd been covering a point of what to call each other? It had felt as though he'd been branding her. Very gently, but very deeply and thoroughly. How badly she'd misinterpreted that mo-ment. Thank goodness she hadn't outwardly responded; she'd be even more embarrassed now than she already was. Quietly clearing the lump from her throat, she laid her serviette across her lap and picked up her knife and fork.

"Do you have a problem with addressing me by my name?"

"Is it proper that I do so?"

"When it's just the two of us, do we care what's proper?"

Her heart jolted and her blood warmed. Her mind chat-tered frantically. "We should," she replied, her voice sounding—thank goodness—far more composed than she felt.

"Why?"

Oh, dear. She took a bite of the roast beef just to give herself time to marshal her wits, to remind herself that, as in the foyer, this was an innocent conversation and that she shouldn't imagine there was more to it than there re-ally was.

"My mother always maintained that crossing the line of propriety was like drilling a small hole in the bottom of a boat. The water that comes in at first is of little con-cern, but it eventually makes the hole larger and the prob-lem far more dangerous."

He nodded and ate a bite of his own meal before observing, "A very wise woman, your mother. How on earth did she become involved with your father?"

"She was a dressmaker's assistant and my father's wife was a favorite client. He began stopping by the shop to purchase gifts for his wife and requested that my mother assist him in selecting them."

"And one small impropriety led to another."

"And another. And eventually to me. Her wisdom concerning men was hard-won from disappointing experience."

"And your experiences with men . . ." He picked up his wine glass and looked at the fire through it. "Have they been more fortunate and rewarding?"

Her heart jolted again, but this time her blood went cold with the realization that the conversation was far more purposeful than she'd assumed. "Why is it that you ask?" she asked warily.

"I am your guardian and responsible for arranging your introduction into society," he said to the glass in his hand. "If there are incidents in your past that might create embarrassment, I need to be aware of them so they can be addressed beforehand."

It was a perfectly logical, perfectly impersonal explanation. But she sensed that there was more to it than that. "I have some difficulty with thinking of you as a guardian," she said, unsure of her instincts anymore and trying to sidestep the issue. "We're much too close to the same age for me to be . . . well, comfortable with the notion of being under your control."

"I'm a good twelve years your senior."

She made the calculations in her head. "You don't look thirty-five."

"Thank you," he said with a smile, setting his glass aside. "The result of wholesome living and gentle pastimes." He picked up his silverware again, adding, "But we've digressed from the original topic of conversation. Are there relationships in your past of which I should be aware?"

She knew how the conversation was going to end and the assumptions he would make as a result. She was also keenly aware of how unfair they were in a larger social sense. Irritated, determined to make her point while she could, she smiled and replied, "I'm sure that my relationships are no more numerous or significant than those in your own past."

His gaze came up from his plate with an almost audible snap. "My past doesn't matter overly much in the marriage market."

She arched a brow. "Becoming a duke tends to erase the memories of indiscretions?"

"Not erase," he said, easing back in his chair and considering her a bit warily. "Outweigh."

"Doesn't becoming the acknowledged daughter of a duke accomplish the same thing?" she asked, pressing toward her point.

"For some," he allowed with a slight shrug. "But not for those who have the finest pedigrees at stake."

"Those who care about pedigrees aren't likely to consider me acceptable, acknowledged or not," she pointed out. "And those who care about marrying a title and a dowry aren't going to care one whit about anything except that. So the specific details of my past experiences with men are rather irrelevant, aren't they?"

Drayton met the defiant, steel-blue gaze and knew that she was absolutely right. And that he was finally feeling the effects of all the wine. The stuff might have been slow, but it was stunningly potent. In another few moments strategic thinking was going to be a largely hit-and-miss affair. Subtlety was already a lost hope. "Are there going to be men peddling paintings or daguerreotypes of you in compromising circumstances?"

"Of course not," she said, somehow sounding both amused and offended by the suggestion.

"Are there likely to be men describing birthmarks to tawdry publishers?"

She arched a brow. "I don't have any birthmarks."

"That wasn't the point of the question."

"I'm well aware of that."

Christ on a crutch. Of all the times for his brain to skip off on holiday . . . She really was far too intelligent and far too beautiful. For a man who'd had too much to drink, it was a dangerous combination that left him with two choices; he could either retire from the field and salvage what little pride was left after doing so, or risk every shred of it, engage her boldly, and hope for an incredible stroke of luck.

"Let's be honest," she said, stripping the decision away from him. "The real point of this entire conversation is whether or not I am a virgin. The answer is no, I am not."

There is a God.

"As to the question of whether that will become public knowledge . . . The answer is that it will only if you choose to make it so. The young man to whom I was engaged is dead. And since he was an honorable and decent man, he took my heart and my secret with him to the grave."

"I'm sorry," he said. *But not overly and deeply so.*

"As am I. I loved Peter very much."

"And your devotion to his memory is what makes the

thought of marriage to someone else unacceptable to you," he guessed, feeling for the first time in months that life might actually go his way for a change. "People often marry for reasons other than love, you know."

"Quite frankly, I think love has very little to do with most marriages," she offered, casually returning to her meal. "At least those that I've seen. Typically, what begins as a glorious bloom of intense physical attraction fades into a purely practical arrangement."

"Fairly quickly," he offered to keep her talking. She was a fascinating creature. So many unexpected facets.

"Seemingly," she agreed. "And then it's a mere matter of service exchanges that don't particularly delight either party, but are acceptable because they're relieved that they don't have to negotiate with strangers for them on a daily basis."

"I never would have guessed that you are such a cynic."

"Hiding it is a necessary professional skill. I make at least a dozen bridal trousseaus every year. Brides don't want to have their breathless illusions of happily-ever-after dashed with reality. If you can't pretend to their satisfaction, they'll take their business to someone who can."

"Amazing," he said, shoving his plate aside, his interest in eating entirely gone. Drinking, though . . . He picked up his wine glass and settled back in his chair, content to just look at her. God, she didn't need a drop pendant necklace to draw a man's eyes to her bodice. How the hell had he ever thought that he could resist her?

"And now that you know all about me," she said, taking a sip of wine, "it's only fair that you tell me something about yourself."

"There isn't much to tell." Well, there was a great deal to tell, actually, but he really wasn't all that interested in talking. If he'd had his druthers, he'd much rather close and lock the dining room doors, sweep the table clean and lay her down on it.

"Your family name is Mackenzie," she pressed. "Scotch, obviously, but I don't hear the brogue in your voice."

Then again, some women considered conversation foreplay. "My father's ancestors came to England with the first King James. In the course of the almost three hundred years since, the Stuart blood that was once in us has been considerably diluted. A good nosebleed these days would be the last of it."

She smiled and then tipped her chin up to laugh outright. His loins tightened instantly.

"My paternal grandfather was your father's cousin," he said, in part to distract himself, in part to keep the game going. "The title had to do quite a bit of backtracking and side-sliding on the family tree to be dumped on my doorstep."

"You make it sound as though you weren't expecting it and don't much want it."

"I wasn't and I was rather enjoying the life I had." *But things are definitely looking up at the moment.*

She laughed again and set her plate aside. And then, to his deep and abiding appreciation, she leaned forward, picked up the wine glass in one hand, propped the elbow of her other arm on the table, and cradled her cheek in her palm. Her eyes sparkling, she smiled across the table at him and said, "I'm afraid that you're going to have to explain all that. It's simply too intriguing to leave as a mystery. How could you not have known you'd someday be a duke?"

He'd explain anything the provocative little siren wanted

to know. "You weren't aware that you had a brother? And that he was killed some six months ago?"

"No!" she gasped, her eyes wide.

Drayton nodded. "His name was Daniel. I suppose it says a great deal, though, that he was always known as Dinky."

"How horrible. How could they do that to him?"

"The name fit him. Like a glove." He cocked a brow and added pointedly, "A very small glove. With sequins."

"Oh," she said, her eyes sparkling.

"Yes, oh. Dinky lived most of his life in Paris."

"Where he'd be far less likely to cause the family embarrassment."

He lifted his glass to her and, as she sipped her wine, he went on, saying, "When Geoffrey died, Dinky was informed of his social elevation and went out with friends to celebrate. According to the French authorities, he was accidentally strangled to death in a drunken . . . encounter."

"Well," she offered with a little chuckle, "it can't be said that the family is boring."

"There being no other direct descendants," he continued, watching her take another sip and wondering what sort of tolerance she had for alcohol, "the queen's men went to the archives and starting tracing the lineage backward, looking for someone to fill Dinky's spangled shoes. In a stroke of pure, rotten luck, my name was the first one that came up."

"No one can make you wear anything you don't want to wear."

"*Au contraire, ma petite.* Two men arrived at my barracks, informed me of my misfortune, stripped me out of my uniform, stuffed me into an ill-fitting suit, and hauled me off to the office of a barrister. All within the span of three hours."

"You were in the military?"

"Like my father and uncles before me," he supplied, "I was an officer in Her Majesty's Royal Regiment of Artillery. Which, as it turns out, was of very little practical preparation for fulfilling the duties of a duke."

Her heart racing at a ridiculous pace, Caroline grinned. *This* was what Simone had been talking about when she'd said that Drayton was a "regular" man. No airs, no prigginess. Oh, but Simone had so much to learn about men. Drayton Mackenzie wasn't regular in any way at all.

"Ah, you only think you're speechless now," he said. "Wait until you hear the rest of it."

"This would be the part of the story relating to the conditions set in the will?"

"Oh, you can't possibly appreciate the conditions of the will until you understand the conditions of the estate in general."

"Which are?"

"Abysmal."

She laughed and drank a bit more wine. "I suspect that our respective definitions of 'abysmal' are wildly different."

"Well, let's just see, shall we?"

"All right," she laughingly challenged. "Tell away."

"There are three physical properties in the estate," he began, absently swirling his wine in the glass. "The first is the London town house. It's in Hyde Park. Very fashionable, you know. It has a staff of sixteen and a payroll that hasn't been fully met in the last eight months. I can only assume that the staff hasn't moved on to other positions because the grocers have continued to deliver food on a regular basis, putting the bills on what is now *my* tab."

He was positively adorable in his frustration. "Sixteen people could consume a great deal of food."

"And they do," he assured her, grinning. "Additionally, because God forbid that anything in this be a pleasant surprise, dear ol' Geoffrey spared no expense in building this monument to his importance, but chose a builder who spent no tuppence he didn't have to in hiring the workers who actually constructed the damn thing."

"Uh-oh," she said, drinking to keep herself from laughing out loud.

"Yes. I've been informed by a structural engineer that if there should be a strong breeze on the same day that there's three inches of snow, it will collapse into the neighboring property."

How he could make it all so delightfully entertaining . . . "Can it be fixed? Made sound?"

He held up his hand and shook his head. "The second property left to me is a strand of shoreline on the coast of Cornwall, complete with a twenty-room mansion that overlooks the sea and which, at some point in the past, I assume, must have been quite lovely. I can only imagine its former glory, of course, because the entire west wall of the house has fallen off and allowed persons unknown to cart away all the furnishings."

Oh, God. She was going to explode in the most unladylike laughter. "And Geoffrey didn't have it repaired?"

"Geoffrey was up to his eyeballs in debt. The cost of building the house in Hyde Park, the expense of keeping Dinky in Paris, and the bills for preventing sixteen people from starving to death in London were the least of his obligations. There was also the duchess. Or more accurately, her expectations, revenge, and the effective use of her dowry to achieve both."

"This just gets worse and worse."

"Yes, it does. More wine?" he asked, snagging the bottle. "It gets easier to contemplate when you've had great quantities of alcohol."

"You said revenge," she reminded him, holding out her glass and letting him fill it. "I gather that the duchess knew about his dalliances."

"According to the barrister—who, by the by, wasn't kind enough to get me drunk before telling me all of this—Brunhilda—"

"Brunhilda?"

"Yes, Brunhilda."

"You're joking!" she accused through her laughter.

"I am not. Apparently she was from Alsace-Lorraine and from a family known for sturdy physiques and their minor claims to Austrian royalty. In any event, her major appeal to Geoffrey was that she came with a huge dowry."

"Ah," she said, lifting her glass in salute. "One of those loveless marriages we were talking about earlier."

"Without, after Dinky's birth, apparently even the practical service exchanges to make it tolerable."

"So sad," she said, drinking. It was wonderful wine. So sweet and smooth and enjoyable. Rather like Drayton Mackenzie in certain respects.

He snorted. "Lady Ryland was apparently the kind of woman you didn't cross without paying for it several times over. When Geoffrey's indiscretions became a public embarrassment, she went to her papa with the tales and, through what was apparently a hideously complicated legal maneuver, he managed to get his little princess control of her dowry. After that, if Geoffrey wanted so much as a new pair of underdrawers, he had to ask her for them."

"Didn't he inherit money of his own?" she asked, fascinated. With the story. Even more so with the man telling it.

"Aside from being a first-class bounder, Geoffrey was also a drunk, a gambler, and the world's worst money manager."

"Of course." She shook her head, polished off the wine in her glass, and held out the empty stemware, smiling and saying, "More wine, please."

He grinned and poured. "Which brings me to the third property I inherited from him. The country estate. Ryland Castle. I have no idea what sort of physical condition the dwelling itself is in. I'll be seeing it for the first time when we arrive there tomorrow. I can tell you, however, all about the estate's financial condition because the barrister felt obliged to bludgeon me with its account ledgers."

She drank and he continued to entertain her with travesty, saying, "It has a staff of twenty-five people who, apparently, are also in no danger whatsoever of starvation. The castle sits in the midst of a thousand acres in the famously prosperous and fertile agricultural region of Norfolk. A thousand acres that have managed, somehow, to operate at a significant annual loss for the last eighteen consecutive years."

Well, that wasn't amusing. Not in the least. She lifted her head out of her hand and straightened to consider him. "How is that possible?"

"Judging by the accounts that have been kept, my one thousand acres have long had the lowest yields of any estate in the region."

"Really," she drawled. "It should be interesting to actually see the harvest come in this fall."

"My thoughts exactly."

Caroline nodded. "Honest accounting should improve your financial situation a great deal."

He snorted again. "The hole Geoffrey dug is so deep it would take twenty years of crop income to even bring the accounts current."

She arched a brow, asked, "Are we at the conditions of the will now?" and took a bracing drink of her wine.

"We are, indeed," he said blithely. "Lady Ryland died a year before Geoffrey did and with her fingers still wrapped tightly around the purse strings. Geoffrey could have her money only if he publicly recognized his bastards and used the dowry funds to see them married off as befitted their new social status."

"The humiliation of it all for him."

"That, the expense and time of legal hoop-jumping, and the satisfaction of controlling from the grave how her husband used her money. It's a complicated procedure for a peer to recognize his illegitimate offspring. It requires mountains of paperwork, a regiment of solicitors, special dispensations to be secured from the government, then gaining the queen's approval—"

"Victoria?"

He grinned. "She's the only queen we have at the moment."

Well, yes, she knew that. It was just that the idea of the queen's knowing all about the sordid details of her life . . . She washed the mortification away with a healthy drink before she pressed on, asking, "She'll have final say?"

"She's already had it. Two months before Geoffrey

croaked off, she waved her scepter over the paper, stuck her signet ring in the wax, and sent it on for the signatures of the elevated—that would be you and your sisters."

Oh, she'd thrown that last mouthful of wine down too quickly. Her head was starting to wobble on her shoulders, making straight thinking a bit of a trick. "Two months?"

He nodded and his smile looked weak. "Geoffrey didn't hire an investigator to actually find his daughters until he was sure he could get something for them. The agent's report was being finalized when the old man died. The agent handed it—and his bill, of course—to me the day after that first meeting with the barrister."

"And the conditions Lady Ryland set in her will passed on to you as the new Duke of Ryland," she guessed.

He lifted his glass and then brought it to his lips and drained it.

"And you said there wasn't much to tell," she accused, shaking her head in wonder. The entire room tilted on an angle as she did. Caroline blinked, smiled, and propped her chin in her hand to put it all back to rights.

"I was still intending at that point to keep the realities to myself," he admitted, his eyes twinkling, his smile wide and easy.

There really should be laws, she thought, forbidding men to look so damn handsome. "Why did you change your mind?"

He laughed softly. "I had a vision of rolling up the drive of Ryland Castle to find a burned-out hulk and twenty-five persons roasting my last fatted calf on the roof of the lone remaining turret. It occurred to me that explaining it all at that point might be a bit more awkward than it would be now."

For Lord Ryland, most definitely. But Drayton Macken-zie had never had an awkward moment in his life. "The castle could be in fine condition," she reminded him. He lowered his chin and cocked a brow. "All right," she admitted, chuckling, "it's not likely. How soon will you receive control of Brunhilda's money?"

He sighed. "I get half of the set-asides for each of you, upon your signatures. The solicitor will arrive at Ryland Castle with the documents the day after tomorrow. The funds will be available in the form of letters of credit he's also bringing along. The remaining halves will be re-leased from trust on your marriages."

She thought about that in the foggy, not-terribly-concerned-about-anything sort of way her mind was working. "It could be years," she eventually concluded. "Especially considering how young and socially with-drawn Fiona is."

"I'm beginning to understand why ol' Geoffrey drank so heavily."

Well, yes, she could, too. It was rather nice to float along not being all that affected by concerns that would otherwise be quite troublesome. Concerns like money and marrying strangers to get it. "Of course, being a duke," she said as the thought drifted through her awareness, "you have incredible potential for marrying well yourself. Just don't pick a Brunhilda and get the money for her up front."

Don't pick a Brunhilda. Not on his life. His tastes were more toward petite, well-shaped blond modistes with earnest eyes and inviting smiles.

"What?"

He blinked and, knowing better, gave her another, more mundane truth. "Who in their right mind is going to give a man like me, with my background, in my financial circumstances, both a daughter and a small fortune?"

"Someone who wants to say to his friends, 'Can't possibly go punting this weekend, Charles. My daughter—the Duchess of Ryland, you know—is having a house party and the Prince of Poofland has asked me to teach him some of the finer points of cribbage."

"Not likely," he countered with a snort. "And the crowning glory on all this is that in the very next session of Parliament, I get to park my arse in the House of Lords and pretend that I don't see the jabbing elbows or hear the snickers of contempt."

She sipped at her wine, her gaze distant. "Go ahead," he challenged to bring her attention back to him. "Tell me it could be worse."

"Well . . ."

"It can't."

"As the recognized daughters of the late duke," she began slowly, "will there be some expectation of presenting us at court? I'm certainly no authority on these sorts of things," she went on, "but isn't being presented a requirement for attending all the balls and affairs where one shops for a suitable spouse?"

He blinked as the reality fluttered down through the haze of wine and slowly sank into what was left of his brain. She'd be presented, back out of the royal presence, and the bidding would begin right then and there. They'd trample each other to get to her. She'd have her choice from among every eligible bachelor in the realm. But only if he could exercise some self-control between now and then. If he couldn't, she'd be a pariah.

"Well," she said in that half-offended, half-amused tone of hers, "I don't think I'd do that badly."

"I was picturing Simone meeting the queen," he lied.

Her eyes went wide. "Oh, dear God in heaven," she laughed, holding out her glass. "More wine, please. Hurry."

He poured for her, knowing even as he did that he should be refusing to do so. He'd had way too much to trust his judgment to control his behavior and she seemed to be rapidly approaching the same point. Things could so easily go to hell in a handbasket from here. It was time to declare dinner done and get a thick wooden door—with a heavy lock—between them.

"You lied to me this morning."

"In the grand scheme of things," he countered, "I hardly think the footman ruse was all that horrible."

"Not that," she said with a smile. "You lied about my father having a change of heart. You said he regretted not acknowledging us before now."

This morning had been another lifetime. Everything had changed since then. "I thought it was the kinder course," he admitted. "Would you have preferred to know then that he was willing to recognize you only because he needed money?"

"Your motives aren't any different than his were."

"In the strictest sense, probably not," he allowed. "But in my defense, I inherited the three of you along with all the other disasters and I'm trying to do the best I can with the situation. For all of us. Yes, I'll get badly needed money for finishing out the process Geoffrey started. But it's not as though you and Simone and Fiona won't benefit from the effort, as well."

"True. But please promise me that, in the future, you won't keep the truth from me in an attempt to protect my feelings. I'd rather be wounded than ignorant."

"If that's the way you want it to be," he offered, dully

wondering if he hadn't just committed a huge mistake. She'd be far more than wounded and hardly innocent if he were ever honest about what he really wanted to do with her.

"And I'm not a disaster," she protested brightly. "I may have a lot to learn about all the social rules and such, but I'm hardly a dimwit. I'm perfectly capable of learning whatever I must."

Oh, she'd be a most able student. The things he'd like . . . He cleared his throat and dragged in a deep breath. It was most definitely time to call an end to the evening. He pasted a smile on his face and firmly said, "I have no doubts whatsoever about either your intelligence, or your ability to dazzle everyone when we return to London for the Season."

Caroline sat back in her chair, stunned and confused and hurt—deeply hurt—by his sudden shift to the distance of formality. "What's worrying you?" she asked. "And don't lie to me. I can see it in your eyes. I hear it in the way you're suddenly speaking."

"It is the fog of too much to drink," he said, rising from the table and refusing to look at her.

"It is not!" she countered, angry that he'd think she was so stupid as not to notice, so pliant that she'd accept his lame explanation. "And you promised, not a full minute ago, that you'd be honest with me."

"There is a line that separates honesty from foolishness," he countered, coming around to stand behind her chair. "You can be angry with me if you like, but I know better than to cross it. As your guardian, it is my obligation to exercise good judgment."

"Not fair!" she declared, throwing her serviette on the table.

"I know," he agreed as he pulled out the chair and she stood. He bowed briefly, stiffly, and added, "If you are ready to retire for the evening, I will escort you to your room."

If he thought he was going to get away with commanding her . . .

⊰ *Six* ⊱

DRAYTON HELD HER ELBOW LOOSELY AS THEY MADE their way down the upstairs corridor, moving to the safety of their respective rooms. She'd made it abundantly clear by her frosty silence that she was not happy. And he was . . . He was well beyond miserable. Everything between his upper thighs and his waist was as hard as a rock and straining for release. Part of his wine-numbed brain was congratulating him on doing the right thing despite his inebriated and agitated state. The other part of it alternated between pointing out that being able to ignore good judgment was why one got inebriated in the first place, and begging him to give up pretending that he was so frigging virtuous.

As they stopped before the door of her room, he released his hold on her and stepped back. She looked up at him, studying his face in the dim light of a wall lamp. Her lips were parted so sweetly, so invitingly. Her breasts rose and fell on quick shallow breaths.

"Good night, Caroline," he choked out, offering her another polite bow. "Pleasant dreams."

She didn't say anything in reply. Which was probably for the best, he told himself as he turned crisply and headed for his own room.

"Drayton?"

He looked down at the doorknob in his hand and debated what to do. And just as she had earlier that evening, she took the decision from him.

"Please tell me what's bothering you," she said softly as she came to stand at his side.

He didn't dare look back down at her; his resolve was tattering by the second. Staring straight ahead at the door, he tightened his hold on the knob, deliberately turned it and pushed the panel open, saying crisply, "Good night, Caroline. Pleasant dreams."

He had one foot in his room when she caught him by the sleeve of his jacket. "It's been a perfectly lovely evening," she said, the low volume of her voice doing nothing to disguise the strength of her determination. "Don't you *dare* spoil it by being imperial."

He blinked. *Dare?* Slowly, he looked over his shoulder at her. "Pardon?"

"I don't much care for Lord Ryland," she answered, still holding him by the sleeve. "He lacks a sense of humor and goes about making declarations as though what others think or want or feel don't matter. I much prefer the company of Drayton Mackenzie. He's an infinitely more attractive man."

He couldn't decide if running away would be an act of cowardice or of wisdom. "He's not a very restrained fellow, though," he replied, unable to get his feet to move. "He has a tendency to act before he thinks."

"That's a good part of his appeal."

"It also makes him a dangerous man."

"Another factor in his favor," she countered. "Lord Ryland is terribly, terribly boring."

Caroline silently sighed in relief as the tension in his

body eased just as it had in the dining room before their meal. From that experience she knew that he'd come to a decision. She searched his eyes, hoping to see a sign that he might relent and tear down the barriers he'd so suddenly put back up between them.

"Boring," he said, cocking a brow. "Ryland's boring."

There was an undercurrent in his voice, a slowly building certainty in his gaze that sent her heartbeat skittering. "Yes, he is," she said, holding her ground, knowing what she was unleashing. "It would never occur to him to be the least bit honest with anyone about anything. It's all appearances and façades with him. It's rather pathetic, actually."

He barely nodded and eased the door wider, holding her gaze as he leaned closer and whispered, "Caroline, you're treading the edge."

"I am well aware of that. Honesty cuts both ways and I'm quite willing to take the risk."

"Really." He let go of the doorknob and reached out to slowly trace the curve of her ear with his fingertip. "Do you have any idea of what the risks are?"

"Yes." She closed her eyes, savoring the pleasure of his deliberate touch. It had been so very long that she'd forgotten how wonderful it felt to have her senses brimming.

"Drayton isn't a very honorable man, you know," he continued, trailing his fingertip down the curve of her jaw, down her throat and to the swell of her breast. "It's that lack of restraint of his."

And the wine, she knew. How something could make all the world fuzzy while, at the same time, so sweetly sharpen sensation . . . It was marvelous. She might regret it all tomorrow, but tonight she was going to enjoy being a woman.

"Stop him, Caroline," he whispered against her ear, slipping his arm around her waist. "Before it's too late."

If he thought advancing the seduction was going to frighten her off, he needed to be informed of just how high the stakes were. She turned into him and slid her hands up the lapels of his jacket. "If he stops, I'll rip his—"

Drayton laughed and pivoted, wheeling them both into his room and kicking the door closed behind them. "Unman me, *ma petite*," he said, grinning down into her upturned face as he skimmed his hands down her back in search of buttons, "and you'll . . ."

The threat was lost, swept aside by the realization that getting her stripped down and on the bed wasn't going to be accomplished as easily and quickly as he wanted. Having spent the day frustrated to one degree or another, and now being so close to relieving it only to be thwarted . . . "Where the hell are the buttons on this thing?"

She chuckled and stepped out of his loose embrace, saying sweetly, "Allow me."

She lifted her left arm slightly, reached across herself with her right, and nimbly began undoing a row of tiny royal blue buttons that ran down her side. Buttons he'd noticed, but had assumed were there for the sole purpose of drawing panting male attention to the alluring curve.

But the dress didn't open as the buttons parted with their holes. "What the . . . ?" he muttered, fascinated as the front ruching of her gown slipped down as a single, separate panel. And beneath it, hidden until that moment, was the line of blue satin-covered buttons he'd been looking for along her spine.

And the feminine form that ruching had hidden and those pretty buttons accentuated . . . It was a glorious sight to behold. His jaw dropped. Not that he cared.

"Women who don't have maids to help them dress," she explained, unbuttoning the lowest one in the line, "have to be able to do and undo the buttons on their own. It's much easier to reach them when they're in the front."

"Let me," he said, gently moving her hands aside.

"If you insist."

Oh, he did. She pressed her arms into her sides to hold the dress in place as he worked his way up, his fingers nimble and efficient and seemingly detached from his conscious mind—what there was of it. He was nearing the top when what he'd been seeing finally registered in his brain. There weren't any petticoats tied about her waist. He glanced down at the opening. There were petticoats, but they'd been sewn into the dress itself so that they and the outer fabric went on and came off as one piece. "How ingenious," he marveled. *And considerate of a man's desperation.*

"Thank you. I designed it myself."

"A woman of many talents," he said, smiling down into sparkling eyes as he undid the last button. He was wondering what talents she had that he'd yet to discover when she lifted her arms ever so slightly, wiggled her hips and showed him.

If he'd been an old man, or one not used to a strenuous life, the delight would have stopped his heart. As it was, his skipped several beats before it slammed hard into his rib cage and began to race.

"And truly exceptional understanding," he whispered in amazement. And in deep, breathtaking appreciation for her creative talent. Her creative, utterly wanton talent.

There was no chemise to obscure the realization that he'd never in his life seen anything so decadently inviting as the white thing that functioned—in a sinfully transparent way—as a corset. As far as he could tell, its sole purpose was to hold in place several short strips of curved whalebone whose sole purpose was to hold her perfectly round breasts up for proper adoration.

"Understanding of what, Drayton?"

His gaze slowly skimmed downward over the white ribbon lacing that held the thing closed. Down over the gentle pillow of her bare abdomen to the small triangle of blond curls to the sheer white stockings gartered high on her shapely thighs.

"Men," he said, offering his hand to help her step out of the satin puddle at her feet. The spark of creativity that flashed through his mind was a pale one compared to those she apparently had, but there was potential in it. He drew her around to the short, flat-topped traveling chest the porter had placed at the foot of his bed. She stepped up onto it obediently and then allowed him to turn her to face him. Just as he'd thought it would, the adjustment for their height differences put all of her within easy reach.

"Perfect," he declared, releasing her hand to unbutton his jacket, strip it off and toss it on the end of the bed behind her.

"I think," she said, setting to work on undoing his tie, "that it's more an understanding of what men appreciate."

A keen understanding. He put his hands on her waist as she began working on getting the studs removed from his shirtfront. "If you'd turn your imagination to the design of men's clothes, we could both be appreciative at once."

"I'll work on it," she said, letting her fingers work on their own as she lifted her gaze to meet his. "Are you willing to be my model?"

"Would that mean that I'd have to let you undress me several times a day?"

"At least a dozen," she replied, a wicked little smile turning up the corners of her mouth. "Perfection is rarely achieved on the first fitting."

He slid his hands slowly downward, caressing the satin curve of her hips. "Would you be dressed like this every time?"

"I could catch my death of cold."

"I'll keep you warm," he promised, moving his hands up and back to explore the curves of her backside. "Are you chilled now?"

Her breath caught. "Not in the least," she whispered, her voice throaty as her fingers slowed and the light in her eyes deepened.

Ah, so easily pleased. He dragged in a lungful of air and reminded himself that distracting her would only delay the shedding of his clothing. He moved his hands back to her waist and left them there. With a motion of his head, he indicated the dress on the floor behind him and asked, "Do you make gowns like that for other women?"

She sighed, smiled at him, and went back to a more diligent effort on his studs, saying, "I've tried, but everyone seems to prefer to go around dressed like onions. Layer upon layer upon layer."

"Surely brides beat paths to your door."

"Actually, not," she replied, tugging his shirt from his trousers. "Brides are usually skittish things. They want twice as many layers as matrons do."

And some of them, from the tales of woe he'd heard, kept adding the layers. Clearly his Caroline enjoyed wearing as few of them as she possibly could. If only he'd known that this morning in the carriage. "Just out of curiosity . . . The brown thing you were wearing earlier today, is it constructed in the same way?"

"All of my outfits are," she supplied to his delight as she turned slightly to take his left wrist in hand. "I'm not an onion."

"No, you aren't," he agreed, placing his hands on her creamy shoulders so that she could dispose of his cuff links. He'd have preferred to put his hands on her breasts, but since that would distract and slow her . . . He moistened his lower lip with his tongue. "Do you design corsets like this one for other women?"

"For some reason, they prefer more utilitarian structures," she explained, meeting his gaze as she blindly tossed his cuff links onto his jacket. "I've never been able to fathom why. They're hideously uncomfortable."

"And not the least bit inspiring," he added as she slipped her hands under his shirt and over his shoulders to push the linen aside.

"Are you inspired?" she asked softly, ever-so-knowingly, as he dropped his arms and let the shirt fall to the floor next to her gown.

She leisurely trailed a fingertip down the center of his chest. "I've been inspired since late this afternoon," he confessed, his body aching from the sweet torture. "Acutely so since you walked into the dining room this evening."

"I thought you didn't notice."

"I noticed," he said tightly as she tantalized the skin along the top edge of his trousers. "And just as a point of information? I've been painfully inspired since that dress puddled on the floor."

She grinned. "In other words, you wish I'd hurry?"

"And a very perceptive woman, too." He caught her hand and stepped away from her touch, saying, "Stay right where you are."

Caroline fingered the ends of her corset lacing as she watched him strip off his shoes. "I gather, since you haven't made a move to pull the ribbon, that you'd prefer for me to leave the corset on?"

"If you don't mind," he said, flashing her a crooked smile as he unbuttoned his pants. "I like it and it won't be in my way."

Oh, he was absolutely magnificent. "And the stockings?" she asked, her knees weakening as the heat inside her arrowed to her core.

"They're not going to be in my way, either."

He stepped in front of her and wrapped her in his arms. The feel of him pressed hard against the length of her . . . "One would think that you're suddenly out of patience," she murmured, twining her arms around his neck as the tide of wanting spilled out of her.

"Imagine that," he laughed as his hands slipped down to cup her bottom.

The gasp of her approval was lost in her moan of surrender as he captured her mouth with his and laid waste to every hope of reserve. She strained into him, consumed with need and driven to demand that he satisfy it. Now. This instant. Before she died of wanting.

He groaned as she deepened their kiss and drew her leg up the outside of his. Powerless to resist, he promised himself command later and lifted her up to mate them in a single swift thrust. The pleasure was intensely immediate, exquisite and mind-numbing. His knees quaked as it shot through him, leaving him frozen, hard and deep inside her, and gasping for control.

"Oh, God," he moaned against her throat as her body tightened around his length and the scent of hot sandalwood enveloped him. And then she shifted, crying softly as she rocked her hips against his, and there was suddenly nothing in the world but satisfying his own urgent need.

Breathless with desperation, Caroline whimpered as he adjusted his hold on her and turned away from the bed. Fearing that he intended to slow their pace, she took his face between her hands. "Please, Drayton," she pleaded as his hardened dark gaze lifted to meet hers. "Now. Right now."

A low growl rolled up his throat and past his lips. Still holding his face, she closed her eyes, lowered her head and kissed him, pouring every measure of her hunger into him. He moaned and the sound rippled slowly through her and then was obliterated by a torrent of surging pleasure. She lifted her mouth from his to gasp up at the ceiling in sheer delight.

Drayton watched her face as he pressed her back hard against the low armoire, bent his knees, slowly withdrew, then straightened to thrust upward again. She gasped again, quivered around him, and threw her arms out and up to grasp the wooden ledge just above her head.

Her slight weight left his hands, and free of the need to hold her upright, he grasped her hips as he drew back and then filled her again. And again and again, meeting her hard and plunging deep each time, reveling in her unstinted passion and the quake of his swiftly coming release.

Their rhythm quickening, her panting growing faster, he slipped one arm around her waist and reached up with the other to take a taut nipple gently between his thumb and forefinger. "Now, Caroline?"

She moaned and he obliged her, squeezing as he drove upward and pulled her hard against him and held her there. Her release came in that instant, her head thrown back as a gasping cry rolled up her throat and her body jerked in his grasp. He closed his eyes and surrendered his will to overriding sensation—her womb clasping him, squeezing him, and drawing him deeper and over the edge of his own exploding oblivion.

Her senses drowsy with the sweetest satisfaction, Caroline sagged in contentment, unable to summon either the strength or concern to keep herself from falling. She smiled as Drayton wrapped her in his arms and drew her close as he settled her gently on her feet. Sighing, she nuzzled her cheek in the crisp hair of his chest.

"Do I need to apologize?" he asked, pressing a kiss to the top of her head.

"I can't imagine what for."

"That was a bit quick and a little rough."

She grinned. "Did you hear me protest?"

"No."

It took considerable effort, but she lifted her head to smile up at him. "Then it must have been to my complete satisfaction."

He laughed and hugged her. "You're a most uncommon woman."

"Is that good or bad?"

"It's utterly delightful," he said, bending just enough to swoop her up in his arms and carry her off to his bed.

CAROLINE BREATHED DEEPLY THE SCENT OF MALE SKIN, then opened her eyes and lifted her head from Drayton Mackenzie's shoulder. Pale light gilded the edges of the draperies. Slowly and gently, she slipped away from his side and out of his bed.

Her clothing gathered up and draped over her arm, she paused at the door between his room and hers, and turned back. He lay sprawled out on the bed, uncovered, and looking sinfully, thoroughly spent. She smiled, remembering the delights they'd given each other. And boldly taken, too, she had to admit.

She tilted her head and arched a brow. How very different it had been with Drayton. With Peter, making love had been an affair of the heart. Passionate, yes, but in a tender and soul-touching way. With Drayton . . . What an amazing thing sex was when there was no love involved. Purely physical, purely in the pursuit of your own body-racking pleasure and knowing that it was just for that one night . . . She'd had no idea that pleasure could be so intense, so . . . She grinned. *Inspiring*.

She didn't know what it said about her that she'd cast all reserve to the wind and not only surrendered to, but fully explored, every carnal impulse that had come over her. And him. She certainly didn't regret it; she'd never felt this physically sated and content in all her life. But it hadn't been a wise thing to do, and good sense mandated that she not let it happen again.

Turning away, she slipped out of his bedroom. The duke's bedroom, she realized as she closed the door softly behind her. The women of her line definitely seemed to be drawn to high-ranking peers. Unlike her mother, though, she'd had the good fortune of having the opportunity arise when the timing of her courses would spare her any lasting consequences.

GOD, HIS FOREHEAD FELT HALF A METER THICK. AND THE pounding behind it . . . He groaned and pulled a pillow over his face to shield himself from the light trying to burn its way through his eyelids. Sandalwood? Did he smell—

He bolted upright and looked around the bed, his head splitting with pain and his heart pounding. The sheets were a twisted disaster, but he was decidedly alone in them. Easing back down, he laid his forearm across his eyes and groaned as the memories flooded his mind.

Jesus Christ. What had he done? What had he been thinking? He groaned again as the answers bludgeoned his conscience. He hadn't been thinking at all. And what he'd done was soak his brain in wine and then leave it in the dining room to come upstairs to make mad, intensely, gloriously passionate love with Caroline. All night long.

And while some of the finer details of his various performances were lost in the haze of alcoholic perception, he could remember quite clearly enough to know that while he'd done a lot of things during the night, taking a French letter from his bags hadn't been one of them. He'd been as stupid, selfish, and recklessly irresponsible as a man could ever be.

There was only one thing to do in the aftermath, of course. He'd marry her and make everything right. If she was pregnant, they'd just have to tell everyone that the child was early and hope it was small enough for the lie to be plausible. And if not, well, it certainly wouldn't be the first eight-month, hefty baby in the history of England.

Yes, it was the honorable thing to do. He'd get up, bathe, shave, make himself as presentable as a complete moral reprobate could hope to look, and then go to her. He'd hold her hand and apologize profusely—in a manly sort of way—for having first intoxicated her and then thoroughly and repeatedly compromised her.

No, he mentally corrected himself. Ravaged. He'd say that he'd ravaged her. While it wasn't strictly true because, as he recalled it all, she'd been a very willing—and active—participant, taking all the blame on himself for what had happened would be noble. And God knew he needed to create all the positive light for himself that he could.

And while he was amending the plan . . . There was no need to mention the thoroughly and repeatedly part. It was bad enough to have done what he had even once. Not that the experience itself had been bad, of course. Sex with Caroline had been nothing short of mind-searingly spectacular. Which was why there had been a repeatedly. But it probably wasn't something she wanted to hear at this juncture. No, she'd be trying to drown herself in remorseful, guilty tears when he found her. The last thing he needed to do was make matters any worse than they already were.

He'd hand her his handkerchief, offer his manly apologies, then slip his arm comfortingly around her shoulders and draw her close to promise that he'd do the right thing and marry her as soon as they could publish the banns and arrange for a ceremony. She'd sniffle and decline his too incredibly noble offer and he'd quietly insist that she accept. They'd go back and forth on that for a bit and then she'd give in and agree that his way was the wisest thing for them to do.

Then, after all that was settled, they'd climb into the carriage and go on to Ryland Castle. They'd greet the staff on the drive where he'd introduce her as his future duchess. She'd happily accept their congratulations and then they'd go inside, get Simone and Fiona situated, take care of any pressing household concerns, and then retire together for another private dinner.

And tomorrow morning he wouldn't wake up with a splitting headache and ridden with guilt. He'd wake up blissfully content and with her right there beside him in the bed, smelling like sandalwood and smiling at him in wanton invitation.

Yes, it was a completely workable plan. In fact, it was bloody brilliant.

⁂ Seven ⁂

"NOW, NOW, CAROLINE . . ." DRAYTON LOOKED AT HIS RE-flection in the cheval mirror and rolled his eyes. Clearing his throat, he shot his cuffs and lifted his chin. "Now see here, Caroline," he said sternly.

No, that wasn't going to work, either. It was too Lord Ryland for anything even remotely positive to happen after that. He straightened his tie, took a deep breath, and then let it out in one big rush as he said, "I can understand why you'd hate me, Caroline."

He shook his head in disgust and looked over at the window. If he had any sort of sense at all, he'd throw himself out of it. But since the fall wasn't likely to be nearly far enough to actually kill him, it would only add to his misery. Damn shame he couldn't catch even the tiniest bit of luck these days. Well, except for last night. In certain respects he'd been the luckiest man to ever draw a ragged breath. Which of course was the reason he was having such a god-awful morning.

Maybe he could just write her a note. *"Dear Caroline. I have behaved badly. Well, not altogether badly as I seem to recall that you rather enjoyed it, but . . ."* No. No, writing her a note was not a good idea at all.

He cleared his throat again, squared up the mirror, and was trying to achieve a smile that looked more cheerful than painful when someone knocked on the door. His first thought was that he'd been mercifully saved from a sad and pointless effort. The second was that it might be Caroline on the other side of the panel. And if it was . . . Drayton cast one last look at his reflection and crossed the room.

He opened the door expecting the worst. And got it. Not the worst that he'd been expecting, but it was close enough that he wasn't going to split any hairs. "Haywood." Friend. Fourth son. Notorious womanizer. God, couldn't anything in his life go well?

Cyril Haywood, as impeccably arranged in a tailored riding suit as he always was in a uniform, adjusted the fit of the crop under his arm and grinned. "Hello and good morning to you, too."

"What the hell are you doing here?"

Haywood's grin widened as he studied him. "Your butler told me where to find you."

Damn Haywood. "That's not the answer to the question I asked and I'm in no mood for your games."

"As I can see," he said, chuckling. He sobered only marginally to add, "I came to preserve your sanity."

His entire forehead creaked as he cocked a brow. "And why would you think that my sanity is in danger?"

"I have six sisters. I know what can happen to a man who finds himself trapped in a circle of petticoats. It's not pretty. I've come to watch your back and offer advice gained from my considerable experience."

Drayton narrowed his eyes, his mind not exactly whirling through all the information. Speed didn't matter, though. Stumbling was quite sufficient to recognize all that hadn't been said, but was in the explanation just the same. The matter with Caroline would have to be slightly delayed. "How," he began, wondering if he really wanted to know. "How do you know about . . ." Hell, all of it. The whole damned mess.

"They've gotten to you already," he said, trying to look horrified but not pulling it off. "You've lost your edge."

"I haven't lost my edge," Drayton countered, wanting to be angry, but as usual, not quite able to keep Haywood's good humor from infecting him. "I drowned my brain last night and I'm suffering the consequences this morning. As you deduced the second I opened this door. I'll be fine by noon."

"They have marvelous coffee downstairs. An urn or two of it will brace you right up." He glanced around the hall, then leaned forward and lowered his voice. "And by the by, my first piece of advice is to never let them drive you to drink. Once your thinking is clouded, you're easy prey and they'll move in for the kill."

Haywood had absolutely no idea of how accurate that statement was. "Coffee's an excellent idea," he said, stepping out into the hall and pulling the door closed behind him.

"That's the spirit, Ryland," his friend said, falling in beside him. "It's very odd to call you that, you know. Ryland. If I forget and call you Drayton or Mackenzie, just give me a good solid kick."

"Call me Ryland," Drayton replied, sliding a hard look over at him, "and I'll call you Cyril."

"Ouch. If you drank enough to be this surly, they must be hideous little monsters."

"How do you know about them?" Drayton asked as they made their way down the stairs. "*What* do you know about them?"

"Oh, it's all the talk at every house party. As the story goes at this point, before the embellishing truly begins, they're the old duke's by-blow daughters and you have to take them in or you don't get old Lady Ryland's money. As for what anyone knows about the girls . . ." He paused in the explanation to smile and wink at a maid at the base of the stairs. As they crossed the foyer and headed for the inn's breakfast room, he went on, adding, "All anyone seems to know is that there's three of them and they're all from the unwashed masses. Their choice of words, of course, not mine."

That was the thing with Haywood. Under all the aristocratic breeze and pomp there really was a sharp mind and a surprisingly egalitarian view of the world. There were no layers to him when it came to women, though. He was a courtly predator from the top of his blond head to the toes of his expensive boots. And all the way to the marrow between. His ability to seduce any female between the ages of eighteen and eighty had always been nothing short of astounding. But now that Drayton had responsibilities on the other side of the man's favorite pastime, it wasn't nearly as amusing.

"I'd avoid the scones," Haywood said as they stepped up to the buffet. "They're as dry as sand. You could choke to death on them."

"Only in my dreams."

"So is what they say true?" Haywood pressed quietly as they carried their steaming cups to a linen-covered table. "Any of it? All of it?"

"It's complicated," Drayton supplied, stalling as he tried to decide just what he wanted to confide, as he weighed common sense against the comforts of friendship.

"Inheritance always is," Haywood observed, putting his crop on an extra satin-covered chair before leaning back to stretch his legs out under the table. He snorted and smiled wryly. "Or at least so my older brothers tell me."

Yes, the respectable ones who had packed him off to be of service to Queen and Country. "Why aren't you with the regiment?"

He interrupted a sip to blithely answer, "Had a bit of a falling-out with Colonel Leighton and resigned my commission rather than make a public issue of it."

Oh, no. He had to ask. The curiosity was just too morbid to deny. "A falling-out over what?"

"The fair Aldys."

The colonel's wife. "Good God."

"And," he added, wagging a brow, "the *delectable* Annabelle."

"His daughter, too?" Only Haywood. "Do you have a death wish?"

"Oh, trust me," Haywood replied, chuckling. "It was worth the risks." He sighed in apparent contentment and then blinked and lifted his cup and saucer, saying, "Since I'm now at loose ends—"

"And unwelcome at home for so badly mangling the military career."

"Well, yes, and that," he allowed with a brief shrug. "No one was terribly surprised. Anyway, I thought I'd catch up to you and see what potential there is for being a duke's toady. I think I'd be fairly good at it."

"What is it that toadies of the peerage do?"

"Fawn, mostly. Tell you how brilliant you are. Let you win at cards. That sort of thing."

"Drink my liquor, eat my food, and smoke my cigars?"

"Of course," Haywood said with a snort. "That goes without saying."

Drayton tilted his head and asked pointedly, "Chase my housemaids?"

"Only the ones you don't want," he replied, his eyes lit with the prospect. "Dukes always get first choice."

Dalliances with the maids? No, he wouldn't have either the energy or the inclination. He'd already made his choice—albeit out of stupidity. There was no changing it and he wasn't all that unhappy about the outcome. No man with Caroline in his bed could claim to be unhappy about it.

But marriage to Caroline wasn't his problem at the moment. Haywood—or more precisely, what to do with Haywood—was. On the one hand, harboring a Lothario hadn't been one of his life's ambitions. Doing so came with all sorts of complications, most of them decidedly unpleasant. On the other hand, having a keen and trustworthy mind at his ready disposal would be invaluable in the days ahead. On that same hand, was also the—

"Mornin', Drayton."

He looked up from his coffee and his musing to see Simone standing at the end of the table. God save him, now that she was clean, her hair combed . . . She was still wearing her boyish clothes, but they'd been laundered and she . . . she . . . she was absolutely beautiful. His heart clenched as he realized that, in just a few short years, men of Haywood's inclinations were going to be storming the doors trying to get to her.

Actually, he realized, as he noted her gaze sweeping Haywood from head to the edge of the tablecloth, God save them. Clearly Haywood wasn't measuring up very well. And Haywood was, just as clearly, stunned by the fact. Drayton grinned.

"Who's this?" she asked.

"A friend of mine from the regiment," he supplied as a wonderful solution bloomed in his brain. "Lady Simone Turnbridge," he said, gesturing openhanded to the man across the table, "this is Haywood."

At his name, the man recovered his poise to half rise from his chair and offer a bow of sorts and say, "A pleasure, my dear."

In typical Simone fashion, she turned away from him. "Turnbridge?"

"Your father's family name," Drayton explained as Haywood blinked at Simone's back. "It's now yours. Congratulations. Where are your sisters?"

"They'll be right down," she answered, putting a hand flat on the table and leaning her weight on it. "We goin' to be leavin' soon?"

"As soon as everyone's had something to eat and the bags are in the carriage."

She looked over her shoulder at Haywood. "He comin' along?"

Haywood snapped his jaw up to swallow and laughingly observe, "Direct little thing, isn't she?"

"I haven't decided about him yet," he confessed, leaning back and considering his friend. "What are your thoughts on him?"

"I watched him ride in a while ago. He sets a horse pretty good."

"I'm flattered, Lady Simone. And may I say that you have a most discerning eye."

She arched a raven-wing brow and looked back at Drayton. "Can I have a horse?"

Oh! Another bloody brilliant plan! "All ladies are expected to know how to ride."

"I'm not goin' to do any of that prissy sideways-in-the-saddle rubbish," she announced, standing straight to plant her feet and cross her arms over her midriff. "I like my neck and don't want it broke."

"Oh, my," Haywood said, chuckling. "You do need my help. Desperately so." Drayton was about to point out that Haywood was going to be the one in need of rescuing when the man's gaze shot past him and lit up like the London Bridge.

"And this must be one of your other little wards," he said, vaulting to his feet.

He knew without looking that it was Fiona. Whose hand was firmly in the grasp of—

"Good thinking on getting the governess, Dray," Haywood said in an undertone. "And your taste is as impeccable as always."

Caroline's. He wasn't ready for this. But since there was no avoiding it . . . He sucked in a deep breath, rose, and turned toward the doorway. They were still at a fair distance, but that didn't prevent him from recognizing several salient facts. Caroline was a vision, a delight of properly encased curves rimmed by morning sunlight. And Fiona . . . Oh, at least he had a few more years before he had to beat the men back from her.

He could say a lot against Geoffrey, but he had to allow that the man had gifted the world with three breathtakingly beautiful females. That the youngest of them had a pronounced limp didn't detract from the overall sum. Doctors these days could work the most amazing miracles and he would spend whatever it took to buy Fiona one.

And then the two of them were close enough for him to see details. Caroline didn't look as though she'd been crying! No, no puffy eyes, no sign that so much as a single tear had been scraped from her cheeks. That stunning realization—and relief—settled his heart back to a normal beat and allowed other facts to flood his brain. She was positively radiant this morning; glowing, serene, tranquil, composed . . . Yes, he'd have to say that altogether, she looked like a woman supremely satisfied. As long as he kept it to himself, there was no reason not to be pleased with his role in her achieving that state.

And, he thought, his gaze skimming over the curves accentuated by the deep plum-colored traveling costume, now that he knew where all her buttons were, he'd be more than happy to see that she was that satisfied tomorrow morning, too.

"Good morning, Caroline," he said, smiling at her warmly as they joined Simone at the end of the table. He looked down into Fiona's big green eyes. "Good morning, Fiona."

Fiona studied him silently as Caroline said easily, "A very good morning to you, your grace."

He looked up to meet her gaze and marveled at the light in her eyes. Amusement. Sultry memory. And a self-possessed reserve that somehow made his knees soft.

"Ahem."

Yes, good call, Haywood. We are in public. He quietly cleared his own throat and began the necessary introductions. "May I present the Honorable Cyril Haywood. The 'Honorable' is a courtesy title, not a statement regarding the quality of his character." He noted Haywood's quick glower, smiled, and finished, saying, "Lady Caroline Turnbridge and her younger sister, Lady Fiona Turnbridge."

"I am utterly charmed, ladies," Haywood crooned, bowing deeply, his gaze flickering to Fiona only briefly to politely include her. It came squarely back to Caroline's as he added, quite unnecessarily in Drayton's considered opinion, "Utterly and devastatingly forever charmed."

Caroline arched a pale brow ever so slowly. "It's a pleasure to make your acquaintance, sir."

Drayton was sighing in relief for having gotten the lines laid down so clearly and firmly while not having to be a complete social oaf about it all, when Haywood stepped away from his chair, pulled it out and said, "Do please join us for a light repast. Do you care for cream and sugar in your coffee, Lady Caroline?"

Damn, he should have thought of that. Caroline, with no polite alternative, was obliged to walk into the man's design.

"Cream, please," she said, smoothing her skirts and surrendering to the gallantry of the blond wolf. Fiona scrambled onto the chair right beside her.

As soon as Haywood strode off to fulfill his first mission, Drayton explained, "He's a friend from the regiment. He wants to come along and be a toady."

"Well," Simone said, watching Haywood, "I 'spose that pretendin' to be a fop ain't quite as bad as pretendin' to be a prig, but why anyone'd wanna do it . . ." She shook her head and shrugged.

Pleased and not the least surprised by the accuracy of her perception, he motioned to a passing footman and instructed, "Substantial meals for the ladies, please."

"At once, your grace."

"Would you care for a cup of hot chocolate?" he asked, looking between Simone and Fiona.

"Ain't never had it before," Simone admitted. "Is it good?"

"Have a seat. I'll get you each one." As Simone's too keen awareness was momentarily diverted, he met Caroline's upturned—and dare he think adoring?—gaze. "We need to talk privately, Caroline," he said as quietly as he could.

"Impossible at the moment."

"Ryland Castle?"

She nodded her assent and turned away to smooth a strand of wispy blond hair off Fiona's forehead. Remembering how those graceful fingers had felt caressing his own skin, he turned on his heel and left before he could make a public spectacle of them both.

"Courtesy title?" Haywood groused as he stepped up beside him at the buffet. "That wasn't necessary, you know."

"Yes it was."

"I could inherit a real title someday, you know."

"Not bloody likely," Drayton countered. "And even if you did," he added, deciding that now was as good a time as any for spiking the man's cannon. "If you ever touch Caroline, friendship notwithstanding, I'll kill you on the spot."

"You've always taken the whole business of duty far too seriously."

"I mean it, Haywood," he assured him. "If you can keep your distance from her, you can come along. If you can't, you'd live a lot longer being a toady for someone else."

Haywood looked over at him. "You're smitten."

"*I* have responsibilities," Drayton snapped as he poured steaming chocolate into the cups.

"No need to get personal." He laughed. "I won't go anywhere near your precious little china doll. The other two, either."

"Oh, you're going to teach Simone to ride," he informed him, carefully turning with the brimming cups and their saucers in his hands. "You do sit a horse better than any man I know."

"Aren't you afraid I might compromise her?" Haywood called softly after him.

He laughed so hard he almost spilled the hot chocolate.

STANDING ON THE DRIVE, WATCHING THE LAST OF THE baggage being loaded into his carriage, Drayton sighed contentedly. Breakfast had been a resounding success even if all he considered was the wide smile and enthusiastic nod Fiona had given him when he'd asked if she'd like another cup of hot chocolate. Add in that both she and Simone had needed only one quick, brief instruction on the proper use of silverware, that Haywood had checked his natural tendency to shamelessly flirt, and that *he'd* been able to keep from leaning across the table and kissing Caroline senseless before carrying her up the stairs . . . Apparently his luck was finally turning. About damn time.

"Did I mention that Aubrey would be coming along to Ryland Castle?"

So much for luck; he should have known better. "No," he said dryly, looking over at Haywood, "you didn't."

"Well, consider it mentioned now."

Drayton followed his gaze, turning to see a carriage making the last turn in the drive and slowing. "Is the entire regiment on its way?"

"Aubrey did say something about his mother packing her things."

"What?" he demanded, whirling about to glare at Haywood. The presumptive bastard!

"The Dowager Lady Aubrey."

"Dammit, Haywood! No games! What are you doing to me?"

Haywood's gaze came off the approaching coach and to Drayton. His smile faded and he said with even, deadly calm, "Saving your arse from your own naïveté. You're squarely in the sights now, Dray. It won't be but a week or so before society finds the range. You need all the help you can get. Be gracious about the offer of it."

"Thank you," he said numbly, but not insincerely.

Haywood grinned, snapped his riding crop up under his arm, and strode off toward the arriving carriage, saying jauntily, "Told you that I'd make a good toady."

Drayton was scraping his hand over his face, praying for deliverance, when Caroline, Simone, and Fiona, side by side by side, came down the front steps of the inn. The sight struck him square in the chest, a thunderbolt straight from the hand of God. He'd never been a good enough man to have earned so much as a sliver of deliverance. In fact, the time had come for him to pay for all the rotten, dishonorable things he'd ever done, said, and thought. And to that justified end, God had sent three avenging angels to show him no mercy.

"Ladies," he said, his head spinning and his knees going swiftly to pudding. He opened his carriage door for them while he still had the ability to move with any sort of dignity and calm.

"Another regimental friend has arrived to accompany us to Ryland Castle," he said, handing Fiona in first. Simone bounded in without his help. He turned and offered his hand to Caroline. With every last measure of his control, he smiled and handed her in, saying, "Since he's in his own carriage, Haywood and I will ride with him and spare you the extreme boredom of our male company. I'll see you all again when we arrive at our new home."

Caroline nodded as she sat and then wished him a pleasant visit with his friends. He closed the door and motioned for his driver to proceed. The carriage rolled off just before the whimper rolled up his throat and out.

❧ *Eight* ❧

HE RALLIED. LARGELY BECAUSE HE DIDN'T WANT TO collapse into a whimpering puddle in front of Haywood and Aubrey. As their commanding officer in the regiment, he'd always had to set the example for them. And now that he found himself a duke to their lesser ranks, the duty of leadership seemed to be even more important. Not that he had the slightest notion, in any sort of specific sense, of where he was supposed to lead them.

"Aubrey," he said, as the footman opened the carriage door and Haywood led his mount to the rear to tie it off. "What a nice surprise."

Aubrey, who, as always, looked as though he'd been sewn into his clothing by a sausage maker, laughed and motioned him in, saying, "Then why do you look like you've been gut shot?"

"In a manner of speaking, I have," Drayton admitted, taking the opposite seat. "A month ago I was happily content, my only obligation being to ably command my company. Today . . ." He shrugged and decided it wouldn't do his leadership image any good to go into the gory details.

"Oh, don't listen to his tales of woe," Haywood said, vaulting in and flinging himself into the seat beside Aubrey.

"He's not only managed to outrank us in the peerage, too, he's also acquired a delightful collection of female wards. The eldest of which, I might add, is stunningly gorgeous."

"And opinionated," Drayton countered. "As well as independent and altogether too . . . too . . ." *Damn delicious*.

"Gorgeous?" Haywood offered.

Well, at least it was a rather neutral observation. "Yes, she's beautiful."

"And the middle one . . . Lady Simone," Haywood went on with a chuckle. "Oh, Aubrey, she's delightfully irreverent. Shockingly plainspoken and appallingly direct. You'll loathe her."

"I'm sure I'll adore them all."

Drayton was trying to think of a polite way of suggesting that Aubrey not harbor any ideas of enjoying Caroline, when Haywood gushed onward. "And the little one. Lady Fiona. A bit withdrawn, but Dray made fabulous progress this morning with a mere cup of hot chocolate. In time, she'll come around. Someday, mark my words, she'll set London on fire."

"No, that will be Simone," Drayton corrected. "And it will be quite literally *on fire*. God help the poor bastards."

Aubrey laughed and shoved a lock of brown hair off his forehead. "You do have your hands full, don't you?"

"You needn't look so happy with the situation."

"Ah," he drawled, ignoring the fact that his hair had fallen right back out of place, "but it's so rare that we're indispensable, you have to allow us a few moments to revel in it."

"Indispensable how?"

"We were born to the peerage."

"We know the rules," Haywood added as the carriage rolled forward.

"And I don't," Drayton summarized.

Haywood grinned at Aubrey. "He's always been quick. I'd have to say that's the key reason he was so tolerable as a commanding officer, wouldn't you agree?"

"Absolutely. That and he isn't the sort to let rank, military or social, be the standard in determining his associations. Most egalitarian sort of chap."

And now that they were done lauding his virtues . . . "What is it that you two are going to get out of teaching me the finer points of being a duke? Aside from the pleasure of making me miserable at every opportunity."

Aubrey laughed. "Oh, you do need us."

"I'm a fourth son," Haywood explained. "Aubrey here is a third. I'm stuck with a courtesy 'Honorable' for the rest of my life and he's going to die a lowly viscount. We're not exactly the sort of men to whom mamas of the peerage scratch and claw for the chance to hitch their daughters."

"But being the good and trusted friends of a duke would change that, wouldn't it?" Drayton guessed.

"Ah, quick indeed," Aubrey granted, settling back into the corner and stretching out his legs.

Haywood sighed in what seemed like contentment. "There is a lovely cachet."

"But only if I manage to pull off being a duke with some aplomb," Drayton pointed out. "If I botch this, you'll go down in smoldering rubble right along with me."

"Precisely," Haywood admitted, looking not the least disconcerted by the prospects of failure. "Which is why we're determined to do whatever needs to be done to ensure that you are the raging success of the next London Season."

Raging success? Hell, he'd be happy if just one person considered him less than a complete embarrassment.

"Which is going to require a considerable amount of preparatory work over the coming months," Aubrey contributed. "By all accounts, your estate is in shambles."

Drayton leaned back and looked between the two of them. "You know about that?"

"Oh, everyone knows about it, Drayton," Haywood assured him with far too much enthusiasm. "But good manners confine them to whispering about it behind your back instead of saying it directly to your face."

"How decent of them."

Aubrey shrugged. "It's all part and parcel of the game. Your task, and ours to help you in accomplishing it, is to give them something else to talk about."

"How you've managed to turn a crumbling, undisciplined estate into a smoothly functioning one on the rise in a matter of mere weeks will do for starters," said Haywood. "We'll move on from there."

Mere weeks? "Uh-huh." God save him from optimists.

"All of which can be largely addressed through building your reputation for hospitality," Aubrey offered. "My mother will be arriving at Ryland Castle in the next fortnight to undertake that part of the mission. As a facet of that, she'll also see to preparing your wards for their eventual introduction to society."

"I hope she has a strong heart," Drayton muttered.

"Tempered steel," his friend assured him. "Now, let's get started, shall we? What do you know about the proper management of servants?"

He considered mentioning that he viewed servants as one of the most unnecessary expenses of his new life, but decided that it would probably open a debate that would, in the end, prove to be a complete waste of time. Eventually, he'd quietly pare the numbers down to a justifiable, supportable number. In the meanwhile . . . "Not a damn thing. Do enlighten me."

"CARRIE?"

Caroline started and opened her eyes to find Simone staring intently into her face.

"We're stopping, Carrie."

It took a moment for the words to penetrate the thickness of her sleep-dulled brain. She sat up straight and looked out the open window of the carriage. She saw trees, a brook, and open fields of ripening grain. "Are we there?" she asked, seeing much the same thing out the other window.

"Not that I can tell," Simone replied. "There's no castle around that I can see."

Caroline scrubbed her hands over her face to chase away the last tendrils of sleep, then took a deep breath and summoned a smile for her sisters. "I'm sorry I fell asleep. I've been a dismal traveling companion for you both."

Simone arched a raven brow. "Didn't you sleep good last night?"

"No. I managed to doze off from time to time, but never for long and never deeply."

"Too excited, huh?"

Quite the understatement, she thought. It was a very good thing the girl had no idea just how accurate it really was. "I suppose so," she allowed as Drayton Mackenzie stepped up to the door.

"Good morning again, ladies," he said brightly, pulling it open. "We thought now might be a good time to stretch our limbs and prepare for our arrival at Ryland Castle."

"Good," Simone declared, bounding out. "I gotta go pee."

He caught her shoulder and stayed her, saying, "You can wait a moment. There are introductions to be made and instructions to be conveyed first. Then you can scamper off to see to nature's calling. Without," he added sternly, "mentioning your intent to everyone, please."

"Prig."

He slid her a threatening sideways glance. Fiona giggled and bounded out the door to stand beside her. Caroline shook her head, wished she had their energy, and accepted Drayton's offered hand.

"Been napping?" he asked quietly.

"I didn't mean to," she confessed as he drew her along the road toward the other carriage and Simone and Fiona trailed behind. "But sheer exhaustion overtook me. Am I a fright?"

He looked her up and down and his eyes twinkled as he leaned close to whisper, "You look positively delectable."

The compliment took her completely by surprise; her mind was hardly paralyzed by it, though. It immediately served up a wickedly wanton, breathtakingly detailed image of the two of them making the rest of the journey to Ryland Castle alone in a carriage. A good and virtuous woman would have silently gasped and blinked the image away as quickly as she could. Caroline arched a brow, admitted to herself that she possessed neither of those qualities, and made mental notes. It was only as the heat flushed her cheeks and her thighs that she brought her vision back to the mundane world of the roadway and the people on it.

Haywood and another man stood beside the second carriage. Both were tall, almost the same height as Drayton.

And both were handsome in a pale and rather parlorish sort of way. But where Haywood was impeccably turned out and arranged, the other . . . Oh, the man needed a realistic tailor and the services of a competent valet. Even then, though . . . She smiled. Neither one of them could hold a candle to Drayton Mackenzie's sheer physical presence. They were men, yes. Not at all boyish. But Drayton was a *man*.

"Lady Caroline Turnbridge, Lady Simone, Lady Fiona," Drayton began ever so formally, his hand cupping her elbow as he stopped before the two of them. "May I present Lord William Marston, Viscount Aubrey."

She dipped her chin in acknowledgment. "A pleasure, your lordship."

"Which is entirely mine, madam. Entirely mine." His gaze slipped past her and he nodded to Simone and Fiona, saying, "Ladies, I am honored."

Simone snorted. "Do all your friends go around pretendin' to be dandy twits?"

Haywood punched Aubrey in the shoulder. "Oh-ho! Told you!"

Drayton sighed. "Make quick work of the next part, Aubrey. Please."

"Of course," the man replied, snapping to attention and smiling brightly. His hazel gaze meeting and holding hers, he began, "We will arrive at Ryland Castle with my coach in the lead and the one bearing you ladies at the rear. The staff should, if they have any sort of proper training at all, be assembled by rank on the drive to greet their new master. Mackenzie will acknowledge their presence with a nod of his head, but make no move to step forward to begin communication until Haywood has handed you ladies from the carriage and you have joined us on the drive."

She looked up at Drayton and quietly asked, "Is he always so . . . crisp?"

"The power has gone momentarily to his head."

"If you two don't mind?" Aubrey shot back.

"Carry on," Drayton said with a tight smile. "We're all ears in anticipation."

"Once we're arranged by our respective social ranks—"

"Which are?" Caroline interrupted.

Aubrey blinked. "Oh, yes. Of course. Pardon the oversight, Lady Caroline," he offered with a little bow. "Lord Ryland will lead. You and your sisters will follow him according to your ages. I will follow Lady Fiona and Haywood will bring up the rear."

"As always," Haywood muttered.

"The butler will introduce himself and the housekeeper," Aubrey went on, beginning to pace, his hands clasped in the small of his back. "Lord Ryland will present us each in turn to them, again according to our ranks. You are to nod in acknowledgment but make no comments whatsoever. It's while he's making the introductions that he'll lay down our respective responsibilities and, as it were, the chain of command.

"Lady Caroline," he said, glancing over at her, "as the eldest of his wards, you will be placed in general charge of the house itself and its immediate grounds. The housekeeper and butler will report directly to you on all such matters. Your decisions will be the rule."

"And if they don't like my rules?" Caroline posed, not quite comfortable with the proposed arrangement. Interlopers were seldom liked, much less appreciated.

"They will either keep their disagreement to themselves or announce their decision to seek employment elsewhere."

Oh, dear. "All right," she agreed, despite her misgivings.

"After that bit of clarification is done, we'll part company for a time. The housekeeper will see you ladies to your rooms, and—"

"I get to pick mine," Simone tossed in hotly. "Drayton promised."

Aubrey cocked a brow and stopped pacing to face Simone squarely. "In public you are to refer to him as 'Lord Ryland.' Not by his Christian name. As to the matter of choosing your own room . . . Lady Caroline will so instruct the housekeeper on your behalf. You are not to open your mouth unless spoken to directly. And if that should happen, your replies will be limited to yes or no. Is that clear?"

"Prig."

His brow disappeared under a shock of brown hair just before he turned slightly, managed a smile for her youngest sister and added, "The same expectations apply to Lady Fiona, of course."

"Ass."

Drayton turned to glare over his shoulder. Caroline smiled at Aubrey and intervened before Drayton could, saying, "That's enough, Simone. Lord Aubrey is only trying to be helpful. I'd rather he be a bit heavy-handed than allow us to make horrible, embarrassing mistakes."

Aubrey's mouth went a bit slack, but she ignored his obvious shock, widened her smile, and prodded him back to the task at hand. "What events should follow the housekeeper seeing us to our rooms?"

"Yes," he said, blinking and clearing his throat. "You will leave Lady Simone and Lady Fiona to the care of their personal maids and accompany the housekeeper on a tour of the household."

"If I might slip a word in edgewise here?" Drayton drawled.

"Certainly."

He looked down at her. "Please make notes as to what needs to repaired, improved, that sort of thing, as you tour the place. I'd like to have a report on just how bad things are as soon as possible. Accompanied, of course, by your suggestions for addressing the deficiencies."

"I think I can manage that."

"I have every confidence in you. You are a woman of remarkable abilities."

Why she heard carnal shadows in the genteel compliment, she didn't know. But it pleased her in a way that had her rational mind reminding her—sternly and, considering the carriage fantasy, a bit tardily—that she'd vowed just that morning to exercise good judgment where he was concerned.

"Ahem."

She looked back to Aubrey and nodded for him to continue.

"We'll meet again for dinner. Lady Simone and Lady Fiona will dine in the schoolroom. The rest of us will dress formally and meet in the parlor at eight to have an aperitif and exchange notes on the conditions we've found."

"Anything else?" Drayton asked.

"Not that I can think of at the moment."

"Good." He looked over his shoulder. "Simone, you and Fiona may wander off a short distance and *gambol*."

As the two took off running, he brought his gaze to hers and added, "Lady Caroline, if I might have a word with you privately?"

"Not too privately, of course," Aubrey instantly instructed as she nodded.

"Propriety and all that, you know," Haywood chimed in. "Stay where we can clearly see you and can vouch that nothing untoward happened."

Ah, yes, propriety. Caroline allowed herself to be drawn off toward the bank of the brook, her good judgment rattling on about the value of exercising restraint and meeting the expectations of decent society. Unfortunately, good judgment wasn't the only voice in her head and the one reminding her of how much pleasure there was to be had in being thoroughly improper . . . Well, the fact that it served up very clear memories as evidence made its arguments the more appealing of the two.

"This is neither the time nor the place I would have preferred to discuss this matter," Drayton said quietly, drawing her to a halt. "But then, nothing has been under my control so far today and I've given up any hope for the optimal."

He cleared his throat twice as she waited, and when he continued to stare off into the distance, she finally prodded, "What would you like to talk about, Drayton?"

He lifted his chin, swallowed hard, and then blurted, "I think we should marry."

The hangman comes for me at noon tomorrow. She couldn't help herself; she laughed outright. His glare said he didn't find the situation nearly as comical as she did. Sobering—with no small effort—she shook her head. "You can't be serious, Drayton. Really, you can't."

"I am."

Yes, apparently he was. "Oh, for heaven's sake," she shot back on an exasperated sigh. "Have you taken complete leave of your senses?"

"Have you forgotten what happened last night?"

"I'll remember it for as long as I live," she cheerfully admitted. "And in case I failed to express my appreciation and gratitude at the time, allow me to thank you profusely now. If we weren't being so intently watched at the moment, I'd kiss your cheek."

"I compromised you, Caroline."

And to think that he'd seemed to so enjoy it at the time. "Wonderfully so," she allowed, her patience with him—with his morose sense of honor—beginning to fray. "But it was hardly a matter of forcing yourself on me and it certainly wasn't as though I were a virgin. There's no need whatsoever to feel the least bit guilty about it all. I applaud your gallantry, Drayton, but it's not necessary."

"Have you considered what would happen to your reputation if anyone were to find out about it?"

Well, considering that Simone hadn't said anything and that Aubrey and Haywood clearly considered propriety a thing still worth worrying about . . . "If you and I don't tell, how will anyone else ever know?"

His jaw clenched and unclenched as he stared off into the distance.

"Drayton," she said gently, mustering all the calm and logic she could, "in all their pontificating on the rules of conduct, did your friends not mention the expectations regarding your marriage?"

"No," he practically growled. "But I'm sure it's only a matter of time."

"Then let me prepare the ground for them. I may not have been born to the peerage, but I've been outside and looking in long enough to have gleaned an understanding of the general principles involved. Peers do not marry for the love of a person, Drayton."

"Honor requires honesty, Caroline," he said darkly. "And the truth is that I don't love you."

"And I don't love you," she countered, wondering why he was so terribly put out about it all. "I enjoyed sex with you tremendously, but that's a separate matter entirely. Peers don't marry for sex, either. They marry for money, choosing whoever offers the most of it."

"You have money."

"So you've said. But it's money you're going to get regardless of whom I marry. There's not one extra farthing to be had in shackling yourself to me. There is extra money, however, if we each marry others. It's a perfectly practical, commonsense matter." *And why you can't see that . . .*

"True, but—" His jaw clenched tight again.

"But what?"

He turned to face her squarely. "The blunt truth of the matter," he said, his voice hard and strained, "is that I'd very much like to continue having sex with you. I also enjoyed last night tremendously."

Well, that did explain a great deal. She blinked and smiled up at him, truly appreciating his candor.

"To such an extent," he said softly, "that if we were alone right now, this conversation wouldn't be taking place at all. You'd be on your back with your skirts rucked up to your waist. Prior to them being discarded entirely."

And it was nice to know that she wasn't the only one struggling with wanton impulses and delightful fantasies. "If our circumstances were different," she began, trying to balance honesty with practicality as her heart raced and her core pulsed, "I wouldn't be all that averse to the notion of being your mistress. But since we're both trapped in the web of social and financial expectations . . . Or opportunities, depending on how you view it . . ." She shrugged. "They say that a sign of an evolved personal character is the ability to resist temptation."

He turned away and snarled, "I'm not that interested in evolving."

Yes, well . . . "Life for both of us will be considerably less stressful in the long run if we can manage it, though. We'll simply have to keep our distance from each other and consider ourselves fortunate to have had one wonderfully reckless night together and that there are no lasting consequences for it."

"Are you sure there will be none?"

"Absolutely."

He looked over his shoulder and cocked a brow. "And if you're wrong?"

"I'm not," she assured him.

He expelled a long hard breath and then lifted his chin. "Well, then I suppose that the matter is resolved."

"Thank goodness," she said, offering him a chuckle that, oddly, didn't sound as relieved as she'd intended for it to. "Shall we collect the girls," she added brightly, in an attempt to disguise the stumble, "so that we can advance on to the glory and potential of Ryland Castle?"

Drayton nodded and turned, offering his arm. Glory, he wouldn't bet on. But potential . . . Oh, yes, there was potential. With it all, he supposed. Not that he cared overly much about fields and crops and tenant rents at the moment. Aubrey and Haywood had staked their claims on the management of those aspects of the future, anyway. And since they were perfectly capable men . . .

He glanced down at the woman on his arm and inwardly smiled. She had the most wonderfully rational and practical way of thinking. A delight, really. And so surprising. Especially considering how it led to his being off the hook for being a complete cad. If only her logic was more than a thin veneer that didn't do a damn thing to disguise her deeply sensual nature. Never in his life had he met a woman so honest about her own hungers, so willing to explore the depths of passion.

Evolved personal character. Such lofty words. Such grand and noble intent. He might have believed she meant it all if he hadn't tasted and ridden the tempest of her hungers last night, if her eyes hadn't sparkled at the prospect of having him lay her down beside the brook and lift her skirts. No, noble and rational didn't have anything to do with what there was between them. At least he'd been honest with her about his desires. If he pushed, just the tiniest bit, she'd be honest, too. She wouldn't be able to do anything else.

Yes, there was definitely potential at Ryland Castle. And he was going to explore it to its fullest limits. If she didn't want to marry him, fine. Fate had made him a duke, fate would determine how and where the affair with Caroline ended. Considering the incredible delights in having her in his bed between now and then, he could live with any consequence.

∽ *Nine* ∽

NO NEATLY CLIPPED HEDGE LINED THE DRIVE, NO OVER-
flowing flower pots framed the front steps. No draw-
bridge, no moat, no turrets—smoldering or otherwise.
Just nine yellowish stone boxes with windows, the largest
of the boxes in the center with four others of varying
sizes and styles attached in a line on either side. There
was a crenelated edge on the front façade of the main part
of the house, though. Which, Caroline supposed, was how
Ryland Castle had been named way back when. Back
when there had actually been a loose layer of crushed
shells on the driveway, before time, wheels, and feet had
packed them into the dirt and made it all as hard as a rock.

She stood on the drive and tried to keep her mind on the
moment. The butler's name was Winfield. The housekeeper's name was Mrs. Gladder. Both were sixtyish,
round, short, and white haired. Thank God he wore
trousers and she a dress; otherwise it would have been
nearly impossible to tell them apart at a glance. They stood
at the head of a pack of shabbily dressed servants assembled in front of the house for the new master's arrival.

Caroline nodded through the introductions as Aubrey
had instructed, and then accepted the housekeeper's

invitation to follow her inside. With Simone and Fiona following hand in hand, Caroline gathered her skirts, summoned a smile she hoped looked at least marginally confident, and walked through the parting mass of servants and up the steps. The foyer was a huge space of white-marbled floors, whitewashed plaster walls, and a smallish chandelier with crystal drops hanging high overhead. And not another thing. It echoed—cold and hollow—as they made their way across it to the central staircase.

It was a wide mahogany and carpeted sweep that led gracefully up to the second floor. The very edges of it testified that at one point, probably the day they'd laid the shells on the drive, it had been a beautiful floral carpet. A dark blue background with peach and sage and just a touch of a dusty blue to accent it all . . . But inside those edges countless footsteps over the years had worn the pattern to a dull, rather brownish and sad blur. Caroline added a new carpet to her list, right behind hedges, stone urns, and lovely plants.

"Lord Ryland advised us of the ages of his younger wards," Mrs. Gladder said as they reached the top and headed down the left wing. "It's been a good thirty years since the schoolroom has been in use and I'm afraid that we've all become a bit behind the times in knowing what supplies are needed to properly fit it out. If you'll prepare a list, the supplies will be gathered as soon as possible."

"The needs are basic enough at this point to be considered timeless," Caroline assured her. "We will need to secure, as soon as possible, the services of a governess and suitable tutors for the girls, though."

"Yes, of course. Mrs. Miller has graciously agreed to leave her retirement to be of service until Lord Ryland can arrange for more permanent help in the schoolroom."

Retirement? Aside from Mrs. Gladder and Winfield, none of the other staff had looked old enough to be anywhere near the point of having their days and nights to call their own.

"Stairs are a tad difficult for her, so I hope that you're not offended that she wasn't on the drive for your arrival."

There was nothing like the discomfiture of being stared at by twenty-four people all at once. Twenty-five might well have pushed her over the edge of silent endurance. "Not at all," Caroline said, wishing that all of the servants had taken their cue from Mrs. Miller.

The *very elderly* Mrs. Miller, she amended as she entered the schoolroom in Mrs. Gladder's black bombazine wake. "Please don't get up," Caroline hastened to say, stepping past the housekeeper to place a restraining hand on a rail-thin arm.

"Thank you, dear, it's most kind of you to be concerned," Mrs. Miller replied, smiling and gaining her feet anyway. "But at my age one often moves just to see if one still can. And while it's something of a morbid curiosity, it does tend to pass the hours."

"I'm Caroline," she said, chuckling, liking the tall and sharp-eyed, sharp-witted old woman. "And these are my sisters," she added, stepping to the side to present them. "Simone and Fiona."

"Ah," Mrs. Miller said softly, looking Simone up and down. "You will have some care for the advanced age and exhaustion of my heart, won't you, dear?"

"I'll try."

"Thank you," Mrs. Miller said with a bright smile. A bright smile she immediately turned on Fiona, saying, "I suspect, little one, that I'm about to lose Mr. Whiskers's heart to you. He's in his traveling basket in my room, too angry with me for putting him in it to come out. I suspect that you could talk him into joining us, though. Would you be willing to give it a go?"

"A kitty?"

Caroline blinked and suppressed the gasp of happiness. Fiona's voice was such a small and breathy sound. But it had been real words, the first deliberate ones Fiona had uttered since she'd joined their odd little family.

Mrs. Miller beamed and leaned slightly down. "A rather underfed one at the moment, I'm afraid. He's just come to live with me and it's my mission to make him fat and lazy and utterly content. You will help me, won't you?"

"Yes," Fiona whispered, letting go of Simone's hand and heading for the open doorway.

"Oh, you're good," Simone said in quiet reverence as their sister disappeared from sight. "Really good."

"Do remind yourself of that," Mrs. Miller countered, standing straight again, "when you begin to think that I've gone completely dotty."

As Simone and Caroline chuckled, Mrs. Gladder softly cleared her throat. "Might we leave the young ladies in your able care, Mrs. Miller? I'd like to show Lady Caroline the rest of the castle."

Caroline caught the quick, fiery look Simone threw her way. "Lord Ryland has promised Simone her choice of rooms," she said to the housekeeper. "Perhaps we could see to that task before we undertake a tour of the public rooms?"

Mrs. Gladder arched a brow. "It's customary for the children to have rooms adjoining the schoolroom."

"And it may well be that one of them will be entirely to Simone's liking," Caroline countered, smiling thinly and recalling Aubrey's advice on the proper handling of dissent. "But she's been promised her choice and a choice she will have."

Mrs. Miller saved the housekeeper the embarrassment of a noticeable surrender by exclaiming, "Ah, I was right!" as Fiona came back into the schoolroom cradling in her arms a gangly black and white cat. It was purring—loudly—and Caroline would have sworn that it was actually smiling. "He's forgotten all about me. The fickle little beast," Mrs. Miller accused as Fiona rubbed under its chin. Motioning for Fiona to share the animal with her, she added, quietly, "Run along and select your room, Simone dear. We'll be fine in your absence."

Mrs. Gladder didn't hesitate to seize the chance for escape. "This way, please," she said, sailing out of the room.

Caroline and Simone had little choice but to follow obediently in her wake. For a little round woman, she could cover ground quickly and she was past the stairs and halfway down the other hall before they caught up with her.

"Lord Ryland's chambers occupy this end of the wing," she said crisply and without a backward glance. "Would you care to see the general condition of them, Lady Caroline?"

Drayton's room? As long as it was something of a group excursion, she supposed that there wasn't anything overtly unseemly about going in there. "If he's not present, I probably should," she allowed. "Should he mention that he'd like some changes made, it would be nice to have some vague idea of what he's talking about."

"He and Lord Aubrey and their friend have gone to inspect the fields and the granary," the older woman supplied as she rapped her knuckles on the wood panel and then promptly proceeded to throw both of the doors wide open.

"Wow," Simone said softly.

Well, yes, that rather did convey the general impression of the room. Shades of plum, rich browns, antique gold. All very masculine colors, all very tasteful and elegant in a subdued sort of way. And the bed . . . It was the biggest thing Caroline had ever seen and it—even with the canopied, heavily fringed velvet draperies surrounding it—was positively dwarfed by the size of the room itself.

"His lordship's private bath is in here," Mrs. Gladder supplied, gesturing toward a door in the far right corner. "His is the only one in the house that has piped water. The bath adjoins his dressing area." She gestured to a door centered on the left wall, adding, "His private sitting room is through there."

Caroline nodded and stepped to the end of the bed to inspect the truly gorgeous gold-tasseled edge of the curtains. "Oh, dear," she gasped, her heart rolling over as they disintegrated between her fingers.

Beside her, the housekeeper sighed. "I'm afraid, madam, that every single curtain in the house is in similar condition. We haven't taken any of them down to be aired in the last three years simply because they would shred if we did."

Caroline nodded her acceptance and stepped back, remembering all that Drayton had told her last night of the estate's finances. "It's a lovely room," she offered. "And clearly it's been prepared to the best of your abilities given the circumstances."

"Thank you, madam," Mrs. Gladder said. Then she turned on her heel and marched back out into the hall, saying over her shoulder, "The next room is the one to which I had your bags brought."

Simone was closing Drayton's doors when the housekeeper pushed open a single wide panel and marched into what Caroline couldn't help but think of as a Pink Rose Riot. She allowed that it probably wouldn't have been so shockingly bright—and wildly floral—had she not just come from the quiet elegance of the other room, but even taking that into consideration didn't make the room any more to her taste. A maid, young and cherry-cheeked, dressed in black and wearing a simple white apron, stood frozen at the armoire, a hanger in one hand and Caroline's blue dinner gown in the other.

"Hello," Caroline said with a smile, quickly noting that all her bags lay open on the flowery bedcover.

"Good afternoon, madam."

"This is Dora," the housekeeper offered. "Her mother was personal maid to the late Lady Ryland. Before joining her mistress to receive their heavenly rewards, she trained Dora for service in her stead."

"And you appear to be very good at it, Dora. Thank you for your obvious care."

"My pleasure, madam," she said with a quick curtsy. "It's very kind of you to notice."

"Your dressing room is to that side with Dora's apartment adjoining it," Mrs. Gladder explained, gesturing to the left. She pointed to the door on the right. "Your private sitting area abuts that of Lord Ryland's through there."

"Another lovely room, Mrs. Gladder. And just as obviously well prepared as the other."

With a curt nod to Dora, the housekeeper swept past Caroline and Simone, stepped directly across the hall, and threw open another door. "Because of its size, this room has generally been set aside for the use of the most honored guests," she said, stepping back so that the two of them could gaze in wonder at another tribute to floral abundance. Violets, this time.

"I would have put Lord Aubrey in here," Mrs. Gladder said as Simone's lip curled in disdain, "but I think it would be better suited for his mother's use."

And Aubrey would be ever grateful for . . . Caroline blinked and swallowed. "His mother?"

"The Dowager Lady Aubrey is expected to arrive within the next fortnight, madam. For an extended stay."

"How lovely," she managed to say, wondering why no one had bothered to tell her before they had the house-keeper. Maybe that was the way these sorts of things were done. It really didn't matter, of course. Not given the larger implications of the announcement. Judging by even what little she'd seen so far, it would take a bloody miracle to have the house ready for company within a fortnight. "It does seem to be the perfect room for a female guest."

"Lord Aubrey has been placed in this next room, instead," Mrs. Gladder went on, pulling the door closed and then marching down the hall.

Someone had really, really liked flowers, Caroline decided as she gazed at an homage to blue delphiniums. And . . . yes, larkspur and bachelor buttons, too. All varying shades of blue, of course. Themes weren't themes if you deviated from them the slightest bit. Either there hadn't been very many male guests at Ryland Castle over the years, Caroline decided as Mrs. Gladder closed the door and moved on, or they'd all been remarkably confident of their masculinity.

"Mr. Haywood has been placed in this one."

Sunflowers. Bright yellow sunflowers. Accented with a ripened-wheat sort of brownish gold and a dull grayish green. But there wasn't enough of the latter two hues to make the overall effect of the room any less blindingly bright. Given that the huge windows faced east, it was a certainty that Haywood wouldn't be able to sleep a moment past the break of dawn.

"Are there any other rooms?" Simone asked quietly, her tone clearly conveying her dismay at the possibilities she'd seen so far.

Mrs. Gladder arched a brow, turned on her heel again and threw open another door. Tulips. In shades of red, leaning decidedly toward orange. The Daisy Room was rather a pleasantly bland surprise by the time they got to it, but Simone was all but swaying on her feet and unable to appreciate it being the lesser of all the evils. Caroline reined in her smile, wrapped her arm around her sister's shoulder, and helped her stagger forward. To the doorway of Fuchsia Peony Hell where Simone actually whimpered and turned a bit pale.

They crossed the landing and began opening doors along the schoolroom hallway. The first of those was . . . Caroline had never seen so many shades of green all in one place before. "Ivy, of course," she muttered as Simone quickly walked away.

Mrs. Gladder was smiling ever so thinly and closing the door rather sharply when, from across the hall, Simone cried, "Oh, thank you, merciful God!"

Well, well, Caroline silently chuckled as she stepped into the open doorway, the vegetation fairy had missed a room. It was the smallest of all the rooms she'd seen, but, like Drayton's chamber at the end of the other wing, it

had been done in subdued, decidedly masculine tones—
dark greens and taupes and little touches here and there
of burgundy. On the wall, between the two windows and
over the bed on which Simone was rolling in delight, was
a set of crossed épées.

"The schoolroom is directly through that door," Mrs.
Gladder supplied, giving a nod in the direction of the
door on the right side of the room.

"Leave the weaponry on the wall, please, Simone,"
Caroline instructed as she backed out of the room and
closed the door. "Thank you for your assistance in selecting her room, Mrs. Gladder. And now that we have that
task done, shall we begin the grand tour? If there's a conservatory, I'd like to begin there, please. I'd like to see
some real flowers."

CAROLINE COULDN'T FORCE ANOTHER SMILE. NOT AT THIS
point. After two hours of one unpleasant discovery after
another, her face would crack and fall off if she even made
the attempt. There was nothing to do now but be honest as
she and Mrs. Gladder entered the foyer together.

"Well, there's certainly a good deal of work to be
done, isn't there?" she ventured, sliding a glance over at
the woman.

"There is indeed, madam," the woman replied evenly,
giving not the slightest indication of how she might feel
about it all.

"I assume you would have shown them to me if there
were fabric inventories in the house."

"Yes, madam. Sadly, there hasn't been so much as a
spare meter for the last five years."

So she'd gathered in the course of the tour. "Are there
table linens?"

"Yes, madam. This way, please."

Caroline followed her through the house, through the dining room and to the large storage room between it and the door that led out into the yard and the kitchen beyond.

"I'm afraid," Mrs. Gladder said, pulling open a set of what turned out to be cedar-lined doors, "that you'll find them all in much the same deteriorated state as the other fabrics in the house."

Yes, she could see the wine and food stains as the linens hung on their rods. "The old duke didn't entertain much, did he?" she observed, taking the cloths out one by one and draping them over her arm.

"Not in the later years, madam. Not in the public rooms of the house."

"Well, we're not interested in setting a table at the moment, anyway. I simply need enough fabric to fashion at least one suitable gown for each of my sisters."

"You intend to cut them up?"

Caroline stopped and looked over at the housekeeper. "Are they suitable for any other purpose?"

She compressed her lips into a bloodless line for a long second and then said, "No, madam. They aren't."

"Not to worry, Mrs. Gladder," Caroline said, going back to her pillaging. "I fully intend to see that huge quantities of fabric are brought from London before the week is out. At the moment, properly clothing my sisters is my most pressing concern."

"Maggie is the castle seamstress. She lives in the village. She's very good and quite quick, but I doubt that she possesses any patterns appropriate for young ladies' dresses."

"Would she be available to come up here this afternoon?"

"I'll send for her immediately."

"Thank you," Caroline offered sincerely, stepping back from the closet, her arms loaded. "When she arrives, please send her up to the schoolroom."

"Will there be anything else, madam?"

"Not that I can think of," she admitted, heading for the main staircase. "Oh, yes, one thing," she corrected, stopping. "Please have additional dinners sent up to the schoolroom for both Maggie and myself this evening. We're going to be too busy to stop to be sociable."

"As you wish, madam."

It took real effort, but she managed to a dredge up a smile. "Thank you for the tour, Mrs. Gladder. I appreciate your time. If there's anything else about which you think I should be aware, please don't hesitate to inform me. Until Maggie's arrival, I'll be about the house, collecting fabric samples and writing out a lengthy list of necessities."

"It would be very nice to have the house restored to its glory again, madam. Keeping it has been a dismal task for so long. I hope the new lord doesn't feel compelled to whittle your list to nothing."

Ah, so Mrs. Gladder wasn't going to be an obstacle. That was nice to know. "He won't," she assured the woman. "He isn't the sort to deny a woman her pleasures." *Private or public,* she silently added as she headed for the schoolroom with the table linens.

DRAYTON FROZE ON THE STAIRS AND ABSENTLY SHOT HIS cuffs as he watched two men roll a potted tree of some sort into place in the foyer below. It was obviously the third of God only knew how many. And there was a large round table in the center of the space that hadn't been there when he'd come in only thirty minutes or so ago. And the brass vase with the tall, fresh flowers sitting in the middle of it was new, too.

Movement on the other side of the sidelights caught his attention and drew him the rest of the way down the stairs and to the front door. Two men were rocking a huge stone urn into place on the lower steps.

"Caroline," he muttered, remembering the way her eyes had sparkled in appreciation as they'd rolled up to the inn last night. "Not letting any grass grow under your feet, are you, woman?"

He closed the door and caught the eye of one of the departing workmen. "Do you know where I might find Lady Caroline?"

"In the study, sir."

He nodded his thanks, got his bearings, and headed across the foyer and down the hall. She was indeed in the study. Sitting behind the walnut desk, her golden hair piled atop her head, dressed in the traveling costume she'd put on early that morning, and looking absolutely ravishing as she scribbled intently on a piece of paper.

"Writing a plea for rescue?" he asked, stuffing his hands in his pockets and ambling across the room toward her.

She looked up, smiled, rolled her eyes, and went back to her scribbling as she answered, "I'm making a list of things I want Jane to bring with her when she comes from London. Hopefully your solicitor can carry it back with him with his legal papers tomorrow. She's going to need all the time she can possibly have."

"What's on this list?"

"For the most part, fabric," she supplied without looking up and seemingly unaware that he'd reached the desk and taken a seat on the outside corner. "Hundreds of yards of fabric. There isn't a square centimeter of cloth in this

house that isn't falling apart from rot. The rugs are thread-
bare. The upholstery is disgraceful. The table linens are
all stained and torn. It's a miracle that the draperies are
still hanging at the windows. Mrs. Gladder showed Simone and me all the bedchambers, but I didn't inspect
any of the interiors except from the doorways for fear of
what I'd find."

"A disaster?"

"Why merely suspecting is somehow more comforting
than actually knowing for a fact . . ." She shrugged and
shook her head. With a sigh, she laid down her quill pen
and looked up at him. "Please tell me," she said wearily,
"that you're getting an obscene sum of money for the
three of us. It's going to take every farthing of a sizable
fortune to make this place respectable."

"Spend however much you wish, dear Caroline. I enjoy making you happy."

She blinked, looked down as the blush colored her
high cheekbones, and then picked up the pen again, saying, "I realize that at some point you'll marry and the new
Lady Ryland will want to decorate to her preferences, but
assuming that you'll choose someone with even marginally good taste, I'll make a start of it for her."

Ah, slightly, delightfully breathless. "It's that bad?" he
asked, crossing his arms over his chest and enjoying the
game.

"It's beyond my worst nightmares. Are there any
changes you'd like to make to the décor?"

"Such as?"

"Well, to begin with," she answered, still writing, "do
you like the colors in your bedchamber?"

"I haven't given it any thought at all," he admitted with

a shrug. "Perhaps we should go there and spend some time privately conferring on the matter. We can start with your ideas on the bedding."

Her hand stilled and she shifted slightly in the chair. After a long moment, she laid down the pen, put her hands flat on the desk, and pushed herself to her feet. "We've agreed," she said slowly, meeting his gaze, "to keep our distance, remember? Leading me off to your room isn't toward that end."

"No, it's not," he readily agreed, deciding not to remind her that he hadn't agreed to the strategy in any binding way. "The end it's toward is ever more enjoyable."

She sighed. "Am I going to have to battle you every single moment for the next few months?"

"Oh, be honest, dear Caroline," he cajoled. "It's your most endearing quality. The larger battle isn't with me, it's with yourself. If you'd just give in, we could pass the time quite pleasurably. My room has a running bath. Did you know that?"

"Yes," she said, gathering her papers into a stack. "Mrs. Gladder told me all about it."

"It's the only one in the house," he added, picking up the quill.

"So she said."

"Please feel free to use it whenever you like."

"I wouldn't dare to impose in such a way."

"You," he drawled, trailing the edge of the feather along the curve of her jaw and freezing her in mid-motion, "my darling Caroline, don't have a cautious bone in your luscious body." He drew the feather down the length of her neck and over the swell of her breast. "Which, in case you need for it to be stated directly, is welcome in my bed anytime. My room is on the other side of our adjoining sitting rooms. The door isn't locked. I checked before I came downstairs just now."

As the pink deepened in her cheeks, she closed her eyes, took a deep breath, and stepped back—beyond his reach. "Thank you for the offer, Drayton," she said tightly. Her smile looked decidedly tremulous as she added, "I'm flattered, but common sense screams for me to decline."

He nodded and handed her the quill, satisfied with what he'd achieved for the evening. Watching her neaten her stack of papers and then pick up the ink bottle, he asked, "Where are you going?"

"The seamstress will be arriving from the village at any moment," she explained, moving around the desk. "We're going to make some serviceable clothing for Simone and Fiona."

"Until dinner then."

She stopped and turned slightly back to face him. "Mrs. Gladder was to have told you. I'm having my dinner with Simone and Fiona, Maggie, and Mrs. Miller in the schoolroom."

Maggie and Mrs. Miller? "Why?" he asked, focusing on the more troubling of the two puzzles.

"As they say, out of sight, out of mind."

"I promise to behave myself."

She rolled her eyes. "I'll have a complete list and fabric samples ready to send to Jane in the morning. If this house is to be in any sort of presentable condition by the time Aubrey's mother arrives, there isn't a moment to waste."

"Is that your way of saying that you intend to actively avoid me for days on end?"

"Yes."

"Caroline," he teased, "haven't you ever heard that absence makes the heart grow fonder?"

"It's not your heart that yearns for my company," she pointed out, walking off.

"True," he called after her, "but it's quite happy to go along for the ride."

He was wondering how lucky he might be when she stopped on the threshold and dashed his budding hopes. "I forgot to tell you something important. Mrs. Miller got Fiona to talk this afternoon."

"Who is Mrs. Miller? And how did she manage this miracle?"

"She's the girls' elderly nurse. A very wise, grandmotherly sort. And she waved an adorable little black and white kitten under her nose. Won Fiona over in a heartbeat. Simone says she hasn't been silent a single second since. Of course, she talks mostly to the cat, but it's a step forward."

"Things are looking up, then," he observed.

"Yes, they are, actually," she agreed, smiling brightly. "Good night, Drayton. My sincere regrets to Aubrey and Haywood for missing dinner together this evening."

"Don't you regret missing dinner with me?"

"No."

Drayton laughed quietly as she walked off. Damn, she was fun to spar with. Always surprising, always a challenge. And amazingly, just as fascinating out of bed as she was in it.

❧ *Ten* ❧

DRAYTON FINISHED OFF THE CONTENTS OF HIS MORNING cup of coffee, set it back in the saucer, and pushed the whole thing out of his way.

"So," Haywood drawled, pacing back and forth in front of the desk, his hands clasped behind his back. "If the tenants are saying that this year's crop is going to be slightly less than last year's because of the timing of the rains . . ."

"And," Aubrey contributed on cue as Drayton continued to work, "if the granary manager is saying that he can't possibly store it all . . ."

"But with the same storage facility in which he didn't have a problem with capacity last year . . ."

"Then the question is where last year's surplus went and whose pocket the proceeds of its sale lined."

Drayton didn't bother to look up at his friends. "Which is exactly the same question we formulated at three yesterday afternoon. And again at seven yesterday evening."

"We're posing it again," Haywood countered, "just to keep it fresh in your mind as you're busily adding up your little columns there."

Aubrey picked up Drayton's empty cup and carried it to the sideboard, asking, "Any conclusions reached?"

"Actually, the conclusion is the one we suspected right from the start," he admitted, laying down his pen and leaning back in the chair. "Thompson's ledger figures don't add up to the same total that the farmers' receipts do. He seems to have skimmed, as a general rule, between twenty-five and thirty percent off each transaction."

"Do Rudman's figures match Thompson's?" Aubrey asked, handing him a fresh cup of coffee.

"Are you expecting them to?"

"Not really."

"As far as I can tell," Drayton said, eyeing the totals on the four separate sheets of paper before him, "Thompson skimmed his portion as it came in from the fields while Rudman took one bushel out the back side of the granary for every five that came in the front."

"That's a fairly hefty loss."

"Between forty-five and fifty percent overall," Haywood summarized, nodding. "Give or take a bushel or two."

"And that's just a portion of it," Drayton went on. "Thompson's rent figures are short—by roughly fifteen percent—compared to the totals recorded on the farmers' receipts."

"He skimmed that, too?" Aubrey asked, leaning over to inspect the sheets for himself. "Good God, the man's a greedy enough bastard."

"What he is is wealthy."

"Well," Haywood said on an indignant huff, "it would seem that your estate manager and the granary keeper have some explaining to do."

"If either one of them has a brain in his head," Aubrey countered, "they spent the night hightailing it for the Continent."

Drayton shrugged. "Only if they spoke with each other to learn that we had possession of both their account ledgers." He sipped while the two considered that possibility and then added, "And only if the farmers happened to mention over pints last night that we'd collected their receipts for last harvest."

Aubrey nodded slowly. "I can't quite envision Thompson and Rudman knocking back a pint or two at the village pub. Can you?"

"They let anyone in there, you know," Haywood assured them. "Terribly low clientele."

"Which means," Aubrey concluded, a grin spreading over his face, "the odds are good that our two thieves are right where we left them."

"More importantly," Drayton pointed out, "they haven't thought it necessary to hide the money they've stolen over the years. Haywood, as I recall, you once studied a bit of law."

He cleared his throat and smiled sheepishly. "A brief but terribly misguided episode of my life."

"Did you happen to last long enough at it to know whether this evidence is sufficient to secure a magistrate's order?"

"If he's an honest magistrate," Haywood answered, "he should be quite impressed with it, actually. We'll need a local solicitor to formally frame the petition, but that shouldn't take but an hour or two at the very most."

Aubrey stepped to the sideboard to snag a bun from the tray, saying, "I should think that the greater trick will be to find a solicitor who isn't, one way or another, in the pocket of either Thompson or Rudman."

Haywood grinned and wagged a brow. "Ah, how incredibly fortunate that ferreting information is my specialty."

"All right," Drayton said, gaining his feet and gathering together all the papers on his desk. "Take a tilt at it, Haywood," he added, handing it all over. "Let's aim for placing our thieves firmly under the court's thumb by noon today."

"With extreme pleasure, your grace."

He was just out the door, the ledgers and papers tucked under his arm, when Aubrey swallowed the last of his pastry and observed, "If the man ever actually focused all his abilities in a single direction for longer than a day, he'd own the world."

Drayton nodded and grinned. "But that would please his family."

"What he needs is a good woman to settle him down and make him focus."

He considered the notion for a moment, then shook his head. "Our definition of what makes a woman good and his are wildly different."

"Oh, I don't know," Aubrey countered with a laugh. "He seems to have an appreciation for Lady Caroline."

Drayton blinked, not the least bit amused. "He hadn't better."

"Oh, not in his usual sense," his friend hastened to assure him. "He actually seems to be in respectful awe of her."

If Aubrey thought that possibility was any more acceptable than Caroline being another of Haywood's casual conquests . . . The matter needed to be addressed directly and seriously. "Has he put you up to making a petition on his behalf?"

"Not yet, but he's decidedly heading that way."

"Nip it before his feelings are bruised," Drayton instructed, picking up his cup and saucer.

"Is that the guardian, the duke, or the man talking?"

He heard the edge in Aubrey's tone and knew that an honest answer would earn him a few pearls of Aubrey's Wisdom of the Peerage. It would be infinitely easier to lie, or even to hedge. But the very idea of finding himself having to contemplate an evasion . . . "All three," he admitted, glaring down at his coffee.

"A few words of advice," Aubrey countered ever so predictably, ever so irritatingly. "The duke needs to take the other two in hand and talk some sense into them. Lady Caroline's an attractive woman, but the duke stands to gain far more financially in marrying a woman of lesser beauty and greater paternal aspiration."

"As the duke is aware."

"And the guardian should be focused entirely on seeing that Lady Caroline marries the deepest pockets and highest title cast at her dainty little feet. Her best interests and all that."

"As the guardian is well aware," he answered tightly. "And Haywood should be, too."

Aubrey lifted his cup in acceptance of the pronouncement and then proceeded straight on to what Drayton sincerely hoped would be his final words on the subject. "The man . . . You need to keep your distance from her so that scandal doesn't prevent either of you from making the most of your opportunities."

"As I am very well aware, Aubrey."

"Yes," his friend allowed slowly. "From what I've seen, you've carefully abided by and acted in accordance with every proper social expectation."

"But?" Drayton prodded. "I hear a 'but' waiting to be spoken."

"I'm afraid that it's obvious that you resent it. Mightily. That's dangerous, Drayton. The cost of losing the battle with temptation would be incredibly hefty. You might want to consider coming along with me in the morning. A week away could do wonders for cooling your impulses."

Running away wasn't going to do a damn thing about cooling his impulses or his heels, much less do anything to ease his irritation. The thought of having to subject himself to a full week of not only Aubrey's well-intentioned lectures, but those of his mother, too . . . God, trapped with the two of them in a carriage for hours on end? For *days* on end? He'd have to shoot himself.

"Mr. John Coleman, sir."

He blinked at the butler standing in the open doorway and smiled in relief. *Impeccable timing.* "Thank you, Winfield." He set aside his coffee cup and shot his cuffs, adding, "Please advise Lady Caroline and her sisters of Mr. Coleman's arrival."

The servant bowed, stepped back and to the side to clear the doorway for the young solicitor from London, and then disappeared without a sound.

Drayton's natural instincts wanted him to stride forward to meet the solicitor halfway and offer a handshake. Aubrey's soft "ahem" reminded him that dukes were supposed to wait while the world scampered to them. "Welcome to Ryland Castle, Mr. Coleman," he said, compromising by taking a single step and sticking out his hand. As Aubrey quietly growled, Drayton grinned and added, "I hope your journey was pleasantly uneventful."

"It was, your grace. And my pleasure to undertake for the business at hand."

Of course he would have enjoyed it. Coleman had struck him on their first meeting as being the sort who enjoyed solving the twists and turns of legal puzzles, but hated the leather-paneled walls that came with them. Thinking that the boy really should have considered a career in the foreign service, he half turned to Aubrey and undertook the tedium of the formal introductions. Both men slightly bowed to each other, exchanged the standard, boring pleasantries, and then looked back at him.

God, it was such a pain in the arse being a duke. So many damn rules, so many expectations. Most of them just patently pointless except to remind people that he was supposedly superior to them in every way. At least there was a command rationale for the restrictions the military placed on its personnel. "I assume," he said, feeling very resentful, "that no problems developed since we last met?"

"No, your grace. I have all of the papers in order. If I may use your desk?"

"Of course," he said, stepping aside and gesturing to the walnut slab. "Would you care for coffee and some pastry while we wait for my wards to grace us with their presence?"

He didn't wait for the man's assent, ignored Aubrey's look of censure, and stepped to the sideboard.

"You are in very deep trouble," Aubrey muttered.

"Then maybe viscounts should think about being hospitable," he countered under his breath, pouring.

"Not that. Look."

He glanced over his shoulder. And, just as it had as he'd stood on the drive at the inn yesterday morning, the world quivered under his feet. He winced and brought his attention back to the overfilled cup and saucer. Putting it down, he snatched up a napkin to dry his hand, and swallowed the lump in his throat.

His wits were only slightly more collected when he turned to face his advancing wards. *Deep trouble?* Aubrey didn't have the vaguest notion of what kind of trouble loomed ahead. How Caroline could manage to look so angelic and so wanton in a demure, buttoned-to-the-throat teal green silk day dress and carrying a sizable stack of papers . . . But God help him, she did. Simone, in a similarly uncomplicated day dress of smoky blue damask, was nothing short of a premonition of London's smoldering fate. Fiona . . . The child was a balm on his ravaged heart. Dressed in a sage green linen smock with a darker green as an underskirt, waist sash, and hair ribbon, cradling a sleeping black and white kitten in the crook of her arm, she was the sweetest, most innocent sight he'd ever beheld. He tilted his head and smiled in sudden realization; she wasn't limping. Heaven only knew how Caroline had accomplished it, but Fiona's grin said that the effort had made the child's world infinitely wider, infinitely more hopeful.

"Ladies," he said earnestly, as they came to a halt halfway to the desk, "a lovelier sight has never brightened this room."

"Oh, stow it," Simone muttered, shifting her shoulders and scowling.

Caroline sighed and Drayton reined in his smile to step closer and lean down. Scratching under the kitten's chin, he asked, "And who is this, Fiona?"

"Beeps."

Oh, such a beautiful, cloud-soft voice.

Simone looked down at the cat. "I thought his name was Mr. Whiskers."

Fiona shrugged ever so slightly. "He says his name is Beeps."

"That's a stupid name for a cat."

"He's very smart," Fiona assured him.

"I can see that," Drayton said, standing straight again. "He has excellent taste in mistresses." Fiona slid a triumphant gaze over at Simone—who rolled her eyes and shifted her shoulders again.

Drayton met Caroline's gaze and blinked, stunned by the heaviness of her lids. The smile she gave him was valiant, but weak—as if every measure of her strength were required to simply stand there and hold on to her papers. He needed to get the business concluded as quickly as possible; she was going to collapse from exhaustion at any moment. "Good morning, Lady Caroline."

"Good morning, your grace," she replied softly. She looked past him to nod slightly and add, "Lord Aubrey."

Drayton dealt with the introductions, presenting Coleman to each of them. When all the pleasantries had been exchanged, he extended his hands, saying, "If I may, Caroline?"

It took her a second to understand what he wanted her to hand him her papers. As he passed to Coleman what were actually detailed drawings and fabric scraps, he explained, "Lady Caroline has prepared a list of items she needs her assistant, Miss Jane . . ."

"Durbin," she supplied, saving him.

"To bring with her when she comes from London later this week," he went on. "If we might impose on you to see that these are delivered into her hands, we would be eternally in your debt."

"It's no imposition at all, your grace," the solicitor assured him. He looked down at the papers in his hands and carefully fanned through the first few sheets. "May I say, Lady Caroline, that you are a very talented artist."

"You're too kind, Mr. Coleman," she countered. "I can sketch to a degree sufficient for designing, but not much beyond that. You should be able to find Jane at my shop in Bloomsbury. It's at Eastcastle and Brenners."

He nodded. "I assume, just glancing through your instructions, that Miss Durbin will require a letter of credit. I'll see that one is drafted for her immediate use." He lifted his gaze to meet Drayton's. "Do you have a general sum in mind for the purchases, your grace?"

Hell, he had no idea how much money he had or how much Caroline's domestic fantasies would cost. And he didn't care, either. Whatever it took to make her happy, he'd spend. "I assume that she's Lady Caroline's assistant because she's proven herself both resourceful and trustworthy. Allow her access to whatever amount she needs."

Caroline gave him the first easy smile he'd seen from her that morning, and he rewarded her by adding, "And please advise her that I'll send my carriage for her on Friday. However, she's to feel free to make whatever arrangements are necessary to transport the goods as soon as she acquires them."

"Oh, yes," Caroline said. "That's brilliant, Drayton. I should have thought of that myself. The sooner we can begin work, the better chance we have of being ready for Lady Aubrey's arrival."

Brilliant? Well, she probably wouldn't think so once she had some sleep, but for the moment he was willing to let her think of him in all the glowingly heroic terms she wanted. He cocked a brow at Coleman and then down at the legal papers.

"Since time is of the essence," the young man said, taking the hint smoothly, "let's dispense with all the legal work." He put Caroline's papers aside, picked up a quill pen and held it out, saying, "Lady Caroline, if you'd be so kind as to sign above your printed name."

She stepped forward, leaned down, signed, then backed away, handing the pen back to Coleman. "Thank you," he said with a slight bow. "I sign here," he went on, leaning over the paper and scribbling himself, "to attest that I have met the minor daughters of the late Lord Ryland and been satisfied as to their having been suitably brought under the care and protection of the new Lord Ryland."

He straightened, dipped the pen, and handed it to Drayton. "Your signature, please, your grace."

It occurred to him as he wrote his name that he was, legally, becoming Simone's and Fiona's father. And Caroline's knight errant. With, if he were being honest about it, the accent on "errant." Rationally, he knew that all of it was a burden he had absolutely no experience in bearing and was likely to bungle on a fairly regular basis for quite some time. Logically, he knew that it would be a heavy responsibility over the coming years and that there would be times when he wondered why the hell he hadn't run for the hills to avoid it all. But as he handed the quill back to Coleman, he felt only the deep sense of satisfaction of having just made the world come right.

"Thank you," Coleman said, dipping the pen again. "And yours, Lord Aubrey," he said, handing it off, "as witness to all of it, please."

Aubrey signed with a flourish and it was done except for the sanding and the folding.

"And with that completed," Coleman announced, tucking the document back into his leather valise along with Caroline's drawings. "I will be on my way back to London to see that the papers are properly recorded and that Miss Durbin receives her instructions."

There was more bowing, more inane pleasantries, and then Coleman was at last on his way, heading for the front door and then northward to London.

"Can we go now?" Simone moaned, pulling at the sleeve of her dress.

"Yes, you *may*," Caroline replied with a sigh. "Mrs. Miller is waiting for you."

As they headed off, Drayton stepped to Caroline's side, wrapped his arm around her shoulder and guided her to a chair, saying, "For God's sake, sit down before you fall down. Didn't you sleep last night?"

"If I did," she answered, stifling a yawn, "it was only by accident and for just a second or two. I simply couldn't let the girls appear before Mr. Coleman in their rags."

"I should have thought of buying them clothes before I collected them. That you've had to go through such torture is entirely my fault."

"And how would you have known what sizes they wear?"

True. "Well, then I should have seen to it immediately afterward."

"One does not walk into an establishment, point to clothing, and say, 'I'll have two of those and six of those. Wrap them up so I may be on my way.' It takes time, Drayton, to make clothing."

"And considerable effort and self-sacrifice," he observed. "Thank you for giving so much of yourself so that Coleman didn't leave here thinking of me as a thoughtless, stingy oaf. Have you had your breakfast yet?"

"No." She pressed the back of her hand to her mouth to cover another yawn. "There wasn't time. We'd just finished the hems when we heard the carriage arrive."

"Let me get you some coffee and a pastry." She murmured something in reply, but he didn't really hear it. Aubrey was leaning a hip against the sideboard and giving him the most disgusted sort of look. Damn, if he hadn't forgotten the man was even there.

"If you don't stop," his friend said quietly as Drayton poured a cup of coffee, "I'm going to retch."

"Do try to make it outside before you do," he countered with a tight smile, picking up the entire plate of pastries with his free hand and walking away. To find Caroline sitting with her hands folded sweetly in her lap and her eyes closed.

"Caroline?" he whispered, setting the food and coffee on the corner of the desk.

"If you're lucky, she won't remember all your pathetic fawning."

"I wasn't fawning. I truly appreciate what she's done." He laid a hand gently on her shoulder. "Caroline?"

"I do believe the expression is dead to the world," Aubrey drawled, chuckling.

Drayton wasn't amused. In fact, a part of him wanted to put a fist squarely into Aubrey's nose. Another part of him, though, simply wanted the world to go away for a while and leave him alone. Slipping one arm under Caroline's legs and the other around her shoulders, he lifted her up and cradled her against his chest.

"Good God! What are you doing?"

"Carrying her upstairs," he explained as she sighed and nestled her face into his neck. "And putting her to bed."

"Do you have even the vaguest recollection of what I said about courting scandal?" Aubrey asked, trotting at his heels.

"I'm going to put her on her own bed, place her in the care of her maid, and walk away. Feel free to tag along to vouch that being kind and considerate needn't compromise a woman's reputation."

"You're besotted," Aubrey accused as they started up the stairs.

Drayton ignored him, deciding that the longer-term interests of friendship probably lay in keeping his comments to himself. If caring for a woman's physical comfort and rest was a sign of being besotted, then, all right, he was. And if it was a sign of being besotted to be genuinely appreciative for all the effort and sacrifices she made to make his house more livable and the opinions others held of him higher, then, yes, he was guilty. About a hundred times over.

And if wanting, in his heart of hearts, to say to hell with appearances and carry her into *his* room and lie down beside her on *his* bed and hold her while she slept was a sign of being besotted, then he was hopelessly and happily gone around the goddamn bend and he didn't give a bloody fig if it took an entire month to come back.

CAROLINE OPENED HER EYES AND STARED UP AT THE ceiling. Either the house was on fire or . . . She turned her head on the pillow and sighed dreamily. What a wonderful life she'd fallen into. A soft, warm bed, a flickering fire in the hearth, a tray of food sitting on the tufted footrest just in case she should rouse from her ease and find herself hungry.

Which, now that she thought about it, she was.

Her back protested as she sat up and pushed the covers aside. It was only as she slid to the side of the bed that her mind clicked fully awake. The last thing she remembered with any sort of clarity was sitting down in Drayton's study. And she definitely recalled having been wearing considerably more clothing then than she was wearing now. She glanced around the room and, not seeing her dress or stockings anywhere, concluded that it likely *hadn't* been Drayton who'd stripped her down to her corset and tucked her under the comforter. No, more likely it had been Dora. And only Dora would have thought to lay her wrapper on the foot of the bed; it was the sort of thought that would occur only to a female mind.

She pulled the cover on, tied the sash around her waist, and padded on bare feet to the chair in front of the hearth to take inventory of the foodstuffs. A cloth-lined basket filled with crusty hard rolls, a little pot of soft cheese, a pair of apples and a delicate silver knife to cut them with, a towel-wrapped silver pot of . . . She tipped back the lid and inhaled the tendril of steam. Oh, dear God, chocolate!

"Just let me eat this," she said, gazing up at the ceiling and grinning, "and then you can strike me dead and I won't say a word."

She'd finished one roll, eaten half the cheese, slurped down a good three quarters of the hot chocolate, and was tossing the apple from hand to hand when she laughed and looked back up at the ceiling. "Whoever had this brought in here . . . Sainthood. Honestly, they deserve—"

The clock on the mantel chimed and she listened,

prepared to count the hours. There wasn't another sound. "One?" she gasped, vaulting out of the chair to check the clock face. Yes, one. She looked at the inky darkness on the other side of the window. She'd slept for how long? Fourteen, maybe fifteen hours? No wonder she'd been so hungry.

Of course now she was full and rested and the only one in the entire house even thinking about what to do with the day. It would be at least another four hours until the kitchen staff began to stir and they were the very first to rise. They'd probably want to kill her if she carried her dishes downstairs and rolled them out this early.

No, she should probably stay in her room and find some quiet activity to pass the time. It had been ages since she'd had the luxury of time to read something other than fashion books. Which, she had to admit, were always more visual fantasies than any true intellectual stimulation. Surely there had to be a book somewhere close at— The sitting room. Yes, she remembered seeing a small bookcase in there.

Pulling a strand from the hearth broom, she lit it and carried it to the lamp on the bedside table. The light was soft and pleasant and in it the cabbage roses on the wall-paper grew huge and seemed to eerily dance.

"Euw," she said, shuddering and carrying the light into the smaller adjacent room. The paper on the walls in there was the same as in the bedchamber, but in the confined space they didn't so much dance as they loomed and pulsed with unnatural life. Caroline put the lamp on the secretary, turned up the wick and focused on the contents of the bookshelf.

Botany. Seven books and every single one of them was on flowers. She glared at the wallpaper, silently threatening to tear it all off and throw it away the very first chance she got.

"Oh," she whispered, grinning and stepping close to the doorjamb. "Just how . . ."

The edge lifted easily, cleanly. "Oh, yes!" she cried happily, pulling a bit harder, a lot more deliberately. The paper separated from the plaster behind it and age-old paste crumbled away, falling to the floor and dusting the tops of her feet. It was only toward the top of the room that the paper began to tear and resist her effort to remove it. Caroline paused, considered the problem, and then smiled. It was a matter of angles and leverage; all she needed to do was stack up some of the furniture so that she could reach higher. She could have every last shred of it gone before dawn.

DRAYTON SCRUBBED HIS HANDS OVER HIS FACE, FROWNED, and worked the kink out of his neck. He was thinking that his days of comfortably sleeping in chairs—no matter how overstuffed—were long over when the sound came through the wall beside his head. He looked over at the plum-striped wallpaper. A rat? The sound came again. A rat the size of a small pony? He scowled, decided against the rat possibility, went to the door that led into Caroline's sitting room, and yanked it open.

He didn't mean to gasp, it was just the sound that came out when his heart slammed up to the base of his throat.

"Hello, Drayton. I didn't—" The pile of furniture under her swayed toward the window on her left and she threw her balance forward to compensate. The back edge of the chair hit the plaster wall with a resounding thud.

"What the hell are you doing?" he demanded, threading his way toward her through the maze of furnishings.

"Tearing down," she answered, tugging the half-loose sheet of wallpaper and sending the stack swaying again, "the world's most god-awful wallpaper. I didn't mean to wake you."

"Jesus Christ, Caroline! Come down from there before you fall through the window."

"I'm not going to fall."

"Yes, I know," he declared, reaching her and instantly throwing his arm around her waist. "Because you're coming down," he added, hauling her back against him.

"Drayton, no!" she squeaked as the paper tore free along a ragged edge. "Oh, damn!"

Off balance, but otherwise infinitely relieved, he pivoted just enough to fall into the chair with her. "Daughters of dukes do not pull down their own wallpaper," he informed her as she glared up at him from his lap. "They order it done by others and then go for a carriage ride."

She threw the sheet of paper on the floor. "How boring."

"How safe."

"I was perfectly safe," she declared, yanking her satin robe closed over her breasts and then flipping the length as best she could to hide her legs.

He grinned and drew the satin over her lower body until all that showed were the tops of her cute little dusty feet. "Do you ever have a waking moment in which you do nothing?"

"No."

"Well, it's time for you to cultivate the skill."

Her breath caught painfully in the center of her chest, Caroline forced herself to look away from the sparkling dark eyes. It was the middle of the night and she was sitting—no, reclining comfortably—half-naked, in Drayton's lap. If she could manage to get out of this predicament with just a tiny little shred of dignity intact . . . "Speaking of cultivating," she began, trying to sound as though she found herself in this sort of situation all the time, "did Mr. Henry get the planters done on the front steps?"

"Yes," he said, obviously fighting a smile. "They were in place by the time Coleman arrived. They look lovely. As does the foyer, by the by. You've been nothing short of a creative dervish since you walked through the front door."

"What about the hedges?" she asked, wondering if it would be possible to just accidentally fall to the floor. Probably not, she decided. Not with his arms around her like they were. "Has the planting begun yet?"

"Henry and his crew were still working on them at sunset. It may take a day or two longer, but the overall pattern is starting to emerge and it's stunningly attractive."

"Has he placed the fountain yet?"

"Fountain?"

Oh, well, sooner or later, his legs would go numb and he'd be forced to ask her to get up so the blood could flow back into them. "It's beautiful. Five scalloped tiers with a simple round finial. Why it was in storage, Mr. Henry couldn't say. It's been there as long as he can remember. We designed the entire Irish knot around it as the centerpiece."

"You're amazing."

Well, so was he. Handsome. Chivalrous. Sweet to little girls with kittens. Generous. And nothing short of breathtakingly intuitive in bed. She cleared her throat softly and deliberately put her mind back on a safer track. "Actually, all I've done is give people permission to do what they've wanted to for ages. Mr. Henry practically danced when I asked if he could do something to improve on the front landscaping. That's when he showed me the fountain."

"Which would explain why there isn't a single drapery left on the windows downstairs."

"Mrs. Gladder has had them torn down already?"

"She's had them burned, too," he said, nodding and smiling. "All of it with a great deal of enthusiasm, I might add." His smile broadened. "And yes, before you ask, the drive has been reshelled. Late this afternoon. And it's deep enough that Aubrey turned an ankle in it when he came back from the village pub this evening."

Well, there was a side to him she hadn't seen yet. "You seem to be rather pleased by that unfortunate event."

He shrugged. "Simone's right, he's a prig. I have no idea why I consider him a friend."

"What's he done to test your temper?" she asked, suspecting that Aubrey had objected to the free rein he was giving her in spending his money.

His smile weakened and his eyes darkened as he stared across the room. "He warned me to stay away from you."

And sitting on his lap was just the sort of thing that Aubrey was worried about. "Wise counsel, Drayton," she pointed out, sliding her feet to the floor and easing out of his embrace. "We should listen to him. He is a good friend."

"A true friend would care about my happiness," he countered, as she perched on the edge of a footstool and told herself that being careful was better than being comfortable.

"What did the girls do with the day while I slept it away?"

He cocked a brow. "You're changing the subject."

"Quite deliberately," she admitted. "What did the girls do with their day?"

"Lessons in the morning," he supplied, stretching his legs out and leaning back to cradle his head in his hands.

"You're right about Mrs. Miller being the grandmotherly sort. I like her. After luncheon, Aubrey, Haywood, and I took the girls out so she could have a hard-earned nap."

"And what did you all do?"

"Simone had her first fencing lesson. She's very good."

"Why am I not surprised?"

"And Fiona found an injured squirrel in the stable."

"Oh, no. I hope she wasn't heartbroken."

He laughed softly and his eyes twinkled. "She splinted its leg and made Haywood find her a cage to keep it safe should Beeps ever rouse enough to have a moment of bad manners and feral instinct."

She laughed and then the implication settled in her brain. "The squirrel is in the house?"

"In her room," he said, nodding as though every home had a squirrel in residence. "It's name is Scutter. Just so you know."

"What if it's diseased, Drayton?"

"Aside from the leg, he looks just fine. And there's certainly nothing wrong with his appetite. Have you ever seen, at close quarters, a squirrel eat? They're the most incredible little machines. It's really more fascinating than you'd think."

She'd missed it. She'd missed standing beside Drayton and laughing with him as they watched Scutter gnaw away at a nut. The loss of that moment, that chance, hurt. Just as it hurt to sit apart from him now and want so badly to climb back into his arms. If only she hadn't been so brave the one time. If only she didn't know just how much she was giving up for the sake of protecting their all-important social reputations and financial prospects.

"What is it, Caroline?"

"I was just thinking," she answered, scrambling for a plausible lie, "that you sound as if you enjoyed the day."

"It was more entertaining than swabbing down cannon barrels ever was."

"Are you missing the military at all?"

"Command is command," he said after a moment. "The satisfactions are different, but also similar in many ways." He shrugged and pushed himself to his feet. "All in all, I'd have to say that I'm adjusting to the sudden change in my circumstances far more quickly and smoothly than I expected."

She stood, too, hoping they could get through parting without too much awkwardness. "You seem to be a much happier man than the one that walked through the door of my shop two days ago."

"Three days," he corrected with a wink.

"You know what I mean."

He nodded and tilted his head to consider her. "You seem to be a much happier woman, too."

Well, yes, but admitting it would just give him too much satisfaction. "I was perfectly happy with my life."

"You know what I mean."

"Yes, I do."

He reached out and trailed a fingertip slowly along the top of her nose. "Could I talk you into coming to bed with me, dear Caroline?"

"No," she whispered as her heart insisted that it would be wonderful if she did.

"Then I had better be putting a door or two between us," he said, letting his hand fall back to his side. "Promise me you won't climb back up there as soon as I'm gone."

"I won't."

He cocked a brow. "Won't promise or won't go back up there?"

"I won't go back up there," she assured him. "I'll work on the lower part of the room. Quietly. So I don't keep you awake."

He glanced over to the open door that led into his sitting room and, with a rueful smile, slowly shook his head. "If you get bored with demolition," he said quietly, taking her shoulders gently in his hands and bending his head.

The brush of his lips was so soft, so gentle it staggered her senses. Never, her mind whispered as she leaned into him, never had she been kissed like this. So tender, so sweet, so deeply longing.

And then she was standing alone, swaying, trying to remember how to breathe as the door quietly clicked closed behind him. She sank down into the warmth of him left in the chair, drew her legs up and wrapped her arms tightly around them, then stared at the door until it disappeared in the haze of tears.

⤞ *Eleven* ⤝

DORA HAD BEEN RIGHT; ESCAPING THE NEVER-ENDING flood of questions for a few hours had been just the thing she'd needed to lift her spirits. It was a perfect day. The sun was shining, the sky was a clear blue, and the clouds were soft little cotton puffs drifting lazily along overhead. Caroline paused in the shaded doorway of the sweetshop and looked up and down the hard-packed street. The village of Ryland was such a delightful change from the noisy, crowded, sooty . . . and well, largely brusque world of London.

Everyone nodded and smiled as you passed them on the street. No one driving carts or wagons or carriages was in a maniacal hurry to get anywhere. Shopkeepers were delighted to chat the time away and eager to give you whatever your merest whim lighted upon. And most amazingly, not only did they never mention the price of things, they seemed almost offended by the notion that you thought they should be paid for their merchandise.

Two hours into the excursion and she was still finding it hard to believe that such an idyll existed, much less that, for all intents and purposes, Drayton owned the whole thing. Not that anyone seemed to resent it. In fact, everyone she'd met had had the nicest things to say about him and, to the person, they'd asked that she convey to him their appreciation for his interest in their lives and businesses. Their obvious surprise at his caring had mystified her until Dora had explained that the two days Drayton had spent in the village and visiting the outlying farms were two days more than old Lord Ryland had ever considered worth his bother.

Dora came to stand at her side, added Mrs. Gladder's bag of horehound candy to their cache, and grasped the wicker handle of the market basket, saying, "Allow me, please."

Caroline sighed. "Oh, for heaven's sake. Three small bags of sweets and a few meters of ribbon are hardly going to strain my arm."

"That's not the point, madam," Dora persisted as she tugged. "It's that ladies don't tote and carry."

"Ladies," she countered, "apparently don't do much of anything except think of things for other people to do."

Dora beamed. "Precisely, madam! Now give it over, please."

Rolling her eyes in disgust, Caroline surrendered the basket and stepped out onto the walkway, thinking that she simply didn't have the temperament to ever be a very good lady. Hopefully there weren't women in London whose responsibility it was to sneak about and peer through windows to be sure that ladies were being appropriately idle. If there were . . . Well, she'd just have to spend the rest of her life at Ryland Castle. No one there clutched their heart and turned pale when she rolled up her sleeves and pitched in to see a task done.

"I think," she began, glancing over at Dora—to find

that Dora wasn't there. Caroline stopped and looked back. Dora stood still as a post, her mouth open, her eyes huge, and her attention riveted on the other side of the street—on two manacled men being hoisted up into the back of a wagon. Everyone around was watching, just as mesmerized as Dora.

Caroline slipped to her maid's side and quietly asked. "Who are they? Do you know?"

"The tall one is Edgar Thompson. He's Lord Ryland's estate manager. The shorter one is Rudman, the granary keeper."

"Are they being arrested?"

"It would appear so, madam."

Well, that had been a stupid question. Of course they were being arrested. A blind man could hear the clink of the chains. "Do you know why?"

"No, madam. But judging by the look on their faces, I'd say that Lord Ryland and Mr. Haywood do."

Drayton was there? She leaned slightly forward to look past Dora and up the main street. And then darted back, her heart pounding. She'd had no idea he could look that lethal, that hard and determined. It didn't help any that he was sitting on the biggest, blackest horse she'd ever seen. And that he'd practically appeared out of nowhere . . . She hadn't done anything wrong. She wasn't in chains and being hauled away. But, God, she so desperately wanted to run. Not that she'd get very—

"Lady Caroline. Dora."

Damn. Caught, she forced herself to swallow and turn to face him.

Edging the horse slowly but deliberately sideways, he closed the last of the distance between them as he asked tightly, "What are you doing here in the village?"

Well, at least he wasn't angry. But he wasn't happy, either. She quickly touched her tongue to her lower lip and dragged just enough air into her lungs to say, "We came down to order paint and do a bit of shopping."

He reined the huge animal to a halt, turned its hind end completely around so that her view of the arrest was effectively blocked, then considered her a long second—for the time it took for Haywood to ease around to her and Dora's backs—before he said, "I distinctly recall mentioning to you how the daughters of dukes are supposed to go about getting things done."

"And I distinctly remember mentioning how boring I found the whole notion," she countered, hating that she had to crane her neck to meet his gaze. It so diluted any pretense of defiance.

He cocked a brow and quickly glanced past her. "Where's the carriage?"

"We didn't bring it. We walked down from the castle. It's a very short walk and a beautiful afternoon and—"

"We'll take you back," he said crisply, shifting the reins into his right hand and extending his left. "Haywood, if you would be so kind as to assist Dora."

"It would be my extreme pleasure. The Honorable Cyril Haywood at your service, miss."

"'Honorable' is a courtesy title, Dora," she said, putting her hand in Drayton's, not having the slightest idea of why other than he'd commanded it.

"I do wish everyone wouldn't feel compelled to mention that fact."

Dora giggled as, his gaze dark and guarded, Drayton leaned down, threaded his fingers through Caroline's, and quietly said, "Turn your back to me."

She did, the movement drawing her closer to the horse

and Drayton's arm over her shoulder. There was a quick creak of leather and then she was gasping, clinging to the certainty of the iron band clamped around her midriff as she flew upward. In the next heartbeat she was planted, still and secure, high above the world and firmly in the circle of Drayton's embrace.

She looked down at her lap, exhilarated. It was almost like sitting with him in a chair. But better because she was so much more closely fitted to him. Shifting ever so slightly to smooth a wrinkle out of the backside of her skirt, she settled her shoulders against his chest, and drew her right leg just a tiny bit higher so that her hips nested perfectly between his thighs.

"Comfortable?"

She thought she heard a smile in his voice and she looked up at him over her shoulder to be sure. It only flirted at the corners of his mouth, but it danced in the depths of his eyes. "Yes, thank you," she admitted, tucking her hands around his forearm as the animal beneath them started forward. "I've never been on a horse before."

"I wouldn't have guessed."

She didn't have to see his face to know that he'd cocked a brow and that he was giving her one of his lopsided smiles. Let him be amused; she was enthralled. Oh, this could so easily be the most scandalous, wanton thing she'd ever done. The warmth and strength of Drayton's body pressed against hers—or hers pressed against his; it changed back and forth with the gentle rock of the animal's gait as it ambled up the road . . . Either way, it felt good. Surely there had to be a way to make love on—She softly cleared her throat and forced herself to think of something else.

"Is there a problem in the village, Drayton?"

"Not at the moment," he answered easily, "but if one develops, I'd rather you not be in the midst of it."

"Do you know why those men are being arrested and taken away?"

She felt the tension shoot through his body half a heartbeat before he answered coolly, "They're thieves. And I've pressed formal charges against them."

Given who the two men were . . . "And the mystery of the low crop yields is solved."

"Yes, but until the evidence is presented in court, there could be resentment in the village. Not that I honestly expect any, but I'd rather err on the side of caution. You're not to come down here again unless you speak with me about it first, understood?"

"Yes," she agreed, seeing his concern and appreciating both that he wanted to protect her and that he was trying not to be heavy-handed in doing so. He'd really come a remarkably long way since the moment he'd walked into her shop and pronounced, *Your life has changed, be deliriously grateful.*

"Thank you for not being obstinate about it."

"I may be stubborn from time to time—"

"From time to time?" he asked, his silent laughter rippling all the way through her.

"All right, most of the time," she allowed. "But I'm not reckless." The words had no sooner left her mouth than she knew she should have swallowed them whole.

"If we were alone on this path, my dear Caroline," he said, casually slipping a finger between two of the lower buttons on her bodice, "I'd prove you wrong."

She'd dared him; of course he'd taken it. It wasn't in his nature to pass up opportunity. And it wasn't in hers to pretend that the feel of his skin against hers was unpleasant.

"You're supposed to call me a cad, Caroline," he said softly, lightly drawing his fingertip over her abdomen. "And then insist that you'd fend off my unwanted advances with every last measure of your strength."

Yes, she knew that. "It seems to me," she replied, closing her eyes and savoring his touch, "that the first lie would only be compounded by the second."

He shifted behind her, twisting slightly. "Your heart's racing," he whispered against her neck. "I can feel it."

She melted into him, her bones softened by the heat of wanting, her will weakening with every step the horse took, with every deliberate brush of his fingertip. Common sense struggled to rally, but its arguments weren't at all persuasive—not when balanced against the promise of desire.

Drayton glanced up to measure the distance between them and the house. And cursed his timing and his luck. They were not only too close to take the seduction any further at the moment, but Mrs. Gladder was standing on the steps, shading her eyes with her hand and watching their approach. It took most of his self-control not to groan in frustration, the rest of it to straighten in the saddle and put his hand on his thigh. He was still trying to think of an excuse that could bring them alone together once they were inside the house when his housekeeper gathered her skirts and dashed down the steps to meet them.

"Lady Caroline! The fabric is here!" she exclaimed, startling the woman in his arms back to reality and crushing any possibility of an afternoon interlude. "And it's from heaven itself! Come see what a wonder your Miss Durbin is!"

She gazed up at him over her shoulder and gave him a tremulous smile. "I'm afraid that my duties call, Drayton. Thank you for seeing Dora and me safely home."

At least she looked sorry about it. There might still be hope. "Stay right where you are," he instructed, his teeth clenched as he reined in the horse and swung down from the saddle.

"I'm tired of Haywood being my only dinner companion," he said, reaching up to place his hands around her waist. As he lifted her down and settled her feet into the shells on the drive he added, "Either you join us for the evening meal or we'll join you in the schoolroom. Or the workroom. Or wherever you think to hide from me tonight."

She considered him, her hands falling from his shoulders to her sides. Slowly she arched a brow. "The workroom. And you're welcome as long as you either assist or stay out of the way."

Then she neatly sidestepped from between him and the horse and turned away. Damn. That hadn't gone as he'd thought it would.

"Oh," she said, pausing and looking back. "Formal attire isn't required." Her eyes sparkled and her smile took on a stunningly delightful wicked edge just before she walked away, adding, "What you're wearing now would be just fine."

He didn't have to look down to know what amused her. Riding breeches never left a damn thing to illusion and his had become uncomfortably tight in the last few minutes. Drawing down the reins, he led his horse toward the stable hoping to hell he could walk off the evidence of his frustration before Haywood finished trying to seduce

Caroline's maid and trotted up to share the details of the successful effort with him. God, there were times when he really hated his life.

OF COURSE, HE HAD TO ADMIT AS HE SWIVELED ON THE stool to move his legs out of a maid's way, his life would be a lot better if he'd quit making stupid decisions. The one to back up his dinner threat with action wasn't turning out to be one of his better ones. He didn't know a damn thing about drapery construction and the process of sewing looked only slightly less tedious than it did masochistic. The combination of the two realities meant that he was of no use to anyone in terms of assistance—and didn't want to be.

Staying out of the way, though . . . Well, he and Haywood were doing their best. The workroom was a sizable one, but with a huge central table having been erected in the center of it and the fifteen, maybe twenty women—it was impossible to get an accurate count—dashing around, it wasn't big enough to be truly out of their way for any longer than a few minutes at a time.

He and Haywood were, however, clearly out of the collective female mind. For the most part. Until a piece of fabric required toting or opening for an examination of some sort and then the square meter of floor space he and Haywood had staked as their own was claimed with a sharp look and not-so-softly cleared throat.

Haywood leaned close. "Have you ever seen anything like this?" he asked quietly.

"No. You?"

"I'm not sure my mother even knows how to sew clothing, much less drapes. My sisters . . . *pffft*." He shook his head. "But even if they did know how to do it, it would never occur to any of them to actually work *with* the servants."

Drayton smiled and watched as Caroline pinned a sheet of vellum to the blue damask laid out on the table. "She is interesting, isn't she?"

"Well, if you're hoping to find a wife like her, you're going to be looking a long, long time."

"Maybe I'll save myself the time and effort and marry *her*."

Haywood snorted softly. "You might want to think on that a bit. I mean, once she has the house redecorated . . ."

Drayton looked at him sidelong. "Are you really that shallow?"

"I just think a trip to the altar should be undertaken only at gunpoint."

Shaking his head, he went back to watching Caroline work. "Your parents must have a horrible marriage to have twisted you so badly."

"Actually, they have a very good marriage," Haywood countered, leaning forward to rest his elbows on his knees and resume his survey of female forms. "Never a ripple of discord and all that. Mother goes her way, Father goes his, and from time to time they meet to ask each other if they happen to remember the name of the last child, the one who was in the artillery corps last year."

"They remember your name," Drayton assured him. "Your mother sends you a gift for your birthday every March. Last year it was book of short stories. And the year before it was a sketching kit. So you don't draw. It's the thought that counts."

Haywood turned his head to meet his gaze. "I was born in August."

"Oh," he said, stunned. "I could see how that might make a . . . Damn, Cyril. I had no idea. I'm sorry."

"*You're* sorry?" Haywood said, chuckling.

They both leaned back and pulled their legs to the side as two maids stepped to the end of the table and cut along the top edge of the vellum pattern. After they'd finished and gone, and as Caroline and Mrs. Gladder carefully cut down opposite sides of the vellum and others folded the length in their wake, Haywood leaned forward again and asked, "Do you care for Caroline?"

Drayton's stomach shifted uneasily. "I like her," he supplied noncommittally. "And as we've agreed, she is interesting."

Haywood nodded and then grinned. "I won't embarrass you by asking whether you find her physically attractive."

He considered denying it, but just as quickly decided that there wasn't any point; Haywood wasn't blind or stupid. As long as his friend didn't push the matter any further, being that honest wouldn't create any problems. "What a good friend and gentleman you are," he allowed.

"When's her birthday?"

"I don't know," he admitted, suspecting that Haywood was going to suggest that he might want to find out so that he got her a present in the right month.

"Does she have a middle name?"

A middle name? Why did Haywood want to know that? He shrugged. "Yes. It's in the report Geoffrey had made on her. I don't remember what it is, though."

"Is she Anglican?" his friend pressed on. "Or maybe one of those Presbyterians?"

"All right," he said on a sigh. "I give up, Haywood. Why are you asking me all these—"

The main doors to the workroom suddenly swung open, stopping everyone in the room mid-motion, mid-syllable, including Drayton. Winfield stepped across the threshold, snapped to attention and lifted his chin to announce, "Miss Jane Durbin."

The butler barely had time to step aside before Miss Jane Durbin . . . well, *exploded* into the room. Drayton was vaguely aware that his jaw sagged, but it was beyond him at that moment to do anything about snapping it closed.

Orange hair. Bright orange hair swept up high and wrapped—several times around—by what looked to be at least half a dozen strips of bright green paisley silk, the ends of which fluttered behind her like the tail on a kite as she swept across the threshold and threw open her arms in triumphant arrival. As wild applause erupted, she grinned and dropped into a deep curtsy of appreciation.

"Whoa," Haywood whispered as her bosom threatened to spill over the lower edge of her neckline. "And thank you, God."

She'd traveled from London wearing an evening gown? Drayton scrubbed his hands over his face and looked back to the door. Why had he been expecting a . . . a . . . *mouse*?

"Jane!"

"Oh, Caroline! You look gorgeous!"

Well, of course she was gorgeous. She also looked decidedly wholesome and respectable and sensible and sane. She didn't look at all like Jane Durbin. God, he hoped she didn't catch something in hugging the woman.

"I'm so glad to see you. I didn't expect you for another day."

"I finished everything and simply couldn't bear to wait another single minute to see you."

The women chattered on as Haywood leaned close again to ask, "Do you suppose Caroline would give me an introduction?"

Drayton looked over at him, amazed. "Do you suppose not having one would make a difference?" Jesus. Of all men, Haywood should recognize an easy conquest when she sailed into a room. Hell, if *he* did, the woman was all but carrying a placard.

"Let me introduce you to everyone."

Haywood jabbed his elbow into Drayton's arm and vaulted to his feet, jerked the hem of his jacket into place, cleared his throat, and struck a ridiculous come-hither pose. Drayton slowly pushed himself to stand and forced himself to smile.

"Lord Ryland and his friend, the Honorable Cyril Haywood," Caroline said, gesturing to them. Drayton nodded as Haywood bowed so deeply that Drayton wondered if he intended to lick his boots. Jane's gaze moved slowly up and down Drayton's body and then slid over to Haywood. She was smiling like a cat full of bird when Caroline took her by the arm, turned her slightly and added, "This is Mrs. Gladder, the housekeeper."

"A pleasure to have you join us, Miss Durbin," his housekeeper said, taking the woman's hands in hers. "There are no words to express our delight with the fabrics you've chosen. They're all beyond our happiest, wildest dreams."

"I assure you that I enjoyed every moment of choosing them. Caroline's instructions and drawings were, as always, simply divine and so easy to work from. I knew exactly what she wanted."

"And this is Dora, my maid," Caroline went on, turning Jane yet again.

"Let's slip out of here," Drayton said, turning toward the door. "I'm not feeling at all well."

"Oh, but that's a beautiful woman."

"Agreed." He stepped past his reluctant, entranced friend, adding, "But it'll be a week before she notices anything except fabric. You might as well cool your heels until then with a good bottle of brandy."

"It might take two," he countered, sighing and falling in behind him.

Drayton stopped at the door, took the handles of both panels in hand and looked back. "Good night, ladies. Happy sewing."

Only Caroline acknowledged his departure. She met his gaze, smiled, mouthed, "Good night," and then turned her attention back to the excited feminine chatter.

Telling himself that he should be grateful for her dedication to the improvement of his property, Drayton closed the doors and headed for the stairs with Haywood on his heels. It wasn't every man, he reminded himself, whose ward and staff happily worked well into the night so that a house could be ready for guests. He should be grateful and thinking of some way to show his deep appreciation.

And he was grateful and appreciative. But he was resentful, too. As well as a bit insulted. To think how she'd melted into him that afternoon and how very close he'd been to having his hungers satisfied, only to have his company declined for fabric and the sisterhood of scissors and thread . . . The fact that she'd chosen to work on the new drapes rather than have dinner with him and pursue their attraction . . .

Yes, he admitted, as he entered the study and headed for the brandy, he was being a bit obsessive about it, but a man with a fragile sense of himself would be crushed by the rejection. At least he hadn't gone that far over the edge. He still had hope. All he needed to do was to get her alone for a few minutes; he could make her forget all about the wonder of new draperies.

"It might take three bottles if you're going to drink the first one all by yourself."

He blinked, startled by Haywood's voice. Damn, he'd forgotten that he wasn't alone. He handed the freshly poured drink in his hand to the man and reached for another snifter for himself.

Haywood waited until they'd both taken a sip before asking, "So, what's troubling you, Dray? If it's my interest in Miss Durbin, I'll defer. Rank has its privileges, you know."

Jane Durbin? Not if she were the only woman left on earth. But telling Haywood that would be too close to a judgment on the man's standards. But confiding the truth wasn't an option, either. It was one thing to admit to finding Caroline attractive in a purely distant sort of way, entirely another to confess his determination to get her back in his bed.

Not that he'd be horribly unhappy about the ultimate outcome of complete honesty. Being forced to marry Caroline would save him from the indignity and embarrassment of being placed on the marital auction block this coming Season. It would also save him from having to figure out how much money she was worth. Putting too much in her dowry would attract every ne'er-do-well from across the width and breath of the empire. Offering too little for her . . . She was going to be humiliated enough in being inspected without adding the insult of being viewed as a pity purchase. Yes, all things considered, it would be ever so much easier if they were to marry each other and avoid the whole mess.

"Or are you trying to remember Caroline's middle name?"

Sometimes Haywood had the most irritatingly smug smile. "No," he replied. "I'm wondering why all the questions you know I don't have answers to."

"Oh, that," Haywood countered with a dismissive wave of his hand as he dropped down into a leather chair. "Just being a good toady and tossing out some conversational possibilities for you. In case you feel the need to work your way toward the 'Will you spend all of eternity with me?' question. You know, soften her up a bit, lull her into thinking that you want to know more about her than whether she prefers long or short stockings."

Long. Very long.

"Not that I'm encouraging the notion, you know. Wouldn't be a particularly forward-thinking move for either one of you."

"In terms of money," Drayton clarified, dropping down in the other chair.

"Is there anything else?"

"Enjoyable company?" he posed, feeling boxed in and surly about it.

"Ah," Haywood countered, lifting his snifter, "but if you marry the right woman you'll have plenty of money to buy all the enjoyable company you want, whenever you're in the mood for it."

The right woman. Meaning, in Haywood's world, a woman from a good family with incredible wealth and no real interest in her husband's desires or his activities in satisfying them. From a logical standpoint, it was the perfect sort of arrangement; unlimited money, a respectable wife, a thriving estate, a legitimate family, and permission, all the way around, to have an affair whenever he wanted. All the things that made a man's life utterly enviable.

Draining his snifter, Drayton pushed himself to his feet and headed off to refill it, thinking that the world into which he'd so unexpectedly fallen was certainly a far different one than the one into which he'd been born. And that he'd be a damn fool to refuse to play by its rules just because he thought they were hollow. Haywood was right; money could buy you anything, anyone you wanted.

Maybe, if Caroline didn't find someone to marry . . . He shook his head to dispel the notion, knowing that men would line up ten deep to offer for her. He had six months to work through and be done with his fascination with her. After that, they would go their separate ways, marry wisely, and never reach back. There were high risks involved between now and then, of course, but other than that, it was the only rational, sensible, logical, financially intelligent thing for them to do.

❧ Twelve ❧

CAROLINE STOOD AT THE FOYER TABLE WITH JANE, watching the carpenters attach the fabric-draped valances atop the high narrow windows flanking either side of the main door. She smiled and congratulated herself on being right; luxurious draperies made all the difference in the world.

The medium dusty blue hue complemented the carpet on the stairs. The richness of the damask itself, the fullness of the panels, the pale gold fringe, and the generous jabots on the valances combined to balance the visual weight of the front doors and the stairs. What had been a cold and echoing chamber was now a welcoming and positive first impression of Ryland Castle. If all the rooms looked so improved when she was done with them, she'd be deliriously pleased. And exhausted, she adding, struggling to contain a yawn.

Wiltson, the estate's head carpenter, came down his ladder and stood back to survey the effect. He gave his son on the other ladder a nod of acceptance and, as the young man climbed down, turned to Caroline and asked, "Will there be anything else tonight, madam?"

"No, Wiltson. We'll declare it a day with this success.

If you and James will leave your ladders, Miss Durbin and I will quickly see to the pleating before we retire. Thank you for all your work. It's much appreciated."

He smiled, nodded, and motioned for his son to precede him toward the rear of the house. As they left, she and Jane gathered up the narrow strips of vellum from the foyer table and went to work on their last task of the day. Climbing halfway up the ladder, Caroline gently folded the width of a damask panel into easy pleats. "How does that look from down there?" she asked. "Too many? Too few?"

"Perfect," Jane assured her, handing up a strip of vellum and a pin. "Tell me about Lord Ryland."

"There isn't much to tell," she said, securing the paper collar around the carefully bunched fabric. "Until he became the duke, he was an officer in Her Majesty's Artillery Regiment. He was just as surprised by his elevation as I was to be recognized as the old duke's daughter."

"Oh, for God's sake, Care," Jane protested as Caroline stepped down a bit to repeat the folding procedure. "We've been friends for way too long for you to even think about lying to me and hoping to get away with it. The way that man looked at you when he left the workroom . . . He had you all but naked. And you weren't blushing. In fact, if they slapped my hand on a Bible and made me tell the truth . . . You were hoping he'd sling you over his shoulder and carry you out."

Of course Jane had noticed that momentary exchange. When it came to men, Jane never missed a thing. Even with her eyes closed. "I was more afraid that he'd actually do it."

Jane handed her another strip of the vellum. "It was not fear twinkling in your sweet little blue eyes."

No, it hadn't been. She'd been remembering the ride together that afternoon, wishing that the fabric hadn't arrived, and regretting that good judgment seemed to have recovered its strength. She pinned the paper sleeve in place, fighting back an unexpected sting of tears. Damn Drayton and the temptation he was.

"Are you all right, Care?"

No. No, she wasn't. She ached—body, mind, and soul. And she wanted—no, needed—to share the burden with her friend. It was either that or walk into Drayton's arms and let him make the world go away for her. She blinked back another searing haze of tears and came the rest of the way down the ladder, saying, "You have to swear to—"

"Take it to my grave," Jane finished, holding up her free hand. She grinned and glanced around the foyer before quietly asking, "Is he good?"

Her mind danced through the memories, sending her heart racing and heating her blood. She closed her eyes, marveling at how her body so keenly remembered the sensation of his touch. "Oh," she sighed, shaking her head and forcing herself to open her eyes and return to the present.

"I knew it," Jane declared triumphantly, giving her a quick hug. "I'm so happy for you, Care. You deserve a good man."

Caroline stepped out of her embrace and to the ladder on the other side of the window. "It was just the once," she clarified, starting up. "Well, the one night, actually. It was the moment and—"

"Apparently," Jane interrupted with a chuckle, "it was a series of moments."

"Well, yes," she allowed, the ache in her core oddly deepening. "But it can't happen again. It just can't."

"Why?"

"Titles, money, and marriage to the best possible combination of the two," she explained, gathering the fabric into pleats.

"So, marry him."

"It wouldn't be advantageous for either one of us."

"What?" Jane challenged, handing up the paper and the pin. "Enjoying rolling around in a tangle with your husband doesn't count?"

"Not really."

"Who made up these ridiculous rules?"

"I don't know," she admitted, stepping down a bit to repeat the process of arranging the folds.

"Well, whoever they are, they should be shot," Jane declared. "And frankly, so should you if you're turning your back on . . . What's his real name?"

"Drayton. Drayton Mackenzie."

"Oh, nice," Jane murmured. "A Scotsman. You know what they say about Scotsmen."

Her heart pounding, Caroline glanced down at her friend. No, she didn't know about Scotsmen, but she did know Jane. And Jane's disdain for any rules that might restrain her pursuit of pleasure. At the moment, Jane was imagining what sort of delights she could find with Drayton.

"You know, if you're sure you're done with him . . ." Jane looked up and then laughed. "You should see your face."

Caroline didn't care how she looked. She glared at her friend, stuck out her hand for the vellum and pin, and said, "Don't you dare, Jane. *Don't* you *dare*."

Jane's hazel eyes twinkled as she passed the supplies. "You said that you can't, you couldn't. Not again. To me, that sounds as though he's free for the taking."

Seething, trying desperately to control the impulse to throw herself off the ladder and paste her to the marble floor, Caroline warned tightly, "Jane, don't test our friendship."

"Then claim him, Care," Jane said with a shrug. "Straight-out. You don't have to love him, you know. And you don't have to intend to marry him, either. All you have to want is to keep him for yourself until you find someone more interesting. Claim him and I won't go anywhere near him."

"All right," Caroline declared, coming down the ladder. She squared up to Jane and firmly announced, "He's mine."

"There," Jane said, beaming, "don't you feel ever so much better?"

"No, I don't," she admitted, turning and grabbing the ladder, knowing she'd been manipulated—artfully.

"You will as soon as you drop him onto the sheets," Jane assured her, trailing along as she carried the ladder to the other window. "Infinitely better. Trust me."

Trust Jane? On anything, with anything, except men. Why hadn't she thought of that before so blithely insisting that she join them at Ryland Castle? Because, the logical part of her brain supplied through the red haze of anger, she'd insisted Jane come along before she'd discovered what a wonderful lover Drayton Mackenzie was. At the time he'd been a pompous ass standing in her shop, making declarations and seizing control of her life. She'd wanted to bludgeon him, and Jane had been the closest thing she'd had to a weapon. Now she was paying for neither one of them having been honest with each other in those moments.

That was the thing about lying and denying, she reminded herself as she went up the rungs. Sooner or later they turned around and bit you. As her mother had always maintained, the truth would eventually come out. And when it did . . . On top of everything that you'd been trying to avoid with the lies and denials was the inescapable fact that you were a coward, too. Better to accept and own the truth from the beginning, no matter how awful it was, than to be caught trying to run from it.

How all that related to Drayton . . . God, it was disheartening to realize that she really wasn't one bit more refined or reserved than Jane when it came to the pursuit of physical pleasure. That she didn't make a regular habit of surrendering to temptation was something of a consolation. A very small one, she knew, because she didn't regularly face temptation. There had been Peter, of course. But in the wisdom of hindsight and the experience of life, she knew now that he had been the love of a very young, very romantic heart. Life together wouldn't have been kind to their matching and they'd have both come to regret the hasty, breathless decision to ease their guilt by agreeing to marry.

Drayton was different. Different from Peter, different from any other man she'd ever met. And God knew that she wanted to be with him, to make love with him again. The truth, the most fundamental, absolute truth, was that she wanted him however she could have him. And that all the rules and proscriptions didn't do one damn thing to change that.

They determined how it would all end, of course. But between now and then she didn't want to lie or deny anymore. She didn't have the strength or the energy for it.

And if Jane's presence was the consequence for being dishonest with each other at the beginning, the consequences of living the rest of her life regretting that she hadn't had the courage to be honest now were just too dismal to contemplate, much less endure.

"Tell me about Haywood," Jane said quietly, intruding on her thoughts. "Is there all that much mystery to him?"

Caroline sighed, and taking the strip of vellum from Jane, answered, "Actually, no. He's a lot like you."

"Really?" she asked, her voice dropping to a mere whisper. "Is he always hovering about like that?"

That? Which implied . . . She looked over her shoulder. Drayton stood at the hall entry to the foyer, Haywood at his elbow. "Yes," she supplied, her heart skipping as Drayton slowly smiled at her. Her breathing shallow, her head light, she swallowed and turned her attention back to the drapes.

"I would imagine," Jane said, laughter rippling through her whisper, "that you'd appreciate having him distracted."

It took a long second for the import of that to sink through the haze of her own sense of anticipation. "For God's sake!" she gasped, looking down, hoping—futilely, as it turned out—to stop her friend from acting on the impulse.

"Mr. Haywood!" Jane called, sailing across the foyer, the pincushion in one hand, the vellum strips in the other, and the tails of her head scarves fluttering behind her. Drayton stepped aside, losing an obvious battle to contain a grin. Haywood remained rooted to the spot, looking a bit, Caroline thought, like a man about to be run down by the queen's carriage—both honored and horrified.

"Might I impose for just a moment or two of your time?" Jane asked, sweeping to his side, twining her arm around his, and tilting her face up to turn the full force of her charm on him. "I need help with something and only a big strong man like yourself will do."

Drayton stuffed his hands into his trouser pockets and made another attempt to control his grin as he stared up at the chandelier. Caroline rolled her eyes as Haywood sighed and looked adoringly into Jane's gaze. "Anything you require, my dear Miss Durbin. *Anything* at all. I'm your obedient servant."

Practically glowing in delight, Jane led him off across the foyer toward the parlor. As she passed Drayton she paused to hand him the vellum and the pincushion, saying, "Here, your grace. Just give a strip and a pin to Caroline when she snaps her delicate little fingers."

She didn't wait for Drayton to accept the responsibility. No, in typical Jane style, she simply assumed that he had nothing better to do and proceeded to haul Haywood off into the shadows of the parlor. Drayton, clearly abandoning any further effort to contain his amusement, grinned and wandered out to the center of the foyer to watch their progress. Caroline couldn't help herself, either. Jane really was a marvel when it came to twisting men around her fingers. Poor Haywood wouldn't know what had hit him until—

The flash of boot soles was accompanied by the sound of the settee rolling over with a heavy thud into the carpet. Caroline turned away, shaking her head, as Drayton threw his head back and laughed outright.

"How on earth did you two become friends?" he asked a moment later, coming to stand at the base of the ladder.

"Quite by accident. We were both shopping for ribbon in the same store and I happened to notice the unique design of her dress and asked her about it."

"Let me guess. It buttoned up the front."

Congratulating him with a nod and a smile, she continued on, saying, "She's taught me a great deal about the practical aspects of design and agreed to be my assistant when Mother passed away. Admittedly, Jane has her share of faults, but no one has a kinder and more generous heart."

He glanced over to the parlor and then back up at her with a quirked smile. "Her generosity is obvious."

"She'd do anything for me, Drayton."

"I'm guessing she'd do—"

"Please don't say it," she insisted, holding out her hand for vellum and a pin. "I'd rather not be put in the position of having to defend her right to make the choices she does."

He nodded and passed her what she required, saying, "Haywood is perfectly capable of taking care of himself. And it's not as though he hasn't encountered more than his fair share of Janes before. You don't need to worry about him."

"I know," she allowed, setting the pin and then backing down the ladder a few rungs.

"Then what are you worried about?"

"Nothing." She winced at the lie and gathered the folds of drapery. But how did one go about telling a man that you'd decided that you were willing to sleep with him? Just coming right out and saying so seemed so . . . so . . . well, businesslike. Almost as if the next words should be "for twenty quid." Perhaps she should climb down off the ladder and just walk into his arms. What she wanted would be obvious; there wouldn't be any need to say a single word.

"It occurs to me that I could easily play this to my immediate advantage," he said softly, stepping closer to hand her the vellum and the pin without being asked.

"Play what?" she asked, distracted by the frantic hammering of her heart.

"But I won't," he went on as she placed the pin with trembling fingers. "When you come to my bed, Caroline, I'll be alone in it. I promise."

He thought . . . ? Of course he did. Haywood wasn't the only man who had met his fair share of Jane Durbins. At some point she'd have to tell him that she wasn't surrendering out of jealousy or fear or even a sense of possessiveness for having seen him first. Not that she knew, in any precise way, why she was surrendering, she admitted as she came down the ladder. It was simply something she wanted to do with every fiber of her being.

He held his hand out, not touching her, but clearly prepared to catch her if she stumbled and started to fall. He didn't step back as she reached the floor. A bare handwidth separated them as she gazed up at him, savoring the scent of his shaving cologne, the heat of his body, the slow, deep cadence of his breathing. God, she wanted to lay her cheek against his chest and feel the beat of his heart, have him wrap her in his arms and hold her there.

"Lady Car-o-line?"

Mrs. Gladder, supplied a small voice in the back of her mind. *Coming from the back of the house.* "It may be a while before I'm free," she whispered, her stomach clenching in disappointment.

"Lady Car-o-line?"

Closer.

Drayton stepped back, putting a proper distance between them. "I understand," he assured her, his gaze smoldering as one corner of his mouth lifted in a weak smile. "Duty before pleasure."

"Unless," she said on a sigh, "you're Jane and Haywood."

"I'm willing to wait," he said softly, handing her the pincushion and the remaining vellum strips just as Mrs. Gladder came from the hall beneath the stairs.

"Oh, there you are, Lady Caroline. Good evening, Lord Ryland. If I'm intruding—"

"Not at all," Drayton assured her, his manner easy and confident. "I was just telling Lady Caroline how very impressed I am with the new draperies. Allow me to extend my awed appreciation to you and your staff as well, Mrs. Gladder. You are all beyond amazing."

The woman blushed and smiled broadly. With a bit of a bobbing curtsy, she said, "Thank you, your grace. I'll convey the message to the others immediately. They'll be so pleased to know that you've noticed their efforts."

"And then, for heaven's sake, let them go to bed," Drayton countered, smiling as he eased away. "They've earned the rest. This will all be here tomorrow."

"Yes, your lordship."

He paused and gave them both a brief bow. "Again, ladies, I'll wish you a good night."

Caroline nodded at his departing back and then smiled at the housekeeper. "There's a question awaiting me in the workroom?"

"Just a few, madam," she answered, sounding sincerely apologetic. "But they can wait until morning."

"Or they can be answered now," Caroline countered, heading for the hallway, "so that we can sleep untroubled and start at a dead run at first light."

IT HAD TAKEN THE BETTER PART OF AN HOUR TO MAKE the decisions and be sure that everyone knew what task they were to undertake first thing in the morning. It had taken another fifteen interminable minutes to try to dissuade Dora from her duties as lady's maid, give up, and let her prepare her for bed. The clock on the mantel was striking half past eleven when the girl finally slipped into her own room and closed the door.

Caroline waited a few more minutes just to be sure that Dora was going to stay there, then climbed out from between the sheets. Pulling on her wrapper, she collected the pile of papers—her pretext in case she faltered or things became a bit awkward—from her dressing table, crossed the carpet, and quietly opened the door to her sitting room.

As he'd promised, Drayton waited for her. The light was pale and somewhere behind him as he leaned against the jamb of the doorway that led into his own sitting room. His jacket discarded, his shirttail out, the front half unbuttoned, and his feet bare . . . She smiled in appreciation for what he'd accomplished for her already.

"I must say," he drawled as she pulled the door closed behind herself, "that, even unfinished, this room is a vast improvement."

Whatever appraisal he'd done had to have been before she got there, she realized, warming as his gaze skimmed over the open front of her wrapper. "Thank you. These are for you," she said, holding out the papers. "Although I'm not sure that this is the sort of reading you'd want to undertake just before retiring. It could well give you nightmares."

"What is it?" he asked, taking them without so much as a glance at them.

"The receipts for what Jane bought." She closed the distance to the same mere breath that had separated them in the foyer. "They're huge sums, Drayton. Obscene."

He slowly cocked a brow and the corner of his mouth tipped upward. "Are you happy with what she purchased? Is the house going to look the way you envision it?"

"Yes. On both counts."

Holding her gaze, he held up the receipts and let go of them, saying as they fluttered to the floor around them, "Then I don't care what it cost."

Whatever her heart desired. And at the moment, he was all in the world that she did. "You make it very difficult to resist you," she accused, reaching out to trail her fingertips along the front edge of his unbuttoned shirt.

"My intention is for you to find it impossible. Am I close to succeeding?"

"Yes," she answered softly even as doubts began to niggle at her confidence.

He grinned and slipped his arm beneath her wrapper and around her waist, drawing her gently against the warmth and length of him. "I assume your maid has retired for the night?"

God, she was on the verge of committing what had the potential to be social suicide. She swallowed and tried to slow the beat of her heart by asking, "Do you have a valet somewhere?"

"Well, in a manner of speaking, yes. He's in London, looking for another employer."

Intrigued by the smile she heard in his voice, she looked up at him. "Why?" she asked, wondering how many women before her had melted at his easy charm.

"I've been dressing and undressing myself—quite ably—since I can remember," he replied, grinning down at her. "I've also managed to shave myself without slitting my throat or taking off my upper lip for the better part of twenty years. I've never needed a valet and becoming a duke hasn't made me suddenly helpless."

"Aren't they supposed to see your clothes laundered and all of that?"

He shrugged and nodded. "I leave them on the end of the bed in the morning and when I return at night, they've been cleaned and pressed and returned to the armoire. I assume one of the maids sees to it. Without the assistance of a valet."

He cocked a brow and his eyes sparkled with amusement as he gazed down at her. "Any more questions?"

"No."

"Are you sure?" he teased. "We could talk about the weather. The farmers are hoping no storm blows in to delay the harvest."

"No, I don't want to talk about the weather," she admitted. "Or the harvest."

"Then we appear to have reached the crossroads of decision."

"We actually reached it this afternoon and again in the foyer just a while ago," she reminded him. And herself. "Now it's simply a matter of which one of us is going to step across the line first."

"As I recall, I stepped first the last time."

He was daring her to make the final advance? "As I recall," she countered, her doubts fading in the face of the challenge, "I pushed you."

His smile faded. With a slow nod, he drawled, "Yes, now that you mention it . . ." He leaned down to press a kiss to her forehead, then stepped back. She was standing on her own, stunned by having been released, when he bowed ever so slightly, said, "Good night, Caroline," and walked away.

She stared after him, her heart pounding in her throat. Common sense told her to run for her room and be grateful that he had better judgment than she did. Pride and desire sent her after him. "Drayton!"

It took considerable effort not to grin, to keep himself from saying, *I knew you couldn't run.* It took another hefty measure to calmly unbutton his cuffs and say regally, "If you don't mind, madam. I'm trying to get undressed for bed."

She arched a brow and the tiniest smile tickled the corners of her mouth. "Oh, really," she replied, shrugging her shoulders and sending the silk wrapper to the floor. "What an interesting coincidence. So am I."

"Hardly a fair contest," he pointed out, opening the rest of his shirtfront, his heart pounding in anticipation. "You don't have any buttons to undo."

She made a little humming sound, stepped close, slipped her hands to the waistband of his trousers and pulled. The fabric tore and the buttons went sailing across the room. "There," she announced, letting go and stepping away. "Now you don't have buttons, either."

"Or pants," he observed, grinning and stepping out of what remained of them.

"You said that you wanted me to be happy."

He didn't remember saying those exact words, but at that moment, he wasn't remembering much of anything except how wonderful she'd felt—he'd felt—the last time they'd been naked together. And then even those memories were gone, obliterated by the promise of now as the simple sheath of her nightgown glided down her body.

He managed to discard his shirt a scant half second before the gown puddled around her ankles. "I win," he declared.

Laughing and stepping into his arms, she asked, "What's the prize?"

"You," he chuckled, lowering his head to lay gentle siege to her mouth.

The fact that he'd won her days ago flitted through her mind and then was gone, swept away by heady delight as he picked her up in his arms and carried her over to his bed.

CAROLINE NUZZLED HER CHEEK INTO HIS ARM, WIGGLED her body closer into the curve of his, and smiled dreamily. Somewhere, no doubt carved in stone, there had to be laws against feeling as wonderful as she did. Not that she was going to go look for them. Aside from the fact that, at the moment, she simply didn't have the physical strength to climb out of bed, she was too satisfied, too happy and content to be bothered by anything beyond her immediate reach. In fact, she decided on a sigh, she'd be perfectly content and happy to spend the rest of her life right where she was. If they ever got hungry, they could just ring a bell and—

Common sense plowed its way through the crack in her illusions, bringing with it the full light and force of reality. Sending down to the kitchen for food for two would be the beginning. Within minutes everyone in Ryland Castle would know that Lord Ryland and his eldest ward were lovers. Within the hour, everyone in the village would know that the sheets had been shredded and thrown out the window for all the world to see. By nightfall, all of Norfolk would be talking about their penchant for making love on the dining room table. Within the week, the tales of sex on the chandelier would reach London and then shoot northward to be the subject of every conversation at every house party from the Cotswolds to the Highlands of Scotland.

One mistake and they'd be branded forever immoral. There would be no recovering their reputations, no advantageous marriages, no money with which to lift the estate out of the morass into which it had been allowed to slide.

God, she hated reality, hated that she was sensible enough to know that she had to surrender to its requirements. If only she'd been sensible enough to have resisted the temptations in the first place. It was easy to give up the unknown, but incredibly difficult to walk away from what you knew was the greatest pleasure you were ever going to have.

The first time she could have blamed on the effects of good wine and the confusion of having her world so suddenly upended. This time, though . . . She'd been sober and feeling not only settled in her new world, but confident in her ability to manage it. Tonight she'd freely and deliberately chosen desire over common sense, passion over convention. It was impossible to regret the intense satisfaction Drayton had given her, but now, looking past it to the high price they might have to pay for it . . . God, one of them had to employ good judgment and find a measure of self-control.

Her stomach twisting into a cold knot and her throat tightening against the rising tide of tears, she shifted her legs and eased her hips away from the warm curve of his body.

His hand slid off her thigh and across her midriff. "And where do you think you're going?" he asked softly as he tucked his hand under her side and drew her back against him.

"To my bed."

"No," he murmured, shifting and drawing her down onto the flat of her back. His arm still cradling her head, he lay on his side and smiled down at her as he brushed a loose curl from her cheek. "It's a long way from dawn and I don't want to sleep alone."

And she did? She sighed and closed her eyes, hoping that it would be easier to hold on to her resolve if she couldn't see the too handsome face of temptation. "This could so easily end in disaster. Either we exercise self-restraint, Drayton, or I'll have to return to London."

"Rather drastic measures, I think," he countered, trailing a fingertip over her lips. "We could take the middle road, you know. You could agree to marry me."

His fingertip glided over her chin and down the length of her throat. Her heartbeat quickened and her determination staggered. "We've been over this before," she pointed out, wishing he would stop, hoping that he wouldn't. "There's no real financial gain in it for either one of us."

"As has been pointed out by everyone with whom I've had any sort of conversation for the last month."

She squeezed her eyes more tightly closed as his fingertip burned a trail over the swell of her breast. "And we don't love each other."

"True," he allowed, drawing a slow circle around her peak. "But that adds a rather nice edge to the sex for both of us, don't you think? A kind of a forbidden quality to it."

"That would be lost if we were married," she offered as her nipples hardened and her core began to pulse.

"Somehow, I don't think that would make the least little difference."

She could hear him smile. And, God, could she feel the wonderful friction of his thumb scrapping so deliberately over her nipple. "Perhaps not in the short run," she pointed out on an embarrassingly ragged breath, "but over time it would."

"Ah," he said quietly, shifting again. "I think you've hit on the central issue, Caroline." His finger lazily trailed a straight path down over her midriff as he added, "Time is our fundamental problem. If we had six months for the passion to run its normal course and fade, we might be able to contemplate the Season with more open minds. At least," he whispered, his finger slipping through her nest of curls, "with minds sated and bored enough to gladly consider other romantic opportunities."

She was going to lose the contest; her body didn't want to win, didn't want to be sensible. Swallowing down a whimper of pleasure, she asked, "Are you suggesting that we be lovers until we go to London next spring?"

"Very discreetly, of course," he said, kissing the hollow at the base of her throat.

"We'd be courting scandal."

"Caroline, darling, we already are."

He shifted again and she knew what he was going to do, knew that she should roll away and keep him from succeeding with the seduction. But she didn't and shuddered with delight as he slowly dragged his tongue over her nipple.

"We should stop," she moaned, obediently shifting her hips beneath the slow slide of his fingers.

"Can you honestly tell me that you don't enjoy the risk?"

No, she couldn't. Not honestly. And knowing that she should lie didn't make any difference. "You've lost your mind."

"I know. And I don't care."

As he kissed his way down across her midriff, across her abdomen, she threaded her fingers through his hair and accepted the fact that she was destined to be thoroughly, irredeemably wanton. At least until the sun came up and he had to face reality, too.

DRAYTON REACHED OUT GROGGILY. FINDING THE BED BE-side him empty brought him wide awake. The sheets were still warm; she'd only been gone for a few moments. A quick glance out the window told him sunrise was a good hour away. He rolled out and headed for the sitting room door, determined to have the last hour no matter what. Why she persisted in creeping away while he slept . . . Was it asking all that much to wake up with her in his arms? Was it such a horrible way for her to begin the day?

The door from her sitting room to her bedroom was closed. Unpleasant possibilities stopped him just before he yanked it open. Dora might be up and preparing Caroline's wardrobe for the day. He was naked. Just striding in . . . No, not exactly a discreet thing to do. He whirled about, stomped back to his room, found his dressing robe, put the damn thing on and went back to her door.

He'd knocked before it occurred to him that he'd need an explanation if Dora opened the panel. Something far less honest than "Please tell Lady Caroline that I'd like for her to come back to bed." Maybe he could say that he'd decided that he wanted new curtains for his room. And of course Dora wouldn't wonder why he felt the necessity to relay that information before dawn and wearing only—

The door opened and he tried not to sag with relief at the sight of Caroline and the empty room behind her, at the realization that he wasn't going to have to be smooth or particularly creative. That she was already dressed for the day registered in his brain just as he asked, "Why did you leave?"

She touched her tongue to her lower lip and drew an obviously fortifying breath before managing a strained smile and saying, "I didn't want to wake you to make a formal announcement of it, but . . ." She moistened her lower lip again and drew another deep breath. "My monthly course has begun. I left because I didn't want to stain your sheets and give the maids something to talk about."

An odd and disconcerting torrent of emotions swept over him. "Well," he drawled, feeling the need to say something, "I suppose that can be considered good news."

"Most definitely."

In some respects, he silently, angrily added. He tamped down the rising wave of irritation and chivalrously asked, "Is there anything I can do for you at the moment?"

"No, but it's most kind of you to—" She glanced back over her shoulder and then turned to him, her eyes wide as she put her hand in the center of his chest, said, "Go!" and pushed him hard enough to rock him back on his heels. He'd barely taken a step back to catch his balance when she closed the door.

Drayton stood there, staring at the wooden panel for a long moment, stunned and feeling more acutely alone than he ever had in his life. And then it passed, evaporated in the heat of anger and . . . and . . .

He clenched his teeth, turned on his heel and stormed back to his room. All right, so it wasn't the least bit rational to be angry and disappointed to learn that Caroline wasn't pregnant. There wasn't anything about his relationship with her that could be considered even marginally explicable, so why should this aspect of it be any damned different?

He was lucky. He had recklessly sown his seed and he wasn't going to have to pay for it. The world was full of men who were, at this very moment, down on their knees begging God and all the saints for his kind of good fortune. If he had half a brain in his head, he'd thank his heavenly benefactors for their mercy and swear to never touch Caroline again.

He cocked a brow and undid the sash on his dressing gown. Or, since it might be considered bad form to promise something you knew was impossible, it might just be best to swear that he'd try to be more responsible the next time he did.

❧ *Thirteen* ❧

THERE HAD TO BE A WATCHMAN POSTED ON THE ROOF, Drayton decided, dismounting and handing the reins off to the waiting groomsman. It was the only explanation for how servants—like the groomsman—were precisely where they needed to be when they needed to be. The only other possibility was that the man had been standing at the base of the front steps since dawn, waiting for his return. Not that it was likely, he knew, taking the stairs two at a time. No one was allowed to stand around and do nothing at Ryland Castle; Caroline's daily task list had achieved domestic renown days ago and had been heading steadily toward the stuff of legends ever since.

As he expected, the front door opened as if by magic. The footman had a new suit? Yes, and so did Winfield, who, quite predictably, stood waiting for him at the foyer table. "Good afternoon, Winfield. How goes the race on the home front?"

"Lord Aubrey sent word, sir. If all goes according to schedule, he and his mother will be arriving slightly before teatime."

Damn, if he'd stayed out in the fields for just another

half hour, he could have missed it. "I assume that you advised Lady Caroline."

"I did, sir."

"To the staff's exhausted regret?"

"She asks nothing of us, sir, that she is not willing to do herself."

And they not only loved her for it, they'd do anything for her. "Where is she now?" he asked, noticing the butler's quick glance at the floor around his feet. Belatedly, and with a wince, he realized that he should have thought to brush off the worst of the grain dust before he came inside. Now someone was going to have to follow behind him and clean up the debris trail before Lady Aubrey got there.

"I believe Lady Caroline has finally retired to her rooms to freshen herself for the imminent arrival of your guests."

Well, as hints went, it wasn't particularly subtle. Drayton smiled and headed for the stairs. "I should probably do the same thing, shouldn't I?"

"Yes, sir," Winfield assured him from behind. "With some degree of haste if at all possible."

Chuckling, stripping off his coat and thinking that the stress of the past fortnight was finally getting to the unflappable Winfield, Drayton took the main stairs just as he had those outside. The newly recarpeted main stairs, he noted yet again. He was amazed every time he went up or down them, awed by how Caroline had managed to have it delivered and installed in the time she had, while doing all the other things she had.

If there was one good thing about Lady Aubrey being just minutes from darkening their doorway, he allowed, opening his shirt buttons as he strode down the hall toward his room, it was that the frenetic activity in his house would come to an end and he'd get to see more of Caroline than the flash of her skirts as she dashed past him. Well, at night anyway. As his luck seemed to go, now that she was done in the house and could relax a bit, he needed to be out in the fields for the harvest.

He pushed open his bedroom doors, stepped across the threshold and shoved them closed behind him. Tossing his dusty coat on the floor at the foot of the bed with one hand, he yanked his shirttail free with the other and headed for his bathing room.

He flung that door open, too. And stopped dead in his tracks as the steam wafted over and around him. His timing wasn't perfect, but it was close enough that he could make something of it.

"Well, hello," he said, stepping in and closing the door as Caroline finished wrapping the bath sheet around her and tucked the end between her breasts. "What an unexpected delight to find you here. Although I distinctly recall you saying that you wouldn't dare use my bath."

She eyed the door behind him, moistened her lower lip with the tip of her sweet pink tongue, and said, "You weren't ever to know."

"Ah, but as chance would have it, I do," he drawled, leaning back against the door. Balanced on one foot, he removed a boot and tossed it aside, asking, "Did I mention the fee?"

"No, you didn't."

He shifted his stance, pulled off the second boot and threw it down beside the other one. "Well, it doesn't matter. I'm sure you won't mind paying it."

She sighed, shoved a damp curl up into the golden

mass piled atop her head, and said, "Aubrey and his mother will be here very shortly, Drayton."

"Yes, I know," he admitted, removing his shirt and tossing it aside. "But I sincerely doubt that he'd be ill-mannered enough to break down the door and bring her in here for introductions."

Her gaze skimming over his chest, her breathing shallow, she softly countered, "It would be ill-mannered of us not to be there to welcome her in the foyer."

"Winfield will explain our tardiness," he offered, slowly but deliberately closing the distance between them until she had to tilt her head back to meet his gaze. God, she got more beautiful with every passing day.

"I really must go."

"There's the matter of the fee, Caroline," he reminded her, reaching out to gently stroke her satin shoulders. "It's not yet been paid."

"Will you accept a promissory note?"

He whispered, "No," as he bent his head and pressed a slow kiss to her throat. God, was there any scent more heady than sandalwood? Any scent more perfect for her?

"Drayton," she chided on a ragged breath as her hands went to his waist. "Why you persist in being so reckless and foolish and—"

He smiled against her skin and continued nibbling his way to her earlobe. "You were saying, dear Caroline?"

"This is beyond stupidity," she murmured, tilting her head to give him free access.

"And well into the stuff of my dreams."

"Your dreams are wicked," she accused, reaching up to twine her arms around his neck.

"Yes, they are. Feel free to expand on them as—" The end of the bath sheet slipped from its mooring and the whole of it slid to the floor at their feet. "Ah, yes," he said, sliding his hands down her bare back. "Just like that."

She looked up at him and then slowly closed her eyes, murmuring, "We shouldn't."

"I know," he agreed, brushing kisses over her lips while quickly undoing his trouser buttons, "but let's anyway."

The knock on the door startled them both. Caroline was already out of his arms and snatching up the bath sheet when the intruder called softly through the panel, "Begging your pardon, your lordship."

Peltham, he silently growled. One of the numerous footmen. As Caroline covered herself again, Drayton hauled his trousers back up on his hips and coolly asked, "Yes?"

"Winfield has asked me to inform you that Lord Aubrey's coach is nearing the village."

"Thank you, Peltham," he said, watching Caroline square her shoulders and lift her chin. "I'll be down shortly."

"I shall so inform Winfield, your grace."

Steam and silence hung between them and in it he was acutely aware of how deeply his body ached, of just how long the fortnight had been and how much he resented all the expectations of their lives. "Car—"

"I really must go."

"All you have to do is walk away," he pointed out. "Or," he added with a smile he hoped looked more seductive than desperate, "admit that you don't want to and enjoy the next few minutes."

"I'll meet you downstairs in the foyer," she said, her gaze on the floor as she quickly glided past him.

He clenched his teeth as the blast of cool air rolled the

steam around him. Damnation, would he ever learn *not* to give the woman a choice? The quiet click of the closing door set him in motion. He stripped off his trousers, threw them aside, and went to draw his bath, promising himself that the next time he found her alone was going to end every differently.

CAROLINE SMOOTHED HER SKIRTS ONE LAST TIME, THEN threaded her fingers and stood staring blankly at the front door. God, she was tired. And the very last thing in the world that she wanted to do at that moment was to smile and play the hostess. Especially for a guest as awful as Haywood said Lady Aubrey was. What was the word he'd used? Formidable? Yes, and demanding, too. The things one did to improve a public reputation . . .

Of course all the paint and carpet and draperies and upholstery and sleepless hours would amount to nothing if her relationship with Drayton ever became public knowledge. What a tangled knot that was. She fully understood the risks in it, knew in an ever so logical way that they were courting disaster and that she'd bear the brunt of it when it happened. And despite that, she melted every time he touched her. Her mind wandered to him constantly and wove from the threads of pure fantasy the most wonderful impossibilities.

She really did need to go back to London, to put some distance between them so the temptation could fade away. The longer she stayed at Ryland Castle, the longer she played mistress and helpmate, the harder it was going to be to watch him court a true wife when the Season began. Not that she loved him, of course. It was more a matter of being comfortable with him, of enjoying his company.

And, if she were to be perfectly and bluntly honest about it, enjoying sex with him. The very idea of another woman sleeping in his bed . . .

Caroline pressed her hands to her clenching stomach and shook her head to dispel the disturbing thought. Yes, she should probably go to London. Barring such an easy escape, she at least needed more than three hours of uninterrupted sleep so that she could think straight. She could design and sew under any circumstances; it was pure instinct and long habit. But controlling her feelings and urges where Drayton was concerned was another matter entirely. The effort was all but impossible when exhaustion made his arms such a welcome haven.

The footfall on the stairs behind her put an abrupt end to her reverie. She looked over her shoulder and watched him descend, realizing that no amount of rest was going to change the fact that Drayton Mackenzie was devilishly handsome. Or lessen the impact of his rakish, confident smile and twinkling eyes. No, distance was the only thing that could possibly save her from herself.

"You look lovely, Caroline," he said as he came to stand beside her.

She swallowed down her heart and managed to get just enough air into her lungs to demurely say, "Thank you."

"And the house is beyond beautiful," he added, absently shooting his cuffs. "I owe you a huge debt."

"No," she countered, chuckling, "you owe London fabric merchants a huge debt."

He grinned as his gaze went to the front door. Or—more accurately—to the sidelights and the sliver of the world visible through them. His smile faded a bit as he cocked a brow. "Good God," he muttered. "Ten pounds says she has *H.M.S. Aubrey* painted on her stern."

A ship? Well, Lady Aubrey certainly wasn't a petite woman in any sense of the term, but to characterize her as a ship? Caroline shook her head, admonished, "Be nice," and drew a breath that wasn't nearly as steadying as she'd hoped.

"She's looking at the house and curling her lip," Drayton observed, his voice low so as not to carry to the footman waiting by the door.

"So did you when you first looked up at the sign over my shop."

"I was going for the effect. Trying to be duke-ish, you know."

"You were obnoxious."

He leaned close to whisper, "I'd be willing to meet you in my room, get down on my knees and offer you my sincerest apologies."

Apologizing? That's what he was calling it today? Her pulse racing, butterflies flitting excitedly around in her stomach, she said, "Here she comes. Please behave yourself."

"I'd rather be apologizing," he countered as the footman opened the door. "I'm sure you'd be pleased by my efforts."

The mere prospect delighted her body. Her core hot and pulsing, she locked her knees, hoped Lady Aubrey thought the flush in her cheeks was from the excitement of receiving a guest, smiled, and said cheerily, "Welcome back, Lord Aubrey," as the man escorted his mother across the threshold and into the foyer.

Aubrey visibly winced, but didn't look at her. His mother did, though. To arch a carefully drawn brow and then pointedly look away. "Mother," Aubrey said, bringing her to a halt in front of Drayton, "I have the pleasure of introducing my friend Drayton Mackenzie, the seventh Duke of Ryland."

"Your grace," the woman said, bowing her head and dropping into a deep curtsy that really was amazingly graceful for a woman of her size and advanced age.

Drayton stuck out his hand and helped her rise, saying gallantly, "Welcome to Ryland Castle, Lady Aubrey. It is a pleasure to finally meet you." As soon as the woman was fully upright he released her hand to take Caroline by the elbow. "May I present the eldest of my wards, Lady Caroline Turnbridge."

God, she didn't know what to do. As weak as her knees were, if she attempted even a small curtsy, she'd topple over and embarrass herself completely. And it didn't help matters any that the woman was appraising her as though she were a . . . a . . . well, a prize ship ripe for seizing. "Welcome, Lady Aubrey," she said, managing a tiny polite smile. "We deeply appreciate your willingness to undertake our social education." *Heaven knows I need it.*

"Then allow me to point out, Lady Caroline," she said crisply, "that it is inappropriate to greet a male guest as informally as you did my son upon his entry."

Oh, God. If this is how it's going to be . . . Be gracious. Don't embarrass Drayton. She locked her knees again and lifted her chin. "Thank you. I obviously have much to learn. Would it be appropriate to offer you some refreshments now? Or should I offer to show you to your room so you might freshen yourself first?"

"The latter, Lady Caroline."

"If you'd come this way, please," Caroline said, turning and gesturing broadly toward the stairs. Apparently something—God only knew what—in that wasn't up to snuff because Lady Aubrey sighed quietly, smiled thinly, and nodded for her to precede her.

They had reached the second floor and were turning to the left when Aubrey's mother said, "You have so very much to learn. I only hope that a week is long enough."

Caroline tamped down the jolt of excitement and worked to sound disappointed when she asked, "A week? Will you be leaving us so soon?"

"A few of my friends will be joining us then," the older woman explained. "It is my hope that you will present well to them at that time. Your entrée into society this coming Season could be eased considerably by their positive recommendations."

"Oh," she said as a torrent of resentment and frustration flooded over her. "How many guests should I prepare for?"

"For how many guests should I prepare," Lady Aubrey corrected. "And ladies do not engage in the preparations. They instruct their housekeeper to see to the necessary arrangements. Twenty, I should think."

Caroline stopped dead, her heart hammering against her ribs and her stomach heaving. "Twenty people?"

"I believe," Lady Aubrey said coolly as she, too, came to a halt, "that is what I said."

"Does that count include their servants?"

"Of course not."

Oh, Lord, she was going to faint. Or worse, cry. She swallowed and dragged in two deep breaths before she had the wherewithal to ask, "How long will they be staying?"

Lady Aubrey gave her another of her strained smiles. "One does not ask such questions, Lady Caroline. It is considered rude to imply that guests are ever expected to leave."

They could be here forever. Twenty people. And if each brought just one servant . . . Add in a coachman and a footman and figuring that some of them might deign to make the trek two to a carriage . . . Sixty. Sixty people to be housed and fed. But it could just as easily be seventy. Or even eighty. Her chest tightening with burgeoning panic, she moistened her parched lips and asked, "If you don't know when people are coming or going, how do you plan ahead for meals?"

"The staff is ordered to prepare for half again the number in residence and make adjustments as your guests' plans evolve from day to day."

"I see." Not that it was a pleasant vision by any means. The amount of food it would take to feed that many people for just a couple of days was staggering. Was there enough in Ryland Castle's storehouse to feed them even that long? When it ran out, where would they get more?

"*What* is *that*?"

Caroline cringed and then turned to follow the woman's horrified gaze, half expecting to see a giant rat dancing a jig on the hall console. "*Who*, Lady Aubrey," she corrected as her blood heated and her panic evaporated. "My sister Lady Simone."

As Simone continued to happily fence with an imaginary opponent on her way toward the schoolroom, Lady Aubrey stammered, "Is she . . . she . . ."

"Wearing trousers?" Caroline finished for her. "Yes. She's never worn dresses and is having a bit of difficulty in making the transition to more feminine attire. This way to your room, please."

"You allow her a choice?"

"Simone can be quite dangerous if provoked," Caroline explained, leading the way down the hall and—not at all nicely—enjoying the woman's distress. "It's wise—not to mention much safer—to offer suggestions and bribes from a good distance and hope she's in an accommodating mood."

"Under no circumstances," Lady Aubrey pronounced regally, "should she be allowed out of the schoolroom while you are entertaining guests."

"I'll see that Mrs. Miller is instructed to tie her up."

"Is instructed to see that she is bound," Lady Aubrey corrected, apparently unaware of Caroline's sarcasm. "To end a sentence with a preposition is a glaring indication of a lack of proper education."

Just get through this and get away. "I'll bear that in mind and make every effort to sound as educated as possible. I wouldn't want any of Drayton's guests to—"

"It is either 'Lord Ryland' or 'his grace' or 'his lordship.' Never his Christian name."

"Of course."

"While we are on the subject of proper grammar, Lady Caroline, I must point out that a lady does not use contractions in her speech. To do so is considered a sign of a lazy intellect."

"Thank you for reminding me," she said tightly as they reached the former violet room. "I shall bear that in mind also." She opened the door and pushed it wide as she stepped aside, saying, "This will be your room, Lady Aubrey. I hope you find it comfortable. If you require anything, please let me know when you come down for tea."

"I will," Lady Aubrey said as she swept across the threshold.

I'm sure of it. Caroline didn't pull the door closed, didn't offer a parting comment. She didn't trust herself to do anything but walk away. As quickly as she could without breaking into a dead run. A week of Mother Aubrey's constant criticism, followed by a possible eternity with twenty of her nearest and dearest friends . . . How very quickly and unexpectedly Paradise had become Hell.

DRAYTON LEANED TO THE SIDE TO BETTER SEE THE FOYER through the parlor door. "Aubrey, who are those other people?"

Aubrey didn't even bother to glance over his shoulder. "If there's four of them, it's the dancing master, the language instructor, and the dressmaker and her assistant."

"A dressmaker?" Haywood said, pouring himself a generous glass of whiskey. "We have two of those in residence already. The redheaded one is scrumptious. But you'll just have to take my word for it because, at the moment, she's in London selecting wallpaper and more fabric."

Aubrey rolled his eyes and countered, "Having a wardrobe designed by a well-known couturier is essential for social success. I'm sure Lady Caroline understands that and will be most grateful that Mother thought to bring hers along. And speaking of Mother," he added, setting his glass aside, "I should be getting up to my room and dressing for tea."

Drayton watched him leave the parlor, thinking that Simone was right; the man was a prig. No, now that he thought about it, *he* was the prig. Haywood was the fop. Aubrey was the ass. God love the girl, she could so accurately gauge people. Although her opinion of Haywood might be different now, especially since he'd taken over the fencing lessons the past two days. Not that her opinion was likely all that much higher, he suspected, grinning; not if the cut in his friend's coat sleeve was any indication of how well he was doing against her.

Haywood polished off his drink and looked as if he were thinking about throwing himself from the roof. "Maybe I should dress for tea, too?"

Drayton shrugged. "Only if you want. I wouldn't be if I hadn't come in from the fields just a while ago." Hell, he wouldn't be dressed at all if the beautiful woman sailing through the parlor doors had shown him any mercy in his bathing room.

"Hello, Haywood," she said, giving him a quick glance on her way to the buffet. "I see that you've been fencing with Simone again."

"She's getting terribly good, you know."

"It's more a case of you being terribly bad at it," Drayton pointed out as Caroline came to his side and picked up one of the crystal decanters.

"Is this sherry?"

He cocked a brow and quietly answered, "You know what happened the last time you drank spirits."

She tilted her head to look up at him. The slow arch of her brow was a warning. "Would you prefer that I kill Aubrey's mother before I pour out the first cup of tea?"

"Allow me," he offered, setting aside his drink and taking the decanter from her. "Just as a point of information and warning, Lady Aubrey brought a dancing fool with her. And a language instructor."

"She also brought her couturier along," Haywood contributed. "And the couturier's assistant."

"Oh, really," Caroline drawled, her brow arching even higher, blue fire dancing in the depths of her eyes.

Handing her the sherry, Drayton said, "Please don't let her turn you into an onion."

Haywood scrunched up his face. "Onion?"

"That's the least of your concerns," she countered, ignoring his friend's confusion. "She's invited twenty of her friends to come visit for however long they want."

"Twenty?"

Seeming highly satisfied by his stunned reaction, she added, "They'll be here in a week."

"Well, the day just gets better and better."

"And the list of things to do gets longer and longer. I don't know how we're going to have rooms for that many guests ready in seven days."

"Maybe," Haywood offered, "you should have Lady Aubrey uninvite them, saying that Ryland Castle isn't yet prepared for guests."

Caroline shook her head and sighed. "I suspect that she'd consider that an act of social suicide."

She looked so tired, so overwhelmed, that it took everything he had not to wrap her in his arms and hold her close. "Better that," Drayton posed gently, "than killing yourself trying to paper and paint every bedroom in this house in the next seven days."

"Don't forget the draperies, carpets, and bedding. They have to be replaced, as well."

"It's impossible, Caroline. Don't even try. It's not worth it."

She stared down into her sherry glass for a long moment. "If we press into service every pair of available and able hands on the estate—"

"No, Caroline."

"Haywood," she said, looking up at him, her pale brows knitted in thought.

"I can't sew," he pleaded, looking as though he might drop to his knees at any moment and actually grovel. "I would pose a great danger to myself and others if I tried. I'm sorry."

She smiled. "Yes, I know. But you can go to London, find Jane, and get her back here as quickly as possible."

Haywood, ever the bounder, did nothing short of sparkle at the assignment. "If it means saving Drayton's social reputation, no journey is too arduous, no task too odious."

"I knew we could count on you," Caroline said, laughing quietly. "You're such a good friend."

"That's toady," he pointed out happily. "I'm a good toady. I'll leave right after tea. Toadies can't travel on an empty stomach, you know."

"Of course not," she agreed. She raised the glass of sherry to her lips, tipped it back and drained the full contents in three quick swallows.

Drayton was still blinking in disbelief when she handed the empty glass to him, smiled her thanks, and headed for the door. "Where are you going?" he called after her.

"To tell Mrs. Gladder that we need to prepare for a siege. I'll be back shortly."

✑ *Fourteen* ✑

HE LEANED BACK AGAINST THE BUFFET, WATCHING HER leave and knowing from experience that there was no such thing for Caroline as a short conversation with the housekeeper. One thing always led to another, one decision creating a ripple in the pond that required more decisions to smooth. What his life would have been like without her in the past weeks . . .

Being a duke was nice, he had to admit, watching Winfield roll the tea cart into the parlor. Servants weren't quite the bane he'd considered them at the start. A large house to call his own wasn't the burden he'd imagined it would be. Neither was the responsibility for managing an estate and the seeing to the livelihoods of everyone on it. And the wards he hadn't wanted . . . Fiona could melt his heart with just a smile. Simone made him ridiculously proud. And Caroline . . . Caroline made him happy.

It was odd how he'd never before in his life noticed how a house smelled apart from the scents of a meal waiting on the table. But since coming to Ryland Castle that had changed. Every time he walked through the front door, he breathed deeply and tried to guess from the air what wonders Caroline had accomplished in the hours he'd been gone. One day it would be the sharp scent of lemons and mellow beeswax. Another day it would be the tang of polished metal. Always it was the crispness of clean air and bright light and the sense that his world had never been as close to perfect as she made it.

He had to be honest, though, and admit that there were times when he resented her devotion to the house. But, he kept reminding himself, there would come a day when it would all be done and their time together could be more patterned and less hurried. They could retire early and lie in bed late, leisurely pleasuring each other all the hours between. He could—

"Will there be anything else, your lordship?"

He could stop staring moonily into the distance and making a cake of himself. "Not that I can think of, Winfield. Thank you." The butler bowed briefly and departed, leaving him with a grinning Haywood. "And what are you so happy about?" he asked, not quite sure he wanted to know.

"The thought of going to London. I think Jane may be the one."

Drayton took a drink of his whiskey. It wasn't difficult to imagine his friend and Jane pledging themselves only to each other for the rest of their lives. Neither was it difficult to see both of them promptly ignoring the fact that they had.

"What do you think, Dray?"

That being honest would ruin a perfectly good friendship. He took another sip of whiskey, wondering how he was going to get out of the awkward tangle. Deliverance came in the form of Aubrey and his mother sweeping across the foyer and bearing down on him.

Drayton flashed Haywood an apologetic smile, set aside his glass, and stood straight. "Lady Aubrey," he said in greeting, noting the woman's quick and decidedly critical glance around the parlor.

"Your grace," she replied with a regal dip of her chin. She looked over at Haywood and arched a brow at what struck Drayton as a bit of a disdainful angle. "Mr. Haywood, isn't it?"

Oh, yes, definitely disdainful. Not that it seemed to bother Haywood in the least.

Smiling, he bowed with a flourish and drawled, "I'm honored and humbled that you remember my name, Lady Aubrey. It's been an entire month."

Aubrey turned a bit pale as his mother's mouth puckered and her eyes bored a hole through Haywood's chest. Drayton stepped into the breach and gestured toward the newly upholstered chair beside the tea cart and said with all the gentility he could muster, "Please, Lady Aubrey, have a seat and make yourself comfortable."

"Where is Lady Caroline?" she asked as her son held her elbow and guided her into the chair.

Rather like a pilot boat putting a man-of-war into a berth. Drayton reined in his smile and answered, "She's gone off to speak briefly with Mrs. Gladder, the housekeeper, about preparing Ryland Castle for our additional guests."

"Yes, I can see that much needs to be done," she said, eyeing the new curtains. "Blue is not the current color of fashionable homes."

She was suggesting that they be torn down and replaced? After all of Caroline's work? The staff's work? Over his dead and rotting body. "I like blue. Very much."

"Magenta is the current rage."

"Magenta?" he repeated, wondering if they were still

talking about the drapes. Magenta sounded like something one drank when visiting a Spanish diplomat.

"It is a dark and rich shade of rosy pink."

"Pink draperies?" He cleared his throat and shook his head. "No. Not in my house. Not in any room where I might see it, anyway. If Lady Caroline wants to follow fashion in a guest room, I certainly won't protest, but I must draw the line there."

"One simply endures the annual fashion decrees with grace, your lordship," she countered, her tone patronizingly patient, "and hopes that the next one is more to their liking."

If she thought she was going to walk into his house and dictate . . . "Blue is to my liking and blue the draperies will remain."

She hesitated for a moment, seemed to check a comment, and then dipped her chin again in her high-toned manner and said, "It is your home, your grace."

Thank you for finally remembering that. With Haywood smirking in a most satisfied way and Aubrey looking as though he might pass out, Drayton decided that it would be best if they moved the social occasion toward its end as quickly as possible. "It appears that Lady Caroline is going to be gone longer than she expected. Would you do us the honor of pouring, Lady Aubrey?"

With another imperial nod, she undertook the duties of hostess, saying, "I assume that you will soon be engaged in finding a new housekeeper."

Drayton frowned. "Why would you think that?"

"If Mrs. Gladder failed to answer the bellpull and Lady Caroline was forced to go off in search of her, then—"

"I don't believe in using bellpulls."

Drayton looked up from the tea cart and watched Caroline advance into the room. Her shoulders squared, her chin high, her stride long and certain . . . And her eyes . . . Oh, God, they were the color of tempered steel.

"Why ever not?" Lady Aubrey asked, clearly oblivious to the fact that she was blithely sailing into a contest of wills.

"Mrs. Gladder and her staff are sufficiently busy with their work," Caroline explained, settling herself on the settee on the opposite side of the tea cart. "That requiring them to leave it to scamper to my side is not only a ridiculous waste of their time, but disrespectful of the contributions they make to the comfort of Ryland Castle and those of us in it. There's—" She smiled thinly. "There *is* nothing wrong with me and I am perfectly capable of walking across the house to deliver instructions or make a request of them."

"Ladies do not go to servants. Servants attend them."

As Caroline's brow slowly rose, Drayton attempted to salvage the situation, saying, "We do things a bit differently at Ryland Castle," as he accepted a cup of tea and a paper-thin sandwich from Lady Aubrey.

"Yes, as I can see and as William has already informed me. Which is why my experience and advice in these matters is so very obviously and desperately needed."

He nodded, pretended that he didn't see Caroline getting ready to speak, and said, "And we deeply appreciate your willingness to share your knowledge with us."

"Unfortunately," Caroline countered coolly, shooting him a warning look, "we find ourselves in a bit of a dilemma, Lady Aubrey. Ryland Castle is suffering from years of neglect and requires a considerable amount of rehabilitation. And while we have made remarkable progress to that end in the last fortnight, we have a horrific amount of work yet to do if we are to be prepared to host twenty guests in one week."

"My dear Lady Caroline," the woman said on a tiny, dry laugh as she handed her son a cup and saucer. "You really must begin to think like the daughter of a duke. This is a simple matter of hiring additional, temporary servants to see the house readied."

Caroline drew a breath, quickly moistened her lower lip, and replied, "There are no extra servants to be had, Lady Aubrey. It is harvest time. Every hand in the village is already hard at work."

"Then—"

"Every hand in all of southern England is already at work," she went on. "Sending to London for servants is not practical. They could not arrive much before our guests do."

Drayton held his breath and wished that Haywood would stop smirking and that if Aubrey was going to do a facer into the carpet, he'd do it now and provide a distraction.

"Obstinance," Lady Aubrey intoned, handing Caroline a teacup, "is not an acceptable trait in a young woman."

"Neither is refusing to accept the requirements of reality simply because they necessitate that she do something more strenuous than wave her hand in command."

Aubrey's mouth fell open. Haywood used his hand to hide his grin. Lady Aubrey stared at Caroline in mute shock. Drayton waited, knowing that Caroline wasn't done with her just yet. She didn't disappoint him.

"I truly regret that the circumstances are as they are, Lady Aubrey," she said with gentle firmness—and, to

Drayton's thinking, showing remarkable restraint in not
pointing out that the stressful circumstances were entirely
of Lady Aubrey's making. "I would much prefer to have
the time to sit at your knee and absorb all the invaluable
wisdom you are understandably eager to share. But for
the next week, it simply will not be possible. I have far
too much to do."

Judging by the amount of blinking and jaw-clenching
that Lady Aubrey was doing, he guessed that she'd never
in her life been set back on her heels quite as effectively.
And he couldn't help but wonder when she'd last been
rendered speechless for so long a stretch. If pressed, he'd
have to wager that it had been an eon or two.

"If I might make a suggestion?"

Haywood was wading into this? Even as Drayton swallowed down a groan, Caroline turned on the settee and
brightly said, "Of course, Haywood."

"Perhaps, while you're otherwise engaged, Lady Aubrey
could focus her social-improvement efforts on Lady
Simone and Lady Fiona."

Oh, God. No. It would be a disaster of epic propor-
tions.

Lady Aubrey huffed. "If the one glimpse I had of Lady
Simone was any indication of their general conduct, I
doubt a week will be sufficient time in which to correct
even the most glaring of the deficiencies."

"Or perhaps not," Haywood muttered.

She'd walked away from an encounter with Simone
unbloodied? The Church would probably want to hear
about that; they were always looking for miracles.

"If you could see that my sisters have the start of
proper wardrobes," he heard Caroline say, "I would be

eternally grateful. I'm afraid that we haven't—" She stopped and smiled thinly again. "I *am* afraid that we *have not* had the time to make either of them more than a single, marginally serviceable gown."

As Lady Aubrey no doubt reeled from the shock of her status being reduced to that of a wardrober, Drayton decided that Caroline had borne enough of the burden for setting the limits.

"Which reminds me," he said, easing into taking his turn. "I've been meaning to say something and haven't had a chance to talk with you. Tell me about Fiona's shoes."

Lady Aubrey looked back and forth between them, but he couldn't tell from her expression whether she was curious or insulted by a conversation that didn't center around her.

"Fiona has a noticeable limp," Caroline explained to her. "Until such time as we can have her examined by a physician, we have compensated for the different lengths of her legs by making her one slipper with a thicker sole than the other."

Having fulfilled the basic requirements of civility, she smiled up at him and went on, saying, "It was a rather slapdash thing, of course, given our time constraints that first day. Simone cobbled it together using several layers cut from old book covers and huge amounts of thread. Since then, she's been working on refining the design so that her sister's more comfortable and less likely to tumble off the platform."

"How ingenious of her," Drayton marvelled. "And kind."

"I thought so. And Fiona was absolutely delighted by even the first design, as crude as it was."

"You know about the crow, don't you?"

"Oh, yes. Tarban." She met Lady Aubrey's gaze again to say, "Fiona collects animals. She has turned the schoolroom into something of an infirmary for them."

Just as he expected, Lady Aubrey pressed her hand to her considerable bosom, shuddered dramatically, and emitted a disgusted, "Ugh."

"She's a very gentle, very loving and tender soul," Drayton said slowly, deliberately. "Great care should be taken not to bruise her."

Caroline glanced up at him, smiled serenely and took a sip of tea.

Again Lady Aubrey reacted just as he thought she would. "One should not dote upon children. It undermines the development of their character."

"Great care *will* be taken not to bruise her."

"As you wish, your grace."

Oh, Caroline thought, reaching for a butter sandwich, *that was masterfully done, Drayton. Masterfully done. Of course, now she loathes you just as much as she does me. Not that we care. And not that it will make the least bit of difference in how long she stays.*

"Pardon the intrusion, your lordship. Mr. Fanes has arrived."

She looked up at the doorway, at the butler standing in it, and wished she'd had the foresight to arrange for an escape. Drayton wasn't merely masterful, he was brilliantly resourceful. Especially so if Mr. Fanes was a wholly fictional visitor.

"Please see him to my study, Winfield. I'll be there in just a moment." As Winfield departed, Drayton placed his teacup on the cart, saying, "Ladies, please excuse me. I must attend to important estate business."

They both nodded as they should.

"And I have to be heading off for London," Haywood announced, returning his teacup to the tray as well. Gathering up all the biscuits and tea sandwiches he could, he smiled, said, "Lovely to see you again, Lady Aubrey," and then took off in Drayton's wake.

Caroline glanced between Aubrey and his mother, smiled, and silently thanked Mrs. Gladder for the advice. Yes, until Drayton married, it was *her* house, and guests remained in it at her pleasure and not theirs. And now that the basic rules had been made clear to Lady Aubrey, they could begin again.

"How was your journey here?" Caroline politely inquired. "Did you have pleasant traveling weather?"

DRAYTON LEFT THE DOORS FOR WINFIELD TO CLOSE AND advanced toward the man waiting in front of his desk. "Sorry to keep you waiting, Mr. Fanes. Please have a seat."

"I would prefer to stand, if you don't mind, your grace. This won't take long at all."

Drayton shrugged, propped himself on the corner of his desk, crossed his arms over his chest, and cocked a brow in permission for the other to begin.

"As you requested," he said, drawing a parchment sheet out of the leather case he'd placed on the chair, "I have drafted the document concerning Lady Caroline Turnbridge's dowry." He handed it over, adding, "All it requires is your signature."

Drayton took it, glanced over it, and then laid it aside saying, "Thank you."

"The final report on the liquidation of her business in London arrived on this afternoon's post," Fanes went on, taking a slim leather-bound file from his case and passing it over. As Drayton flipped through the pages, the solicitor added, "I have taken the liberty of perusing it and can see no problems or unresolved issues. The statements from the bank regarding her account are included as an addendum to the report itself. As you expected, the sum is not significant at this point, but will grow over time if left to accrue interest. The bank has projected the totals forward in yearly increments."

"Thank you." He laid it aside, asking, "And do we have a docket date?"

"Yes, your grace. The first trial begins two weeks from today. The second three days after that." He produced more papers from his bag and handed them over, explaining, "Your summonses were delivered to my offices yesterday."

"So the Crown has decided to try them separately?"

"Yes. The prosecutor will be the same for both actions."

Three days apart, huh? It certainly gave a new meaning to the concepts of swift and certain justice. "He obviously expects them to proceed quickly."

"Actually, your grace, given the overwhelming volume and strength of the evidence against them, he expects the men to plead guilty and throw themselves on the mercy of the bench the eve before a jury is selected. Not that mercy is likely. He believes the judge will impose the fullest penalty the law allows."

"Which would be?"

"Life imprisonment, your lordship. With their assets and accounts seized by the court to be counted toward full restitution."

Eighteen years of bold thievery amounted to a great

deal of restitution. "Do you know anything of their family situations?" Drayton asked. "What would become of their wives and children if they're incarcerated?"

"I can make discreet inquiries, if you would like, your grace."

"Please do," he instructed, nodding slowly as he considered and weighed all the facets of the situation. "And prepare documents deeding their homes and personal possessions back to them."

Fanes drew his shoulders back and softly cleared his throat before saying, "As your solicitor, I am bound to point out the consequences of such a magnanimous gesture. While it's true that their London bank accounts contain the lion's share of the ill-gotten proceeds, forfeiting the houses and personal possessions will have a considerable impact on the court's effort to make you whole. A negative impact, sir."

Drayton shrugged. "I won't be known for putting women and children out on the street. I don't care what it costs to act with good conscience."

The man apparently needed a few moments to consider the notion, but eventually he quietly sighed. "It is your decision, your grace."

"Yes, it is, and I've made it. Please draft the documents. I trust that you'll advise me if my testimony isn't required by the court?"

"I will, sir."

"Then it seems that we're concluded for the day," Drayton observed, coming off his desk. "Thank you, Mr. Fanes."

"My pleasure, Lord Ryland," he said with a crisp bow.

Drayton watched in silence as the man picked up his leather satchel and headed for the study doors—which, of course, opened like magic as he drew near them. Leaving Winfield and the footman to see the solicitor on his way, Drayton looked down at the papers the man had delivered.

The summonses were of no concern; either Thompson and Rudman pleaded guilty and made his testimony in court unnecessary, or they didn't. Justice would be served one way or the other. The papers for Caroline, though . . . He picked up the report on the liquidation of her business and turned to the summary pages. The sum total of her mother's life and the first twenty-three years of Caroline's were paltry, less than half of what his annual commission had been as an artillery officer. Even if left untouched and allowed to grow for twenty years, it wouldn't amount to a third of what had been spent just on the new draperies for Ryland Castle. She could never live on it. Not well, not as she deserved.

He picked up the dowry settlement and read it through, noting the sum and the terms under which she could have access to them. The former was substantial, the latter simple and short; if she didn't find a husband in two years, she could have her dowry and do with it as she pleased. If she wanted to open another dress shop, she could afford to make it the biggest and best in all of England. She could go her own way for the rest of her life and never want for a thing.

Drayton considered the line on which he was to sign, binding himself to the agreement they'd made that first morning as they'd done verbal battle across the counter of her shop. Not once since then had she mentioned the conditions she'd set for their truce—even while more than living up to her pledges. He was honor bound to sign the thing, to keep his word just as she had hers.

But he didn't want to. Deep in the pit of his stomach,

misgivings and sadness and worry churned and coiled into a cold knot. It was the strangest, most inexplicable mixture of emotions. Especially considering that he knew full well that Caroline's life was hers, the decisions affecting the course of it entirely hers to make. She deserved the freedom to make choices that would make her happy and the dowry settlement gave her that. He should be relieved to know that she wouldn't be forced into a loveless or—even worse—an abusive marriage to avoid poverty.

So why, he wondered, staring blankly at the document in his hand, did he want so badly to toss it into the fire and deny that he'd ever agreed to have it drafted?

With no signs of an answer stumbling from the recesses of his mind, Drayton shook his head, muttered, "When in doubt, don't," and deliberately laid it aside.

REVELING IN THE SOLITUDE, CAROLINE ATE THE LAST two biscuits on the tray, washed them down with tepid tea and then set her cup and saucer on the cart. Fighting off a huge yawn and sternly telling herself that she didn't have the luxury of time for a nap, she rose to her feet and turned to face the parlor doors. Mrs. Gladder had said fifteen rooms would be sufficient for twenty guests. Fifteen divided by seven was . . . was . . . God, her brain was so overwhelmed, so tired that she couldn't even do simple arithmetic.

She closed her eyes, trying to see the problem on an imaginary slate. Two, with some left over. Two rooms a day on average. Possible. If they worked and slept in carefully orchestrated shifts, if there weren't any surprises or problems. But all it would take was one thing going wrong and the chances—

"Is teatime over already?"

Drayton. She opened her eyes to find him standing halfway between the door and the tea cart. "Yes," she said, giving him all of a smile she could muster as she moved toward him. "Would that it never have happened at all."

"But it had to, sooner or later," he replied, his smile soft, beckoning. "And you established yourself as the mistress of Ryland Castle without direct insult or bloodshed. I'm very impressed."

"You didn't do at all badly yourself," she pointed out as she stopped in front of him.

"I rather enjoyed it." His smile slowly faded as his gaze searched hers. "I suppose," he said quietly, almost sadly, "you're off to strip wallpaper and tear down more curtains."

She nodded. "And roll up rugs, dress down beds, and organize the painters and paper hangers."

"Do you ever think of me as you race hither and yon?"

"Never."

One dark brow cocked upward. "Really," he drawled.

She knew what he was going to do and, in defense of her good judgment, it did suggest that she step beyond his reach and then bolt for the rear of the house. But she chose not to listen to it, chose not to run from the momentary comfort and pleasure he was offering. As his arms slipped around her waist, she stepped into him, twined hers around his neck and tilted her face up for his kiss.

His possession was no less thorough, no less melting for its gentleness. A spark ignited in her core and instantly grew to a hunger that burned in every fiber of her body, that moaned in frustration as he lifted his mouth slowly from hers and whispered, "Do you think of me?"

"Constantly," she whimpered as he kissed her eyelids. "Most inappropriately."

"Where are Aubrey and his mother?" he asked, laying a burning trail of kisses to her ear.

"Walking the gardens."

"Where's Dora?"

"Guest wing," she supplied breathlessly, her body aching.

"I promised myself," he said, easing back and deliberately taking her arms from his neck, "that I wasn't going to give you a choice the next time I found you alone."

"But you are?" she asked as her mind cried, *I choose you.*

He nodded. "Your bed or mine."

Her heart soared. "Right now?"

His grin was instant and went from ear to ear as a wicked light danced in his eyes. "I hadn't thought of that, but I'm willing if you are. Would you prefer the floor, the settee, or on the tea cart?"

"Not here!" *On the floor or the settee. The tea cart rolls.* "I meant going upstairs now."

"I like the idea of right here."

Oh, God, so did she. Tremendously. "They'll come back at any moment," she said, her heart racing and core pulsing. "Our gardens aren't very big."

"Then it's your bed or mine. Decide."

"Yours."

"Just for the sake of appearances," he said, grinning as he released her and stepped back, "I'll give you a minute's head start."

She nodded and turned. And had taken all of three steps toward the promise of satisfaction when she heard familiar voices in the foyer. She stopped dead in her tracks, her heart twisting and her spirit withering.

"Son of a—"

"Bitch," she quietly finished for him as tears welled along her lashes. Through the shimmer she saw the two dark shapes step into the frame of the parlor doorway. Not daring to look back at Drayton, she dragged a ragged breath into her lungs and willed the tears to dry.

"Lady Caroline," Mother Aubrey said, "a woman's reputation is her most valuable possession. As the sponsor of your formal presentation and the coming Season, I must insist that you never let yourself be found alone in the company of a man. Not that I am in any respect implying that your behavior is untoward, your grace."

"Of course," he said tightly. With, no doubt, a formal, perfunctory little bow.

"Lady Caroline, perhaps now would be a good time to introduce me to your sisters."

Caroline nodded, forcing a smile on her face and her feet to move. It didn't do any good to resent Lady Aubrey, she reminded herself as she led the way to the schoolroom. Neither did it accomplish anything to resent the expectations and requirements of her new life. No, the only useful purpose for her anger was to use it to shore up her resolve to find a way around it all.

❧ *Fifteen* ❧

CAROLINE SCRUBBED HER HANDS OVER HER FACE AND
then blinked at the yardage computations again, hoping
that they'd make sense this time. They didn't, not any
more than they had any other time she'd stared at them in
the last five minutes. She expelled a long, slow breath,
trying to collect her mind and make it focus on the task at
hand. It refused, again.

God, if only the imaginings weren't so good. Her
pulse had been skittering for the last two hours. Her entire
body ached from the strain of it, and deep in the center of
her chest there was a bubble of something that felt almost
like panic. Common sense had insisted that it would go
away if she forced her attention outside herself. It had
also promised that her fantasies would fade away, her
heart would slow, and she'd get a great deal of work done.
So far, common sense had been ladling out of a crock.

The rattle of keys announced Mrs. Gladder's return to
the sewing room and the arrival of a much appreciated
distraction. "And?" Caroline asked as the housekeeper
came to her side.

"The last of the wallpaper is down and being hauled
out for burning. The walls are being painted in three rooms

and repapered in three more. The rest are in varying stages of being cleaned and aired and readied for either paper or paint."

Fabulous news. All of it. Which really bordered on being too good to be true. "Was there any plaster damage in removing the paper?"

"Only a slight bit that will be fully repaired before the hour is out and sufficiently dry to paper over in the morning."

"Then we're ahead of schedule."

Mrs. Gladder smiled and very sweetly said, "Yes, we are."

"Just as you predicted," Caroline allowed, chuckling and relieved that it was all going well enough that she could admit that her fears had been unfounded. Why she wasn't thrilled and delighted by the situation, though . . .

"You should be dressing for dinner soon, madam."

Dinner with Drayton. Unfortunately also with Aubrey, and his mother. "I really don't have the time for such things." She looked back down at the drapery sketch and the measurements. "For the life of me, I can't calculate the yardage on these jabots."

"We'll manage it without you."

No doubt better and more quickly; her total contribution this evening had been to simply take up space in the workroom. "It's a terrible thing to be dispensable, you know."

"You are hardly unneeded, madam," the housekeeper assured her. "But I truly believe that you would be better served to play the hostess for an hour or two."

"Which would be your polite and indirect way of saying that one must defend the rules once they've been established?"

Mrs. Gladder smiled. "One should never surrender the field either too soon or too confidently."

"Point taken," Caroline said, nodding. Gathering her skirts in her hands, she headed for the door. "I'll be back as soon as I reasonably can."

"There is no need to hurry, madam."

Well, yes there was, but it didn't have anything to do with paint, wallpaper or draperies. If she hurried, she might find Drayton in his room dressing for dinner and willing to be sidetracked for a few minutes. If she had to go through the next few hours trying to suppress the bubble in her chest at the same time she had to make polite conversation with Lady Aubrey . . .

"Just in case," she said, pausing on the threshold and looking back over her shoulder. "Could you come to the parlor around ten with a question of some sort?"

The housekeeper smiled knowingly. "One that requires you to leave it to make a considered appraisal of the situation."

"Thank you, Mrs. Gladder. You're a godsend."

As the woman chuckled, Caroline resumed her course. She managed a sedate pace all the way to the front of the house and even up the staircase, but once her foot touched the upstairs carpet, anticipation broke through the dam of reserve. Her skirts fisted in her hands, she dashed down the hall to her room. Two seconds after closing the door behind herself she was standing in the doorway of Drayton's.

His clothes—the ones he wore when out riding—lay in a neat heap at the foot of his bed, a soggy bathing sheet atop them. The woodsy scent of his shaving cologne lingered in the air to taunt her. Fighting back a wave of frustrated tears, she turned on her heel and went back to her own room to get ready for what she knew was going to be the most miserable evening she'd ever had to endure.

THE FLASH OF BLUE AT THE EDGE OF HIS VISION BROUGHT Drayton's attention up from the glass of whiskey in his hand. Caroline. Coming down the stairs. God, he had the fondest memories of that blue satin evening gown. He glanced over at the mantel clock and then back to Caroline, wondering just how adventurous she was feeling. Not very, he guessed, noting the tilt of her chin and the thin line of her mouth as she crossed the foyer and headed toward him. Then again, with the proper plying, cajoling, temptation . . .

He met her at the threshold, handing her his whiskey and saying, "You look like you could use a good bracing."

She glanced at the amber spirits for a second and then up at him. Something—anger? frustration?—sparked in her dark eyes as she arched a brow. Her lips parted. And then she drew a deep breath and deliberately looked away to ask, "Where are the others?"

"Still dressing for dinner," he supplied, trying to fathom her mood. "You missed passing them on the stairs by less than a minute."

"What? They've left us unchaperoned?"

Resentment. And so tense she was close to tears. "For at least the next fifteen minutes," he assured her. He had two ways to go; the first would leave her thinking he was a kind and sensitive man and the second leaving her not thinking at all.

"If only it were twenty," she said morosely, taking a huge drink of the whiskey.

As she gasped and shuddered, Drayton smiled and stepped behind her. "As inspired as I've been the last few hours," he whispered against her ear as he reached around her to cup her breasts, "I can do quite a lot with just ten. Would you like for me to prove it?"

"This isn't wise," she murmured, leaning back into his chest.

Nibbling her earlobe, he asked, "But it is ever so enjoyable, isn't it?" as, beneath the satin, her nipples hardened to tease his palms. He kissed his way down to the creamy curve of her shoulder, delighting in the sanction of her soft sighs. Sliding one hand under the edge of her bodice, he caught a hardened nub between his fingers. His other hand slipped down over the flat of her midriff to the hem of the ruched panel. "Tell me how much you want me to stop."

"I should."

"But you can't," he told her, moving back to her ear as he continued to tease her nipple with one hand and began to open the hidden buttons with the other.

She moaned quietly and melted closer against him. Turning her head, she grazed his lips with hers and raggedly whispered, "The doors. Someone could see us."

If that was all the objection she was going to offer . . . "Then let's move out of the sight line," he said, easing his hands free of her dress.

"You don't fight fairly," she accused as he took the whiskey glass from her and set it aside.

"I'm not the least bit interested in fighting with you, my dear Caroline," he admitted, drawing her toward the far corner of the room and into the space between the wall and the backside of a chair. "Can't you tell?" he asked, stepping behind her again, glancing at the mantel clock and then putting his mouth and his hands back to their tasks.

"Yes," she whispered. Reaching up, she twined her arms around his neck as he freed her breast from the confines of her bodice and opened another button.

"I love your sensibilities on dress design," he said, gently pinching her nipple and slipping his hand into the opening to lay his palm on the soft warm pillow of her bare abdomen. "It makes you so wonderfully accessible."

"That wasn't," she protested, turning her head to nip at his chin, "my primary motivation."

He slowly slid his hand off her abdomen, moving it downward and countering, "But you can appreciate it, can't you?" His fingers slipped into the moist curls and arrowed to the hooded nub nestled in their midst. "Ah, yes," he murmured, as she choked back a moan and her knees buckled. "You do."

There was no denying it, no denying him. Or her own desperate need. "This is wicked," she gasped, grinning as wave after sweet wave of pleasure rippled through her body.

"And you're enjoying it immensely."

She could feel his smile, hear it in his voice. "God, yes. Aren't you?"

"As a prelude, it's quite good," he admitted, his fingers gliding along her cleft. "Do you know how long I've wanted to do this to you?"

"Since teatime?" she guessed breathlessly as they slipped inside her and her muscles tightened in welcome.

"From the very beginning, dear Caroline," he crooned. "But in the last hours fantasy has become need."

He was asking for permission, giving her a chance to escape if she wanted to. "So has mine," she whispered, turning her head to kiss him. "Whose shall we make real first?"

"Mine," he moaned against her mouth as his hands eased their delicious torment to take her arms from around his neck.

No. No, she'd die if she couldn't have release. "Drayton, what—"

"Ssssh," he whispered, placing her hands on the chair back in front of her. "Not a sound or we'll be caught. Or do you want to be caught, dear Caroline?"

She gasped as he lifted the back of her skirts. "This is too outrageous even for—" No, it was perfect, she admitted, closing her eyes, shivering in delight as his hands skimmed over the tops of her stockings to the bare skin of her upper thighs and then upward to caress the curve of her backside.

Yes, it was beyond wanton. Yes, it was dangerous. And she'd never in her life wanted anything more intensely, more immediately. If he didn't get his trouser buttons undone in the next two seconds, she'd—

The growl of her frustration slipped past her lips, twined with a moan of gratitude as he filled her with his heat and power. Her knees weak, her senses reeling, she sagged forward, surrendering her mind, body, and soul to the sheer brilliance of the pleasure, to the breathlessly swift spiral of satisfaction.

Drayton closed his eyes and threw his head back, clenching his teeth and swallowing a groan as she shuddered in achievement and pulled him blessedly to his own. God, for as long as he lived . . . Breathless, his heart pounding and his body quaking, he forced himself to think beyond the heady pleasure, beyond the desire to lay her down on the floor and do it all over again. Later, he promised himself, holding her hips and withdrawing. After dinner. And slowly. Much more slowly, he vowed, easing her upright as he stepped back and let her skirts fall between them.

With one arm around her waist, he held her steady as he quickly buttoned his trousers. Her head fell back against his shoulder, her blond curls bright against the black of his dinner jacket, the soft curve of her sated smile thrilling his heart. So honest in her wanting, so unaware of how rare a creature she was. Feathering kisses along her brow, he reached around her and gently eased her breast back into her bodice.

"Seven minutes," she said on a sigh as he turned her in his arms and drew her against him.

"You looked at the clock?"

She tipped her head back and smiled lazily. "You didn't?"

He grinned in admission. "With eight minutes left for that delightfully naughty flush of satisfaction to fade from your cheeks before Mother Aubrey arrives."

"You're reprehensible," she accused, her eyes sparkling and the color of her cheeks deepening.

"I won't argue with you. As long as you'll admit to being perfectly, lusciously willing."

"Too willing," she countered, sighing and stepping from his arms.

"That's *not* possible, Caroline."

She laughed softly and turned slightly away to adjust her bodice. "You bring out the absolute worst in me. Common sense doesn't even so much as whimper in protest when I am near you."

"For which I am eternally grateful," he allowed, stepping up behind her and slipping his arms around her waist again.

"Drayton," she murmured, tilting her head out of the

way so he could better kiss her shoulder. "This is insanity and we both know better than to keep taking the risks."

"Apparently the bloom is off the satisfaction already." He laid a lingering kiss on the curve where her shoulder swept up into her lovely neck, on the spot where a touch always melted her knees. "I promise to do better next time."

"There can't be a next time," she protested on a breathy whimper as she sagged back against him. "Please don't make me be the only sensible one."

Why the hell she was suddenly feeling guilty for the pleasure they so easily gave each other . . . If he had another seven minutes, he'd gladly use them to prove to her that she didn't have any more sense—or regrets—than he did. But since he didn't and he knew that words wouldn't make a damn bit of difference, he decided that he was better off deferring the contest of wills until later. Until after dinner when he could ever so slowly and deliberately make his point.

He kissed her in the sweet spot one more time, and as she shivered, he stepped back to take her hand and lead her out of the corner, saying, "We'll continue our negotiations after we've retired this evening. I'm going out to smoke a cheroot so Mother Aubrey's sense of propriety isn't strained."

"There's nothing to be negotiated, Drayton."

"We'll see."

"No we won't."

He stopped and let go of her hand. Taking her chin gently in his hand, he tilted her head up until her gaze met his. "Have I mentioned how utterly alluring I find your obstinance?" he asked, noting the confusion in her eyes, but not letting it deter him. "Challenges are so incredibly stimulating for the imagination."

"I think I could easily loathe you."

"That could be an interesting edge," he said softly, taunting her lips with a feathery kiss just before releasing her. "I can't wait to see what it feels like. You will promise to bring it to bed with you tonight, won't you?"

Caroline watched him walk away, her refusal caught in her throat, hopelessly snared in a simple net of possibility that she didn't dare give voice to. No, she didn't love him, she assured herself as she buttoned her dress with ridiculously trembling hands. She was smarter than that, more self-possessed. They hadn't just made love; they'd had a kind of sex that was, at best, a rather simple bestial exchange. And yes, she'd enjoyed it. Immeasurably and wickedly, she had to admit. Her body had been sated, delightfully and quickly and quite thoroughly. For all of a few seconds.

Until he'd put their clothing back to rights, wrapped her in his arms and held her close. Desire had blazed to life again as she'd looked up at him. And deep in the center of the renewed wanting had been the horrible flicker of first realization. She'd tamped it down, tried to be rational. She'd called an end to their affair even as she knew that if he eased her to the floor, she'd go without a fight.

Whether she'd driven him out to smoke his cheroot or he'd always intended to go didn't matter. He'd left her alone with her chattering mind and her sinking heart. And it hadn't made any difference at all. In fact, in the silence and solitude the tiny, dreadful spark of possibility had become a pulsing, undeniable reality.

She wanted to spend the rest of her life making love with Drayton Mackenzie. And only him. If he didn't feel the same way about her . . . Caroline swallowed down the bubble of panic and marshaled her pride. If he didn't want her the same way, she'd survive. She'd do what she had to do, what she was expected to do. When he announced that he'd given his heart to someone else, she'd smile and wish him the best and then go back to the life she'd had before he'd turned it upside down and inside out.

Yes, that's exactly what she'd do. She'd stay as far away from him as she could, becoming the best excuse maker the world had ever seen in the effort to keep the distance between them. Because if she didn't . . . Because, until the day she died, if he gave her one of his easy, seductive smiles and nodded toward the corner of any parlor, she'd glance over her shoulder to make sure his wife wasn't anywhere around and then she'd go with him. She'd be his mistress, whenever, however he pleased.

No, she couldn't do that. She couldn't live with being responsible for the ache of another woman's heart. But until the day came when she had to exercise good sense and self-denial . . .

Caroline closed her eyes and drew a deep breath. Maybe she was just too tired to think straight and was being foolish and overreacting. Maybe if she stopped fighting the attraction, if she simply surrendered to desire whenever it struck . . . It could burn itself out. Become so routine and boring that his marriage to someone else would be nothing short of a blessed escape for her. Yes, that was a perfectly likely outcome. One Drayton had posed right from the start, she realized. And since he had considerably more experience than she did in such matters, she could trust that he was right.

Feeling considerably more settled, Caroline opened her eyes. She picked up the glass of spirits Drayton had set aside earlier and took a healthy sip As before, it seared a path down her throat and took her breath away. She had no idea what kind of liquor it was, but it clearly wasn't the sherry that good and virtuous women limited themselves to sipping from dainty glasses.

But since she wasn't a good and virtuous woman, at least not at heart . . . She took another drink and decided that she didn't mind being the kind of woman Drayton Mackenzie wanted in his bed every night. Defiance and impropriety definitely had their rewards. Even if just for a short while.

"AND OF COURSE THERE WILL BE A BRIEF DISCUSSION OF making the seats in the House of Lords subject to the vote," Aubrey said as the footmen cleared away their dinner plates. "It's a perennial issue. For the life of me, I fail to see why anyone of reasonable intelligence would expect a member of the upper chamber to surrender hundreds of years of privilege so he could stand before the masses and sell himself like a tin of tea. You'd think that . . ."

Aubrey went on, but Caroline wasn't listening anymore. You'd think, she mused, watching Drayton swirl the wine around his glass, that Aubrey would notice that he wasn't the least bit interested in who had what seat in Parliament and how they'd gotten it. Or in what the Conservatives planned to do to block enactment of the Liberals' anticipated agenda. Not that Drayton was any more interested in the Liberals' expected plots to overturn the very foundations and traditions of the British world.

His gaze met hers across the length of the table as Aubrey droned on. Too far away to see the depths of his eyes and gauge the nature of his thoughts, she offered him a slight smile of commiseration. Although, quite honestly, Aubrey's soliloquy wasn't yet anywhere near the length his mother's had been on the importance of being seen in all the right places, wearing the right fashions, and talking with the right people. After the first ten minutes or so of the detailed list of names, Caroline hadn't paid any more attention to her than Drayton was now paying her son.

Clearly, she and Drayton were destined to be the misfits of London's elite social and political circles. Not that they'd be ostracized for their nonconformity and allowed to go away to live in peace at Ryland Castle. No, according to Lady Aubrey, rank had its duties and one of the most important of them was to sacrifice themselves to profitable matrimony and beget another generation of titled Englishmen. It was the British Way and to not shoulder their burden would lead to the certain and swift downfall of the Empire.

Unfortunately, if there was anything else she'd gleaned from Mother Aubrey's dinner dissertation, it was that Society was never inclined to be either patient or merciful with those who stumbled along the way. Considering that neither she nor Drayton had been born to tread the path that lay ahead for them . . . Like dinner tonight, they'd simply have to make the best of it and try not to let on how utterly boring they found it all.

And, she added, hearing the jangle of approaching keys, arrange their escapes well in advance. Drayton's brow went slowly up as Mrs. Gladder came into the dining room. He hid his smile around the rim of his wine glass as his housekeeper flawlessly executed the plan, then stood and lifted his glass in salute as Caroline begged the necessary apologies before leaving him to fend for himself.

She and Mrs. Gladder were well outside the dining room when she asked, "Is there really a concern with the paint color?"

"Of course not," the housekeeper replied, chuckling. "The captains of British industry should be properly jealous of our efficiency."

"And do those working through the night need clarification of their tasks?"

"I tossed that one in just for good measure."

"I was hoping so," Caroline admitted. "Would you think terribly of me if I begged for a few hours' sleep?"

"Not at all, madam," Mrs. Gladder assured her. "No one has earned a good night's sleep more than you have."

"Then I'll thank you for my timely rescue, urge you to get some sleep yourself, and promise to be of assistance first thing in the morning."

"Pleasant dreams, Lady Caroline."

Yes, she'd get to the pleasant dreams, she promised herself as she headed for her room. Eventually.

OLD PEOPLE WERE SUPPOSED TO TIRE EASILY, HE SILENTLY groused, making his way down the hall toward his room. Not stay up until the new day started. Of course Lady Aubrey hadn't spent the day in the fields with the harvest crews and she wasn't going to rise at dawn to sally forth for another one. No, the most strenuous thing she'd done all day was leisurely cut her meat at dinner.

Caroline, he silently declared as he passed her room, could run circles around Aubrey's mother. On virtually no sleep at all. And not only look positively beautiful while doing it, but drive him mad with wanting whenever she crossed his path. Not that she crossed it nearly often enough to please him. Once the harvest was in—with luck, late in the week—he'd have the time to figure out what her usual paths were and make sure he placed himself on them.

He slipped into his room and closed the door, unbuttoning his coat as he crossed to the foot of the bed and let his eyes adjust to the darkness. He blinked and turned his head. And grinned. Caroline, sitting in his bed, her golden hair tumbling over her shoulders, waiting for him and wearing nothing but a welcoming smile and a bit of sheet. There was a God and He was good. "Well, hello," he drawled, stripping off his jacket and tossing it aside. "I thought we were going to cry quits and put the insanity behind us."

She shrugged. "Well, yes, that would be the rational thing to do."

"I gather that you've decided that you don't want to be rational?"

"Not when it comes to you," she answered, as he sat on the edge of the mattress and yanked off his boots with what he hoped looked like confident nonchalance. "Being wicked and wanton is infinitely more enjoyable."

Oh, yes. He stood up, turned to face her, pulled out his shirttail, and opened his cuffs. "There's a considerable difference between being wanton and wicked, you know."

"Really," she drawled, letting the sheet fall away and shifting onto her hands and knees. "Do enlighten me."

Oh, as though she didn't have a deep and intuitive understanding of the difference already. Blindly working the studs out of his shirtfront as she ever so deliberately crawled across the mattress toward him, he realized that she was turning the parlor table on him. His heart hammering and his loins hardening, he resigned himself to the tragedy of being ruthlessly and deliciously seduced.

"'Wanton' rather implies a willingness to be compliant," he began, wishing the damned shirt studs would just melt. "To happily follow where led along the path of carnal pleasures. Which certainly isn't a bad thing, you understand. Wicked, on the other hand, implies a delightful bit of independence and assertive creativity along the way."

"I had no idea," she said as she stopped, sat back on her heels, and looked up at him. "Do you have a preference?"

"I can appreciate both," he answered, his hands still as he watched her slowly moisten her lower lip with the tip of her tongue. "At the moment, though, I'm drawn—"

His breath caught as she boldly held his gaze while reaching out and undoing the top button on his trousers. And then the second. He swallowed hard and broadened his stance in a futile attempt to get the room to stop swaying around him.

"You're drawn to what, Drayton?" she asked softly, undoing the third and last button.

You. "Wicked."

She released his gaze, hers trailing slowly downward as she skimmed her hands over the bare skin of his hips and pushed his trousers aside. "I hope I don't disappoint you."

"I'm sure you—Oh, Jesus," he moaned as she lowered her head and took him into her mouth. The room swayed harder and he desperately broadened his stance again. Her murmur of appreciation vibrated through every fiber of his being. His knees quaking, he threaded his hands through her hair, closed his eyes and arched his back, surrendering himself to the exquisite torture, to the perfect rhythm of her assault.

Pleasure after pleasure shot through his body, each bolt stronger, each deepening his need and pulling him closer and closer to the brink. And then it was suddenly too close, too compelling. "Caroline," he pleaded, gasping, tightening his hands in her hair, trying to still her. "I can't—"

She took him deeper, past the tattered edge of control, and into the blind and mindless oblivion of soul-shuddering completion.

The strength ebbing from his body on sated waves, he marshaled what was left of it to open his eyes and step back from her. She looked up at him and slowly, wickedly, knowingly smiled. His senses staggered, his heart reeled. And desire gently swirled up from the depths of satisfaction.

"Caroline," he whispered, gathering her in his arms and easing them down on the bed. "Sweet God, I can't get enough of you."

"I'm sure you can if you really try."

No he couldn't, but if that was her fantasy, he wasn't going to ruin it for her. No, he was going to enjoy the hell out of it, out of her, for as long as he could convince her to stay. And then he'd figure out some way to get her back here again tomorrow night.

❧ *Sixteen* ❧

CAROLINE ABSENTLY BUTTONED HER BODICE AND STI-
fled a yawn as she read another passage in the book lying
open on her dressing table. Frowning, she read it again.
Yes, right there, in black-and-white and according to
Godey's, a person was supposed to be fully aware of another person's history and social ranking *before* an introduction. How one was supposed to know all that, they
didn't say. But they were adamant that the order, course,
and conversational content of all proper introductions
were dependent on the respective importance of everyone
involved. The consequences of committing a mistake in
the process, *Godey's* claimed, was too hideous to describe
in print.

What a godsend that the responsibility for doing the introductions according to form would fall to Lord Aubrey—
being the highest-ranking person who knew both them
and the guests. His mother had no doubt given him *his*
copy of *Godey's* while he'd still been in nappies. *The
poor man,* she thought as she flipped back to the section
on the rules governing parlor and dining room seating
and conversation. *It's no wonder that he's a stick.*

She was reading yet another passage on the importance

of rank in the peerage when there was a familiar, quiet knock on the door. "Come in, Dora," she called, gratefully abandoning her attempt at social edification.

Her maid barely crossed the threshold before stopping to give her a quick, bobbing curtsy. "The carriages are coming, Lady Caroline. They should be here within the half hour."

"Thank you, Dora. Are Mrs. Gladder and Winfield aware of that?"

"Yes, madam. They're collecting all the servants to change uniforms and then assemble on the drive for baggage duty."

Of course. The household staff was nothing if not impressively well organized. Thank God. If they had been even marginally undisciplined, Ryland Castle wouldn't be ready to receive guests. "Has anyone thought to send word into the fields?"

Dora nodded. "Mr. Haywood said it was properly the work of a toady and took off some time ago to retrieve Lord Ryland. I haven't seen them, but they should both be back here already and dressing."

As soon as she could, she'd check to make sure Drayton was indeed going to be ready in time. If anyone thought she was going down into the foyer and face the expectant masses without him . . . "And with that," she said on a sigh that was part resignation and part relief, "I suppose we're as ready as we can possibly be. With a few minutes to spare for a deep breath or two."

Again Dora nodded. "Miss Durbin said to tell you that she has just a few minor details to see to in the servants' quarters, but that she expects no one to catch her at it. She'll join you in the parlor for tea after she's freshened herself."

Caroline nodded, vaguely recalling having read something in *Godey's* about the protocol of commoners in a
social gathering of peers. Was it that it wasn't to be done
at all? Or was it acceptable as long as the unanointed remembered their inferiority and fawned appropriately?
God, it was all so complicated. And so utterly artificial.
"We should all sleep like the dead tonight," she said,
wishing they were to that point already. "Lord knows
we've earned a full night's rest. Thank you so much for all
you've done, Dora."

"I've done no more than my fair share, madam. None
of us have. We can't have people saying bad things about
our lord and lady. Or Ryland Castle."

Discipline *and* devotion. Caroline managed a smile. "I
can only hope that I live up to my part."

"You'll do fine, Lady Caroline," her maid assured her
brightly. "You're three times the lady that Lady Ryland
was. And ten times kinder."

"Thank you, Dora," she whispered, feeling suddenly
and completely overwhelmed by all the levels of expectation.

"If you don't need me for anything . . . ?"

You could push me out a window. Or maybe shoot me.
Caroline smiled, hoping that it passed for serenely confident. "Not at all."

"Then I'll be off to get a clean apron and cuffs so I'm
not an embarrassment to you."

The door closed and Caroline expelled a long, slow
breath. Marshaling her resolve, she crossed the room and
passed through the connecting sitting areas. As always,
the private door into Drayton's room stood open.

She entered to find him standing in front of his armoire, wearing only a crisp linen shirt and a bath sheet

wrapped around his hips. He held up two suits and grinned. "I was just on my way to ask . . . Black or purple?"

"It's a deep plum," she pointed out, dropping down onto the foot of his bed.

He shoved the black suit back into the cabinet, saying, "I'll take that as your preference."

Since either would be perfectly fine, she simply smiled and watched him quickly dress. It wasn't in any way as satisfying as watching him disrobe, but she enjoyed the play of his muscles as they were hidden by fabric and promised herself a reversal of the process as soon as she could manage it.

How late did houseguests usually stay up? *Godey's* had made it clear that a good hostess was expected to be the last to retire in the evening, seeing to her guests' every need and whim until they couldn't possibly come up with another. Barring extreme illness, of course. Only then could a hostess plead off her duties. Caroline lifted her hand and brushed her fingertips along the length of her throat. Why, yes, she decided, smiling, she could feel a cold coming on. It would probably strike in full soon after the ladies had retired to the parlor after dinner. Perhaps a half hour or so.

Then again, she realized, finding a way to escape the ordeal wouldn't necessarily result in more pleasurable pursuits unless Drayton could find an excuse to do the same. And both of them sneaking off, albeit separately, would set tongues wagging. *Godey's* never missed a chance to mention the importance of living a virtuous life and maintaining a spotless public and private reputation. One mistake in judgment, real or simply perceived, would set the course of a woman's life spiraling into the darkest depths of prostitution. Not that the editors were ever tasteless enough to use such straightforward language; they were so very good at inference that it wasn't necessary. The family's public shame over her fall, though . . .

Drayton fastened his cuffs and considered Caroline's heavy sigh. "Is there a problem?" he asked.

She shook her head and gave him a faint smile. "How is the harvest going?"

"Very well," he supplied, pulling on his shoes and thinking that the harvest was the least of her worries. "And I'd much rather be swinging a scythe than playing host to a horde of people I don't know."

"Frankly, so would I."

He reached for his suit coat. "Remind me again why we're doing this to ourselves?"

"Because we are members of society and must be perceived as worth knowing."

"Why?"

"I'm a bit fuzzy on that part," she said as he put on the coat and fastened the buttons. "I get various complicated explanations from Mother Aubrey—along with rolling eyes and a heavy sigh—every time I ask. The underlying theme of all her dissertations, though, appears to be that it's financially profitable for everyone."

"If that's the case," he suggested, stepping in front of her and extending his hands, "why don't we just nail some banknotes to the front door along with a note saying we'll see them all in London sometime?"

Allowing him to pull her to her feet, she laughed softly and countered, "*Now* you think of that?"

"You are beautiful," he murmured, gazing into her up-turned face.

"For an exhausted woman?"

"No qualifiers at all." He gently squeezed her hands and bent his head. "Just beautiful," he whispered across her lips.

As he drew back, she sighed softly and shook her head. "I don't know if absence makes the heart grow fonder, but it obviously makes the eyes more forgiving."

Nothing either impaired or affected his eyesight. She *was* beautiful. And he was more than willing to make the effort to convince her of it. "How long do we have before the locusts descend?" he asked, wrapping his arms around her shoulders and drawing her against him.

Her brow went up and the light in her eyes danced in anticipation. Her lips parted ever so enticingly and heated his blood in the most wonderful way.

The knock at the door instantly chilled it. And startled them both.

"Drayton?"

Damn. Haywood.

The doorknob turned.

"Not long enough," she said softly, hastily stepping out of his embrace and darting toward the safety of the sitting room. Drayton quickly turned and stepped to the side, placing his body between the opening door and the path of her retreat.

"Yes?" he asked tightly as Haywood pushed the door just wide enough to step onto the threshold.

"Have you by any chance seen Lady Caroline?" his friend asked with a dark look before glancing meaningfully over his shoulder. "Or know where she might be?"

Drayton stowed his frustration and crossed the room. Haywood retreated only a half step, pushing the door wider and turning sideways to allow Drayton to see into the hall behind him. Aubrey's mother stood in front of Caroline's door. Judging by the high arch of her brow . . . "Is there a problem, Lady Aubrey?"

"Lady Caroline is not answering my knock."

Bless Haywood. "Perhaps she's in her sitting room and can't hear you," Drayton said, thinking fast. "Allow me to check."

He left both of them standing where they were and stepped to the other door in his room. Caroline was waiting there for him.

"I dozed off while reading," she said quickly, "and you had to wake me."

"Sounds entirely plausible." He caught her hands and stayed her for a quick kiss. "I'll see you downstairs in a few minutes."

She was gone with a nod and a rustle of silk, not looking back as she dashed through the sitting rooms and closed the connecting door of hers behind her. Drayton considered the panel for a moment, not liking the barrier, but understanding the prudence of it. God help them both if Lady Aubrey saw it standing wide and made assumptions. Not that they'd be wrong, but it would be—

"My lips are sealed."

Drayton wheeled about to find Haywood leaning ever so nonchalantly against the armoire, an ever so grim tightness to his smile. Drayton silently walked past him, pasted a false but easy smile on his face, and stepped into the opening of the other door.

"I was correct, Lady Aubrey," he said, even as Caroline opened her door and the other woman looked away from him.

"My apologies," he heard Caroline say. "I was relaxing with a book and dozed off. Is there a concern, Lady Aubrey?"

Leaving her to manage the woman on her own, Drayton stepped back into his room to deal with his unexpected caller. Haywood made no move to depart; he simply stood there studying him with a cool, level gaze. "Don't you have somewhere else to be?" Drayton prodded.

"Not at this precise moment."

Resigned to enduring the inevitable, Drayton ambled to the bureau asking, "Do you mind if I finish dressing while you lecture?"

"Toadies don't lecture," Haywood replied. "Bad form to be critical and all that."

"But?" Drayton pressed, threading his watch chain.

"Just a reminder that it's always the woman who pays the price for scandal."

"Noted, Haywood. Only a complete cad wouldn't be concerned about the consequences for his partner and take every precaution to avoid discovery. If you hadn't walked into my private quarters uninvited, the secret would still be a secret."

"True, my suspicions would still be nothing more than suspicions."

Drayton tucked the watch into its pocket on his vest. "Have we been careless?"

"Only in that neither of you can keep from being obviously happy in each other's company. And that you often speak to each other with mere looks the way old married couples do. It all rather implies a relationship deeper and more personal than that of a proper guardian and ward, much less that of two relative strangers."

"I'll make a point to be unhappy and uncommunicative in the days ahead," Drayton promised. "It shouldn't be all that difficult." As Haywood cocked a brow in silent comment, Drayton added, "And I'll be counting on you to act as my chaperone."

His friend slapped his hands over his heart and looked up at the ceiling. "An elevation of my status. Yesterday a common toady, today . . ." Grinning, he let his hands fall to his sides and brought his gaze down to meet Drayton's. "You can count on me. I'll do my best to keep you distracted, frustrated, and surly. No one will ever guess that Lady Caroline has made you a happy man."

Yes, Drayton allowed, nodding and heading for the door with Haywood on his heels, he was a happy man. By and large. A home that anyone would consider well appointed and comfortable. An estate that was well on its way to becoming profitable again. A good friend at his side. And beautiful, delightful Caroline in his arms.

Yes, if it weren't for the rapidly approaching horde of strangers and the social expectations for his and Caroline's respective marriages, he'd consider his world utterly idyllic. The strangers would eventually grow bored and move on to disrupt someone else's life, of course. But the expectations weren't going to go away with them. They would always be there, making certain that his happiness was only temporary. Given that reality . . .

A virtuous and prudent man would—firmly, deliberately, and gallantly—set Caroline aside for the sake of protecting her reputation and prospects. A selfish, unconscionably hedonistic man would hold her close for as long as he could and hope they could be careful and discreet enough to escape scandal and ruination. Proof, as though he needed it, that he was considerably less than the man she deserved. Thank God Haywood was there to see that he didn't do something incredibly stupid in the days ahead.

AS MOTHER AUBREY OPENLY CONTEMPLATED THE EXPLA-nation for her whereabouts, Caroline stepped back and opened the door wide, asking, "Would you care to come in?"

"Am I to assume," the older woman intoned as she swept into Caroline's bedroom, "that your private chambers are attached to those of Lord Ryland?"

"Through our respective sitting rooms," she supplied, wondering why Lady Aubrey hadn't considered the possibility before.

"And the doors are not locked?"

"There are no keys. At least not that we have been able to locate. Given all the other work that has been necessary in the past few weeks, replacing the old locks with new ones has not been a priority." She motioned to the pair of chairs placed before the banked hearth. "Would you care to have a seat?"

Lady Aubrey gave a crisp nod and lowered herself into one of them, saying, "I think it prudent, prior to the arrival of Lord Ryland's guests, to touch upon the more important aspects of your public presentation and conduct."

Well, it was a reprieve of sorts. At least it wasn't an inquisition regarding her private conduct.

"I have observed since my arrival that you have been instilled with an understanding of good, basic manners. Which is fortunate and far more than can be said for either of your sisters."

A compliment followed by a barb. How very typical. "I am sure they can learn. With the proper instruction."

"A lady is always optimistic," Mother Aubrey said with a tight smile. "Which is one of several important caveats that bear mention at this time."

"Such as?" Caroline asked, hoping she sounded more willing than she felt.

"Ladies do not stride as you are wont to do, Lady Caroline. They glide. Ladies do not laugh, they titter politely. Ladies do not ask personal questions of others. Nor do they offer personal information about themselves. Should one of Lord Ryland's guests comment favorably on the various appointments of Ryland Castle, the draperies, for instance, although I doubt very much that it is likely, you should nod appreciatively, smile, and make no mention of the details of how they came to be. Under no circumstances are you to mention that you in any way personally participated in the process of their acquisition or creation."

Oh, God forbid. "I understand."

"I suggest that your best approach to navigating the days ahead is to affect a retiring demeanor and to practice keen observation. Never be the first to act or speak in any given social situation. If you diligently follow the path of others, you will be far less likely to make a disastrous misstep."

"I certainly would not want to do that."

Mother Aubrey arched a brow and pursed her lips until they were a bloodless line. It took a long moment, but she rallied to tartly instruct, "Ladies are never sarcastic. It implies an unpleasantly critical nature. Which is most unbecoming and not a characteristic that men seek in a wife."

"Of course." *I wouldn't dream of being anything more than the perfect adornment.*

"Those who will soon arrive are of the oldest, most

influential families in England," Lady Aubrey went on. "The opinions Lord Ryland's guests form of you in the coming days will be the foundation of the reputation that precedes you to London and your formal introduction to society with the advent of the next Season. It is of the utmost importance that you conduct yourself in a manner that leads them to form glowingly favorable impressions. If you fail even marginally in that endeavor, you will be at a distinct disadvantage in the competition for a suitable husband."

"And if I fail spectacularly?" she asked before she could think better of it.

Lady Aubrey blinked—twice—before snapping, "Ladies are not flippant. They take seriously the requirements society places upon them in the interest of their betterment and security."

How thoughtful and caring of society.

"A woman's reputation is her fortune, Lady Caroline. How she protects, nurtures, and trades upon it determines her lot and happiness in life. I would advise you to do all within your power to use wisely the exceptional opportunity you have been given by your late father."

"May his soul rest in peace."

"Indeed," the other woman said with a momentary bow of her head. "Take care, Lady Caroline. Do nothing, say nothing in public or in private that you would not want all of England to know about in the most scathing, most salacious detail."

Good judgment suggested that she simply nod and keep her mouth shut. After countless days of frantic work, though, she was too tired to listen to it or care about the consequences. "Are Lord Ryland's approaching guests known to be window peepers and vicious gossipmongers?"

The brow went up again. "A lady does not cast aspersions," Lady Aubrey said icily.

Hypocrisy at its finest. "Unless she has cause, apparently," Caroline pointed out. "However slight or imagined it may be."

Aubrey's mother rose to her feet as Caroline wearily gained hers. "Ladies do not provoke conflict," she advised. "It is even more unbecoming than sarcasm and flippancy. You are courting disaster with your defiant attitudes, Lady Caroline."

Yes, I know. Now go away. Caroline summoned a smile and all the contriteness she could muster to reply, "I shall do my best in the days ahead to stifle my natural tendencies and blend with the wallpaper whenever possible."

Lady Aubrey looked her up and down before promising darkly, "I will be watching you carefully to be sure that you do."

Thinking that she should consider herself fortunate that Mother Aubrey wasn't putting her on a leash, Caroline went to the door and opened it. "Thank you for your concern, Lady Aubrey," she offered in a less-than-subtle end to their exchange. "And your words of wisdom," she added as the woman sailed regally past her and into the hall. "I appreciate the instruction."

Lady Aubrey muttered something about pearls and swine as Caroline was closing the door, but this time she let good judgment rule. Standing alone inside her room, she scrubbed her hands over her face and sighed. If all the women about to arrive at Ryland Castle were like Aubrey's mother . . . God give her strength. And the haven of Drayton's arms.

Yes, she reminded herself as she dropped her hands and squared her shoulders, she could get through anything as long as she knew that at the end of the day, Drayton would be waiting to hold her and willing to make all the trials and tribulations of their world disappear.

Only a reckless fool would openly defy convention and invite ruin. And since she was no fool, she would ably manage the charade, would artfully maintain public appearances and meet every social expectation. She would be the embodiment of ladylike grace and refinement, the *Godey's* ideal woman—above reproach and suspicion and the slightest possibility of scandal—come to life. When outside her and Drayton's rooms.

But once the doors were shut behind them . . . She made a mental note to keep the draperies closed and the doors locked. And to stuff the keyholes. In private, the only expectations she intended to meet were Drayton's and her own. It was a reward they'd both earn each and every hour of the interminable days to come.

Resolved, Caroline smoothed her skirts, lifted her chin, and left her room to begin the most earnest and calculated performance of her life.

❦ Seventeen ❦

HE WAS WAITING FOR HER, JUST AS HE HAD BEEN EVERY night for the last fortnight. How a man could look so seductive just sitting in a bed, his back propped against the headboard while he read in the pale lamplight . . . All right, it probably helped some to know that under the sheet he was gloriously naked—and glorious—but after ten straight nights it wasn't surprising enough to account for how her breath still caught at the sight of him.

"Get dear Dora tucked in for the night?" he asked as she came around to what had become her side of the bed.

She removed her wrapper and nightgown and laid them on the foot of the bed, saying, "Actually, I just pretended to be asleep long enough for her to slip out. I think she's meeting Lord Henry's second footman for a midnight stroll in the gardens."

"And you didn't stop her?"

Caroline smiled as he drew the covers aside for her. "I'm hardly in any position to pass judgment on anyone else's affairs," she explained, sliding in and scooting across the wide expanse of mattress. As always, he laid aside his little blue book, picked up the glass of wine they shared, and had it ready to hand her when she arrived at his side.

As she snuggled her bottom against his hip and leaned back against his chest, he wrapped his arms around her and nuzzled his lips in the hair at her temple. It was silly to be so thrilled by the little things they did that made conversation so unnecessary, but she was. Smiling, utterly content and happy, she tipped her head back and met his lips. As always, his kiss melted away all the tensions of her day and left her sighing in appreciation for how amazingly good he was at making her feel so perfect.

"Speaking of affairs," she said, settling back against his chest and taking the wine glass from his hand. "Which I vaguely recall that I was. I gather Haywood and Jane have ended theirs?"

Tucking her head under his chin, he wrapped his arms around her midriff as she sipped. "He discovered this afternoon that Jane has fickle affections."

"Really?" she drawled. "I'm shocked."

"Then that makes the two of you the only ones in the world. According to him, he went to meet her for a rendezvous and found that Lord Linden had beaten him to it."

"No doubt," Caroline quipped, "while Lady Linden was rendezvousing with Lord Vernon in the conservatory. These people aren't even discreet, Drayton. It's to the point that I knock before I open the doors of my own armoire."

He laughed softly, the sound and the feel wonderful as it passed through her. "You know Lord Handen?"

"Round, bald, about a head shorter than I am, and the master of all he surveys?"

"That would be the one. Simone says he likes to wear a saddle and bridle."

"No!" She turned in his arms to look up at him. "How does—?" He cocked a brow and she settled back again, saying, "Never mind. The answer's obvious."

"Simone is actually an incredible font of information about our male guests. Lord Renning prefers to watch through a peephole in the armoire. Lord Ralls prefers a crowd. And Lord Sillings is required to pay as he crosses the threshold because simply contemplating his choices is more than enough for him."

"She's not contemplating blackmail, is she?"

"Who knows?" he said, taking the wine glass from her. "I can either run the affairs of an estate or I can control her. There aren't enough hours in the day to do both."

"How are the *affaires d'état*?" she asked as he drank.

"French?"

She nodded as he passed the glass back to her. "Lady Aubrey brought the language master along, remember? Having run out of excuses to avoid it, I had to spend an hour with him this morning under the watchful supervision of Mother May I. After which I had to spend *two* hideous hours with the dance master. Also under supervision."

"I thought all ladies like to dance."

"Yes, well." She drank a bit of wine and then confessed, "I seem to have a slight problem with being led."

"Really," he said, laughing silently.

"You'd think the man would just give up, let me lead, and keep his feet out of harm's way. It can't be very good for one's professional prospects to be known as the peg-legged dance master."

He laughed outright, hugging her close. "It's not funny,

Drayton," she chastised, grinning. "The poor man is in considerable pain."

"Sorry," he said, not sounding the least bit sincere.

"You didn't answer my question," she reminded him as he took the glass from her. "How are the *affaires d'état?*"

"*Très bien.* Which is French for Mr. Fanes was right when he predicted that Rudman and Thompson would plead guilty and throw themselves on the mercy of the bench."

"So there won't be a trial?"

"No, thank God." He handed her the glass again, adding, "At least their wives and children will be spared a little public humiliation."

Yes, that was good; for the innocents and for Drayton. Their tears had been weighing heavily on his mind. But in the way that a blessing often created a curse . . . "Well, I'm relieved for the families, but *you* get to tell your guests that the wildly anticipated social highlight of their week has been canceled. *I'm* not going to do it."

"We could just keep the news to ourselves," he suggested, "let them all go on their merry way to court and lock the doors behind them."

She nodded. "And pretend that we're not here when they wander back. It could work."

"Or not," he countered. "With our luck, they'd just camp on the lawn, bathing in your fountain and eating your shrubbery."

And peering through the windows, their noses against the glass and their hands cupped around their eyes. She took a sip of the wine and shook her head in wonder. "With a few exceptions, they really are a strange lot of people, aren't they?"

"And who would those exceptions be and why haven't I met them?"

She smiled. "Lord Betterton seems like a solid sort of man. Polite, sober, rather given to reflection. At least more than the others."

"Please." He snorted. "Betterton missed his calling. He should have been a deacon in the Church of No."

The Church of No? She grinned. "Oh, he can't be that bad."

"I'll prove you wrong."

He pulled an arm back and shifted under her, forcing her to quickly sit up so she didn't spill their wine. She was turning her head to see what he was doing when a pile of little blue leather-bound folios landed on his lap. "What are those things?" she asked as he eased her back against him again. "Aubrey's always carrying a handful around these days."

"Issue position statements," he answered, sorting through them with one hand. "And Aubrey always has a fistful of them because he's taken it upon himself to be my political tutor. Politicos must have an opinion on everything, you know."

"No, I didn't. But to be perfectly honest about it, I've never paid Parliament much attention at all."

"Well, you should have," he said, apparently finding the one he wanted. He propped the book in her lap and flipped through the pages, adding, "They're probably the ones who decided magenta was this year's proper color."

She frowned. Magenta? He wouldn't know magenta from violet. "What are you talking about?"

"Never mind. Read this," he said, holding the open book up for her at eye level. "Third paragraph down on the right-hand page."

She read, blinked, and read again. "A wife should submit to her husband in all things?" She looked over her shoulder at him. "What if he's an idiot?"

He smiled and winked. "Keep reading. You're not to the best part yet."

"And if she is willful and acts without his *permission*?"

"Read on."

Her jaw sagged. "Oh!" she squeaked, reading it again, not believing her eyes. "Oh!"

"I think you're there."

"He is within his *God-given* rights to drive her from his house and take her children and her property as a punishment for her evil ways? Oh, my God!"

"I'm sorry, but apparently God is only for men," he said, letting the book fall closed as he took the wine glass from her slackened hold. "Make a note, darling Caroline, to find yourself a husband who won't mind lending you his from time to time."

"If I'm supposed to be submissive and surrender my good judgment," she countered, "it's not going to go well and I'd be much further ahead to not marry at all." She took the folio from his hand. "What issue is this drivel all about?"

"The continuing debate over married women's property rights and whether they should have any."

"And Betterton wrote this?" she asked, skimming a few passages that were just as unbelievable as the others.

"Yes."

She tossed it down with the other books in his lap. "Well, he needs to do a bit more reflecting than he has to this point. Does Aubrey think that's the position you should support in the House of Lords?"

"Apparently. All of these are pretty much in the same vein. Different subjects, of course, but still very much against anything that might alter the established order in a noticeable way."

"You're right about Betterton. I've formally and permanently crossed him off my They Seem Relatively Normal list."

He chuckled and settled his arms back around her. "Who's left on it?"

"Lady Gregory," she replied, snagging the glass and taking a healthy drink.

"Lady Gregory?"

"Yes. She's so . . . effervescent, so lively. She always has something pleasant to say. Lord knows, the conversation never lags when she's around. And honestly, if she could focus her thinking for longer than five minutes at a time, she could run circles around me in getting things done." She looked over her shoulder at him. "Did you know that Lord Gregory spent five years in the foreign service attached to the embassy in Nassau?"

"Uh-huh." He cocked a brow. "Did you know that Lady Gregory sniffs her lively effervescence up her nose every few hours?"

"Sniffs?"

"You're so worldly," he chuckled, planting a kiss on her forehead and hugging her. "Coca, darling. It's a powder that makes her so energetic. She acquired the habit in the West Indies. And has taken it to excess."

Coca. She'd never in her life known anyone who had actually used it. Of course, no one she'd ever known could afford it. "How do you know all that?"

His eyes sparkled and his smile went lopsided. "She offered to share with me. And no, I declined the kind offer."

Oh, there was more to the story than that and she knew it. "What else did she offer to share with you?"

He laughed and bent his head to give her a quick kiss. "I limit my romantic conquests solely to blondes with smoky blue eyes and some meat on their bones."

Satisfied, she settled back in his arms with a sigh. "She is very thin. You could stuff a mattress with all the padding in her dresses. Poor thing. I feel sorry for her now."

"She thinks she's perfectly happy."

"What she is is perfectly bored," Caroline countered. "They all are, really. They're more demanding than young children. No offense to young children, you understand."

"Of course." He tucked her head under his chin again. "I assume that Lady Gregory remains on the list so that her feelings aren't hurt. Who's left with her?"

"Lord Bidwell," she supplied halfheartedly. "But I suppose that you know of some dark secrets lurking beneath his polished, terribly educated façade."

"He and Lord Ablin are traveling together for a reason."

"But they're both married."

"Then either their wives are deaf, dumb, and blind, or very good sports."

"Oh, I give up." She drained the wine glass. "They're all strange. Do you know that not one single married couple in this house is sleeping with each other? Every one of them is having an affair."

"Boredom is a way of life for some people."

True. Not that she'd ever known it was possible until the hordes had descended on Ryland Castle. She'd learned a lot about a great many things in the last few days. "Do you think Lady Aubrey knows about . . . well, any of it?"

He cleared his throat softly and lazily answered, "I have no idea. Why don't you ask her for us?"

"Thank you, no." Lady Aubrey didn't have conversations. She pronounced, instructed, monitored, corrected, interrogated, and guarded. Oh, did she guard. From dawn to midnight, day in and day out. Thank goodness the woman slept at night. If she ever availed herself of Lady Gregory's coca supply, there'd be no escaping her, no respite from the dreary expectations.

"Why is it," she mused, "that everyone is obsessed about a woman's reputation being untarnished before she's married and then don't care at all once she is?"

It took him a moment, but he eventually cleared his throat to say, "Huh?"

Caroline smiled. "You're asleep, aren't you?"

"Wide awa . . ."

Chuckling softly, she turned in his arms and reached across him to put the empty wine glass on the night table.

"Don't go," he murmured, his hand skimming over her backside. "Please."

"I'm not," she promised as she gathered up the books and set them beside the glass. She turned down the wick in the lamp until the light went out. "I'll be right here when you wake up."

He muttered something too thick with sleep to be understood, gathered her back into his arms and rolled them both onto their sides. Her head lying on his arm, Caroline threaded her fingers gently, slowly through his hair. What an interesting man he was. So different from all the others she'd ever known. She smiled. How deeply she'd hated him the day he'd walked into her shop. Her smile widened. How intensely they'd made love that same night.

As she looked back, it seemed insane. Normal people didn't go from loathing each other to being passionate lovers in the span of a single day. Of course, what she'd loathed had been his attempts to be something, someone, he wasn't. But he hadn't been able to sustain the façade, and as it had crumbled and she'd seen the real man behind it . . .

Her smile faded. As amazing as it was, somewhere in that first day, she'd handed him her heart. And then gone through all the days and nights since pretending that she hadn't. She'd spent hours and hours thinking about him, about being with him, and telling herself that it wasn't anything more than a keen appreciation for his skills as a lover and the thrill of a reckless, forbidden desire.

Without knowing it, he'd done his part in preserving the illusion. He'd smiled at her, teased her, taunted her, and tempted her. Relentlessly, wonderfully, and so deliciously that falling into his arms and letting him satisfy the hunger was all she thought of, all she needed and wanted.

Until that evening in the parlor when she'd hardly been able to stand in the aftermath of the pleasure and realized that it wasn't enough, that she wanted more. That she wanted a life with him. How close she'd come to having her own façade crumble in that moment and how desperately she'd scrambled to save it. She'd declared the need to be sensible and called an end to their affair. And in the moments after he'd called her bluff and walked away . . . How confidently she'd assured herself that she was wrong. How boldly she'd committed herself to letting passion run its course until it ceased to exist.

She studied his face in the darkness and knew that she'd been lying to herself all along. It had never been a

simple matter of sex purely for the sake of physical satisfaction. Not for her. She just hadn't been able to hear the
whisper of her heart and soul over the pounding of her
blood and the strident demands of her body. No, that
wasn't entirely true, she admitted, closing her eyes. She
hadn't wanted to hear them.

It was one thing to surrender to physical temptation.
The thrill of it was undeniable, the satisfactions so heady
and deep. And she knew how to manage the life that came
after the passion faded and died and you were left alone.
She'd watched her mother do it and she'd learned that it
was perfectly survivable.

But loving a man, heart and soul, was another matter
entirely. When the passion was gone and you were left
alone with a love that wasn't wanted . . . She knew nothing about surviving that. Nothing at all.

She swallowed down her fearful tears and took a long,
deep breath. She couldn't run away from this, couldn't
deny that she'd committed herself to the most dangerous
journey she'd ever take. There was nothing to do but accept the truth and hope the day never came when Drayton
walked away. Hope that somehow, someday soon, he
would look at her and hear a whisper from his heart, too.

And if he didn't . . . She wouldn't think about that.
She'd live every moment as it came and be happy. She'd
make good memories, collecting them and holding them
close in her heart. And hope that she died a very old
woman in Drayton Mackenzie's arms.

≈ *Eighteen* ≈

A COSTUME BALL, CAROLINE SILENTLY GROUSED AS SHE
stood in the back doorway of the butler's pantry and
watched the rain puddle in the yard. Of all the stupid,
ridiculous things . . . Obviously these people didn't have
enough responsibilities to keep them productively occu-
pied. And of course it never occurred to them that she did
and that planning a costume ball for their distraction might
just be a bit more than she wanted to deal with. More, she
silently snarled, than *with which* she wanted to deal.

A good hostess grants her guests' every wish.

Well, she hadn't been able to pull a scandalous trial out
of a hat for them four days ago. And she'd been trying to
part the clouds and stop the rain—and their whining—for
the last two. God, what she wouldn't give to have them all
wish to go home. That she'd happily see make happen before the hour was out. But, since there was still food and
liquor in the house, the odds were they weren't going anywhere else anytime soon and that she was going to have
to make the best of it. And beg the exhausted, harried staff
to do the same.

Winfield and Mrs. Gladder had taken the news rather
well, considering; Mrs. Gladder managing a weak smile

and a weary assurance that it would be a lovely occasion, and Winfield turning a bit pale, rocking back on his heels, and somehow not swearing. She'd left them after that, thinking that they probably would prefer to cry in private.

Now, five minutes later, she eyed the kitchen and regretted her offer to inform Cook and the kitchen staff that, in addition to the already constant work of feeding the army encamped at Ryland Castle, a banquet feast loomed on their horizon. If they didn't attack her with their cleavers, she'd be extremely lucky. Or not, depending on how she looked at it. People who were dead or seriously maimed were allowed to beg off planning stupid parties.

So did people who couldn't be found, she decided, her gaze going to the stable. No one was out riding in the rain. And the stable boys were over in the conservatory, helping Mr. Henry as they always did on days when no one was riding. Just her and the horses and a blessed, desperately needed stretch of solitude. Gathering her skirts, she lifted her hems above her ankles and dashed across the open space.

She was soaked to the skin and chilled by the time she reached the doors and slipped inside. The warmth and the earthy scents swirled around her in an instant. She smiled down at the tendrils of steam rising from the sleeve of her dress.

"Hello."

She turned, her heart dancing, to find Drayton leaning back against the wheel of a carriage, his booted ankles crossed and his arms folded across his chest. No jacket, no tie, the neck of his white shirt open just enough that she could see a few crisp dark hairs.

Solitude wasn't all that wonderful, she decided, moving toward him. And certainly not the only thing that could calm her spirit. "What are you doing here?" she asked.

He grinned and opened his arms for her. "Hiding. What are you doing here?"

She stepped into them, twined her arms around his neck, and smiled up at him. "Hiding with you."

"You looked decidedly frustrated when you came in."

Well, that was then. Things had improved considerably in the moments since. "If I hear the words 'ladies do not' and 'a good hostess always' one more time, I'll scream."

"Is there anything that ladies are allowed to do?"

Oh, when he smiled that crooked little smile of his . . . Threading her fingers through the hair at his nape, she happily replied, "What very few things I'm permitted to do are hideously close to tortures. Do you know that Lady Aubrey actually made me walk about the upstairs hall for thirty minutes this morning with a book balanced on my head?"

"It must have been painful."

No, it had been a little thing that had slipped off at the slightest wobble, but if he thought she'd been in pain . . . "And she finds my dress designs far too unconventional to be even marginally acceptable."

"I hope you're drawing the line with her right there and holding it."

"I hate my life." She grinned. "Well, most of it, anyway."

"You just dislike having restrictions placed on you."

"Dislike?" She arched a brow. "I passed dislike at noon three days ago. I have since progressed into full-blown resentment."

"It'll be all right, Caroline. I promise."

"No it won't," she countered, reveling in her pessimism. "I swear to God, I'm going to run off with the first eligible bachelor I can find in London. Just to escape her."

"Don't do that," he asked, planting a little kiss on the end of her nose. "If she's that bad, I'll send her and her legions packing."

"She's trying to be helpful," she admitted, feeling a bit guilty for her criticisms. "In her own, tightly corseted way."

Drayton shook his head and drawled, "No, go back to hating her. It's nice to have you loathe someone more than me."

She laughed and tugged at his hair. "I don't loathe you."

"Really?" His smile curved upward. "Damn. I was looking forward to that."

"I know you were," she teased. "That's why I decided to go back to simply not loving you."

His eyes sparkled and his smile went wide and wicked. "I'll take that. I have very fond memories of being callously, selfishly used by you."

"And you'd gladly let me use you so again. Right this very moment if I want."

"I can make you forget all about being frustrated and resentful."

Oh, yes, he could indeed. He could make her forget the world beyond them even existed.

"Oh, darling Caroline," he murmured, angling his head to the side. "Do I see a flicker of temptation in those lovely blue eyes of yours?"

"Lady Aubrey says they're nondescript."

"What does she know?" he asked, shifting his stance to draw her closer against him.

"She says that my mouth is too large."

"I know for a fact that it's just the right size."

"And that my breasts are too small," she added, feeling her nipples tighten and her breasts strain against the thin lawn of her corset.

"Anything more than a handful is a waste."

"She says that I'm unremarkable in every way and that it will take a miracle for any man to notice me among the potted palms."

He cocked a brow and slowly ran his hands down over her backside. "Really," he murmured, his eyes darkening as he settled her hips against his. "Let me assure you, darling Caroline, that Lady Aubrey doesn't know a damn thing about what men find attractive."

His need pressed hard into the pillow of her abdomen, her body quivering in anticipation, she smiled up at him. "You bring out the absolute worst in me, Drayton."

"I hope you're not expecting me to apologize for it."

"No, I'm not hoping for that at all."

"What are you hoping for, Caroline?"

She slipped her hands down over his shoulders and in across the broad planes of his chest. Opening a button of his shirt, she said, "That you don't have anywhere to be for the next seven minutes. And that you have a fantasy about a carriage, too."

"Oh, yes," he murmured, taking her hands from his shirtfront and drawing her along to the carriage door. "Allow me to assist you inside, Lady Caroline."

DRAYTON SMILED. GOD, SHE HAD INCREDIBLY GOOD FANtasies. Of course, when he could feel anything other than intensely drugged satisfaction, it was likely to be a neck crick and leg cramps. Thinking to shift a bit to prevent it, he forced his eyes open. And promptly forgot all about the prospect of pain.

Straddling his hips, her skirt rucked up to her waist and her bodice and corset opened and spread wide, she leaned back against the wall of his legs with her eyes closed and her lips curved in the sweetest, sated smile. She was . . . His mind stumbled through the words, trying to separate them from swirling emotion. Magnificent, yes. And breathtaking. Delicious, bold, exquisitely intuitive. Everything. And his.

Yes, his. He reached up to stroke the pads of his thumbs over the taut peaks of her breasts. Only his. For as long as he could keep her. And damn the selfishness of it, damn the possibility of scandal. He didn't care.

"I think," she murmured dreamily, covering his hands with hers and pressing them hard against her breasts, "that our seven minutes are gone."

"A good half hour ago." And it was going to be another half hour before he let her go for even a short while. He shifted his hips beneath her, thrusting upward and quickening the return of his erection.

She sat up, and still holding his hands over her breasts, rotated her hips to draw him deeper as she softly whispered, "People are probably out looking for us."

"They can wait another seven minutes," he declared. Rolling her over onto her back, he gently pinned her hands over her head, bent his head and slowly dragged his tongue over the hardened, tender peak of her breast. "They can wait forever."

SOMETHING WAS DIFFERENT. SOMETHING HAD CHANGED. She could feel it in the silence hanging between them as she tied off her corset ribbon. Something that made the satisfaction deeper, more complete. And, well, heavier, too. She glanced over at him while she buttoned her dress front, hoping to see a hint of it in his eyes. And found only a wickedly handsome, half-dressed man reclining into the corner of the carriage, his eyes closed and his expression far away. Deciding that she was the only one aware of the new current, she bent down and retrieved her shoes.

"Caroline?"

She looked over at him, but his eyes remained closed as he went on, saying quietly, "I don't love you, but I will admit, quite readily, that I do love having sex with you. You are the most incredible woman I've ever known."

I don't love you. Her heart aching, she forced herself to smile as broadly as she could and say breezily, "Thank you. I find you rather appealing, too. In a casual but intensely physical sort of way. It's going to be very difficult to find another lover who's as good at pleasing me as you are."

He cleared his throat, sat up, and reached for his boot, saying, "I'm sure you'll inspire him to all new heights of manly performance."

She didn't want to inspire anyone but him. "I'm selfish enough about my pleasure to hope so," she said, keeping her secret. "Thank you, Drayton," she added, opening the carriage door and letting herself out while she still had the composure to maintain the façade. "I feel infinitely less frustrated now."

He nodded and she blew him a kiss, then turned, gathered her skirts into her trembling fists, and summoned every last shred of her strength to walk calmly away.

"GLAD ONE OF US ISN'T FRIGGING FRUSTRATED," HE growled, sagging back into the corner of the carriage and staring blankly at the roof. *"In a casual but intensely physical sort of way."* Goddammit, there wasn't anything casual in how he felt about her. Not anymore.

No, he didn't love her. He'd been honest about that. But she *was* the most incredible woman he'd ever met. She was intelligent and funny and irreverent. She whirled through life, confident that she could do anything, make everything around her perfect and right. And she could. With amazing poise and competence and ease. He respected her honesty and her integrity. He trusted her judgment. He was, when it came down to the fundamental truth of it all, in awe of her. And the sex was damn good, too.

"And I'm not sharing her," he growled, setting himself in motion. Snatching his boot up from the floor, he rammed his foot into it and threw himself out the open door so that he could put his clothes on straight. She'd go looking for another lover when hell froze over and not one day before, he vowed, yanking up his trousers and ramming his shirttail in.

"In a casual but intensely physical sort of way." Casual, he silently snarled, buttoning up. That made him the only goddamn thing in her life that she considered—

He blinked and looked past the haze of his anger. And silently swore. "Aubrey," he gritted out as his mind raced through what might pass for believable explanations.

"Yes," his friend said, leaning back against the wheel of the carriage and staring off toward the end of the stable. "I saw Lady Caroline leave a few moments ago. Fixing her hairpins as she went back to the house. Not that her effort was disguising much."

All right, so they'd been caught. It wasn't the end of the world. Aubrey had had his fair share of dalliances. "I trust that you'll be discreet about it."

"I'll hold my tongue. But it's only a matter of time

before it's someone else who catches the two of you together." He turned his head to meet Drayton's gaze. "Or haven't you noticed that your house is teeming with people who have far too much time on their hands and no particular loyalty to you?"

Drayton crossed his arms and leaned his shoulder against the stable wall. "I sense a lecture barreling my way."

"You've made a lecture pointless," Aubrey countered, turning to face him squarely. "I'm afraid that what you sense bearing down on you is an ultimatum."

"Oh?" *This should be interesting.*

"You've crossed the line with one ward, Drayton," his friend said, sounding genuinely regretful. "How long do you think it will take for the story of your affair with Lady Caroline to be transformed into one of an affair with Lady Simone or one with Lady Fiona?"

"Oh, please, Aubrey," he said, coming off the wall and heading for the stable door. "That's beyond ludicrous."

"As you and I both know," Aubrey said firmly, stepping into his path. "But what matters is that it's not beyond people to tell the tale as though they'd seen the debauchery with their own eyes."

The bastards. "Then we'll give them something else to talk about," he snarled. "Caroline and I will just run off to Gretna Green and be done with it. Now get out of my way."

Aubrey didn't budge. "Would it be too much to ask that you use just a bit of common sense in the situation?"

"Marrying her solves the problem." *So would killing you.* "How much more common sense is necessary? Move."

"Yes, it does solve the immediate problem," Aubrey allowed, standing his ground. "I will concede that. But I do ask that you think about the longer-term consequences."

"God," he groaned, throwing his head back. "Don't tell me that I'm going to have to hear another homage to the importance of money."

"It would be a waste of breath. You have absolutely no respect for wealth."

All right, he'd let Aubrey make his goddamn point and then he'd tell him one more time to get out of the way and let him pass. If he didn't, he'd knock him on his ass and step over him. "So what is it that you'd like me to take into consideration?"

"Do you love Lady Caroline?"

Jesus. He hadn't been expecting that question at all.

"Or is it more a matter of loving the risk in having an illicit affair with her?"

"Well, that's no small factor in it," he admitted. "As for loving her . . ." He shrugged. "I think that perhaps, in time, we could grow into love."

"Or perhaps you couldn't. Do you want to be shackled for the rest of your life to a woman you don't love?"

Drayton tilted his head to the side, amazed that Aubrey would even think to argue from that standpoint. "Have you not noticed the general quality of the marriages in temporary residence at my house?" he asked. "It seems to me that no one marries for love."

"No, they don't," he answered. "They marry, for the most part, for money."

And here they were, as always, back to the power of the almighty British pound. "You said you'd be wasting your breath."

"Look, Drayton, you're a good friend," Aubrey said on a sigh. He went back to his regretful approach when he added, "If you loved Lady Caroline, if you firmly believed that it would stand the test of time, then I'd step aside and wish the two of you only happiness and the best of life. But you've admitted that you don't, and so I can't let you make a huge mistake without trying to prevent it."

He wouldn't be talking marriage at all if Aubrey had just agreed at the beginning of the conversation to keep his frigging mouth shut.

"Glower at me all you like," the other said. "It doesn't change the basic facts of your situation. If there's no love involved in the decision, you'd be a damn fool to marry without getting all the money and prestige you can for the sacrifice."

"It's mercenary."

"It's realistic," Aubrey shot back. "And marrying Lady Caroline is not only an easy way out of you having to play the marriage market game, but highly unfair to her."

"Unfair?"

"Good God, man," the other retorted, flinging his hands up in clear exasperation. "The woman is the daughter of a duke! And not at all unattractive!" He raked his fingers through his hair and drew a deep breath before he added more calmly, "Somewhere on the Continent, Drayton, there's a prince who's going to come to London for the Season, see her, and think that she'd be the perfect queen for his little kingdom. Not to disparage your high rank and all that, but you really can't match that sort of offering."

Oh, God. He hadn't thought of that. In his mind's eye he'd always pictured men like Aubrey and Haywood courting her. Men she'd treat kindly, but never take seriously. But a prince who could offer her a kingdom, a fairy-tale life . . . "It's her decision," he said even as his heart told him that she deserved to be a queen.

"As I fully understand," Aubrey allowed quietly. "But don't you think that she'd be better able to consider the merits of every proposal if she isn't sleeping in your bed when she receives them?"

The world under his feet sagged and turned to mush. It took every dram of his resolve to keep his balance. Two futures unfolded before his eyes and it took every battered strand of his self-control to hold back the cry as he faced the only one he could choose.

"All right, Drayton. Here's what we're going to do," Aubrey said. "We're going to pack our bags and retire to London. Tell everyone that the Mayfair house needs repairs that you have to oversee. Or that you have to prepare for the opening of Parliament. Either excuse will suffice. The important thing is that you're going to end the possibility for scandal and let matters between you and Lady Caroline die so that both of you can make decisions with unclouded vision."

God, he ached. To the center of his bones, to the cold hollow of his soul. "And if I don't fall into line?" he asked, knowing that he was going to, that it was the only kind and fair thing to do for the sake of Caroline's future happiness.

"I don't know," Aubrey said glumly. "I guess somehow prepare Mother for the fact that her son is going down in infamy as the loyal and stalwart friend of England's greatest pervert."

The *H.M.S. Aubrey* would roll over on her keel. But not before she'd formally disowned her pilot boat. "The stable boys are in the conservatory today," Drayton said, leaning back against the carriage, his body suddenly leaden. "Go fetch one of them to get a coach ready for us."

"Thank you, Drayton."

He nodded. "There may come a day when I can thank you, Aubrey. It's just not today."

"I understand. I'll be back shortly."

No. No, Aubrey didn't understand. Drayton wasn't even sure himself how deep the wound went, how long it would take for the emptiness to fill and and the aching to fade. He'd never in his life felt this way. It was nothing like the pain that had come with his parents' passings. There had been a naturalness to those good-byes, a sense of having traveled all the road with them that had been destined. This . . . His throat tightening, he swallowed hard and expelled a long, slow, steadying breath. He'd get through it. He'd do the right thing even if it killed him. He'd make a clean, swift, merciful break and not look back.

LADY AUBREY LOOKED DOWN AT THE NOTES CAROLINE was dutifully making. "What about congealed eel? That is always popular."

With whom? Caroline silently asked, her stomach roiling as she wrote it down on the menu.

"Lady Caroline? Might I speak with you privately for a moment?"

Drayton? In the house in the middle of the afternoon? Her heart skittering, she looked over to the parlor door. Yes, Drayton. Dressed in a dark suit, a greatcoat draped over his arm, a hat in his hand. Her stomach clenched. Oh, God. Something was wrong. She could hear the tightness in his voice, see the tension in the hard line of his shoulders and the width of his stance.

"I'm afraid not, Lord Ryland," Mother Aubrey answered even as Caroline gained her feet. "The rules of propriety, you understand. Lady Caroline's reputation must be protected."

"Thank you for the reminder, Lady Aubrey," he said, bowing slightly to the matron. "We'll stay well within your sight."

"I can see that you're dressed for going out," Caroline said softly as they walked together into the foyer. "Is there a problem in the village?"

He shook his head slowly and waited until they reached the center table before saying, "We've been caught, Caroline."

No. Oh, no, no. This can't be happening. Stop talking to the wall. Look at me, Drayton.

Ignoring her silent pleas, he kept his gaze firmly fixed on the plaster between two of the potted fig trees. "Aubrey's delivered an ultimatum as only Aubreys seem able to do. And since, as much as it pains me to admit it, he's right, I'm leaving for London as soon as my bags are put in the carriage."

She could do this; the only other choice was to lie down and die. She forced herself to breathe and willed a wholly false calm into her voice to ask, "How long will you be gone?"

He hesitated, raked his lower lip with his teeth, and then flatly replied, "When you and your sisters come back to the city for the Season, you'll take up residence at Lady Aubrey's town house."

Her heart tearing, tears clawing at her throat, she could only whisper, "So we're done."

"We both know that it's for the best."

"And we've always known that this day would come sooner or later," she added as she was supposed to, as a blessed numbness crept slowly through her. "Have you said your farewells to Simone and Fiona?"

"Yes." He cleared his throat and lifted his chin a notch higher. "Fiona cried. Simone . . . Well, let's just say that she dubiously broadened her little sister's vocabulary and leave it at that."

"She's young," she offered in her sister's defense. "She doesn't understand how one must do the sensible thing regardless of how difficult it may be."

"Precisely. We found ourselves unexpectedly thrown into a world neither one of us finds particularly comfortable and—"

"Found comfort in each other," Caroline supplied quietly, vaguely troubled by the absence of clear memories. Were they gone forever? Wiped away like the sums on a schoolroom slate? Or were they simply floating out there somewhere in the graying edges of the foyer?

He nodded ever so slightly and cleared his throat again. "Now it's time that we accept where we are, who we are, and do what's expected of us. I appreciate all that you've done—are doing—to improve my standing."

"As I appreciate your concern for my reputation," she lied. How easily it had slipped off her tongue. How sincere it sounded. A new talent.

"The men will line up around the block once you get to London. You'll have your pick."

I've already picked. And been denied.

"But, in the event that none of the men are to your liking . . ."

She stared at the leather folio in her hand, dully wondering how it had gotten there and oddly intrigued by the fact that she couldn't feel it.

"We made a bargain that first day," she heard him say as though from a great distance. "I would see your business settled fairly and have a document drawn up allowing you access to your dowry portion if you choose not to wed. In exchange, you would accompany me and fulfill the terms of Lady Ryland's will. You kept your end of the bargain, and now I've kept mine."

It had been nothing more than a bargain to him? An exchange of services. A contract made and kept. How very foolish she'd been to let it become more to her than that. She should have known better.

"The money from the settlement of your business is yours regardless of your decision on marriage. It's been placed on account in both our names with my signature required for you to gain access. I didn't want it to be possible for a husband to take what's rightfully yours. If you ever have need of the funds for yourself, for your dreams, I'll sign at your request."

Ah, dreams. No, she'd never do that again. Losing them hurt too much. Slowly, thickly, she realized that there was silence hanging between them. Had he said something? Was he waiting for a reply? "Good-bye, Lord Ryland," she said, hoping it was what he expected to hear.

"Good-bye, Lady Caroline."

She didn't see him walk away, she felt it. A cold emptiness unfolded in her soul, growing larger with every step he took, pushing back and walling away all other feelings. At the click of the door latch it crystalized, hard and impenetrable. Deep inside her, tears welled and froze. Wave after wave of them rose and surged, each piling hard against the one before. Her chest tightening, the pain growing with every ragged beat of her heart, she put the folio on the table, turned and moved toward the stairs while her legs could still hold her.

"Lady Caroline, we were planning the menu for tomorrow evening."

"Serve whatever you like," she said, gathering her skirts, fixing her gaze on the upstairs landing, and starting up.

"It is your responsibility to decide."

"I've decided that I'd very much like everyone to go

somewhere else for dinner. Preferably on their way to live in someone else's house."

"A good hostess does not ask guests to leave. It would be incredibly ill-mannered to even hint that they'd outstayed their welcome."

A good hostess. Ladies do not.

"Lady Caroline!"

Ladies do not stride, they glide. Ladies do not laugh, they titter. Ladies do not cry, they sniffle. Ladies do not cry. Ladies do not cry.

"Good afternoon, madam."

Ladies do not ask, they instruct. "Lock the door, Dora," she said, standing in the center of her room, not quite remembering how she'd gotten there. "Don't let anyone in. If Lady Aubrey wants to know where I am, tell her I've died."

"I can't say that, madam!"

Caroline wrapped her arms around her midriff and closed her eyes. "Then tell her I'm not feeling well and don't want to be disturbed."

"Shall I summon a physician?"

"It's nothing a physician can fix," Caroline said softly, wishing that a simple balm or poultice could ease the horrible ache in her soul. "I need to be alone for a while. I'll be fine in time, Dora."

"Are you sure, madam?"

No, not at all. "Yes. Thank you for being concerned."

"I'll be in my apartment. If you need anything, ring and I'll come."

Caroline nodded and listened to Dora slip away. In the silence there was only cold emptiness, her frozen sea of tears, and the tiny voice of hope whispering, *maybe*. She turned and walked through the sitting rooms and into Drayton's.

The fire was banked in the hearth, the bed made, the draperies drawn back from the windows to admit the golden autumn light. She crossed to the armoire and opened it. Then stepped to the bureau, pulled open the drawers one by one, then went into his bathing and dressing rooms.

In the end, she stood at the side of his bed, straining to hear the whisper of hope again. It refused to offer her anything more, refused to deny the truth. It was over. Forever and always done. Drayton was gone. He'd taken all of his things with him, leaving her nothing to hold, nothing to remember, nothing to wrap the fragile wisps of her hope around.

She reached down and smoothed a wrinkle from the coverlet. Then up to adjust the edge of the sham covering a pillow. Drayton's pillow. On Drayton's bed.

Maybe . . .

She slid onto his bed, covering his place in it, gathering his pillow into her arms and holding it close, pretending it was him, willing him to come back to her. "Please," she murmured, pressing her face into the pillow. "Please, Dray—"

The scent of him poured through her and struck her to the core, shattering the icy walls containing her pain. Choking on the surging tide of tears, she buried her face deeper in his pillow and sobbed as the memories flooded back.

I don't love you.

❧ *Nineteen* ❧

THE JANGLE OF KEYS? CAROLINE TORE HER GAZE FROM the flames dancing in her bedroom hearth and turned her head in the direction of the sound. Yes, it was Mrs. Gladder. Moving from the door to the window on the opposite wall. "I instructed Dora that no one was to be admitted."

"So she said." She threw the curtains wide in one smooth, ruthless movement.

Caroline flung her forearm over her eyes, shielding them from the intense sudden brightness. "I don't want the draperies pulled back."

"And I don't want to trip over the furniture."

It sounded as though . . . Caroline drew her arm back just enough to peer out through squinted eyes. Yes, Mrs. Gladder had dropped down into the facing chair and was studying her across the tea service. Her eyebrows were knitted and her mouth was pulled to one side as if she wanted to smile and frown at the same time. Caroline covered her eyes again. "I didn't give you permission to sit," she said, trying to deflect the approaching lecture.

"My dear girl, one begins as one means to go on, and it's far too late for you to decide to be a duchess with me. And while I will publicly defer to you as befits your rank, in private you and I will speak just as frankly about all matters as we do the making of draperies and the painting and papering of walls."

So much for the imperial approach. "I don't want to talk at all."

"What *do* you want to do?"

Be miserable and die. Alone.

"A point of information for you as you sit there and contemplate . . . No ones dies of a broken heart."

How did she know what she'd been thinking? Caroline lifted her arm and peered at her again.

"Oh, yes," Mrs. Gladder said, rolling her eyes. "It's such a wonderfully tragic way to achieve revenge. But the truth is that only fragile, delicate little girls have hearts weak enough to be at risk. *If* they had the fortitude to fall in love to begin with. Which they don't. And on the chance that no one has ever said so, allow me to be the first to inform you that you are not any more a little girl than you are either fragile or delicate."

The suspicion of which had flitted through her disappointment just a while ago when she'd found herself still alive as the sun had come up again. She let her arm fall into her lap. "I'm not as strong as you think I am."

"If you're feeling weak, it's largely because you haven't eaten anything in the last four days."

Well, that was probably true. Still . . . "I'm not hungry."

Mrs. Gladder sighed softly, studied her for a few moments, and then said firmly, "Lady Caroline, men have been incredibly stupid and done magnificently stupid things since the dawn of time. It is simply part of their natures. It is part of our natures to watch their follies, clean up the debris left in their wake, and decide whether we want to accept their apologies when they finally realize what complete oafs they've been."

"Some of them never realize they've been oafs," she countered. "And some of them would choke to death on an apology."

"Would you put Lord Ryland in either of those categories?"

Drayton was certainly capable of reflection. And expressing his regrets. Both of which had been evidenced the morning they'd stopped along their way to Ryland Castle and he'd asked her to marry him. If only she hadn't been so quick to be rational. "No," she admitted. "But then, he doesn't think he's done anything at all stupid this time. He thinks he's being incredibly noble and protective."

"Trust me, my dear," the housekeeper said, arching a brow and smiling. "If he's been sleeping alone for the last three nights, his sense of nobility and gallantry is crumbling by the second."

She *knew*?

"Oh, for heaven's sake, Lady Caroline," Mrs. Gladder said, shaking her head. "Haven't you ever wondered why you and Lord Ryland found so many opportunities to be alone and undisturbed?"

"It wasn't just good timing?"

"The entire staff has worked very hard to ensure that love had every chance to grow and bloom."

The entire staff knew? Oh, God. Caroline swallowed down her mortification and managed a tight smile. "Not that it worked out very well, but I appreciate the effort."

"One of the other natural traits of women is our ability to exercise patience," Mrs. Gladder went on. "It's God's way of ensuring that enough males survive to continue the human race. Lord Ryland will come to his senses. It may take a while, but he will."

So *she* said. "And if he doesn't?" she countered peevishly.

"One day, one hurdle at a time, Lady Caroline. The task of the moment is for you to pick yourself up, dust yourself off, and get back to living your life. Your house is full of unruly guests and—"

"Unruly?"

"Last night Lady Gregory organized a Tribute to Norway evening. Lord Henden pretended to be a reindeer and gave sleigh rides on upturned ottomans, ending in the foyer where everyone spent the better part of two hours bobsledding down the central staircase on silver trays."

Caroline snapped her jaw closed and swallowed. "You're joking."

"It would have gone on all night if Lord Vernon hadn't borrowed a couple of neckcloths, tied trays to his feet and attempted to ski down."

Oh, no. "Was he badly injured?"

"Frankly, I couldn't tell whether he'd been knocked unconscious or finally been overcome by all the whiskey he'd consumed. In either case, the Tribute to Norway was immediately reorganized into Rescue in the Alps with Lord Henden playing the part of the St. Bernard. As a point of information, not a one of them can decently yodel."

"Dear God." They'd all gone insane.

"All of which is a minor concern," Mrs. Gladder assured her crisply. "Of greater importance is the fact that your sisters are a bit worried that you've contracted some dread disease and are going to die before the week is out."

"No!" Oh, God, she hadn't been thinking of anyone but herself!

"I've assured them otherwise. As have Mrs. Miller and Dora. Lady Aubrey, however, contends that Lady Fiona's crow has given you a vicious flesh-eating parasite."

Of course. Her irritation surprisingly strong after having lain dormant for days, Caroline snapped, "She's such a brick."

"I tend to agree with you."

"Where was she when all of the Norway nonsense was going on?"

"She retired to her room with a headache immediately after supper."

"Headache, my Aunt Fanny. She let them run amok in the hope it would drive me out to put an end to it. Where was Haywood during it all?"

"He was entertaining Lady Vernon in the library. But all of that is beside the point," Mrs. Gladder countered gently. "The point is that it's time for you to pack your understandable heartache into a trunk and take control of Ryland Castle and the people in it."

"I suppose you're right," Caroline agreed with a sigh. "Even if it's just for Simone's and Fiona's sakes."

Mrs. Gladder gave her another of her half-frowning smiles. "It's not quite the resounding commitment I was hoping to hear, but it's better than nothing. If it helps any to know . . . There's power to be had in having men come crawling home to discover that they haven't been missed."

Caroline snorted. "Dukes do *not* crawl."

"Well, then it's probably a good thing that he's not much better at being a duke than you are at being a duchess."

Well, that was true. In part, she amended as she remembered the morning he'd walked into her life. "Oh, but when he puts his mind to it," she replied, her irritation surging back, "he can be . . ." The memory of his leaving struck her. But this time, unlike every time it had since that afternoon, it didn't send her reeling into tears and utter misery. She drew a long slow breath as the realization settled in her brain.

"Yes?" Mrs. Gladder quietly pressed.

"Insufferable."

"Which is simply stupidity," the housekeeper pointed out, "with a particularly irritating, pompous edge."

"Drayton's being a duke," Caroline said, sitting forward in her chair, her mind turning over everything he'd said as he'd closed the door on their affair. "I can't believe this. Of all the thickheaded—"

"Tea?"

"Yes, please. If he thinks he's going to get away with this, he really does need to be informed otherwise. Are those lemon biscuits?"

"Yes," the housekeeper replied, putting three on the saucer before handing it to her. "This batch is especially good," she added, taking one for herself.

Caroline washed the delicious cookies down with solid drinks of wonderfully hot tea as she considered what to do. Going to London, grabbing him by the lapels, and shaking him until his teeth rattled had a great deal of appeal. As did simply walking into his bedroom, dropping her nightgown, and letting him apologize in the sweet haze of satisfaction.

Of course that whole plan depended on walking in and finding that some other woman hadn't dropped her nightgown first. Everything changed if Drayton had decided to play the duke as a way of ending a relationship that was growing more complicated or restrictive than he wanted. Maybe the change she'd sensed in the carriage had been his having reached the decision to end their affair and go looking for another.

Of course, if he hadn't been thinking that at all and was simply having another bout of feeling ridiculously noble . . . He'd certainly seemed happy when they'd been together in the stable. And all the days before then, too. Were men prone to changing their minds in a single second? Did they go from contented to desperate to escape in the blink of an eye?

"More tea and biscuits?"

Caroline nodded, handed back her cup and saucer, and decided that she needed an outside, objective viewpoint. "Do you think he loves me?"

"Yes," Mrs. Gladder instantly replied. "But whether he knows it or not is another matter," she added, dashing Caroline's elation. "Do you love him enough to wait for him to figure it out?"

"What if he never does?" she posed, frustrated. "What if he's old and withered and lying on his deathbed before he smacks himself on the forehead and says, '*By George, I love Caroline*'?"

Mrs. Gladder chuckled and handed the teacup back, saying, "It is nice to have you back, madam."

"You didn't answer my question, Mrs. Gladder. What if he never realizes it?"

"One day, one hurdle at a time, Lady Caroline," she answered, rising from the chair. "There will be a crossroads. There always is. When and why, we can't tell in advance. But you'll know it when you get there, and the course of action will be clear. In the meantime, there's

nothing to be done except live life as normally and fully
as possible."

"Thank you, Mrs. Gladder."

She grinned and headed for the door, saying, "A housekeeper's work is never done."

Apparently the daughter of a duke wasn't allowed a
respite, either. She had to bring the guests under some
sort of control before they reduced Ryland Castle to rubble, and she also needed to reassure her sisters that she
wasn't going to die anytime soon—all without trying to
worry about what she was going to do if Mrs. Gladder was
wrong about Drayton and the likelihood of a natural solution presenting itself. Maybe, if she was really lucky,
Drayton was already on his way back, an apology in
hand, and life would be perfect again before supper.

HIS HEAD THICK AND POUNDING, DRAYTON CROSSED HIS
arms over his chest and considered the wall of his study.
Or, more accurately, what was left of it. As holes and
piles of debris went, it was pretty impressive and clearly
not something he'd dreamed. No, apparently he had actually picked up the madeira decanter and pitched it as hard
as he could at the portrait of dear ol' cousin Geoffrey.
And, judging by the headless painting pitched off to the
side, hit it dead on. An amazing bit of accuracy considering how drunk he'd been.

He glanced over at the buffet and then back to the
holes and the soggy plaster and general wreckage on the
floor and furniture beneath it. Yes, there were the shat-
tered bits of the brandy decanter. And those of the one
that had held the gin. The port and whiskey and rye decanters were there, too. And the sherry. That had been the
last one to go, as he recalled. The one he'd launched while

telling himself that there wasn't any point to keeping sherry around if Caroline wasn't going to be there to drink it. After that, he'd thrown anything that hadn't been nailed down, until his arm had gotten so tired that he'd stumbled upstairs, promising himself that he'd start back up again as soon as it was rested.

He rolled his right shoulder and used his hand to massage the sore muscles as he slowly shook his head and decided that last night was as low as he really could allow himself to go, that two weeks in an alcohol-induced stupor was sufficient. He smiled ruefully. Not that he had anything left to drink even if it wasn't.

"Lord Aubrey, sir."

But, he amended, scrubbing his fingers through his aching hair as Aubrey came into the room, if the man intended to stay and press more position papers on him, he could send one of the servants out for more. There was no such thing as being too foggy when Aubrey was around.

"What's this?"

"My attempt at redecorating. Are you impressed?"

"Oh. Not the wall. This."

Drayton looked over his shoulder to find Aubrey standing at the desk, a familiar piece of heavy parchment in his hand. "An invitation," Drayton replied.

"I can see that."

"Then you can probably also see that it's from Lord Gladstone and that he's asked me to join him grouse hunting this weekend."

"Are you going?"

Well, since the moment had to come sooner or later . . . "Yes."

Aubrey tossed it back down on the blotter. "Good God, why?"

"I'd like to hear the Liberal position on issues."

"Why?"

"Why not?" he countered, dropping unceremoniously into one of the pair of leather wingbacks in front of the crackling hearth.

"As a duke," Aubrey countered, lowering himself into the other one, "the Liberals' policies are not in your personal financial interests."

"Whose interests do they champion?"

"Largely everyone's except those of the titled and the very wealthy."

"Isn't that what Parliament is supposed to do?" Drayton asked, trying very hard to keep the sarcasm out of his voice. "Act for the betterment of the majority of Englishmen?"

"You are a reformer?"

"I have no idea," he admitted with a shrug of his sore shoulder. He went back to massaging it, as he added, "But I do know right from wrong and that's how I'm going to decide my vote on issues that come to the House of Lords. I don't care which party it pleases or displeases."

"If you vote consistently Liberal, you'll regret it socially. You'll be largely cut out."

As will those around me, which is what you're really worried about. "And why would I want to socialize with people whose primary concern is not fairness, but their own self-interest?"

"It's not what they believe or do, it's what they are . . . titled. And whether you like it or not, you're one of them."

He considered how honest he wanted to be and decided that since it was a morning—no, late afternoon—of new beginnings, that he might as well start with all of his slates clean. "Having a title to flaunt would seem to be the only thing we have in common," he replied. "Beyond that . . . No, Aubrey, I'm not one of the divinely chosen. I'm a duke purely because Dinky couldn't put on a façade long enough to get an heir."

"I think perhaps it would be better if we continued this conversation when you've been sober for longer than an hour."

"Aubrey, make a note," he said kindly but firmly. "I'm not willing to surrender my conscience, my sense of right, and human decency under any circumstances—drunk, hungover, or sober." He gave his friend a couple of moments to mull the pronouncement before he added, "And make another note while you're at it. We can either agree to disagree at this point and let politics be a subject we don't discuss, or we can cry quits on our friendship."

"Politics is important, Drayton."

So much for hoping Aubrey would choose the easy way out for both of them. "As I'm coming to understand," Drayton said, slowly nodding. "I'm also coming to understand that a man's politics is the truest reflection of who he is. His stances on ideas and policies tell you everything you need to know about the depth of his character and his capacity for empathy. Whether he'll give you the shirt off his back or slit your throat for your shoes."

"If you think that society expects, much less rewards, integrity in its politicians, you're incredibly naïve."

Drayton drew a slow, deliberate breath and unclenched his teeth to ask, "That makes it acceptable to act only in self-interest?"

"And the interests of one's friends and social class in general. Of course, one shouldn't be flagrant about it."

Drayton stared at him as astonishment gave way to momentary disbelief and then slid into a roiling mixture of disgust and outrage. The self-serving shallow son of a bitch. And Aubrey actually thought he should be one, too. Drayton gripped the arms of his chair as part of his brain suggested that there'd be a great deal of satisfaction in beating the hell out of him, and the other half insisted that he wasn't worth the effort or the split knuckles.

"Pardon the intrusion, your grace."

"Don't apologize, Banks," he said as he pushed himself to his feet. "You've just saved Lord Aubrey's nose."

As Aubrey rose and casually put the chair between them, the butler cleared his throat and went on with his duty, saying, "There is a Miss Jane Durbin at the door. She says that you know her and would be willing to receive her."

Jane? His heartbeat quickened even as he told himself that if something horrible had happened, Jane would have said so at the door. Or just given Caroline's note to the butler. "Please show her in, Banks."

"Very good, sir."

"You know," Aubrey said caustically, "it might do you a world of good to let her . . . distract you."

"If you want to leave here with your teeth, Aubrey," he quietly warned as his anger sparked hotter, "keep your mouth shut."

The damn fool started to reply, but Jane—dressed in wildly bright purple—sailed across the threshold just in time to cut him off and save his sorry, undeserving ass. "Good afternoon, Miss Durbin," Drayton said, forcing himself to put his anger aside for the time being. "This is a pleasant surprise."

"Lord Ryland," she said, stopping a good arm's length away and dropping him a quick curtsy. "Lord Aubrey," she said, giving him a mere nod.

"What's brought you to back to London?" Drayton

asked. "Surely Caroline hasn't found another room in need of redecorating."

"Actually she's redecorating, your grace."

"Already?"

Jane winced slightly. "Perhaps the better term would be 'repairing.'"

"I assume," he drawled, mentally bracing himself, "that you're going to explain?"

"Several ottomans were torn during the reindeer rides on Tribute to Norway night and have to be reupholstered," she supplied.

Reindeer rides?

"And, a few nights after that, one of Lord Ablin's magic tricks didn't go quite as he'd hoped. Apparently he mixed together two powders he shouldn't have and when he added the water to his hat . . . Well, he's lucky to still have both of his hands. His eyebrows will grow back eventually. The parlor ceiling plaster is already repaired, but the furniture under that part of the room has to be reupholstered, too. And then—"

"Is Ryland Castle still standing?" he interrupted.

"It was when I left yesterday afternoon, your lordship."

Well, there was good news. As long as he knew that this wasn't going to end badly, he could be patient in hearing the story. "And then what, Miss Durbin?"

"There was a small fire during the costume party the night before last. Lord Henry came as Mount Vesuvius and when he erupted, a few sparks caught in the drapes of the ballroom and up they went."

A fire. "Was anyone hurt?"

"Just Lord Henry when Caroline knocked him aside to get to the drapes and pull them down before the flames could spread."

His heart tripped. "Is she all right?"

"Caroline is a cat, your grace," Jane assured him with a wave of her hand and a chuckle. "Nine lives and always lands on her feet."

Yes, he could see that. "Was Lord Henry seriously hurt?" he asked, not because he particularly cared, but because it was the next logical and socially expected question.

"Not so much seriously as embarrassingly," Jane answered. "Lady Sillings—who had come as a Vestal Virgin, which no one guessed—attempted to catch him as he staggered back. She got her hands on his rocks and was doing nicely at hauling him upright when his costume had a bit of an avalanche. He went reeling right into Lord Bidwell, who was rushing over to help Lady Sillings. Unfortunately, Lord Bidwell had come as Marc Anthony, complete with sword. Lord Henry's been standing to dine ever since."

"Anything else?" he asked warily.

"Nothing that began or ended in damage."

He knew a hedging answer when he heard one. "What about injury?"

"Well, there was the time Scutter escaped his cage."

Again his heart raced. Fiona. God, she loved that squirrel. It took conscious effort, but he managed to calmly ask, "What happened?"

"Scutter made it down the stairs and into the foyer with Lady Fiona and Lady Simone in pursuit just as Lady Ralls and Lord Betterton were coming back from their afternoon ride. They opened the door to come in and Scutter made a run to get out. At the sight of a squirrel limping at her, Lady Ralls, twit that she is, fainted dead across the doorway. Lord Betterton, valiant moron that he is, tried to bludgeon Scutter with his riding crop, but kept missing and hitting Lady Ralls."

"Fiona?"

"The girl has quite a voice when she's angry," Jane supplied. "And she's utterly fearless."

When it came to defense of helpless animals, yes, Fiona would take on the world and not think twice about it. Drayton sighed and pinched the bridge of his nose. "I'm afraid to ask about Simone."

"The brass vase off the foyer table," Jane supplied, grinning from ear to ear. "From the center of the room. Hit him square in the chest. Knocked him clean off his feet and right out of the house. Which, of course, ended his attempt to be a hero."

Well, at least she hadn't run him through with a cutlass. "And Scutter?"

"A bit shaken up by the whole thing, but otherwise unscathed."

Thank God. Fiona would have been devastated. "All of this in two weeks?"

"It hasn't been the least bit boring, your grace."

An explosion. A fire. A stabbing—albeit accidental. An assault with a brass vase. Oh, yes, and whatever the hell reindeer rides were. No, boring it hadn't been. "Does Caroline need me to return to throw out the Huns?" he asked. "Is that why you're here?"

"Oh, no, your grace," Jane quickly replied, reaching into the side seam of her purple skirt. She produced some folded pieces of parchment and handed them to him, explaining, "When Simone and Fiona heard that Lord Ralls was bringing me to London for fabrics, they asked me to deliver letters to you and I said I would."

"Thank you," he said, glancing down at them. Three. There was one there from Caroline, too. He brought his smile under control, cleared his throat, and met Jane's gaze. "When you return to Ryland Castle, please give my regards to Caroline and tell her that if she needs anything of me, she has but to ask."

"I'll certainly do that, your grace," she promised. She sighed and shook her head slightly and then gave him a little smile. "Although I'm sure you've noticed by now that Caroline isn't inclined to think of any situation as being beyond her ability to manage or endure all by herself."

"I have," he admitted, half wishing that Caroline had it in her to be helpless about something, anything.

"Well," Jane said breezily, "since Lord Ralls is waiting in the carriage for me, I really must be going now."

"Safe and pleasant travels, Miss Durbin." He lifted the notes in his hand. "And thank you again for delivering the letters."

She gave him a bright smile and another curtsy, then turned and said, "Lord Aubrey," as she walked away.

Aubrey. Damn. Out of sight, happily out of mind. Deciding to keep him that way for a while longer, Drayton opened the first of the letters. The penmanship was atrocious and the ink spots numerous. In the upper right-hand corner was a clear paw print. Drayton grinned and read the short note.

> Dear Lord Ryland,
>   Scutter is safe. Tarban can fly.
>   Deebs is fat. I miss you.
>   Lady Fiona Turnbridge

And he missed her, too. Horribly. His chest tight, he cleared his throat and went on to the second note.

Where Fiona's letters had been round and full, these were angular—as though they'd been written either in great haste or under great duress. The penmanship was slightly better than Fiona's, but the ink spots were even more numerous. Some of them looked a bit deliberate. One tiny one . . . He angled the paper into the fading afternoon light. Yes, that was definitely a hangman's noose.

> *Dear Lord Ryland,*
> *All is well here. We are in good health and spirits. I hope you are enjoying London.*
> *Your ward,*
> *Lady Simone Turnbridge.*

Drayton chuckled. Definitely duress. And probably dictated, too. Simone would never have thought of saying anything like that, much less spent any time putting it down on paper. God love Mrs. Miller; the woman was a saint for trying.

He opened the third letter and his smile faded. The handwriting was clearly Simone's. There weren't any ink spots, though. Not a one. And no pictures, either. Setting aside his disappointment that Caroline hadn't thought to write, he angled the paper into the light.

> *Dear Drayton, I surched Lady Awbree's rume*
> *an dent find yor balz. I think Lord Awbree has them.*
> *Simone.*

Ah, yes, that was the real Simone. He read the message again, appreciating both her keen perception and her persistence. She'd been right all along; he just hadn't seen it.

"Anything of great import in the correspondence?" Aubrey asked.

Yes, but he wasn't going to share it with him. "Deebs is fat."

"That's good to know. Would you like to go out clubbing this evening?"

"I'd rather eat glass," he said, moving to his desk.

"You cannot sit in this house day in and day out doing nothing but supporting England's distillers."

"I'm supporting Scotland's distillers, too."

"You're missing the point," the other snapped, his irritation obvious.

Drayton dropped down into his desk chair and laid the notes aside, saying, "I'm ignoring the point, Aubrey. And you. Very deliberately."

"I'll be at White's if you decide that you've had enough of living like a mole. Think before you publicly commit yourself to a liberal political course, Drayton. If you don't, you'll quickly regret your lofty ideals."

"Advice noted," Drayton replied, opening a drawer and taking out several sheets of stationery. "Enjoy your evening at White's."

Aubrey left without—uncharacteristically but wisely— saying another word. As soon as he was gone, Drayton leaned back in his chair and cradled his head in his hands. God, he hated being in London. He hated this house. He hated the life he was living in it. He wanted to go home. To be with . . .

He looked at the letters from Fiona and Simone as he considered the realization. Not since his parents' passing had he had a home. Yes, he'd had a place where his bed was; the regiment provided all its officers with billets. But a real home, a place his heart actually yearned to be?

Somehow, without his being aware that it was happening, he'd put down roots and made a claim to Ryland Castle. It was home. It was where his family was. Fiona and her little zoo. Simone and her wild ways. And Caroline.

It wasn't the physical he missed. Well, he did, horribly, but not as often as he missed the everyday, very public pleasures of her company. The way the color of her eyes changed with her emotions. The expressiveness of her smile, the way she tilted her head back to look up at him. He missed watching her, talking with her, laughing with her.

He swallowed the knot in his throat. If she'd ever felt any affection at all for him, he'd crushed it in walking away from her. There wasn't enough alcohol in the world to drown his guilt or numb his regrets. Or erase his memory. For as long as he lived, he'd remember the hurt in her eyes and the sadness in her voice as she'd tried so hard to play the part of the accepting mistress.

If only there was a flaw in the logic that had driven him to sanity. If only there was some way that he could reasonably ask her to give up all the possibilities in the world for him. Weighed against all that she could have . . . What did it matter that he loved her?

❧ *Twenty* ❧

CAROLINE DREW ANOTHER WILTED LILY FROM THE
arrangement on the foyer table and considered what was
left of the arrangement. After she had plucked the faded
blooms, the front side of it looked a bit empty; the result,
no doubt from bearing the brunt of the frigid blasts that
accompanied every coming and going of Ryland Castle's
guests.

What they all found to do that required them to enter
and leave the house a half dozen times each day, Caroline
didn't know. And didn't care enough to discover. Her
only hope was that at some point, they'd go out and not
come back in. Christmas was only a month or so away.
Surely they all had somewhere to go, some family who
would pine horribly in their absence.

Perhaps, Caroline mused, she could begin mentioning
the approaching holidays in casual dinner conversation
and work her way toward inquiring as to where everyone
intended to spend them. Just to give them all an extra
nudge along the road, she could talk about shopping and
lament as to how few true luxuries there were to be had in
the village, how the goods to be found anywhere else
were ever so much more interesting and varied. Maybe, if

it looked as though no one ever planned to pack a bag and leave on their own, she could organize a complicated scavenger hunt. In London.

London. Where Drayton was. In the big, lavish house her father had built in Hyde Park. It was probably too much to hope that he wandered its halls and rooms and wished that she were there with him, but she did anyway. Not that there was ever so much as the slightest hint in his letters that he was feeling anything except terribly frustrated with the repairs being done on what he referred to as Geoffrey's White Elephant and obsessed with properly preparing for his first session of Parliament. No, odds were he hadn't missed her at all.

With a sigh, she gathered up the flowers she'd pulled from the arrangement, wondering what Drayton's plans were for Christmas. Did he want to spend the holidays with them? In London or here? Or had he already made arrangements to pass them in the company of others? She really should write and get an answer before inquiring of the guests what their plans might be. In asking them, she opened herself to the expectation of sharing hers.

The cold air struck her, cutting through her skirts to chill her skin. She turned to see which one of the guests had realized that it was approaching time for another free meal. She arched a brow as Simone stomped past her, leaving the door wide open so that Lady Aubrey could charge in after her.

"What's wrong?" Caroline asked, pivoting.

Simone came to a sudden halt at the base of the stairs and whipped back. "Lady Aubrey says I have to ride sidesaddle or I can't ride at all! That I'll be ruined forever if I ride astride."

"There are physical . . ." the woman hotly countered, somehow managing to pant and glare as she bore down on the girl. "Consequences . . . that . . ." She stopped between the two of them, her back to Caroline and breathlessly declared, "Well, we needn't go into the specifics."

Simone threw a tangle of black curls over her shoulder. "The cherry might pop and deprive some man of the greatest thrill of his life?"

Lady Aubrey started, gasped, then moaned and crumpled where she stood.

"Simone!" Caroline cried, dashing forward, thinking to break the woman's fall to the hard marble floor. The intent didn't take into account Lady Aubrey's greater weight and the time it would take Caroline to reach her. She got a handful of riding habit, for just a moment, and then it was pulled from her grasp. "Oh, no," she moaned as Lady Aubrey became a fashionably attired unconscious mass at her feet.

"Have I killed her?"

"No, she's still breathing."

"Well, there's a disappointment."

"Simone, please," she chastised. "Would it really be too much to ask that—" She froze, appalled. "What are you doing?"

"Sneakin' one of her cheroots," Simone announced, removing a small tin from the woman's skirt pocket. "Amazin' what good stuff money can buy," she added, taking a twist and a match from the container. She struck the match on the bottom of the tin and, seemingly oblivious to Caroline's shock, drew the fire into the end of the little cigar. She puffed twice, shook out the match, and then held out the cheroot, asking, "Wanna pull?"

"No!"

She shrugged, clamped the bit of tobacco between her teeth, and stared down at Lady Aubrey as she said, "Look,

Carrie, before the tugboat comes around, there's something you need to understand. All this . . ." She gestured to the house around them and met Caroline's gaze. "All the dancin' lessons and talkin' lessons and all the fancy dresses and sidesaddles in the world ain't gonna make one bit of difference in the end. My da may or may not have been the old duke. Hell, given how I don't look anything like you and Fiona, odds are he wasn't."

Her heart pounding, Caroline pressed her hand to the cold pit of her stomach. "But you've been legally recognized, Simone. It doesn't matter."

"Yeah, it does," Simone countered, ambling over to sit on the stairs. Calmly, ever so matter-of-factly, she explained, "The duke wasn't my da and my ma was a whore, Carrie. I was ruined the day I was born and no amount of paper is ever gonna change that. You can call me 'Lady' and give me a last name, but ain't no one ever gonna look at me and not see where I come from."

"They will overlook it, Simone."

"Not for real," she quietly shot back. "They'll just pretend to 'cause that's the only way they're gonna get Drayton's money. And if you think otherwise, you're just lyin' to yourself, Carrie. We ain't nothin' more than some man's way up the ladder." She nodded toward Lady Aubrey. "Do you think she'd even talk to either one of us if we wasn't attached to Drayton?"

No. She wouldn't have so much as acknowledged that they existed.

"Admit it, Carrie. She wouldn't, would she?"

"No, probably not," she allowed.

"No 'probably' to it." She pulled on the cheroot and sent a cloud of blue smoke toward the ceiling. "Ridin' astride ain't gonna matter one whit, Carrie. Hell, I could

ride astride buck naked through Trafalgar Square and it
wouldn't outweigh Drayton's money."

She was right, of course. But still ... "You'd just be
making your own life terribly difficult," Caroline pointed
out. "Unnecessarily so."

Simone smiled wryly as she stared at Lady Aubrey.
"But not nearly as difficult as I'd make it for the tugboats
of the world. Every time they have to talk to me, look me
in the eyes, smile at me and be nice, they'll know that *I*
know just how low they'll go for money." She slowly
lifted her gaze to meet Caroline's. "How we *all* know that
underneath all the fancy clothes and fine airs they ain't
one bit different from a Cheapside whore."

Leave it to Simone to so smoothly, coolly cut to the
core of brutal truth—and not only accept it, but use it to
her advantage.

"But that's just my way of lookin' at all this," Simone
went on, puffing on the cheroot again. "Your ma wasn't no
whore so you got better odds of it going easier for you."

"No, I don't," Caroline admitted, her knees starting to
shake. She crossed the foyer and dropped down beside
her sister. "Not really."

"So what you gonna do?" Simone asked as they both
stared at Lady Aubrey. "Keep dancin' to her tune? Or call
your own?"

A quavering voice in the very farthest corner of her
brain said she'd be better off following Simone's advice.
Clasping her hands together, hoping that Simone wouldn't
notice how they were trembling, she managed a weak
smile and an even weaker chuckle. "I don't think I have
the courage to ride astride and naked through Trafalgar
Square."

Simone snorted, flicked the ash on her knee, rubbed it into her pant leg, and then held out the smoking bit of tobacco. "Wanna pull while you think about it?"

She didn't really, but took it, telling herself that every journey of defiance began with a single small act of nonconformity. "This tastes horrible," she said, sputtering out a tiny puff of smoke and holding it out for her more daring sister to take.

Simone pushed her hand back toward her. "It helps to think of it as wastin' someone else's money."

Caroline took another small puff and was amazed that it didn't make her choke this time. "You're right," she said, handing it back again. "But just the same, I don't much care for it."

Simone blew another cloud toward the chandelier and drawled, "What's the most outrageous thing you've done since . . . ?" She shrugged. "Well, since whenever."

Making love with Drayton in the parlor. She blinked as the memory played through her mind. Heat flooding her cheeks, she expelled a long breath and said, "I don't think I can tell you about it."

"You musta enjoyed it."

"I did," she had to admit.

"Did Drayton?"

She whipped around to squarely meet her sister's gaze. "Simone!"

"Oh, hell, Carrie," she countered with a chuckle. "I've known from the very beginning."

"Oh, really?"

Simone nodded and took another pull on the cheroot. "The night at the inn on the way here."

All right, her sister knew. Just *how* she knew . . .

"Have another pull," Simone said, passing the tobacco twist as she leaned forward to study Lady Aubrey. "Are you sure I didn't kill her?"

"We don't have that kind of luck," Caroline pointed out. She managed to blow a fairly decent stream of smoke this time and then passed the cheroot back, pleased with herself.

"Aw, luck's what you make out of the bits and pieces you come across."

True. But what was lucky one day had a way of becoming a burden the next. The trick was to know from the beginning what was going to turn bad and what wasn't. A month ago she would have said that being recognized as the daughter of a duke was the most wonderful thing that could ever happen to a woman. In the span of a single day she'd gone from a meager existence, a narrow bed in the corner of a workroom, and hoarding a little bar of scented soap to . . . to having everything she'd ever dreamed of and never thought possible. A huge home to make beautiful, two wonderful sisters, sharing a bed with Drayton.

And then Drayton had left. She still had everything else that made a world golden. She could still appreciate how far she'd come. But now the luck felt largely empty and these days she smiled and laughed only because she was expected to.

"So what you gonna do, Carrie?"

"I don't know," she admitted. "I wish I did."

"Well, just 'tween us, sleepin' alone in his bed and dreamin' about him seems like a real pathetic way to spend the rest of your life."

Caroline sighed and blinked back tears. "Is there anything you don't know?"

"Yeah," her sister drawled. "Why the two of you think

doing what everyone expects you to is more important than doing what you want. Seems to me you make each other happy, and why you'd be willing to be miserable . . . I don't know why you'd do that."

"Because," she began. The tears spilled. Angrily wiping her fingers over her cheeks, she said, "It's about money, about marrying as much of it as you can and then using it to . . ." It was about surrendering your life and your soul and your happiness for money. "Oh, God."

"And the light dawns," Simone whispered. "'Bout damn time. So you goin' to London after him?"

She didn't have any choice. She had to know for sure, had to hear Drayton say of his own accord that she didn't make him happy, that he was willing to sell his life to the highest bidder. If he could do that, then she would let go of hope. If he couldn't . . . God knew she could create a scandal without even trying. If she actually put her mind to it . . . Her heart pounding, her knees quivering, she stood, saying, "Go have a carriage readied. I'll pack our things."

"Who's all goin'?" Simone asked as she came to her feet.

"You, Fiona, me, Mrs. Miller, and Dora."

"Gonna be cozy."

Yes, it was. Especially with Fiona's menagerie. "Where's Haywood?"

"Probably still standin' in the stable, holdin' the reins and waitin' to see if Lady Aubrey wins."

"A change in strategy," Caroline declared, eyeing the front door, mentally mapping her course. "You go tell Mrs. Miller and Fiona that we're leaving. I need to speak with Haywood. And then find Mrs. Gladder and let her know."

"All right." Simone turned to go up the stairs, then paused and looked back over her shoulder at Lady Aubrey. "We just gonna leave her there?"

She was tempted, but her conscience squirmed and she relented just not to have to fight with it. "We should probably at least loosen her laces," she said, stepping over and squatting down beside the woman. "Help me roll her onto her side."

Simone huffed, but did as asked, grunting with the effort and grumbling, "If we ever run out of whale oil . . ."

"That's not kind," Caroline pointed out, undoing the lower buttons of Lady Aubrey's riding habit and then plucking loose the strings holding the scant petticoat around her waist. The laces of her corset exposed, Caroline picked first at the knot of the upper half, then abandoned the effort for an attempt to undo the lower one. "There is no way to get these untied," she finally admitted, sitting back on her heels in frustration. "There's absolutely no give in them at all."

"Here."

Caroline blinked as the light danced along the edge of the slim knife Simone held out for her. She took it, asking, "Where did you get this?"

"I've always had it," her sister supplied with a grin. "It was a christening gift."

God help the world, Caroline offered up, trying to get the point of the knife under one of the laces. Failing that, she drew a deep breath and simply sawed her way through. The last thread gave way with an audible pop.

The laces sang as they whipped through the grommets. Simone snatched the knife from her hand and jumped away, crying, "Stand back, she's gonna blow!"

Rolling her eyes, Caroline said, "Perhaps we should put her in Mrs. Gladder's care," and watched as Lady Aubrey moaned and feebly lifted a hand from the floor to her brow.

"Be right back."

As Simone ran for the rear of the house, Caroline eased the woman onto her back, asking quietly, "Are you feeling better, Lady Aubrey?"

For a second the woman simply looked up at her, her gaze clouded with confusion. Then she blinked and the haze disappeared as she laid a hand on her midriff. Her voice was hot steel as she demanded, "What have you done?"

"We couldn't get your laces loosened, so we cut them."

"You have ruined my corset?"

"Just the lower laces."

"How dare you!"

"Well," Caroline drawled, gaining her feet, "now that we know your expectations, next time we'll just leave you lying where you fall. Would you like assistance rising, or would you prefer to spend the rest of the day there?"

"I do not like your tone."

I don't care. Caroline bit her tongue. Mrs. Gladder and Simone saved her from having to bite it in two.

"Lady Simone tells me you're leaving for London within the hour," the housekeeper said to Caroline as she came across the foyer.

"Sooner if possible."

"Have we arrived at the crossroads?"

"We have, indeed. And you were right. The course of action required is very clear."

"What?" Lady Aubrey gasped from the floor.

Simone leaned over and informed her, "Carrie's had enough. We're goin' to London so she can be with Drayton."

"If you leave this house, I will refuse to sponsor your coming Season," Lady Aubrey threatened, apparently unaware that lying flat on her back at their feet didn't do much for making it terribly intimidating.

"I don't want a Season," Caroline told her. "I have never wanted a Season."

"What you want is to create a scandal that would be the complete ruination of the Turnbridge name!"

As though that were even remotely possible. "I'm simply carrying on as my father before me," she replied, smiling thinly. Walking toward the rear of the house, she called back, "I leave her in your hands, Mrs. Gladder. I'm going to speak with Haywood and order a carriage readied."

The wind was quick and stinging and by the time Caroline reached the bottom step and headed toward the stable, it had cut through both her dress and her anger. Folding her arms across her midriff, she walked along the rear of the house, her teeth clenched and her mind chattering. There was no need to think of something scandalous to do or say once she reached London. She'd seen to that in the foyer of Ryland Castle. Between the determined efforts of Lady Aubrey and the other guests, the story of her outrage would probably get to London before she did.

As Simone had predicted, Haywood was standing just inside the stable door, holding the reins of an unsaddled horse in his hands. He dropped them at first sight of her and shrugged off his coat. Draping it over her shoulders, he asked, "Was it bloody ugly?"

"Actually, Lady Aubrey went over in a dead faint two seconds into the brawl," she supplied with a sigh. God, she was suddenly so tired. She nodded toward the man's saddle on the nearby stand. "Lady Simone will ride however she pleases, Haywood."

"Oh, God. Are you sure you've thought this through?"

"Saddle her a horse for traveling," she instructed, nodding. "You can teach her to ride on our way to London."

"London?"

"Yes, London," she repeated, squarely meeting his darkening gaze.

"I should try to talk you out of this."

"But you're not going to?"

"Well, scandal isn't entirely bad," he said with a half-hearted smile. "It does get people's attention, and as long as you're not the scandal-ee, being noticed can advance one's public recognition in a rather positive way. After a bit of time, of course."

She sighed and shook her head in dismay. "Do you ever think of anyone other than yourself?"

"Well," he said slowly, tilting his head to the side as he considered her, "would you rather I mention that Drayton might not be all that thrilled to see you?"

"No," she assured him. "Thank you for sparing me. I apologize for accusing you of being self-centered."

"Well, now that the cat's poked its head out of the bag," he said, "we might as well let it all the way out. He's a man, Lady Caroline. He's not likely to have closed himself up in his room and tried to forget you. At least not alone."

It had been delicately, kindly put, but the impact was none the less for the effort. Her heart aching, she swallowed her fear and admitted, "I have thought of that possibility.

But hearing it actually put into words is a bit more disconcerting than I expected."

Haywood looked genuinely regretful when he said, "I'm sorry that we're not nobler creatures."

"Still," she said with a shrug, "I have to go to London. I can't bear another minute of wondering. If he's forgotten me or replaced me, then at least I'll know that and I can get on with my life without him."

"Do you think that's possible?"

Bless Haywood. Under all the spit and polish and predatory tendencies, there was a very soft heart. "If it has to be, it will be, Haywood," she promised him. "Pride will save me. It always has." Taking his coat off and handing it back to him, she said, "Saddle Simone a horse, please. And could I get you to have the coach readied while I go pack our things?"

"Not quite so fast," he admonished as she started to turn away. He waited until she'd squared up to him again to ask, "Is Lady Aubrey coming along?"

He really had to ask? "No. She's not invited."

"All right," he said slowly, his gaze fastened on something in the distance. "I'll see you safely to London on one condition. You'll agree to go to my brother's home and not Drayton's."

"Isn't he at his—or someone's—country estate like everyone else?"

"Well, he is, but his wife isn't," Haywood explained. "Margaret hates the country and always stays behind in the city. She'll be a suitable chaperone. And I assure you that she's considerably more tolerant than Lady Aubrey."

Anyone would be more tolerant than Lady Aubrey. Caroline considered the suggestion, the fact that she'd be essentially moving into a stranger's house just as strangers had moved into hers. To be guilty of preying on the expectations of hospitality . . . She didn't know if she could do that. It wasn't as if she didn't have anywhere else to go. Of course, if Drayton had taken a mistress and she were to walk in unexpectedly and find them together, it would be horribly embarrassing. Not to mention acutely painful.

"Did I say that I must insist that you go to Margaret's?"

She nodded, focusing on a growing glimmer of understanding. It wasn't so much that Haywood thought a chaperone would be an effective deterrent; he knew them better than that. "Going to Margaret's instead of going to Drayton's," she ventured, "will give you time to warn him that I've come to town for a reckoning."

His smile was small, but hugely guilty. "Well, yes, and that, too."

And save me the pain of actually finding another woman in his arms. "You're really very good at manipulating people."

"I try to use a light touch at it whenever possible."

"All right, Haywood," she conceded. "I'll exercise some common sense. Just for a while. I'll go to your sister-in-law's."

He smiled broadly and gave her an exaggerated bow. "Then I shall see that Lady Simone's horse and your coach are readied at once, madam."

"Thank you, Haywood." She left him, but got only as far as the stable threshold before pausing and looking back. "And a cart, please," she added, her mind whirling through all that needed to be done and how to best manage it. "For the baggage."

"Women," he grumbled, his eyes sparkling. "Could you have Winfield pack my bags?"

✺ *Twenty-one* ✺

"AND WITH THAT," LADY HAYWOOD SAID IN QUIET TRI-umph as the young man walked away from them, "your dance card for the evening is filled. You have done beauti-fully, Lady Caroline. Beautifully."

"All I've done is nod politely and say 'I am looking forward to it, sir.'"

"Not every woman can do that, you know," she coun-tered, gathering her skirts. "I'm going over to speak with Lady Rhys for a moment. I'll be right back."

"I won't move from the spot. Or talk to strangers."

Lady Haywood stopped and turned back. "Unless, of course, the first dance begins before I get back. Do you remember which one Lord Rufus Collins is?"

The one with the feet as big as boats. Caroline nodded, then watched Haywood's sister-in-law flit off to speak with the patroness of this evening's gathering. Which was, now that she had a moment alone to fully consider it, an interesting affair. According to Lady Haywood, Tris-tan's wasn't as glorious as Almack's and not nearly as difficult to get into for an evening of dining and dancing. Two factors that made it, according to Lady Haywood, the perfect place to begin an assault on the pillars of London society. To that end, Caroline was to eat like a bird, smile pleasantly at the men Lady Rhys brought over for formal introductions, and allow them to sign her dance card while saying as little as possible. Be absolutely circumspect and preserve the feminine mystery, as Lady Haywood had put it.

The feminine mystery might have everyone watching her every move for one that wasn't circumspect, but Caroline considered the high reputation of Tristan's to be the more intriguing puzzle. The décor was nice—although the gold-fringed magenta curtains were a bit loud for her taste. The orchestra seemed to be good. The food was edible and plentiful and the tables were set attractively. It was the tables, Caroline decided. Placed practically end to end around three sides of the dance floor three rows deep, well, it was the same arrangement that could be found in any reputable social club. The only difference between Tristan's and Walton's in Bloomsbury was the degree of extravagance. And the pretensions of the patrons.

"Lady Caroline. This is certainly a surprise."

And speaking of pretensions . . . "Aubrey," she said. "You're looking well," she added, sparing him a brief glance before her gaze went past him in search of Drayton.

"And you. Where is Mother?"

"She's not in London," she provided, bringing her attention back to him. "At least that I know of. I abandoned Ryland Castle to her and her guests yesterday morning. I can only hope they don't burn it to the ground before I get back."

He considered her for a moment and then asked, "Why are you here?"

Well, that was blunt. "Would you like to hear something pleasantly dishonest, or the truth?"

Clearing his throat, he looked out over the dinner crowd. "I assume Haywood came back with you. Is he here this evening?"

"Actually, he's out and about looking for Drayton, to warn him of my return to London. Apparently he's been a good thirty minutes behind him all day. He was terribly frustrated at mid-afternoon. I can only imagine what he's like now." She quickly moistened her lower lip and then boldly asked, "Do you have any idea of where Drayton might be?"

"I've heard that he had a meeting at Westerham's club and then was going for supper and some gaming to Lanter's club. As for his more private plans after that . . ." He shrugged.

He'd *heard*? He didn't know for sure? Interesting. It seemed to imply a falling-out. No doubt over politics. As for the "his more private plans after that" and the shrug . . . Hardly a subtle insinuation that Drayton might be out—as men so euphemistically put it—chasing skirts. And an obvious deliberate effort to wound her.

"Well, I'm sure Haywood will eventually track him down," she offered breezily, refusing to let the thought trouble her. She'd come this far for the truth and she'd simply have to take what she found—good or bad. There was no point now in worrying which it would be.

"Pardon the intrusion, Lord Aubrey," a voice said from behind them, "but I believe I have this dance with Lady Caroline."

She glanced down. Yes, Lord Boatfoot.

"He's the third son of a baron," Aubrey muttered as she accepted the other man's arm.

"It doesn't matter," she tossed back over her shoulder. None of this mattered one single whit to her. All she was doing was killing time. And hoping not to permanently cripple anyone while she did it.

JUST TWO MORE DAYS, DRAYTON REMINDED HIMSELF AS HE climbed the steps and his driver took the town car down the drive and toward the carriage house. Meetings with the architects and contractors all day tomorrow, dinner with Peters and Masters tomorrow night to go over the preliminary legislative drafts, and then a round of meetings to present them the following day.

After those obligations had been fulfilled, he'd be ready. For Parliament when it convened after the Christmas holidays. And for going home until then. Only heaven knew what he'd find when he got there and how everyone was going to feel about his coming back through the door. Hopefully, the gifts he'd spent the day buying would smooth out any rough spots. Simone would love the new épée and Fiona would be delighted by the fancy cage he'd found for Scutter.

Caroline, though . . . That had proved to be a tough one. Nothing seemed quite right. The diamond and sapphire tiara had had some appeal, but imaging the look on Caroline's face when faced with the request to actually wear it . . . He'd winced, had it put back in the case, and abandoned the whole idea of a grand symbolic gesture. Of course that meant that at this point he didn't have anything to give her except himself. A sorry gift if ever there was one.

"Good evening, Lord Ryland."

"Good evening, Tilden," he said, tugging off his gloves as the footman closed the door behind him. "Have the packages arrived?"

"They have, your grace. And been placed in your study." He stepped up to take Drayton's hat and added, "Where we also placed Mr. Haywood some time ago."

Drayton froze, looking down the hall. "Haywood?"

"Yes, your grace."

Leaving the footman standing there holding the hat, he headed down the hall, his heart pounding furiously as horrific scenes played out before his mind's eye. Fiona attacked by a wild—rabid!—animal. Simone putting her eye out with any one of the weapons she didn't know how to use nearly as well as . . . Oh, God, Caroline falling off a ladder. Or sick. Or blown up by one of Lady Aubrey's idiot friends.

He charged into the study to find Haywood's coat lying over the back of the nearest chair and the man himself leaning nonchalantly against the buffet, a drink in his hand and his gaze fixed on the battered wall.

"Damn, Drayton," he chuckled. "You have some big, mean mice in this house."

"Hello and why aren't you at Ryland Castle?" he asked, stuffing his gloves in his coat pocket. "What's happened?"

"Gawd," he answered, shaking his head. "What *hasn't* happened lately?"

"Then why are you here?"

"Because," he said pointedly, lifting his glass in salute, "Lady Caroline's come to London."

Drayton stared at him, vaguely hearing himself say, "What?" as his mind chattered excitedly and his heart raced in earnest.

"Caroline's come—"

"Where is she? Upstairs?"

"I insisted that they take up residence at my sister-in-law's. Margaret—"

"They who?" If she'd brought that band of barbarians with her . . .

"Lady Caroline, Lady Simone, Lady Fiona, Mrs. Miller, and Dora," Haywood supplied to his utter relief. "And all the animals. Margaret—that's my sister-in-law—insisted that Caroline go with her to dinner this evening at Tristan's."

Tristan's. He knew where it was. And what it was.

"It's not Almack's, of course," Haywood went on. "But she—Margaret—desperately wants to trump Lady Aubrey in sponsoring her—Caroline—and said it would be the perfect place to introduce her to what society remains in London at the moment. To get her feet wet, so to speak. Well, more like damp actually, but you know what I mean."

Oh, yes. Put Caroline out there and then whistle the sharks in for dinner.

"She practically cackled at the possi—"

"*Which* she?"

Haywood blinked. "Which she what?"

"Cackled!"

"Margaret," Haywood said. "Lady Caroline doesn't cackle." He frowned and then shrugged. "Of course, I never thought Margaret did, either. She sounded positively evil, Dray. I had no idea. She's always been such a mousy little thing. Of course, I've never seen her when John isn't about so—"

"Why is Caroline here?" he asked, frustrated enough to damn the rudeness and cut to the chase.

"It's not for me to tell you. She should properly be the first."

It was Drayton's turn to blink. Possibilities tumbled one over the other in his head, most of them ridiculous and dismissed out of hand. But one was entirely within the realm of feasible. Delightfully so. "She's pregnant?" he guessed.

Haywood's eyes went huge. "She is?"

"Jesus, you're a plank," he declared, turning on his heel and heading for the door.

"Are you going to Tristan's?" Haywood asked, dogging his heels.

"What do you think?"

"Why?" Haywood asked, pulling on his coat as he followed Drayton through the darkened halls and rooms toward the rear of the house.

"To see Caroline!"

"All you're going to be able to do is look. Maybe exchange a few polite words over a cup of punch. It's very public."

"I'm a duke. I can do as I damn well please, when and where I please," he declared, pushing open the servants' door and striding out into the rear yard. "John!" he called to his coachman. "Don't put the carriage away!"

Haywood trotted up beside him. "Well, I must say that you seem to have spent the last few weeks growing a bit more comfortable with wearing the title. Although that attitude may not be for the best considering that those who are at Tristan's tonight are the same ones who'll go to Almack's during the Season. They can make a mountainous scandal out of a single grain of sand. If you look at Caroline for even a heartbeat too long, it will take her years to live it down."

"I'm not going to look at her too long," he replied, motioning his driver into the box. "I promise."

"What are you going to do?"

Drayton yanked open the door. "You're welcome to toady along and find out."

As Haywood threw himself inside, Drayton looked up. "Tristan's, please, John. And hurry."

CAROLINE SIPPED THE TEPID PUNCH AND WONDERED whether the next man on her dance card was going to have any more sense than the previous six had had. It seemed to her that at some point one of them would notice the others nursing their injuries and, in a moment motivated by pure self-preservation, remember that he'd asked another woman for the dance first. But, apparently, it wasn't going to be the next one. She smiled to acknowledge his glance from across the room. If they were both lucky, he wouldn't be able to escape the elderly lady chattering away at him.

She sipped again and let her gaze wander. Lady Rhys was certainly in a hurry to get to the door for some reason. Caroline turned to see what it might be and smiled. Setting her punch cup on the end of the table, she watched as Drayton bowed to Lady Rhys, said something decidedly brief and then stepped around her and swept the ballroom with his gaze. It met hers, locked, and set him in motion. Oh, he was magnificent, and if any of the other men present had brains in their heads they would know that they didn't stand a chance against him.

There wasn't much of a crowd between them, but what there was of one parted to let him pass. One or two of the men spoke to him and while he acknowledged them with a dip of his chin, he didn't let them delay his advance in the slightest. Their gazes followed him, then darted to her just before their wives tugged on their sleeves and they bent down to whisper.

Well, she allowed, smiling, so much for the hope of behaving impeccably this evening. He'd violated at least half a dozen rules since he'd come through the door. And, judging by the way the light was sparkling in his eyes, he didn't care how many more he broke before the evening was done.

For a second she thought he was going to open his arms and her heart thrilled. But he stopped a surprisingly and perfectly proper distance in front of her, his arms at his sides. Even as she struggled with the disappointment, he slowly gave her one of his lopsided, heart-melting smiles and her world came right.

"I see that Haywood finally found you."

He nodded. "May I have this dance?"

"I believe, sir," said an imperious voice from her left elbow, "that my name is next on Lady Caroline's card."

Before she could do or say anything, Drayton squared up to the man, cocked a brow, and smiled. "Allow me to introduce myself. I am Lord Drayton Mackenzie, Duke of Ryland. And you are?"

"Surrendering the dance, your grace," the other said, sounding as though all the air was going out of him at once.

She felt a bit sorry for the man, whatever his name was, but not enough to offer him even a quick apology over her shoulder as Drayton took her elbow. "That was certainly effective," she observed as he escorted her to the dance floor. "A bit imperial, but effective."

"I've grown very weary of all the games," he replied as the orchestra began to play a waltz. "In fact, my patience is gone."

"As I can see," she said breathlessly as he whirled her into position and instantly moved them into the brightly colored circle of gliding, spinning dancers. She stared at the studs in his shirtfront, trying to catch her breath and marveling at how smoothly she was moving, how her feet just seemed to know where they needed to be, where he wanted them to go. What a difference it made to partner with a commanding, certain man. She closed her eyes and smiled, feeling lighter than air and not worrying about the other dancers, not caring where he took her and if they never came back.

Drayton stole a glance down at her face as he moved them to the inside edge of the ring of dancers. So beautiful, so perfect in his arms. As if she'd been made just for him. The very thought of another man touching her, making her smile so sweetly . . . His chest tightening and his blood racing far faster than the waltz tempo, he committed himself to the greatest risk he'd ever taken. "Why are you here, Caroline?"

Her smiled broadened. "I'm bored with mashing the toes of the dancing master at Ryland Castle and came here looking for new men to maim."

All right, if she didn't want to give him a straight answer right away, he'd accept it. He'd been the one to put the time and distance between them and made her understandably wary. "Find any of interest?"

"Just one."

"Oh?"

"Unfortunately," she said, opening her eyes to study his shirtfront, "I'm not sure if he's interested in me. Which makes it all decidedly awkward."

Well, if she was referring to him, he could end awkward right here and now. If she was talking about someone else, they were going to take awkward to all new heights in just a few moments. "You could send Haywood out to make inquiries on your behalf," he suggested. "Believe it or not, he can actually be discreet when he puts his mind to it. Of course," he quickly added, "he can also be decidedly thick when he puts his mind to it, too."

Haywood, would you please go ask Drayton if he loves me? I'll be hiding behind this palm until you get back. How ridiculous. "It seems to me," she said, finally looking up at him, "that sending someone to ask personal questions on your behalf is rather cowardly. Not to mention more than a bit childish."

"I tend to agree," he offered. "If you don't know someone well enough to ask a personal question yourself, then you really don't know them well enough to be asking it. I hope you know that you can ask me anything at all. Or tell me anything for that matter."

"Well," she began, her eyes sparkling, "I should probably let you know that Lady Aubrey threatened to withdraw her sponsorship if I left Ryland Castle."

"I'm sure that gave you pause for all of a second or two," he replied, wishing he'd been there to see that exchange. Lady Aubrey was probably still recovering from it.

"Less than that, I'm afraid."

"Because?"

He pressed his hand into the small of her back and she happily obeyed, closing the space between them until her bodice lightly brushed the lapels of his jacket as they moved in tandem among the other dancers. "Largely because," she said, gazing up at him, delighting in their boldness, "I've discovered in recent weeks that there are worse fates than the possibility of scandal."

Drayton grinned, his heart soaring with certainty.

"What could possibly be worse than scandal?" he asked, slowing their dance and easing them apart from the other dancers.

"Doing what others expect you to do," she answered softly, lifting her gloved hand from his shoulder to brush the backs of her fingers along his jaw. "And pretending that you're not absolutely miserable for the effort and sacrifice."

Knowing that her touch had made pretending to be dancing pointless, he drew them to a halt, caught her hand in his and brought it to his lips to press a lingering promise against it. "And you were miserable at Ryland Castle?" he asked as she gazed adoringly up at him, as the orchestra played on and the smooth swirl of dancers around them faltered and came to an abrupt, stumbling stop. "You've been missing the wonder and gaiety of London?"

She shook her head. "I came to London because I miss the sound of your voice and the way you smile, the way you shoot your cuffs. Because I miss your integrity and kindness, how you surprise me and anchor me and make me laugh. Because I'm so very tired of sleeping in your bed alone and waking to find that you've been there, holding me close, only in my dreams."

"Do you love me, Caroline?"

She smiled and truth shimmered from the depths of her eyes to wrap gently and forever around his heart.

"That would be incredibly foolish and shortsighted, wouldn't it?" she whispered.

"Not to mention financially indefensible," he allowed, releasing her hands to place his on her waist.

"Yes, exactly." She twined her arms around his neck and smiled up at him, her heart brimming and sure. "You haven't fallen in love with me, have you?"

"Oh, no," he offered, shaking his head. "Foolish and indefensible and all that. But I do love sex with you."

"Yes, there is that," she said brightly.

"And how I love watching you cut out fabric and pin paper bands around drapes," he added, his voice a whisper that twined through her soul. "I love how the color of your eyes turns to steel blue when you're angry and how it turns to smoke when I kiss you. I love the sound of your laugh and all the shadings of your sighs. But most of all, I love your honesty and your courage and how you believe that nothing is impossible."

"I don't believe, Drayton. I just hope with all my heart."

"And what impossible hope of your heart has brought you to London?"

"That you might ask me just one more time to marry you."

"Oh, darling Caroline," he murmured, slipping his arms around her and drawing her full against him. Bending his head, he brushed his lips over hers and amid the storm of gasps and choked cries of outrage, grinned and whispered, "You're going to have to."